A PHILOSOPHY OF THIEVES

Also by Fran Wilde

The Canarvier Files
A Philosophy of Thieves

Bone Universe
Updraft
Cloudbound
Horizon

Gemworld
The Jewel and Her Lapidary
The Fire Opal Mechanism
The Book of Gems

Clock Star Rose Spine

The Ship of Stolen Words

Riverland

A PHILOSOPHY OF THIEVES

FRAN WILDE

EREWHON

an imprint of Kensington Publishing Corp.
erewhonbooks.com

Content notice: *A Philosophy of Thieves* contains depictions of body modification, body horror, murder, coercion, drugged interrogation, coercive pharmaceuticals, prison, kidnapping, and class-based oppression.

EREWHON BOOKS are published by:

Kensington Publishing Corp.
900 Third Avenue
New York, NY 10022

erewhonbooks.com

ISBN 978-1-64566-194-8 (hardcover)

First Erewhon hardcover printing: October 2025

10 9 8 7 6 5 4 3 2 1

Printed in the United States of America

Library of Congress Control Number: 2024943943

Electronic edition: ISBN 978-1-64566-196-2

Edited by Diana Pho
Interior design by Kelsy Thompson
Images courtesy of Shutterstock and Noun Project

The authorized representative in the EU for product safety and compliance
is eucomply OU, Parnu mnt 139b-14, Apt 123
Tallinn, Berlin 11317, hello@eucompliancepartner.com

For Gregory Frost, writer, friend, teacher,
who believed in this story before anyone else.

The Cocktail Job

AT HALF PAST five on Tuesday evening, the Canarvier family announced they were robbing Dutton Change Corporation's office party.

Because Jayson Dutton was midway through his founders' award acceptance, few guests noticed the thieves' calling card at his feet. They were dazzled by their host's newly chipped hand—which glowed the pale green of pre-turbulence money—and the award-worthy invention displayed nearby.

Only an observant few pointed at the card, and the word *Canarvier* printed in elegant gold lettering on thick cream-colored fabricant.

The name of the most infamous thieves in New Washington glittered momentarily before the card dissolved into a yellow puff of dust.

"Dutton Change Corporation and the Dutton family have much to celebrate this quarter. This award—as you've seen on our feeds—confirms our role as key players in keeping global disaster at bay. I'd like to thank our investors—gathered here tonight—for their support as we make the world less turbulent." Dutton coughed as the calling card's dust rose and expanded beside him. The cloud obscured both Dutton's hands and the invention: a sturdier air purifier for New Washington and Enclave citizens. It even dimmed the shine on the founders' medallion draped over the shoulders of Jayson's formal suit.

"Welcome, everyone. Enjoy the party!" The host's last words were muffled by his guests' gasps.

Dutton's investors—some with chips that glowed to match their cocktail silks and suits—and the Change Corporation's white-coated engineers took cautious steps backwards. "Are the vents blocked?" "Is this an attack?" "In New Washington?"

To their relief, the company's new air purifier whirred, sucking the dust away admirably. But the gold cloud lingered long enough for hidden lasers to write "Beware the Thieves" in the blurred air.

At that, guests shrieked and patted their pockets. It was already too late.

At twenty-eight minutes to six, Daxian Canarvier slid behind an overstuffed coat rack and crammed himself, along with a bundled tablecloth, into the antique air vent. No one was chasing him yet. But the trick, as King Canarvier always taught his kids, was to get ahead of the crowd.

The vent traverse was a long, patient crawl, and Dax had promised King he'd go slow, careful, and quiet. Noise from the party obscured the metal grille's slight rattle as Dax slid it back into place.

At first, the noise of congratulations, murmured

gratitude, and toasts had been loud enough to cover what Dax was up to. The noise of success signified how far the city, and other cities like it, had come in the past thirty years, after the Mess, or, depending on who was describing it, the recent Turbulence. Success meant power and security. Both of which Jayson Dutton had now achieved: a newly glowing Enclave chip was confirmation.

Soon, the feeds said, a Dutton might sit on the Recovery Court, along with illustrious families like the Lius, Morenos, and Benfords.

When Jayson Dutton's personal assistant had offered the Canarviers the job, King had laughed and accepted. "No better way to celebrate success than with thieves."

To Dax, it was a micro-heist. A minor job for major talent. The gig might keep the family's bus going and pay the rent on their city apartment share for a month or two, but it wasn't the glorious assignment that would set the Canarviers up for life: Dax opening his own pop-up in New Washington and inheriting the family business officially; Nan quitting both her bookkeeping and cleaning service hustles; Roosa's tuition at Miss Farmer's paid so she didn't have to help cater parties. And King? What King wanted was the glory, the art, the spectacle, and the one thing he couldn't have: his wife.

Dax listened to Dutton's partygoers shriek with delight at being part of a robbery—even a small one—while he hauled their watches and jewelry deeper into the air vents.

He crawled the guts of the building's fifth floor. The party's noise pulsed against his palms and knees.

The building's vents were filled with snags and an industrial cleaning scent that didn't quite eliminate the acrid city smells. The white catering tablecloth Dax pushed in front of him held trendy vintage wallets and the kind of recovered and validated jewelry that New Washington's citizens loved. It grew gray and greasy in the metal crawlspace.

Dax's sommelier uniform became equally fouled. He wanted to sneeze, but it wasn't time for that.

When the calling card dropped, according to terms laid out in the Dutton contract, the Canarviers had twenty minutes left to grab everything they could, without getting caught. Dax stifled his sneeze with pride.

He'd scored the beats for this heist himself: card drop, vent traverse, guest chase, shaft jump. King had double checked everything, of course. But the closer the clock ticked to five fifty, the more Dax looked forward to his father clapping him on the back for a job well done.

True, King would also hand him the laundry to soak overnight in the apartment sink. *No laundry service for the Canarviers, no sir. Not when we can spend all our winnings on improving our art.* Dax grumbled, but he really didn't mind. The artistry was part of the family's mystique. But the grime would be tough to get out.

A fan turned somewhere down-vent, sparring with the filter in his cheap service mask. His nose and throat tickled. Dax bit down hard on the sneeze. *Just a few more minutes.*

"See, we do just fine without Roo," he whispered, more to distract himself than to criticize his sister. They were a team, even if she'd found her way into a fancy Enclave academy with real teachers. They were a family.

"Quiet when performing this close to guests," King's voice staticked in Dax's ear.

Sorry, Dad. Dax knew his silence would be taken as contrition.

King picked him to take over the family trade—not the public business, which was a hodgepodge of hustles and pop-ups cityside under the name of Vane—the real business. The Canarviers' entertainment troupe. If Dax led a successful heist—even a small one like this—the Canarviers would thrive. Maybe even branch out to other cities around the reclaimed world. With or without Roosa. Dax would get to direct the entertainments, with the bigger take that came with the responsibility. He loved performing, but he adored the payoff even more.

I wasn't that loud. Besides, sending one of Aanand's automatons down the left vent while I went right covered up any noise.

Dax closed his eyes, imagining what he'd be able to buy when the job was done. Once they sold their take back—with a thieves' markup—to the investors gathered in Dutton's office, paid off their suppliers, the rent, and the bus repairs. Maybe he'd get a preloaded New Washington citizen's band for a whole weekend. Hit the clubs, get some ideas for his own pop-up. Maybe he'd even take a real bath at a hotel with a working desalinator, rather than his bi-weekly sand scrub.

He smiled, then relaxed his jaw. The sneeze erupted. His ah-CHOO pushed its way down the vent and out the grille.

Perfection. Even King had no criticism to share over the comms.

The party's noise changed tenor. "I heard one!" "Over here!" The searching guests shifted directions.

Dax's eyes slowly opened. He smiled in anticipation. The reality before him—another stretch of dusty vent barely wide enough for his shoulders, that tasted like metal—could be dealt with. Profit—even cocktail sized—awaited.

Four minutes left. The guests yanked at the grille far behind him, then tried to cram themselves into the air vent. This was their chance to catch a thief.

Dax inched forward, toward the intersection with the elevator shaft. On his wrist, next to his deactivated workband, King's analog timer read thirteen minutes to six. Other crews used the clocks on their tablets, but King swore by the Timex he'd found in a dump on New Washington's outskirts. Whoever ran the job got the watch. *Can't beat analog,* King always said. *Traditions are important.*

Finishing this heist—success was moments away—would put Dax one step closer to the Timex becoming his for good. A Grand Heist, like the one at the Graves estate next week that he'd seen King looking at, was the kind of performance that would put them over the top. That was the kind of glory the Canarviers deserved.

Especially if Nan and King stopped fighting about it and actually put in a bid.

Dax was very careful never to say things like that out loud. Everyone knew King Canarvier was superstitious about discussing heists, contracts, and family matters.

Through the network of vents that wove the reclaimed office building, Dax listened to the rising chatter of Dutton's guests closing the chase. They could sense time was running out to get their things back. And, even better, to get the reward that came with catching their own thief. Even if they didn't really send them to lockup.

Far behind him, a woman groaned. "I think I'm stuck." Galvanized steel creaked as a weight was pulled free.

Dax checked his watch again. Almost time to jump.

Dutton's guests were slower in the vents than he'd expected. His knees ached from the cold metal and he was looking forward to getting back on his feet.

Less than two minutes left. Good enough, or should be. He risked a whisper. "Give them the finish, Dad."

King didn't reply. Not the "One minute, forty seconds," Dax expected. Not a lecture about being artists and how details mattered. Usually, he'd say: "The job ends precisely when the client says." But he didn't say it. Dax waited. He wouldn't be the reason they got nicked and the job turned illegal.

King's rules kept the family in business. They'd heard thieves in other protected cities copied their act. Or tried to. Dax respected that. *But what difference does a few moments make to people as rich as these? Who throw away money for sport?*

The Timex's fast hand twitched. One minute. *Come on, Dad.* At this point in the party, guests were as likely to catch each other as they were the thieves. With under a minute to go, the air was nearly electric.

"Give them every second they've paid for," Nan's voice crackled after a long pause.

The vent finally screeched behind Dax. Closer now. A high-pitched voice bounced off the ancient aluminum. "I'm through! There are tracks!"

Amateurs. Dax reached the elevator shaft as the vent began to shake. The burden of several well-dressed guests made the shaft supports groan. They followed the path Dax had left in the grime. *Fifteen seconds. Time to jump.*

He clipped himself to the pulley cable King had strung. Netted his stolen goods in the counterweight bag. Then Dax said a small hope that Nan had calculated the weights right and jumped into the ancient elevator shaft.

With a soft zip, the goods went down and Dax rose, just like they'd practiced. Three floors down, Nan would hook the sack and tuck it into her cleaning cart, then resume vacuuming another corporation's hallways.

That had been Dax's idea. A good one. King himself said so. Even Nan had approved.

As time ran out, Dax stood on the neighboring building's roof, watching well-dressed engineers and investors crawl beneath office desks, jump stairwells like in old movies, and shine cuff lights into the basement's depths. Their movements grew more frenetic as the last seconds ticked down.

The air felt cool on Dax's sweaty neck.

Finally, the Canarviers' closing card bloomed in the Dutton's window. A little late. A purple "The thieves have the time and yours too. With that, we take our due."

King said the cards, and especially the verses, set the Canarviers apart as performers. Dax didn't think he was good at rhymes, but King had pressed him to try. And it worked.

The partygoers cheered and laughed as they got up and dusted themselves off. Then they began to applaud their hosts. Jayson Dutton and his family bowed as if they'd crawled through the vents themselves, which they certainly had not.

"A cocktail heist isn't nearly as good as a Grand Heist, but it's all right." Dax didn't hide the pride in his voice as he whispered to King and Nan.

He took a deep breath, looking up at the dust-dimmed stars. Waited for King to say *A job well done,* like he did with Roo's heists. The earpiece stayed silent. Dax's unease grew.

At a quarter past six, Dax turned away from the Dutton's windows and leapt to another rooftop, landing gently on the balls of his feet. Always good to practice the skills. He descended three fire escapes and dropped the last gap between ladder and sidewalk silently. Right beside an old janitor carrying a bag of trash.

Even in the reclaimed world with all its marvels, someone always had to take out the trash.

"At least a million, Nan!" Dax felt like shouting. "Performance done and done well too!"

"You counted in the middle of a heist, Daxian?" Nan's voice stung more than her swat on his bicep. "Never do that. Bad luck."

"Nan, come on . . . we did well." He really wished someone would say that back to him.

Nan patted Dax's shoulder with a gloved hand. "Where's your father? I had to trigger the calling card remotely."

"I thought he'd be with you." That was the plan. "Dad?" Dax tapped his earpiece like he was waking the fabbed tech from a nap.

But King stayed silent. The air beat down around Dax's ears as Dutton's better guests left the building in sleek roofhopters. The shiny carbon-fiber hulls lifted them out over the rebuilt city and the seawalls to their floating homes and domed mansions nearby. *Platinum folks, slumming.*

New Washington began to hum with the night's music and smell of pop-up food. Dax's mouth watered. A few citizens captured autocars on their slow, silent circuits of the streets. They tapped their bands on the windows before ducking inside. The cars swung automatically toward destinations of choice. The best homes in New Washington were still underground. Dax and Nan pushed themselves into the shadows as a car sank into a grate nearby, before the streets settled again.

The odd sound of small wings beating the air made Nan suck in a breath. A city MilPol drone was pacing toward them.

Before the drone could turn the building's corner, Nan and Dax stuffed their haul into a dumpster. It was the kind of trick that still worked in a pinch. People avoided garbage in order to keep themselves away from disease and dust. The pair sank down in the bin's shadow.

When the drone had passed, the streets went as silent as Dax's earpiece. *Where is King*?

They walked, keeping to the shadows, until they arrived back at the aboveground tenement pushed up against the city walls. Entering the tiny apartment they rent-shared with several other families from the Skirts, they shucked their uniforms and service masks in the hallway and scrubbed the outside grime off as best they could.

"He'll be all right. He's always all right." Nan coughed until her handkerchief was black.

"Time to fab another mask before we go back," Dax said. The Skirts were unfiltered, and he worried about Nan. "Now that we have the credits?"

She winked at him but didn't answer. Settled by the window to watch and wait, leaving the small cot in the bedroom for Dax. In his memory, she'd never found it useful to worry aloud about anything.

When the sun rose, King was still gone.

Nan, wearing a pair of cleaners' coveralls, slapped a new workband on her wrist, donned her old mask, and walked back to the office building by herself in time to clock in, and then change to meet Dutton's assistant.

During her absence, Dax burned up a handful of screen credits to watch the heist fee hit the family's account. He tapped a few more to show the latest feeds on the apartment's screen. Educational shows were free, but not much else. Dax paced, clenching and unclenching his hands, as he scanned gossip channels, fan groups, and municipal reports.

The feeds wove news and rumor with immersives—video, audio, documents—each bit taking a micropayment. The rarer, the more views and comments, the more expensive. He couldn't afford to access everything. He waved off a cheap batch about a founders' ship party that had been going for a year. Another skein of clips and reactions to Trenton's sea-calming tech. Finally found one clip of Dutton's speech. But nothing about the heist. Or a captured thief. *We weren't showy enough to catch on*, Dax groaned.

Nan returned after the city and Enclave transports had left the neighborhood on their morning circuit. "Sold back the guests' belongings at a nice markup. The client was pleased with the show."

"But nothing in the news," Dax said. *And no King,* he didn't say.

It was nearly time to hand the apartment over to the next family: Dax's best friend Aanand and his dad, Amos.

Nan turned a grim look on Dax, her eyes clouded with worry. The apartment's single light bulb deepened the creases on her cheeks. "You call at the precinct. I'll get Roo."

New Washington City Feed

Municipal Mudlarkers group
(full citizen band required)

Mudlarker 3421: Found this before it was sequestered—anyone heard anything?

New Washington South Wall Precinct Dispatch

Precinct Report Dossier: Illegal Burglary at Dutton Change Corporation,
Assault on Judge: 7 p.m., Tuesday [date redacted]

- ·Victim Name & Title: [Redacted], Judge
- ·Employment: Unified Recovery Court, Protected Cities
- Injuries, Losses: Access Band/Dossier/[Redacted] Records
- ·Contact information: [Redacted]
- ·Assailant Name: Kenneth Vane, aka "King"
- ·Occupation: Event Planning, Catering, Rare Books Trade, Sanitation Contractor
- ·Former Employment: City of New Washington, Reclamation/Recovery Public Works
- ·Address: New Washington Tower 14 [to be verified]
- ·Citizenship Status: Citizen Renter

Testimony: Victim states assailant approached threateningly at the conclusion of a founders' award celebration. Victim moved to evade. Assailant grabbed them by the right arm and removed from their person several documents [not recovered] and an access band [recovered by witness]. Victim alerted MilPol.

Witness (Citizen, Enclave): On the evening of [redacted], just before 7 p.m., I observed the suspect leaving a midtown office building in the company of a Recovery Judge. In the shadows between buildings, there was a scuffle, then the figures separated. The judge seemed injured. I alerted MilPol.

Charging: Assailant has prior complaints and instabilities on record (see attached documents). No verified crimes. Suspicion of aliases; maintains renter citizenship under given name of Kenneth Vane.

Supporting documents from city records: one employment termination letter, one dissolution of marriage contract document, fourteen resolved suspicions dispatches, one documented protest action. Incorporation documents, reclamation tithe receipts: Vane Bookkeeping, Vane Cleaning and Salvage, Vane Catering and Planning, Vane Antiques.

Mudlarker 224: Haven't heard a peep—will keep an eye out.

Mudlarker 4457: A judge attacked? Bet we'll be seeing more MilPol drones on the streets. And in the Skirts too.

Mudlarker 224: good.

The Safe Approach

In the small bedroom of their apartment share, Roosa Canarvier tested her borrowed ball gown. Her hands settled against the bustier, pressing her lock picks, watch, and data tablet securely against her ribs. The seamstress poofed her silk skirts, rendering the bustle's many pockets invisible.

I am supposed to be presenting my final exam at Miss Farmer's, not preparing to rob an Enclave house. Roo waved the thought away before the seamstress saw her worried expression. The fitting was taking precious, but necessary, time.

In an hour—maybe less—the Enclave van would pass by. If she missed it, there wouldn't be a ball, or anything else, to go to.

Sasha Limére, a Miss Farmer's classmate and the genius seamstress currently at work on her bodice, couldn't know all of what she intended to do over the next few days.

"Sasha, I've never worn anything so nice." The designer's signature augmentations at the gown's lower back and sleeves shifted from butterfly cutouts to feathers on command. They didn't quite reveal enough to get Roo thrown from Mason Graves's fancy house and Evangeline Benford's birthday weekend, but it was a near thing.

Roo's blue eyes reflected in Sasha's gold-rimmed lenses as the seamstress took her measure. "Enclave parties have extraordinary standards. Those who can afford to ignore the rules will be the first to notice those who can't."

Sasha was right. Roo couldn't afford to ignore anything, but she needed to look like she could. Although, at the moment, she was having a hard time ignoring the brown-eyed seamstress sitting very close to her knees, so focused on her handiwork that there was a tiny dent between her eyebrows, just above her freckled nose.

Sasha caught her staring and winked. "Just take care of the outfit. I don't present finals to Miss Farmer until next week, but I won't have much time for repairs."

Roo stared at her hands, her cheeks burning. "I will take care of it. If you're certain."

Sasha waved the idea away with a programming-mesh-covered hand. "You are my friend. Your family needs you to attend this event. And I can get a real-world test of the wardrobe before I turn it in. I'm the one who's grateful."

Even in the predawn light, Sasha's smile was warm and encouraging. At her gesture, the gown pinged softly, then whispered, "Reconstitute?"

"Cancel." Sasha spoke quickly. "Sorry. The new fabric is very sensitive! I'll silence the audio now."

"Worth it," Roo said. "I'm relieved to have your expertise." *Along with a promise not to ask too many questions.*

When Nan had messaged about her father's illness and the need to be on the next work van for New Washington, Roo had worried she might not see Sasha again. Or be able to complete her own final project. She wasn't the only one who worried. As she closed her work down, her advisor had frowned.

"Miss Vane, can you afford to dote on a relative this close to exams? Your project isn't complete. You have class requirements as well."

Roo—Roosala Vane to everyone at Miss Farmer's—had practice keeping her temper, especially around her advisor, but the word "dote" made her nostrils flare. "Thank you, Mr. Kerr-Moulthrop, I promise you I will finish it. The project is important to me. So is my father."

Her advisor had dedicated his life to helping the offspring of good Enclave and city families secure full employment on the Enclave side of the wall after graduation. He'd pressed his lips together beneath his waxed mustache, then began, "Your problem of identity perpetuation across interruptions of service and ownership is not a simple database hack, Miss Vane. You haven't sorted half the shared-packet issues—" when Sasha, at the desk next to Roo, interceded.

She'd stared down the advisor. "Have a heart, sir."

Kerr-Moulthrop sighed, but waved his hand. A chip in his palm glowed, acknowledging Roo's dismissal.

Sasha whispered, "You'll be back in plenty of time to finish. I'll help you study. Anything you need, message me."

What she couldn't tell Sasha, or anyone, was that when she reached the city, she met Nan outside the MilPol precinct. Afternoon sun filtered through the clouds, turning nearby buildings and overhead walkways golden. Dax hurried down the precinct stairs to them. "He's still being processed, couldn't talk to him. The charges are actual, illegal burglary—someone at the Duttons' claimed he attacked them. Someone important."

Nan groaned quietly.

Roo stared at her brother and grandmother. "That's not his way. We can fight it. We have citizen's bands for exactly this purpose."

"This isn't King's first accusation," Nan replied. She

was right; that was an industry risk—and it made the eventual punishment worse. With infractions on his record, the fact that he also shared a single renter's citizenship with multiple families under the Vane name put King, and all of them, in danger.

Dax pulled them away from the steps. "I got an officer to agree to take his case off the feeds for a week. Told them it was a hardship. It took the rest of our haul from the Duttons. They made it clear that without another hundred million credits they would be shipping him to Alaska next Sunday."

"That's only five days." Not enough time to call in favors, Roo knew, especially when King was usually the one to manage favors. "We have to do a gig, fast."

Dax looked intently at Nan. "There's one gig coming up we could bid on."

"No." Nan whispered the word. "I can pick up extra shifts. Do the books for *Enclave & Towne* or the court—both pay well." Even as she said it, her brows knit together. She knew extra regular work would never be enough, fast enough, to get King back.

"What's the gig?" Roo pressed.

Dax pounced on her question as if he'd had this argument already. "Mason Graves is throwing a birthday party for his girlfriend—a whole weekend! A real Grand Heist! He put out a request for proposals two days ago, and Nan and King have been fighting me about it ever since."

"That girlfriend," Nan said, "is Evangeline Benford. We don't mess with the Benfords. They own too much of the city and the MilPol. Not to mention the Enclaves. Plus, Mason Graves uses kinds of biosecurity that are far too risky for us. We could lose everything. No."

"Nan—" Roo looked at her grandmother. "We'll lose everything if we *don't* try. The job makes sense." She had to admit, she'd seen Mason and Evangeline on the feeds a few times at Miss Farmer's. They looked like they had plenty worth stealing.

"There's no time to prepare!" Nan protested. She ticked problems on her fingers, as if trying a case before a MilPol judge. "Without your father, who'll do the fast talking, the distractions? The dazzle? Who will double-check the beats? Make the calling cards? The aliases? Costumes? I can't drop the clients I've lined up this week—we need the credits to pay the extra days at the apartment so MilPol continues to think he's a citizen and a Vane. No. This is too fast, especially with only three of us, especially without King."

"We can do those things," Dax said. "We did the last job with three. We did great."

Except you lost King, Roo thought, but didn't say.

Before Nan could argue with Dax, Roo jumped in. "I'll do the beats, the costumes, the aliases, and case the location. You sort the contracts and the acrobats like always, Nan. We can do this. King's trained us to do this. It's the only way."

"What if this is some sort of trap?" Nan grabbed their elbows and walked between them back to the apartment. "If another troupe set King up? Or a vendor? Someone King's angered? Lord knows there are plenty of those. I can't be at the house long—not if I'm holding the apartment and getting the aerialists together." Nan stood before the apartment door. "Who will run the job?"

"I will," Roo and Dax said at the same time. They looked at one another and both spoke again: "No I will."

Dax reached for King's watch in his pocket. "I've got the Timex."

His fingers came up empty. He stared open mouthed at Roo, who held the watch, grinning. "Fine. But only because you're older."

Roo bristled. Dax narrowed his eyes.

"You can't run a job and fight too," Nan said. "That will make this disaster even worse."

Roo counted to ten silently. Dax was supposed to inherit the troupe. But he'd lost King. She needed to make sure this one job went right, one last time. "Nan, make the bid, get the job. Let us help dad. We'll run it perfectly—you'll see." Roo turned pleading eyes on her grandmother. "Let us do what we're good at doing."

Nan shook her head but muttered, "You're going to need fancier clothes than the last job." She settled at the small apartment table, before her screen, and opened a bookkeeping task that was blinking red—late. "Let me finish this and then I'll see what I can do."

She was going to let them try.

Dax whooped, not bothering to conceal his excitement. As they waited, Roo drew out a list of initial beats, based on her favorite previous heists. She remembered King, whooping and dancing around Nan's rebuilt bus in the Skirts, the first time she'd escaped an event on her own. She'd made it all the way home, her pockets filled with silverware.

She turned to the costumes. "I know who to call for clothes."

Sasha Limére was already the fastest seamstress on either side of the wall. Even while pursuing her studies at Miss Farmer's, she took commissions from the Enclave and the city to support her tuition. When Roo called, she worked all night to finish her final design early.

And now she was here, in the Vanes' tiny apartment well before dawn for the fitting.

She inspected Roo's appearance with a skilled tailor's eye.

Roo tried hard not to fidget. Her right hand touched her left wrist and the charms attached to the simple chain there. The cool glass baubles—discreet smoke-throw charms that Nan and King had presented to her after her first successful Grand Heist "for emergencies"—were real metal and glass, not fabricated carbon. They caught and tossed the light against Roo's tan arm in soothing ways.

"Lovely." Sasha gazed at the charms appreciatively. She wouldn't understand what they truly were, but fabbed baubles could never capture the light in this way.

Suddenly Roo had no idea what to do with her hands. *Lovely*, Sasha had said. The word lingered.

"I bet they'll bring good luck." Sasha looked up at Roo. "They complete the look. It's stunning." She paused and took a breath. "My work, that is. Please be sure to take good care of it."

"I promise," Roo said, a bit too forcefully. *Stunning. Lovely.*

Roo needed stunning. Everyone–King, Dax, and Nan–depended on her making a flawless entry to the party. The beats she'd choreographed had her front and center at the ball, after spending a night in the house's walls, working her way into Graves's security systems. *If I can get into the house. If we get the job.*

Each day King stayed in the hold was a risk–if the precinct caught on, they'd all wind up in Alaska, instead of safe on the family bus in the Skirts. They had to get the job. Roo and Dax had to be perfect. No sign of Skirts dust, no hint of their lives in the caravans that circled the city–for an entire weekend.

From where Roo stood, a tiny sunrise mirrored off the Enclave's distant dome and reflected in the opposite building's windows. Their tower was too near the city wall to see the sea directly, or the road between the city and the Enclave's airlock, but she could get this glimpse of twice-reflected dawn. The only other thing the shared apartment overlooked clearly was the Skirts: a slow and barely tolerated moving camp that rode the ancient Belt Way's remains around New Washington.

Sasha tucked her hemming tools away with a snap, pulling Roo's attention from the window. She lifted the invitation to Evangeline Benford's twenty-first birthday weekend from the bedroom's dusty dresser. Pulled the dance card from the envelope. "Very grand. How did you get this lucky?"

Roo smiled. "Better not to say." Her heart skipped. Sasha thought she–they, her family–was grand. At least momentarily.

Sasha's quiet snort lifted the tension in the sparse room. Roo used that exact phrase when working on a commission that roused her classmates' curiosity. "Fair."

In truth, the engraver for the Graves event had an apartment share one floor down, thanks to King. He'd made an extra invitation set, right down to lifting the digital security badge of a declined RSVP, thinking Roo was trying to break into the gossip feeds.

Sasha was making similar assumptions. New Washington society followers had Graves and Benford firmly set as an item. Fans waited breathlessly on an engagement.

"Let me in on your cut if you get a ring shot." Sasha winked. "I hope this helps your family." She checked off the events. "Masked ball, brunch, concert, banquet, and . . ." she wrinkled her nose, "A hunt? Lawn tennis? That's a bit showy. Let's hope the terraform holds." Sasha tapped a finger against her lips as she read the invitation through. "Dress codes for everything. Black gown and gloves for the ball. Do you have a fancy mask?"

Roo nodded. She planned to get one at the Graves house.

"Can't forget gloves." Sasha emphasized the last word so that the fabric listened. She pointed her finger at Roo's bare hands.

At the gesture, Roo's sleeves extended beneath her bracelets, seamlessly connecting around her fingertips. "Save augmentation," the seamstress finished, smiling softly. Her wire-rimmed glasses tinted blue for a moment, then turned transparent again. Roo's fingertips tingled. She stared at them. *Focus.*

When Sasha lifted her head, she was all business. "The fabric's flexible enough to accommodate the weekend. I added a singlesuit you can modify for the tennis. But do remember to let the fibers rest between big changes, and recharge occasionally in the sun. You'll be fine. You'll fit right in." She chuckled and began tabulating the rental and security fees on her reticule's abacus, which she'd designed herself. "Go ahead, try it."

"Conversion A." Roo snapped and tied hidden gathers on the skirts, activating a transformation. The cloth folded into undetectable, slightly padded silk cargo pants. It took ten seconds to transform the garment's lower half. She'd need to be faster. A tug at the gloves' smart fabric retracted them. The feeling was like a moth's wing brushing her fingertips—until the fabric looped over her thumbs.

She pressed a hidden tailor's button to change her top's color to a workaday cream that looked and felt like canvas. The corset detailing became pockets and seams. Sasha hadn't just made her a gown. She'd built Roo a wardrobe suitable for anything. Even a Grand Heist. "Show me the next conversion?"

Pounding at the apartment's front door startled them both. "Someone's quite early!" Sasha whispered. Roo nodded, her heart in her throat. It could only be MilPol, checking on King's residency and identity.

Dax answered the door and stepped into the hallway. Roo was glad the wall muffled the voices. When the door closed moments later without extra visitors, Roo relaxed. They'd been right to stay in the apartment, even though it cost them. *Had Sasha noticed?* She wasn't sure.

Dax coughed from the threshold, making her jump again. "Wrong address." He smiled. "Hello there, miss?"

He took a step toward Sasha, hand out. A cocky grin revealed the gap between his front teeth. His nails were tinged with grime.

The seamstress smiled a quick acknowledgement. "I should go as well." She pinned her hat back on and raised her outdoor mask. "I have one more client call, and then back over the wall before class if I'm taking notes for both of us today. Give me your pass."

Roo handed Sasha her student wristband. "Never felt so lucky to not be chipped."

Most who came and went in the Enclaves had ordinary workbands that held citizenship and account data. Several of Roo's and Sasha's teachers and classmates had Enclave chips that allowed them to come and go freely and pay for anything they wanted without an account tabulation. It was impressive, as long as their families remained Enclave owners. A big insolvency the previous semester had resulted in multiple bandaged hands, and fewer chips.

"Band checks wherever you go? No thank you. I can't wait to earn one." Sasha beamed happily at the space between them, eyes on future successes. Sasha's reputation was immaculate. Her inventions, brilliant. Roo was wearing the proof. All of that, plus years more work might earn her a founders' award someday, and the chip that came with it.

"As long as you don't mind being traceable," Dax said.

Too late, Roo stepped firmly on his foot.

Sasha sucked in an offended breath and then tipped her head at Roo. "For now, I will agree it is convenient for you." She swept past Dax, pausing long enough at Nan's worktable to collect her security fee.

Roo followed her out, glaring at her brother as she did.

The seamstress disappeared through the door into the still-dark city. The door's weight ground closed against dust in its hinges. When Dax murmured, "Next time why not visit us in the Skirts?" Only Roo could hear it.

"She is doing us a favor!" She whirled on her brother, the past day's stress winning over her usual controlled demeanor. "As am I."

"Exactly my point," Dax said. "Would you rather have stayed over there?"

"Grandson," Nan said from the table, her face lit by an event-bidding screen, "do you want us to do this job together, or not?"

"More than anything," Dax replied.

"Then keep your ego out of your mouth." Her tone was

even. She did not turn from the screen. Both Roo and Dax could see the tension in her jawline. She was scared. Her son gone. MilPol knocking at the door before dawn. But was there more?

"What aren't you telling us?" Roo asked quietly. She didn't have much time before the work van arrived, but doubt tugged at her mind. Very few things scared Nan.

"This is not a game, not a mere performance. This is a gamble against people who make the rules. There's no room for errors," Nan began. Her voice shook. "Or pride. Look at where that got King."

"Sorry," Dax stammered. "We will make this work, Nan. We promise."

Roo understood then how much King's arrest had shaken Nan. The new troupe dynamics—everyone having to fill in for King's expertise at a rush—that's what was driving her grandmother's worry. She squeezed Nan's shoulder, trying to comfort her without embarrassing her. "We will."

King would have made a rousing speech or a rallying joke. Roo had no time for either.

She pushed her feet, covered by the wardrobe's socks, into a well-used pair of work boots by the door. The apartment came with several pairs, none new enough to resize properly any longer. Her feet sloshed in them until Sasha's socks thickened to compensate.

She reached for her day mask, its outer layer speckled with grime. The apartment's allotment bulb highlighted a problem: the outfit, when paired with the mask, looked too clean for work. As did Roo.

A drawback to being over the wall for the past six months. Although she wore the right uniform and a hacked workband, the lines where city dust should set deep into her skin weren't there any longer.

Dax elbowed her back. His own ocean-colored eyes—like their mother's, King had said frequently—twinkled. His grin was an echo of King's. He looked more like their father every day: Broad shoulders, dark skin, darker curls. Give him enough time, Roo thought, and he'd try for King's handlebar mustache, or a subtle goatee. He, thankfully, hadn't yet had the time.

"Spotless," he said. "Let me." His Skirts mask was caked with dust. As she held her breath, he tapped it over her knees and elbows. The dust settled into the seams. "Much better. The drive will help too."

Now Roo's skin itched, and she couldn't complain. Canarviers were proud to be from the Skirts.

"The apocalypse happened," King was fond of telling other Skirters. "It just wasn't evenly distributed. We might be few, compared to city folk, but we remember."

The city and the Enclave had already forgotten in order to move into the future. *I'm changing too, getting used to life in the Enclave.* Roo couldn't admit that to anyone. But she was also gaining connections King wanted. She turned twenty in three months; before that, she had to graduate from Miss Farmers' and finish a final project that would secure her a spot on the Enclave side of the wall. Or maybe even with the Reclamation Court. She still hadn't told her family that she was working on a way to trace identity and property lost in the Mess, both Nan's and others. She'd wanted it to be a surprise.

"That dust will do until it's time to clean yourself up," Nan said, stopping Dax from shaking his mask over Roo's head. Her voice was encouraging. "If only King were as careful."

The space where King used to be felt like a balance missing from a watch. All the other parts kept trying to find ways to work, but had a hard time connecting.

She hugged her grandmother. "We'll get him." Then she turned to her younger—but only by a year—brother. "Ready to work?"

"Ready to dazzle," Dax replied. "Just like last time."

The van was going to arrive in moments, but she couldn't

let his words slide. "Maybe less dazzle, more technique," she said. "Dutton Change Corporation was not in the Enclave."

"The client wants two high-visibility thefts each day, or a total of six across the weekend. Stick with the plan, no additions, no deviations," Nan reminded them.

"I will!" Dax growled. They were pushing each other too far with worry.

King kicked each job off by reciting the beats. Roo tried it, to reassure herself and everyone else too. "The plan is: confidence, fool the house, friend of a friend, all that glitters . . ." She waited for her brother to join in, but Dax sulked. "Come on."

"All that glitters, baker's dozen, falling star . . ." Her grandmother tapped the screen, negotiating now with the client. "Dax—"

"All that glitters," Dax finally said, only naming the card-drop beat. One of his first responsibilities. "I'll have both calling cards ready when I see you."

"I'll come as soon as I finish work," Nan said. "Or sooner if anything goes wrong."

"It won't," Dax said confidently.

"It might." Roo fiddled with one of the sparkling pins Sasha had placed in her hair. They were too fancy for the outfit, but she hadn't wanted to change them. "Without a win, King goes to the water mines Sunday night. You know what happens to people in Sitka, even if they make it, especially after—" after *Ma disappeared.* She didn't say it. "Promise me—"

Roo paused. Dax stared at his shoes, hands curling into fists. "Falling star, dropped melon, apron scam. Disappearing banquet. Exeunt, pursued by a thief." He looked up. "Roo, we've done all of these at least once. What if we find a safe? No one's ever done that at a party."

Nan stopped working on the negotiations. She stared at her grandson. "No safes."

Roo figured he'd been joking. Enclave safes were highly trained in how not to be found.

Nan tapped her earpiece. "Work van, six blocks away."

"Did Graves sign yet?" Missing this van would screw up timing for the rest of the heist. Roo rolled a smoke charm between her fingertips. *We'll get the gig and get you back, Dad. I promise.*

"Not yet. They're arguing security now. Enclave folks want safer thieves than last season. Imagine." Even as her grandmother worked, Roo watched the tablet counter for screen time costs. It rolled with each moment the negotiations dragged on. Beside it, King's case number, with his MilPol fees increasing by the second. Waiting cost too much. Mason Graves needed to hurry up and decide.

She rested her head against Nan's. The smell of the Skirts' sand laundry wrinkled her nose, but she lingered. "Graves will sign. We're the best." *He had to sign.* Roo couldn't watch those counters rise any longer, knowing how little was left in the family accounts. Knowing that the only thing she could do to help King depended on Graves deciding to let her do it. "I have to go."

She jerked the straps on her pack tight, and double-checked her tools with quick fingers. Picks, a flat card packed with screwdriver and cutters, a rolled-up tablet, microprojector, drill, protein bars.

She tucked a tendril of hair back behind one of Sasha's pins. Maybe she was nervous.

Dax reddened in the extending silence. "Van's turning the corner."

"Good. Dax, see you tomorrow. Wine delivery at five." At least they were sure of that connection. The sommelier was a friend of Nan's. "Card drop at seven. First take before the ball ends. Nan, see you on sweep, Saturday."

"Got it." Nan's white hair had pulled from its bun. In the light, her bronze complexion was tinged green. *Was she feeling okay? No. One too many worries.* Nan would say if she needed help. "I'll send the haul estimates once you send me the guest list. I'm about to lock the contract. In addition to the mandated spectacles, I'm afraid we had to compromise on a few capture techniques. Plus, they wanted a guarantee that the full troupe would be on site. No understudies. And the owner's suite is off-limits."

"How can we manage multiple spectacles with so many restrictions? They're being ridiculous—" Dax began, but Roo cut him off.

"We will manage." They had to. "I can set a workband to King's specifics." Her first hacking chores as a Skirts kid were changing the citizen bands' ID specs for apartment residency. A repetitive but necessary task. Graves's negotiation demands might be unsettling, but they couldn't stop now. *Even if he was asking about understudies. What did he know about King?*

Roo opened the door and glanced out. Three floors below, a dark van lumbered down the street, steaming in the dawn. A few apartments had lights on, and Roo saw shadows emerging from the buildings. Hurrying to score a seat.

Dax and Nan accompanied her to the door. Their message was clear: *We are a team, no matter what. We are a family. We're Canarviers.*

But the message was silent without King there to say the words. That hurt. Roo hugged them both. "I'll get you the guest list before dark, Nan."

She would have to jump two flights of stairs to make the van.

"Good. I'll share your data with Dax. Then we're radio silent until we get this done." She made a shooing motion and turned back to the contract.

Cursing slightly as she eyed her first jump, the fire escape rattling, Roo unwrapped a new workband from the apartment's cache near the door, then pocketed three more. She slapped the carbon fab strip on her wrist and hustled to join the growing line of workers below.

While his girlfriend prepared to sneak back to her family estate on the other side of the Enclave green, Mason Graves tried to focus on the thieves' contract negotiation.

He heard her pad softly around the bedroom. Then a creak as Evangeline leaned against the office door, murmuring, "Always working."

"Always, Ev," he replied. He sipped his morning vitamin shake from a recovered crystal glass and tried to compose himself. He'd almost said "love." Tried for a more jocular tone. "I do have to run a business while I plan your party."

"Don't worry, I understand." She tapped her polished fingernails against the door. "But you don't have to close the door while you work. It's just me."

Mason paused. He liked to work alone. Even Holt, his security chief, mostly stayed out. How was it possible he could feel Evangeline's pout—that soft lower lip, her sad eyes, her long, dark lashes nearly brushing her perfect cheeks—even through the office door. A real, recovered wood door, too. Not fabbed.

He couldn't refuse her anything. Not while he was trying to win her hand. "Of course. Habit." He pushed a button on the desk.

"Would you like to remove your no-interruptions boundary?" Llyria, his house, asked him. Mason had set the house's voice to be soft, a little like Evangeline's. But only in his office. "You have 419 messages waiting. Two urgent messages from Dr. Karen Tsalta."

"Just Evangeline for now," Mason said.

The latch clicked. The double doors swung open.

Evangeline padded barefoot across the thick carpet in a silk pajama set the color of night, carrying an expensive pair of matching slippers. "Habits are a sign of a deliberate mind. Society loves such things. So does my father."

Her platinum bob was tucked under the hood of her robe. She hadn't gone so far as to do makeup, but she'd dabbed a bit of gloss on her lips before she made her entrance.

Mason smiled as her pout turned subtle grin. Her robe slid to reveal a bare shoulder. She didn't pull it back up.

"I'm very deliberate when it comes to business, Miss Benford. Even though my wits seem to scatter every time you're around." The office was where Mason felt focused, ready to take on everything his business or the complexities of Enclave society threw at him. But now, all he could feel was the narrowing distance between himself and her.

"I am very deliberate, Mr. Graves." She winked. "Especially about when I come here. If Papa knew . . . well, I wouldn't have bothered if I thought I couldn't distract you from work."

"Oh, you're distracting." Mason stared at his screen, then back to her lips. They curled, softly, in the tiniest of smiles.

If the feeds discovered that the only daughter of Sam Benford, Enclave builder and rumored heir to one of the founders' Enclaves floating off the east coast's new reefs, was sneaking from her family home to Mason's newly built estate? The resulting public outrage, not to mention the Benford family's embarrassment—her aunt was a Recovery Court Judge, for land's sake—would be a very expensive and public upending of Mason's plans.

Plans that included a party in two days' time, a strategic partnership between the Enclaves and Graves Biosecurity, and Mason's proposal to Evangeline.

This morning was the kind of risk that Mason would have ridiculed in any of his rivals only months ago. But he couldn't help himself. When she was near, he felt unstoppable.

"I can stop working on the party." Mason spun the contract on the tablet so she could see it without coming around to his side of the desk. The top drawer held the ring he'd leveraged so much to get his hands on. The kind of ring, he'd been assured, that would dazzle Enclavers. As much as Evangeline had dazzled him. "We don't really need thieves, do we? No one knows I'm considering it, except the thieves."

Instead of teasing him back, Evangeline tugged the fabric of her robe tighter. "We can't not have thieves! The Andersons didn't. They said what happened at the Lees' was too much, and everyone's still calling them cowards. You must. *We* must. Mason Graves is not a coward, nor is Llyria so poorly leveraged that you can't withstand a little thieving."

Mason raised an eyebrow. Evangeline had her pick of wealthy suitors—both locally and abroad. She'd declared them all too dull for her taste and picked the entrepreneurial hard-driving upstart instead. This party felt like his final test.

Was he wealthy enough to weather an event as expensive as a Grand Heist without liquidation? He would be shortly, even if he wasn't now. "Who are the Andersons? Are they on the guest list? The Lees most certainly are not."

The Lees were evicted from the Enclaves for insolvency after their last party, which made everyone uncomfortable. Even as Evangeline's crowd treated vice like sport, and the feeds ate it up, no one liked someone who couldn't handle the consequences.

"No, but we should invite the Duttons. I know he's an ex, but it's good form with the founders' award." She leaned forward, serious now. "You're the youngest Enclave investor in years. You've got no family nearby to back you. You need to prove yourself. Plus, you can show off your new inventions. Everyone's already saying it's brilliant and daring to bring back the masque."

The Duttons. Jayson had come too close to winning Evangeline too recently. He'd also received a founders' award. Mason marshaled his expression. How he hated giving competitors—past or present—even the slightest opening.

But Evangeline knew this world better than he did. If

she accepted his proposal, they'd be all right. Better than all right. Yes, the feeds went on about his age—although Mason would never admit that he checked them. He'd made his first trillion credits at twenty-five. *Lost them right after, but no one knew that.*

Also, the feeds were quite fascinated at how much Sam Benford's sole heir seemed smitten with Mason, at least currently.

She tilted her head, grazed her even, white teeth against her full lower lip, and gazed at him through her lashes. "If you—if *we*—throw a weekend party without hiring thieves, there will be talk. If we succeed? Papa will be impressed. Besides, I've never caught a thief. And I want to."

Mason rubbed a hand across the back of his neck. She was right, he couldn't avoid this. Not if he wanted to win Benford's official approval. He didn't have his own entry on the social register, but that green chip would definitely come with Evangeline's *yes,* after his proposal was certified. "All right."

Before he could rise to meet her, Evangeline moved to his side. Her silk-wrapped hip brushed the desk drawer. She rubbed a bare foot against his calf. "Who are you negotiating with?"

"Rockville and the Canarviers."

She smiled, without committing to one or the other. But he thought her eyes sparkled when he'd said "Canarviers." "Everyone else dropped out when they saw what biodata we were collecting. These two didn't, though they're balking on artistic grounds."

She peered at the proposals. "That's tradition. It's sporting."

At almost twenty-one, she would come into a large Enclave portfolio on her birthday. The rest would be hers when she started her family. She already sounded like the elder generation of Enclavers when she said words like *tradition.*

As he'd grown his business and his fortunes, Mason had viewed traditions as traps, impediments to possibility. But that smile swayed him.

"Biodata is standard-hire stuff," he protested. "Holt agrees." Besides, it was his biodata tech—the latest scanning, slapcuff technology, and safe enhancements—that made him who he was. The feeds called him a wild genius, though he barely paid attention. The wildness was part of the reason he hadn't managed a founders' award yet—those were for inventors who brought order back to the world, apparently. Mason represented the reality, even decades after the Turbulence, that chaos existed.

"If you don't want thieves," Evangeline said carefully, "we could go garbage diving, maybe find some treasures worth saving."

Mason's stomach churned. Certain games currently fashionable in the Enclaves were, even with protection, far too uncomfortable. He'd cobbled his first scanning tech from discarded components on the outskirts of Denver. Those garbage dives were the stuff of Mason's nightmares, not entertainment. Though he wasn't superstitious, he wouldn't have any Mess-relics in his home, only verified objects with Recovery Court provenance. He hated that others played at it.

I'm about to contract with thieves to rob Llyria and my guests, gambling with the fortune I am fighting so hard to build, in order to impress the Benfords and their neighbors. Am I just as bad?

Evangeline's foot stopped rubbing his calf. She stared at him. Waiting for a decision.

"Artistic tradition," Mason grumbled. "Lucky for us, these aren't real thieves." The outraged Rockville and Canarvier representatives kept reminding him they were expert entertainers. *Damn the Enclaves' love of spectacle.* "Will your aunt be at the party?"

Judge Minerva Benford, like all of the Recovery Court Judges, was as anti-spectacle as it got in New

Washington. She hated parties like this. But she'd renounced her shares of the family inheritance and accepted the judgeship in order to strengthen Evangeline's future majority. The weekend honored that happy event. Surely she'd attend to celebrate the success of her plan.

When he'd first met the judge, soon after arriving in New Washington, years ago, he'd been wary of her. For a fee, she'd helped verify the provenance of a few baubles he'd told her were what remained of his own family's fortunes. She'd looked over his few pieces of gold and still-working tech. Tutted at his explanation. "I do pity families like yours, who emerged from the Turbulence successfully, only to falter while divvying up control. We Benfords have carved a clear path for the future."

Back then, she'd barely spared him a moment outside the courthouse. As his company began taking off, however, she'd been the one to introduce him to Evangeline, and to help him obtain the ring.

He'd grown to like her. Mason felt sure that she took a long view, as he did.

"I have asked Aunt Min to come, even if it's only for a moment," Evangeline said. "After that terrible attack at the Duttons'–imagine, someone daring to assault a judge! She's only grown more vocal about the impact of vice on New Washington."

As he'd worked his way up in the city, courtesy of the sale of those trinkets, Mason had seen Minerva again on a public history feed. She'd clashed with Sam after a Benford business partner in the Enclaves got robbed for real during a party years ago. She'd said vice could destroy the Enclaves.

"She's not wrong," Mason said carefully. He'd seen what vice could do to so many surviving cities on his trek east from Denver as a teen.

"But she wasn't exactly right either, Mason! Just look at us now. Thriving." Evangeline slid closer, her arms stretched wide. "We'll have such fun."

Back then, Sam Benford had traced and purchased back every guest's lost items, waving it off as "hardly anything." Bids for Enclave shares and available property skyrocketed, even faster than when the domed estates first launched. Families living on the ocean toyed with the idea of returning. Benford bought out the partner and created an Enclave family trust. Gossip flew. *How much did the old man truly have locked away? And* where? *He doesn't have enough close family to create a respectable safe.*

Benford would never tell anyone. Not his sister. Nor, according to Evangeline, his only daughter.

Meanwhile, everyone who hadn't attended, or wasn't invited to the party, wished they had been. The feeds clamored for details. Smart event planners began to cultivate thieves of their own. Every few years, someone even risked a full Grand Heist. Guests found it thrilling to catch thieves. At first, they tried to send several off to Alaska as real criminals, but Minerva had put a stop to that.

By the time Mason's Enclave estate was ready for occupancy and he'd begun dating Evangeline, the game was tradition. Minerva had, temporarily, stopped speaking publicly against it. And the tradition was so popular, more hosts began contracting with Graves Biosecurity. Usually after a performance.

Still, he hated it, as much as Minerva did. "But we shouldn't risk offending her, then–" He had many reasons to want to stay on the judge's good side.

"She'll come, even with thieves about. She loves me." Evangeline pointed out. "Besides. *I* want them."

"Ev, they are stipulating ridiculous things. No recourse for losses during the event. No duels with the artists, either on the premises or afterwards, in perpetuity. No live-tracking losses on the guest feed, just a daily accounting. Performers to set the price on returned goods."

Unlike the detailed contracts with the musicians, caterers, fire-eaters, aerialists, and everything else a birthday party for an Enclave girlfriend required, this arrangement was all or nothing. A huge risk.

"Not taking a risk is an even bigger risk." Evangeline was rather brilliant at strategy, despite her sheltered upbringing. Mason hadn't expected how much he'd like her, when he'd first started on the path toward partnership with the Benfords. Now her foot pressed against his leg. "Give Holt some of your new products, if you're nervous. You know he loves this stuff. But don't let him wreck the game. I must go."

The sun was just rising. She was right. "I'll absolutely talk with Holt."

"Sir, did you need me?" Holt's voice shook Mason's subdermal com, summoned by his name. "I've got the due diligence you requested. Canarvier may be the weaker team. One of their members hasn't been seen for days. Authorities are strangely quiet, even when I incentivized them."

Mason was one for taking full advantage of weakness. He tapped his teeth together, muting Holt. "I do like a challenge."

He caught Evangeline's ankle and tugged it gently toward him, to make sure she was paying attention. Then he touched the screen to send one last set of terms to the Canarviers. "All arranged. Tell no one."

Evangeline laughed and put her arms around his neck. "And what of a winner's prize?"

She'd been raised entirely in the Enclaves, no expense spared on tutors and mentors for business and the arts, and parties. An upbringing modeled on pre-Mess standards, as with so much in the Reclamation and Recovery. She had high expectations for him, he knew.

Mason had learned to anticipate those expectations. "I haven't forgotten."

He tapped two fingertips on the desk. A hidden door to the valet's room slid open, revealing his safe. "Come in, Gabriel."

Gabriel was a rental, sadly, and a bit old at thirty-eight. But he was a green-chipped member of society, as all safes were.

When put through his paces, Gabriel had proved himself to be fast and easily able to avoid capture or disassembly. Both important safe-trade duties, post-Mess.

Mason had added a Graves Biosecurity upgrade for free. Safe positions paid very well, especially those with the latest modifications and a loyalty record. It was a coveted position in families who hadn't settled the honor on a younger sibling or cousin. Gabriel had appreciated the bonus, though he'd refused the self-destruct add-on.

Stifling a yawn, the safe stepped into the office. He bowed to Evangeline.

Evangeline looked thoughtful. "How nice to meet you."

"This is temporary, I assure you," Mason said, but he noticed how comfortable Evangeline seemed with the idea of a rental. *Is that what Sam's using?* Benford didn't contract with Graves for safe-supplies, so Mason was as in the dark as everyone else. *For now.*

He held out his hand and Gabriel opened his jacket, revealing a cache in his side where a useless organ had once resided. Gall bladder. Gabriel had several spaces available for hire, but this was the one he'd agreed to upgrade.

The cache was sterile, titanium coated. When Gabriel handed Mason the blue velvet-wrapped contents, they were as cool as the room. Body temperature- and chemical-proof. The upgrade was a beta, though Gabriel didn't need to know that, and it was working well. Mason made a note to have one added to his own future safe, once he gained enough relatives.

He unfolded the velvet. Inside, seven jeweled, brooch-sized gold peacock feathers gleamed. "I had the big two made for you. The rest are prizes."

Evangeline's mouth hung in a pretty "O" for a moment. She recovered quickly. "Astonishing. I almost want to win them all for myself."

"You would never be such a rude hostess." Mason ran a hand across her arm. He shivered as she looked down at him, her hair haloed by the robe's hood. "If we do catch all the thieves, I promise you an even better prize."

He imagined his ring on her finger. A perfect end to the weekend.

With unfiltered delight, Evangeline clapped her hands. The sound echoed in the office. She bent and kissed his earlobe, whispering, "I can't wait."

Mason waved a hand to dismiss his safe while they said goodbye. Gabriel stepped silently back into the valet's quarters. The man wasn't bad, for a rental. People had been known to adopt rentals. Just not *established* people.

He reached for her waist, but she slipped off the desk. "Time to run, before the house wakes. Pick me up before lunch?"

They would tour the New Washington seawall, try a new pop-up, and visit Graves's research lab at Public Works, avoiding the party planners' takeover of the house for the night.

Two floors below, a cook ran a blender in the distant kitchen. Five a.m. and Evangeline was still here. But his people wouldn't gossip. They wouldn't dare sell a story to the feeds. A stray feed drone high outside? Still a risk. "Hurry then."

He listened to her footsteps fade on the service staircase. Her shadow crossed the dew-flecked lawn. The Enclave's dome-perfected haze-free sunrise sparkled as she ducked through the gate between his property and the green. Large enough for concerts and sports, the green was currently planted with cherry trees that provided a decent cover for Evangeline's circuit to the Benford estate. As she disappeared, Mason's ability to focus returned.

It will be much easier when she can stay. When she was

safe at home, she messaged him: the sound of her blowing a kiss tingled against his cheek.

"Holt. Have the roofhopter ready at eleven."

"Absolutely, Mr. Graves." Holt's military-crisp respect and experience with the Benfords—he'd worked with them before coming to Llyria—buoyed Mason's confidence. He was definitely going to be among the established people.

New Washington City Feed

Benford Fan Group Number 45

[Log] Fifteen images of Evangeline Benford and her father, Sam Benford, walking the lawn at Centenaire, their home near New Washington—[UPDATE: Images redacted. Account deleted.]

[Log] Videos of Evangeline's suitors' applications and dates, including her latest visit to the hit pop-up, Mango! Check out her custom trench coat. It's raining in New Washington! [UPDATE: Videos redacted and renounced by alleged suitors. Account deleted.]

[Log] See the Benford family at work!

Miss Minerva Benford is a Recovery Court Judge—a great sacrifice! Like all judges, she renounced her inheritance and family chip. She certified she will produce no heirs. As Recovery Court Judges oversee valuable property from the Turbulence, ensuring return to rightful owners—plus, successions, sales, mergers, and the city's feed network in order to reduce risk of viral attacks that wiped out most interconnected feeds—this is wise and responsible. In short, judges like Minerva Benford maintain and improve the fabric of society for the future, not just for one family.

Sam Benford focuses on philanthropy and development. His vision for the New Washington Enclave continues to astound protected cities around the globe.

The Benfords' only heir, daughter Evangeline, is preparing to come into her majority and assume more direct control of the family businesses: primarily real estate and services. Click here to view some of her recent charity work in the city.

They are all art museum benefactors.

[Log] Listen to a former Benford private tutor talk on the educational feeds about best business practices, and then hear what he has to say behind the scenes [micropayment required]. [UPDATE: Audio declared fraudulent. Account deleted.]

[Log] Get to know Evangeline's friends—What's the glue that keeps them so close? Hint: it's fashion! Learn how to make your own Evangeline Benford style board, or, for an additional fee, learn how to teach others! [UPDATE: Account suspended.]

[Log] Official Evangeline Benford press releases and images [contents: three interviews, 2,014 approved photos, one series of approved designer recommendations, an interview with a new artist Evangeline discovered on her last trip to New Washington (file 567d].

The Confidence Game

CRAMMED BETWEEN A laundress and a young gardener, Roo let the work van's familiar sway over the reclaimed highway lull her. The road was cracked and pitted, as recovery engineers had their hands full with the seawalls and large air filters. The van was designed to compensate. The rise and fall of conversations soothed her after the tension in the apartment.

It had been a long time since she rode with an early shift. When the van screeched to a halt well before the wall, Roo jerked fully awake.

Two MilPol officers boarded, masks up. A man in the row ahead of her seemed to shrink in his seat. Her gardener neighbor shivered and stuck his hands in his coat pockets.

"Bands!" One officer held out a scanner. The second followed behind. Arms extended up from each row. The scanner beeped in passing. Then most handed small trinkets and food to the second guard, who pocketed them.

Roo groaned. King had always slipped an honorarium or two in their pockets before a job, just in case. Roo didn't have anything. Worse, she hadn't prepared gifts for the weekend. King handled that part of the work, shaking hands and passing small packets of homemade tea and found objects to their new homes.

Nan was right. Their troupe was missing a whole layer of knowledge.

The officers reached her row. Scanned workbands. The seamstress offered a sewing needle, tucked into a fabbed thank you card. The gardener held out two wrapped packets. "Mom's homemade fruit bread." He saw Roo's face. Added, "For both of us."

The second guard lifted her visor and unwrapped one. "Lucky I like fabbed fruit," she said as she chewed. She was Roo's age and resembled a girl who'd graduated from Miss Farmer's with a security focus last fall. She didn't recognize Roo.

When the guards were through, one shouted, "Vane!" Three heads jerked up. Roo stared straight ahead. Vane was a very common name. Apartment shares made it more common. "Simon Vane."

Two rows ahead, a man tried to bolt from his seat and shove his way out. The guards caught him gently, one at each elbow. "Easy, friend. Just a question about your prior employment."

Roo fidgeted with the edge of her sleeve. As the guards stepped from the van, her relief barely made a dent in her nerves.

"Valo," the boy whispered.

"Roo," she answered. He'd done her a kindness. "Where do you work today?" With a long ride to the Enclave's exterior dome, talking could distract them both. A roofhopter made short work of things, but those were for Enclavers. Everyone else took the roads as they came.

Valo nodded at Roo's band, glowing from the scan. Her location code matched his own. "Same. Graves's residence."

Enclave estate codes were displayed on workbands. Owners' names weren't. "You've been working there a while?" *Was this a competing thief?* She needed to find out.

The boy grinned. "A month."

The laundress leaned in. "Llyria? Big party this weekend. I put in for the security check, maybe I'll catch extra work."

"It's brand new. Not much needs washed, yet," the boy teased.

"Cleaned, though." Roo relaxed into the banter. Llyria was an ostentatious name for a home. "Lots of that. Any good places to nap?" The staff always knew what the house system didn't.

The gardener shrugged. "I know gardens, not rooms. Started on landscaping, now I'm in flowers. Owner's security and bio-scans don't miss a thing."

The laundress paled. "Oh, well."

Roo's data skills kept their records clean, though Dax and King's shenanigans had occasionally exceeded her abilities. Would their aliases hold this time? Nan would hate it, but Roo had asked Dax to source some bio-masking. Contacts, putty sculpting, and dyes created in the Skirts always made Nan nervous—she despised biologics. "Why alter your features when that's all you really own?" Even the stuff that Dax's best friend Aanand made got complaints.

Dax had picked up several sets of contacts and hair tint anyway. He'd passed them quietly to Roo when he shook the dust over her outfit. She wondered what colors, and how long they'd last.

They crossed the wall. The van quieted as the sea barrier glittered on the tinted windows. Roo shaded her eyes as the pale plains receded. In the distant hills, she saw a glint, a whisper of dust on the air: MilPol drones, heading for the Skirts. Hopefully Nan's bus was safe.

With a lurch, the van bumped up onto smooth pavement and each workband beeped twice as the van moved through the Enclave's outer drone field. The suspension stopped creaking.

"Enclave roads," the gardener said appreciatively. Roo didn't reply. Her eyes were on the terraforming, especially the trees. She loved how they reached for the sky. On this side of the walls, she felt lighter. Like someone who was used to trees. Someone who was friends with people like Sasha. Someone who had a future. Today, that feeling was laced with dread.

For King, I'll risk every tree. Every friend.

When she stayed quiet, the boy ducked his chin. "I forget my manners."

Digging unasked into others' business. Something Nan taught her grandchildren to shy away from. Manners saved lives. Having lived through the Mess with a five-year-old son, Nan knew more about that than Roo ever would.

"We can't all be founders," Roo whispered to him.

The gardener chuckled. "Nah, my dad's up there." He gestured at the van's ceiling, leaving Roo to guess whether he meant dead or mining. "Ma scrapes by on a few hustles. This job saves the both of us. You?"

"I wish I was a founder, or at least offshore," the laundress said. "Somewhere with fabs big enough to print everything—even medicine—and drones to fly anything anywhere I want."

The boy laughed, but Roo knew it for truth, not a fantasy. Offshore families and companies—usually the same thing—had retreated to a safe distance before the Mess really got started. Now, many of their goods came to the protected cities by drone on regular delivery days, and even more went to the landside Enclaves. Before Nan caught them at it, Aanand had been showing Dax how some of his family's hustles in biologics and reclaimed gear came from drones they'd shot down themselves.

When Roo and Dax were much younger, the free feeds shared songs about important families—founders—sheltering scientists, supporting their research when the universities closed. About other families with their own rocket pads mining asteroids. And others focusing on stabilizing the protected cities. Roo wondered if Valo knew the tunes.

She hummed a verse of "After Tensions Cooled and Seawalls Rose" from a popular kids' feed.

"The Recovery Court learned/ What is what and whose is whose," the laundress and Valo whisper-sang, rolling their eyes and chuckling at the shared memory. Roo joined in too.

When the local feeds declared the Mess over for New Washington—as every company and philanthropist gave themselves awards to signify it—they celebrated citizens living useful, secure lives: running the vertical farms and start-ups that founders might buy into; working for the Enclaves; or living there, if they received a founders' award. By the time King was raising two children with Nan's help, most everyone wanted to be useful to the Reclamation and Recovery, often thanks to those songs.

Those who stayed in the Skirts, or found themselves in Alaska or the moon, didn't get songs. Roo closed her eyes to avoid thinking about where King could end up.

She leaned into the turn as the Enclave road split. One stretch of pavement headed toward Miss Farmer's. She watched the long curve of smooth road disappear. *I should be in class right now. What if Kerr-Moulthrop was right?*

Her family had used hard-won heist wins to get Roo the right outfits and baubles for Miss Farmer's. To buy her a chance to apply for the scholarship. To fix her teeth. No one in the Skirts had nice teeth these days—except the very few residents Nan's age who were older than the Mess. Bad teeth, patched and fabbed clothing, poor manners? Anyone in the Enclaves or New Washington proper knew that didn't belong. And all of it cost money to fix.

Have I just thrown all that work away?

When she was in the dormitory at school, she missed the Skirts in the same ways. The ancient-electrical buzz of Nan's bus; the woody-salt smell of King's salvaged books. The rocking sensation of always being slightly in motion. Wherever she was, at school or with her family, the pull of the other place always felt so strong.

On the way to her first heist in almost a year, Roo knew both could disappear.

They were coming to the second Enclave gate. She needed more data to make this performance work.

"Gentlepersons!" The driver's bellow interrupted before the gardener could reply. "We are approaching the Enclave residences. Have your badges out. Stay quiet so you don't miss instructions."

Roo could recite the next words in time with the driver, thanks to the work-study mandated by her scholarship. "You are not to take anything from the Enclave except yourselves. You are not to speak unless spoken to. You are to be useful. Should you have any questions or concerns about anything you are asked to do, please file with Enclave Resources using your workband."

"At which point," the laundress whispered, her breath tickling Roo's ear, "Resources will put a black mark on your file and feed you to the nearest exit or woodchipper, whichever is closer."

Roo couldn't help but laugh, causing the bus driver to glare at her row in the rearview. "And then your accounts will be charged for the woodchipper use."

The gardener snorted. Then he said quietly, "The best places for a break are in the chrysanthemum garden shed, behind the roses. And by the green, in the trees. Can't be seen from the house. The cooks are nice. Don't cross security. The head guy is a nasty piece of work."

Perfect.

A band scan, the purple disinfection glow, de-dusting, and they were inside the airlock gates. Roo's fingers brushed her sleeve again. The edge felt rough. When she peered at it, she saw Sasha's neat stitching. A tiny message in the hem: "You've got this."

Roo felt her cheeks warm with her friend's kindness. She did have this. She had to.

They passed the Veleutner mansion on the left, the Benford compound's imposing gates on the right. Acres of green lawns, rolling hills, and enough trees to ease Roo's heart. The terraforming here was a beacon for the future. That was the Enclave's true purpose. All the feeds said so.

"There's a price to pay for dreams," King had cautioned before she'd left for Miss Farmer's. He'd loved to teach and tell stories over meals. Dax had long ago escaped the table for another vehicle slowly making the rounds of their community. But Roo hung on King's words, the stories pulled from ancient books he'd rescued. "You're playing with stacked odds: your dreams, someone else's everyday. From Prometheus to Sophie Lyon. We pay the thieves' price to play." She'd heard him say that so many times.

But this time, he'd lifted his glass—precious, clean water, not fabbed protein drink—to his daughter. "You are beyond that price, my dear. You will take us into the future, while Dax builds our present and supports our past."

Her heart lifted at the pride in his voice. She'd felt ready to exceed his every dream.

And when I was distracted, the price came due. King paid with his freedom.

Roo pulled her service mask up, just like everyone else disembarking the van.

With one difference. She was here to change the odds.

Evangeline lifted a tiny gelato spoon to her lips. "This is exceptional! Lemon!"

The pop-up, Citrus, was new. Its New Washington-banded owner, a young woman in her late teens, beamed at the heiress. "All real fruit, nothing fabbed. I contract with the vertical farm by the seawall, and several Enclave greenhouses."

Evangeline leaned forward conspiratorially, "Including Benford greenhouses, I suspect."

The owner beamed. "Yes!"

Watching his girlfriend light up the shop, Mason appreciated Evangeline's people skills. The vendor would talk on the feeds (until her posts were redacted due to Sam Benford's love for privacy), and among her friends and colleagues about how wonderful she was. Word spread; it always had. Ev wove her family's business with her private life with a confidence that came from infinite resources and dedicated tutors. *Hard work,* he realized, *can look easy, but it was still work.*

"The cooling systems for this place are a wonder of innovation," Mason observed. The collection of dry-ice storage maintained a rolling tray of pink and yellow gelato containers at perfect temperature. Even in a shopfront that was mostly curtains to cover empty shelves, this kind of resourcefulness was impressive. "Did you design the storage?"

The vendor shook her head. "I contracted that."

"Who from?" Mason knew many contractors in New Washington. Most didn't make their own dry ice. He had a person at his lab for that himself. He glanced around the shop again, wondering what else was hidden there.

The shop owner stammered, "I can find their card. They were doing me a favor but they're quite good."

Evangeline nudged him. "It's all right, Mason. Enjoy your gelato." She tilted her head at his untouched cup. He hated cold things—his teeth couldn't abide them—but it would be rude not to try it, and Evangeline didn't know about his teeth. He put the spoon to his lips, avoiding the dental work he'd paid so dearly for a few years ago. "Delicious." Strawberry. It wasn't too terrible. Maybe the implants were finally syncing with his nerve endings properly.

A bell sounded near Evangeline's palm. "I must go; Valencia wants to do tea and outfit coordination. Don't be late tonight!" She waved at the owner and stepped out on the street, where a car appeared and swept her to the next destination. Mason held out his wrist to pay and saw that Evangeline had already chipped the exorbitant cost.

His face clouded. Evangeline knew his money was just as good as hers, but she'd paid anyway. Was it the band? When he caught the owner watching him curiously, he smiled. "Isn't she spectacular? I'd love that card. If the cooling system creator is available, I'm always looking for apprentices."

The vendor patted her pockets and then lifted her hands, her smile faltering. "I'm afraid it's not with me. I can send it when I have it."

Then he understood. Whoever built this wasn't available, either because they'd been working off books as a side hustle, which could get them fired, or because they weren't a citizen.

"Not a problem." Mason recalibrated his afternoon schedule. He made a note to tell MilPol to look into the situation. Order in the city required vigilance. Anyone knew that.

On the street, he lifted his mask. He would walk to the laboratory. It was close by, and walking always righted his mind. From his early days near Denver, he'd walked miles without a complaint. A few blocks wouldn't hurt now. Besides, he should check in at Llyria.

"Holt."

"Sir," the answer came quickly. "Do you need the roofhopter?"

"Not yet. Visiting the lab, and then dinner and a show. How are the security checks coming?"

"I appreciate your checking, sir." Holt's voice echoed on the walls of Llyria's main hall, until the sound-cloaking kicked in. Military standard, Holt's tech drowned conversations in white noise. In person, Mason found it irritating, like being followed by an attentive ghost. Over the subdermals, it was soothing. "We've finished additional checks on the house staff, caterers, and musicians. No one uncounted in the house or grounds. Your entertainers will pose a definite risk, but we'll know where they are."

A crash interrupted the call and Mason nearly jumped off the sidewalk, looking for an oncoming car or a MilPol drone.

"Sorry, sir. Designers are still here. Dropped box of stemware."

"We won't be liable for that."

"I'll make sure it's not on the itemization for the weekend."

Holt was thorough. He allowed none of the largesse Evangeline tended to wave away as if it didn't matter. "They're installing the rugs and furniture you selected."

While Mason's bedroom and office at Llyria had been comfortably arrayed before Evangeline ever visited, and the kitchen had been stocked with energy and vitamin drinks and enough health tech to alarm the staff, he hadn't paid much attention to the main rooms in the house until he needed to. A weekend's worth of guests required furnishings, and Mason had spared no expense–renting only the best recovered antiques when he couldn't buy them straight out. He let the planner choose most of it.

Llyria's twenty bedrooms, ballroom, kitchens, and game rooms would be polished and prepared to match the grandeur of the estate Mason had salvaged from the drowned Hamptons and had fully restored and expanded. "Good."

Thinking about the work being done in his absence wiped the vendor's expression from Mason's mind. He enjoyed feeling in control, and Llyria–the entire Enclaves–gave him that feeling. That was the secret to the place's popularity: the beauty of the homes and the static-drone filtration domes, the successful terraforming, and the orderly staff. The Enclaves embodied control over a still chaotic world.

No one would know how long it had taken Mason to work his way into New Washington society, and Denver before that. Far from the salt and silt of his childhood. No one could know how far he'd leveraged his companies to make this work.

Mason was never one to shy from winning, and investors had spotted that early. The Benfords were only the latest part of the plan. That it had taken a much larger cut of his fortunes than Mason had expected was no matter. He'd gain it all back soon enough.

"Sir, two small details." Holt said it as if nothing was small. "We have detected one thief on the property. Would you like them removed or watched?"

"Tag everyone you suspect and watch them. There will be more than one thief, and they can lead us to the others. Meanwhile, suspect everyone." *Smart of me to think of that.* Mason smiled in the confines of his mask. He walked faster. Almost to the lab, though the heat and the new shoes Evangeline had made him buy were becoming unbearable.

"Very good, sir. Though Miss Evangeline and Mr. Sam are beyond suspicion." Holt carefully enunciated the words.

"Absolutely," Mason hurried to agree. Holt had been in Enclave employment long enough to have help crafted the staff loyalty oath. Military college educated, trained in corporate espionage, with an unfortunate affinity for the forbidden. Which is why Benford had to quietly let him go—he'd been caught managing an illicit pain feed piped in from the Denali mines. Mason had paid off MilPol to keep him from a one-way transport to the moon and erased his record. He'd secured Holt's loyalty with an additional and hefty share of Graves Biosecurity. When Mason succeeded, now Holt did too. Still, the man had continued respect for his former employer. It was endearing. "Continue."

"I hoped there were new items you could loan me from the lab. Is the new bio-surveillance ready? Or Safeware 2.0? A tool that can be used quietly in tandem with the guest and staff databases?"

Mason stopped just before the laboratory doors. Holt's enthusiasm had been profitable in the past. He'd recently discovered that diluted Safeware had temporary applications in interrogations. That got MilPol interested again. Winning their business back would be a coup after the trouble with his former partner, Rylan Stonecliff. But tandem use with guest data? That was skirting a delicate line.

Keeping a database of guests—likes and dislikes, names and offspring—was the mark of a conscientious host. He and Holt had expanded theirs for Llyria to a much more delicate thing: relationships, alliances, dalliances, indiscretions, DNA. Mason was sure other families kept similar data, though no one spoke of it, even in private.

"Safeware is purely for use in safe compliance, Holt. And only for the best families. We will not be crossing that line. I'm at the lab now and will see if there's anything else you can use."

"Yes, sir."

"Have a camera-map and war-room model prepared for my return, and make sure we don't overcorrect. This is supposed to be a party. Evangeline will never let us hear the end of it if we offend the guests. She wants the weekend to be perfect. We will triumph in both security and entertaining."

When he captured the thieves and won the weekend—Mason couldn't think of it any other way—it would be the perfect moment to propose. In front of her friends. With her father in a public position where he couldn't refuse if she said yes. And she would say yes.

Mason could see her perfect lips forming the word.

"Understood, sir." Holt's tone was conciliatory. "We'll

make sure it is. And are you certain you do not want to move the safe?"

Three small questions, not two. "Where would you have me move Gabriel? It would be a sign of weakness to do so—and I won't give anyone the satisfaction of saying I'm not one hundred percent dedicated to the weekend. Besides, he's superbly trained. You said so yourself. And there's no place more secure than a Graves home." Mason mimicked the feeds. "Unless it's a Benford home."

"As you say, sir."

Mason clicked his teeth to dismiss Holt. He'd reached the lab, a tower at the Reclamation and Public Works facility's east corner. While he'd built his business on scans and workbands, he'd secured this research space with several new safe support contracts. It was delicate work. Safes were family.

Before Safeware came on the market, a few betrayals had made the feeds and been quickly erased: safes taking side gigs without permission, and one—rumored—family coup with a trusted safe at the center of it all. That was much rarer now.

Still, with competitors, including Stonecliff, entering the local biosecurity business, Mason was increasingly hearing, "We already have this. Anything new?" It was infuriating.

But Mason wasn't one to give up. To eliminate the competition, or at least get out ahead of them again, he'd dedicated research resources to products that guaranteed increased safe compliance and family loyalty.

He'd invested in Dr. Tsalta's lab, buying it away from a company town. Tsalta's papers were intriguing, and dense. Mason knew dense science was key to making investors feel the research was important. He himself was still getting up to speed. But leaders didn't need to understand all the details. They needed to hire the right people. That was Mason's skill.

For the first time, Mason noticed how dusty the walk had been and regretted his choice. His mask had overclocked. When he pulled it off, his face was ringed with a light sheen of sweat and grime. Worse, the shoes Evangeline had brought him looked dirty. The dark, vat-grown leather was speckled with dust. He hated new shoes.

"You walked, sir? I thought you would call." His chief scientist greeted him at the door.

"You said it was important." He was not going to be questioned about his habits, even by someone as distinguished as Dr. Tsalta. "What has happened?"

"There's a variant in the Safeware 2.0 formula cycle." Tsalta's dark skin glistened at the temples.

A problem. Now. "We can't have problem variants. We need to standardize production. Our investors expect formula deliveries by month's end. We must keep them happy." Mason felt panic rise, even as he emphasized the word *happy* for his chief scientist.

Evangeline expected him at dinner with her father. But Safeware was paying for the dinner, the party, the ring, the wedding. Llyria. His future. It couldn't have problems.

Dr. Tsalta shook her head. "The variant's not necessarily a problem, sir. It has interesting outcomes."

"Tell me."

"When you requested escalating safe loyalty compliance beyond pheromone influence, we began experimenting with modified antibodies. These help match controlled cells with that of a related controller on a level several orders of magnitude beyond Safeware."

"Yes, I understand." Dr. Tsalta was speaking too much science. "Cut to the point. The interesting outcomes part."

She said something that sounded like "post translational modifications to the enzyme."

The phrase made Mason press his fingers to his temple. "Translate please."

"In the early twenty-first century, scientists saw that sugars couldn't be exactly replicated on all assays and variants might occur, especially when—"

Mason held up a hand. “You’re saying this batch isn’t like the previous batch. What does it do?” They arrived at the observation deck over Tsalta’s lab. He peered down at the white-capped workers.

“No, sir, with respect that’s not quite—” Dr. Tsalta stammered, pointing at several rows of purple-capped ampoules. “We can still make the Safeware stronger than before.”

“Good.” He would make it to dinner with Evangeline after all.

Then Tsalta held up five orange-capped tubes. “But this variant—we’re still running tests—seems to allow a safe to improve the longevity of the relative they serve quite remarkably. The impact on the safe isn’t good, but—”

Mason stopped. “We might have a formula that allows safes to boost family longevity? You should have said that first.”

“Yes sir, I wanted you to understand the complexity—”

He let her go on, cursing that he did not have more time to spend at the lab. But that would mean canceling the damned party. No, he had to find a way to have both. “Step up the research, but tell no one beyond your group.”

Business must move forward, no matter the price. And someone would pay a very high price for this.

When Dr. Tsalta turned to speak to her staff, Mason pocketed two orange-capped ampoules to study on his own.

New Washington City Found Footage Group

(Citizen Verified Subscription Required)

Subscriber 2342: Hey, is this real? MilPol encrypted transmission garbage had bits and pieces. I tried to stitch it back together best I could.

House Feed Video Surveillance, Samuel and Serena Benford Residence, New Washington Enclaves
pre-market [date redacted]
Redacted from public records, per Chipped Citizen Request.
Annotated privately by investigators following new case requests [date] [date] [date]
Redacted permanently on date. Marked for bit-level destruction.
Film timestamp 0:00:20am [date redacted]

At the sound of silver sliding into carryalls, Serena Benford drops the screen she'd been working. She rises from her reading nook, her toned, amber arms spread wide for balance. Her cream shift sways from the motion, her fingers splayed on the closest bookshelf. What she wears, her bare feet, her dark curls let down for a quiet evening, indicate a wealthy woman readying for bed. Her alarmed expression—wide eyes, open mouth—makes it clear: she hadn't been anticipating this. No one had.

[film breaks at this point]

Subscriber 32234: The Enclaves are very safe. That is their main selling point. If this is real, Benford buried a crime in favor of keeping it out of the feeds.

Subscriber 123: That's not unusual for Enclavers. Especially Benford. Have you seen the unauthorized fan feeds? They get flatlined daily.

Subscriber 2342: Hang on there's more:

Video: Serena Benford grabs the nearest heavy object, an oversized book.

Subscriber 783: did anyone find the receipts/reclamation certificate for that book? It looks old?

Subscriber 2342: Not yet.

Video: The book, *The Annotated Alice*, is large enough to smash a large bug, and possibly to stun a burglar if she swings it hard enough with both hands. But she doesn't yet move.
Splice to second camera, same timestamp: the thieves sorting through the family's silver.

Subscriber 2342: I bet they came in through the unfinished construction—you can sort of see it out the window.

Video: Serena lifts the book and prepares to face the robbers alone. Almost alone. Serena puts a calming hand to her belly. She takes a deep breath and walks from the lavishly appointed rooms of her married life, past locked bedroom doors. [video breakup]

Video: Serena moves quietly down the stairs. She is barefoot. On the stairs, she curses and holds a corner of her gown to her nose with her free hand. She applies pressure as she descends the back staircase, hurrying.

Video: Serena is a shadow in the main hall; now a ghost in the parlor nearest the dining room. As the larger burglar—masked, male from shoulder and hip breadth—tries the library doors, the smaller assistant pauses at a new sound. A whisper of feet on a marble floor, then a silence that is more present than not. The assistant slips through a door.

Subscriber 3232: After all they'd been through, the Benfords. How hard they'd worked to build a safe future together, for themselves and the world, this moment absolutely haunts me.

Subscriber 425: You seem to be in the wrong feed, you are looking for a Bedford Fan Feed, perhaps?

Subscriber 3232: As a citizen, I can feed however I want, thank you. You?

Video: The smaller burglar moves behind Serena like a second shadow. A dark pillowcase descends over Serena Benford's head and, because she is taller than her attacker, drags her down and backward in the process. Serena struggles wordlessly for a moment, then goes limp. The larger burglar appears and lifts her in his arms. The assistant carries an equally heavy load of valuables from the estate. No ransom ever came. None of the valuables ever discovered.
From the rooms above, faint on the surveillance, a small child cries, as if waking from a nightmare, for her mother.

Subscriber 453: That can't be real.

Subscriber 6788: Who's the Benford fan?

Subscriber 723: Unknown.

Subscriber 32234: If the videos are suddenly disappeared, it is. Benford's been obsessed with takedowns since Evangeline was a child. My theory is . . .

[feed deleted]

Fooling The House

Roo peered from the chrysanthemum garden shed window. The work van, filled with day-shift gardeners, housekeepers, and laundresses, passed by, then its lights receded down the dark road. Roo had picked up her seatmate's skill list on the van ride and copied it to her own band. Did a full day's work, then ducked into the shed. An extra band of Roo's accompanied the van home, attached to the underside of the laundress's bag.

The gate would register that the cleaner had left the Enclaves with the shift.

But laundresses worked odd hours. Graves had several on call for the party, according to the staff database she'd pulled from the network while hiding in the shed. Better still, she'd found three out-of-service dragonflies—two with damaged wings and one with a melted circuit.

Pollinators and spies both, dragonflies were wired to certain patrols around the Enclaves. They picked up pollen on microstatic wings, interfered with feed-snoops, and recorded the properties. The Enclaves loved multitasking.

With her toolkit, Roo fixed the dragonflies to her own purposes. She pocketed parts of one, all of the second, and sent the third back out into the garden. It hovered in the mane of a purple-and-white chrysanthemum, iridescent in the gloaming. Then it followed a party planner from the house, through the gardens. "I won't take responsibility for entertainers I wasn't consulted on," Roo heard the planner say on her tablet. "I understand, Mr. Graves. It's your choice." The planner walked to the road, where a private car picked her up. The dragonfly returned.

The evening fell quiet, except for Roo's footsteps on the gravel. It was time to see if Llyria would let her back inside.

Her uniform turned a brisk white. She lifted her indoor mask. Shifted a stolen shed basket, topped with two outdoor tablecloths, to her hip.

Head down, she rounded the hedge and walked with purpose toward the basement service entrance.

"Bit late for laundry." A stocky man with military bearing spoke as she almost stepped on his feet. He'd seated himself in the shadows to watch the planner leave.

Roo froze. So much for the house being the first test.

"Scan." The man grabbed her wrist and ran a gloved hand over the glowing ID. House security, for sure. "Eyes too."

Roo, her eyes tinted brown by Aanand's contacts, winced at the sudden brightness from the man's flashlight. "I was asked to do some confidential cleaning. Extra contract work."

She'd overheard a gardener and one of the cooks on break talking about a young lady's early visit.

"You make sure that stays confidential." The man let her arm go. Roo resisted the urge to rub where his fingers had gripped. She felt a sharp poke through her sleeve. Had he just put a tracer on her?

She ducked her head, but he caught her chin with his other hand, studying her eyes. She knew the contacts wouldn't show in the light, but it was uncomfortable. "Not much to look at."

Roo leaned in, loosening his grip. "If I may, sir. I'm running behind."

"Go on then, designers left a mess in there for you."

"Yes, sir. Pleasure to serve, sir."

He harrumphed and turned on his heel. Roo walked the remaining few steps, heart pounding. She placed her wristband on the doorframe, forcing her pulse to a more elevated beat. The threshold sensors would clock her as the scared laundress that the stocky guard expected. The door buzzed and swung wide.

Once inside, Roo shoved fabric into one of the industrial washing machines and turned the other two on for good measure. She set dryer cycles on timers. In the ensuing clatter, Roo made a nest for herself in a pile of nearby laundry. She dropped the tracking clip from her sleeve into the fabric. Opened her tablet.

Intent on intimidating her, the guard hadn't noticed the scrap of dragonfly wing on his shoe. Now she could watch him, the same way he thought he was watching her. The wing glowed on her rudimentary map of the estate, filling in unknowns as the man walked a circuit through the house, then to an interior room on the lowest floor, where the signal disappeared.

High-level security bunker. Maybe that was the man the gardener had called a piece of work.

She dropped the laundress band in the basket with the tracker. The machine's hum gave them a false signal.

In the thick tumult of the dryers, with the house asleep, Roo climbed into the laundry chute and allowed herself a moment to breathe. She'd made it into the house, but now she had to get into the network.

The security scan told her Llyria relied on band and biosecurity to keep strangers out. With several more layers likely beyond that. To fool the house network into thinking she belonged—in each of her aliases, Roo needed a backdoor. *Time to go old school. The house's eyes and mind, its cameras and data servers go first. Then the guest list.*

She adjusted her third workband, the heat of her fingers tracing a pattern on the display that triggered the band's second role: silencing. Llyria's band and tag security couldn't see her now, if she was careful.

"Conversion H," she whispered to her wardrobe. Sasha had made her a full feed-journalist kit. The result exceeded Roo's hopes.

At her command, seams smoothed and fabric, no longer white, mimicked the laundry chute's walls and shadows. She splayed her hands and feet against the vertical shaft and crab-walked up to the first floor. The cloth rippled and Roo hoped she was a ghost on her opponent's systems.

If King had been able to, he would have bribed his way in with the designers and planners. He would have set up entrances and exits for Roo, copying keys, adjusting security points with a little gaffers' tape here, a bit of putty or a mirror there. Leaving a window open to let the fresh paint air out. That's how they'd done it before. Tonight, Roo had only herself.

She pushed the chute door open into the kitchen, which should have been still warm from the day's baking. Instead, she saw tins set out on a prep table with labels: breakfast, lunch, dinner. Each had a scoop and a scale beside it.

Mason Graves wouldn't survive Enclave society if anyone found out he liked fabbed energy shakes and Mess-survival meals. Roo stifled a laugh.

Crates and boxes waited in the hallway and pantry beyond, ready to transform the space with catering for the weekend. Roo stuck her head into the main hall, listening for footsteps. She heard ticking instead.

Roo had seen pendulum clocks illustrated in King's

books, but she'd never heard one in person. It was an odd, regular beat, more expansive than King's watch. She traced the sound to a tall clock at the main hall's far end. In Llyria's silence, the ticking mimicked words—almost as if King himself were there. *Focus. Move faster.*

The clock wasn't wrong. Roo refocused. With the first night's masque centered on the ballroom, cameras would be set up there already. Enclavers liked to control their own feed media—even if some publicly railed against it. Roo guessed the ballroom was behind a big set of doors opposite a grand staircase at the middle of the main hall.

She popped one of her charms and let it spill smoke across her path. Security beams crisscrossed the marble floor. She lifted two pins from her hair and pulled the crystal beads off. Rolled several in front of the beams to shift them out of her way. The beams parted.

By the time the ornate, antique clock began sounding the new hour—its ticking replaced by a series of startlingly loud gongs that made her tense and nearly fall—Roo hung invisible near the ceiling of Llyria's biggest public room.

The rococo wall sconces' patterns faded from her gloved fingers. Her bespoke singlesuit now matched the hues of the gilded mural.

Graves apparently couldn't decide between a modernized Public Works style and rococo, both of which Roo had studied with King. The mural's unfortunate artist had been required to blend both into taupe, pink, and red pastoral scenes. Sheep-in-a-meadow and workers-building-seawalls played across Roo's wardrobe, camouflaging her. She made notes for Dax, in case he wanted to work the art into the calling card.

Stacks of chairs were her only audience as Roo snuck up behind one of Graves's media nodes. If eyes were the windows to the soul, cameras were among the easiest ways into a modern house's network. She tapped into the camera's feed, tracing where it sent its data. This one went to a small PR node as well as security. Both connections ran through the basement office that was still a void to Roo. She'd get there.

Back at Miss Farmer's, Sasha had noticed how good Roo was with systems. Sitting at a neighboring console, she'd watched Roo speed through basic databases. "Where'd you learn that?"

Roo couldn't say the Skirts, because everyone thought she was from the city. "My Nan. She built bookkeeping databases before the Mess. Still works on them."

"Don't show too much competence." Sasha eyed the instructors. Sasha's particular skill, Roo had learned quickly, was camouflage. "Or they'll have you teaching here. Lay low and you could get a bona fide founders' gig on the other side of graduation."

Founders' gigs meant espionage. Roo's heart had raced at the thought. A position with an independent investigator was among King's highest hopes, and hers. Founders raced each other to find ways to rebuild the world. Work like that could take her beyond New Washington. Beyond entertainment as Roosa Canarvier, artisan thief, and Ro Villon, aerialist. Beyond side hustles and keeping her reputation spotless as Roosala Vane. As she got closer to graduating from Miss Farmer's, Roo hoped she could level up her fortunes, and her family's. Espionage would do that.

All after this heist.

Roo attached an extra camera to the panel before her, covered in more of Sasha's spectacular fabric. It blended with the wall coverings and merged with the existing media node. Redirection was one of her favorite parts of a Grand Heist. She adjusted the connections on the media panel until it accepted her camera as one of its eyes. First small step accomplished. It was time for a bug.

Footsteps echoed beyond the ballroom doors. *Dammit.* Her tablet showed the dragonfly wing right outside. Roo pressed herself close to the ceiling and held her breath as the door cracked open.

The stocky man peered in. Behind him, another guard.

A subdermal conversation buzzed. Then, "Boss says no one should be in the house this late. Bag them and take them to interrogation."

"Yes, Major Holt." The second guard stepped inside. She moved a flashlight around, dazzling Roo's eyelids. "All clear here."

"The signal came from nearby. Check the kitchens."

"Yes, sir," the second guard said.

The doors closed. A heartbeat later, Roo heard a crash. Someone running. *Who else was in the house?* It had better not be Dax.

She stayed as still as she could until the hall clock chimed the quarter hour. She had eighteen minutes until the laundry was finished. Sixteen hours until her brother was supposed to arrive. She'd barely gotten her first objectives in place. She had to risk the bug.

She slid her hand to the singlesuit's pocket and pulled out the next dragonfly. Holding it close to the panel connected the drone to Llyria. Before it could send any data, Roo pressed it against her own tablet, swapping its passwords through a code tumbler she'd created for school. After a long moment, a network thread appeared on her basic map of Llyria.

She had dragonfly-level access to the house. Not much, but it was a start.

She recoded the bug to look like a house drone on the network and let it hover beside her as she worked her way deeper into Llyria. From the ballroom, hallway, and garden cameras, she found a last-minute connection to PR consultants. Modifying one of those, she could see the main floor. The staff maintenance logs, less secure than they should be, were next. A security sandbox node. She wouldn't touch that, in case it was a trap. Instead, she accessed maintenance, inserting a party planner's request for the morning and rescheduling two sprinklers.

Even without King, she could open a few windows of her own. Once the requests were accepted, the extra code she'd worked in would percolate through the system.

She checked a last camera angle and used her new access to peer into the hallway and kitchen. No security visible. She rolled up and stowed her equipment. The clock sounded another partial melody. Half past.

A high vent between the ballroom and the main hall turned her clothing silver. Roo considered exploring the private rooms above, via the main staircase. Best not press her luck. Not yet.

She retraced her path, picking up crystals as she went. Leapt a boot-smashed bead and single ray that had broken through. She continued to the conservatory gallery, then the service stairs.

By the time Holt's security located her, she was sleeping on a pile of warm laundry in the basement.

"You can't rest in the laundry!" The guard Roo had seen earlier shook her awake. "Badge!"

Roo presented her arm, having swapped back the laundress's badge. The sweep cleared her. "It was late. I missed the van."

The woman shrugged. "Not my problem; there's staff cots if it happens again." She pointed toward the basement. "You seen anyone else down here?"

Roo shook her head. It was the truth. "What's happened?"

"Nothing to worry about." The guard took the stairs to the basement staff quarters. Toward security.

If they were still chasing thieves, she had everything to worry about. And more work she needed to do before her brother showed up—if he wasn't already caught.

Digital paper and thin tablets littered Mason's wide desk: perimeter monitoring patterns, biosensors, components of the weekend's security plan; new schematics for Graves

Biosecurity's product upgrades and investor foresight statements. Titanium safe caches, bio-scanners, and the DNA-controlled slapcuffs and seals MilPol loved had made Graves's fortune. Upgrades and new research were how he'd keep it.

After meeting with Tsalta, and a dinner where he'd been admittedly distracted, he'd tried and failed to stay in town. He'd dreamed of sand—swirling through Denver, overwhelming his home, drowning him. He'd woken up choking on his pillow. Evangeline slept peacefully beside him, and did not stir when he rose from the bed and left the room.

He'd returned to Llyria before dawn. Holt took him to the basement to observe the thief before they reviewed the video of the capture together in Mason's office. *Securing What's Yours,* the Graves corporate motto, had never felt so personal.

If only I could use the footage for PR. "You weren't supposed to catch the thief that hard, Major."

Holt shrugged and brushed at the carpet with his toe. "Little brat ran."

"You're lucky it was someone trying to get feed material. No contract, no standing, can't file for losses. Totally illegal. How did he access Llyria for a month, Holt? When he recovers, get him to tell you that before you send for the precinct."

"Yes, sir," Holt answered, gravely serious. "I've brought in extra staff and started re-scanning workers. Should we keep the interrogation room open?"

"Yes, but don't tell Evangeline. Or Benford." Mason looked over his desk, distracted by what Dr. Tsalta had told him. "We've bio-locked this office?"

"Correct, sir. And someone will be watching at all times. Plus, as you said, Gabriel has his own defenses."

Mason nodded. "It isn't unheard of for a little corporate espionage to happen during a party. Perhaps we should set some additional traps."

Holt, who'd trapped a spy embedded at Graves's own office a year before, grinned. "I'd be glad to."

That spy had gone to Alaska by way of MilPol. The person who'd allegedly hired him, Graves's own CFO, Rylan Stonecliff, had been a deeper problem. Mason had once thought himself lucky to work with someone like Stonecliff—a member of a founder's family, due to inherit. It was a hint of things to come: investors—which did happen—and a founder's medal of his own—which didn't. After the arrest, he and Stonecliff agreed to part ways, with little of the public acrimony the feeds devoured. But Mason still seethed.

Evangeline didn't, and wouldn't, know. In the manner of old families, the man was close to the Benfords. "Did Stonecliff RSVP?"

"He's at sea, apparently."

"Thank the founders for that." Stonecliff would love to know about Mason's conversations with Dr. Tsalta.

Mason flexed his toes, then each foot. His left heel was starting to blister. Could he find someone on the staff with the same-sized feet, who could walk the property to break them in? He needed them for the masque: the planners had programmed them with the first dance choreography. "What shoe size are you? Nine?"

Holt shook his head, jaw clenched. "Size eleven. How may I assist you?"

"You can't, more the pity. I look forward to your next briefing."

Mason waited until he was sure his security chief had gone. "Llyria, lock the office."

He opened the lid of his desk. He'd had a small lab installed there as Llyria was being finished. A hobby lab, yes, but its crystallography machine had a hand-etched X-ray diffuser inside, customized with exquisite glass and brass fittings. The lab was both a thing of beauty and a useful tool. Mason could point to it any time a potential investor called him a fraud. *Did frauds have things like this in their Enclave homes? Did they know how to use them? They did not.*

Mason's early years had been conveniently lost in the Mess, but he was no fraud. He withdrew from his pocket the ampoules he'd taken from the lab.

Multiple sample sheets and a careful application of an antique eyedropper later and the machine was humming. Mason made a few notations and checked that the ampoule caps were re-sealed. He took a few calls. Answered messages from his backers.

When Benford's clock tower chimed a distant four o'clock, and the antique clock sounded downstairs moments later, Mason looked up, alarmed at how much time had passed.

If he lingered much longer, the evening's first events would begin without him. He'd promised Evangeline he would be ready by six. She needed to be his focus, at least for now.

"Gabriel," Mason summoned his safe out of an abundance of caution. "I'll need to rent another cache for the weekend, until Monday. Do you have additional space?"

"Of course. I have a small hip cache available." A large number appeared on Mason's desk. He thumbed approval and Gabriel flipped a tactical pocket flap open. Mason handed him the ampoules. "These will fit, thank you sir."

"I doubt I'll need them until Monday, but if I get a moment, I'll call on you. They're bio-locked. Put it on the company tab. Meanwhile, one of the feathers, please. And the other item?"

"Of course." Gabriel closed the second cache, securing the ampoules inside. He passed Mason a feather and a small box, then closed the primary cache. "Safe as houses."

With the variant secured, and the crystallography calculations due to take at least a day, and his surprises for Evangeline in good hands, Mason gave a satisfied sigh as Gabriel retreated to his room. "Good to get a little work done." The weekend stretched out before him. Perhaps, instead of catching the thieves all in one decisive swoop on the first night, he might, for showman's sake, let things go as long as Sunday morning, before breakfast. He could present the thieves trussed on the table. That would give his guests, and Evangeline, a thrill.

He closed his desk, sweeping the remaining documents into secure drawers. Then he bio-locked everything. *Can't be too careful, not with thieves coming. Even the fake kind.*

Dax was uncomfortably late. Vanier Wines had booked him on a one pm Enclave van, thinking it was a favor for King. He was looking forward to the dust-free, air-chilled ride on smooth roads.

But at quarter to one, Dax was still seated deep in New Washington's main MilPol precinct. He'd paid for a quarter hour, and then another. The last credits were ticking down. The cheaply fabbed chair scraped at the backs of his knees. King sat on the opposite side of the static barrier, saying nothing.

"This wastes good credits, Dad. Tell me who you think framed you. If we don't know, we can't fix or avoid it."

King scrubbed at his face, dirty and exhausted. Shook his head slowly. The sight of his only parent in such a state shook Dax to his core. He had no memory of Cere Canarvier, aside from the stories King told about their mother at bedtime. He couldn't stand to lose his father too.

"Who's to say the same thing won't happen to any of us?" Dax didn't care that the guard heard him. Everyone asked questions like this. He cared that King—who loved to tell a good story—wasn't answering. He leaned his elbows onto his knees, his hair falling into his eyes. "Seriously."

King leaned forward so that his posture mirrored Dax's. His eyes said 'don't press me' even as his body sagged. He didn't wave the conversation private. He couldn't until Dax's credits ran out. His prisoner number glowed on his sleeve through the static, even as the barrier's disruption made the rest of him look gray and washed out, like a cheap projection on a bad comm.

"Fine. But give us information—something to fight with." Dax, about to go radio silent for a Grand Heist he couldn't tell his father about, wanted to yell, but he kept his voice level. There was no more money to bribe the guards with. Maybe they wouldn't move King into the big hold—the one randomly swept by Alaska-bound transports needing ballast—until Sunday morning, but if anyone learned King wasn't a full citizen before then, that would immediately change the situation. Whoever had done this to him was still out there.

King blinked. His hands moved together and apart in the shadows of his knees. Once, and then again, faster.

The family employed a long-established combination of codes and signals, as other methods of communication often broke down. Modified Skirts signs, mixed with blinking patterns based on old Morse, a few sound-signs. Dax was terrible at Morse, but he could still make out his father's wishes clearly: *Keep Roo in school. Help Nan. She's frailer than she looks.*

This shook Dax more than his father's silence. King made speeches that rallied friends and neighbors to his causes. He did not give up. But now he was. Did he have a different plan? Or was he in deeper trouble than Nan thought? Dax closed his eyes, then blinked back. "What did you do, Dad?"

King stared. Then spoke one word: "Go." The credit timer dinged. Dax had no more funds to feed it. Unless King opted to accept more time on his own account, the visit was over. King did not opt to accept. The barrier turned white.

Dax, late for the job that might save his father, shook his head. "How can we help you if you refuse to be helped?" *Was that what King intended?* Infuriating. Dax gathered his comms from the guard, traded his visitor band for his workband at the precinct entrance, pulled up his outdoor mask and began to run.

Will I make it? Has Roo been able to finish her setup tasks and King's, both?

Although he caught the van by the barest of margins, Dax sweated almost all the way to the Enclaves.

When he arrived, security had already set up a checkpoint in the driveway. "Move fast!" A guard shouted. The line of staff and entertainers for the first night's events inched forward, letting Dax finally catch his breath after the pell-mell run and the van's speeding, jolting journey—the driver's only indication that Vanier had made her wait off schedule. Finally, Dax reached the front.

"Name and job?" A blank circle with space for a visual ID appeared on the young guard's tablet. The man's body blocked the way into the service entrance.

Behind Dax, the van pulled away, abandoning him and seventeen crates of wine to the back driveway of Llyria, next to a long line of contractors waiting to be verified.

"Charlie Barringer." Dax smiled his most winning smile, knowing his eyes had to carry it. He'd tucked his dark hair into a complicated bun beneath his cap—no hint of curls showed. His mask covered his dimples. And his contacts let his eyes sparkle with a hint of green.

"Employer and title." The dry-voiced guard raised his eyebrows, glancing at a timestamp in his heads-up display. Dax could practically read his thoughts. *Two o'clock, hours more to go.* Instead of checking catering crates and city workers, the guard probably wanted to be doing fancier work with drones for MilPol.

"Vanier Wines. Sommelier's assistant." Dax reached into his satchel for proof: a tiny bottle of Vanier's best. Boss's idea. Perfect at a time like this, even if guards weren't supposed to take honoraria.

He proffered his wrist so that the guard could scan

his workband. The guard palmed the bottle, then slipped it into his Graves Biosecurity jacket. When he scanned Charlie's brawny arms and khaki pants, he was smiling. Then he moved to the crates.

"Service quarters are in the bunker, two floors down. Grab a shower." He gestured with his chin at the wine. "This will take some time. I'll ping you on the house feed when it's ready to move."

Dax figured a few more bottles wouldn't make it. Price of doing business in the Enclave. "How do I get on the house feed?"

"Mask."

Dax carefully lowered his day mask without protest. He looked into the bio-scan. He caught the guard looking at him intently and wondered if, with his catering jacket, he was also a nice vintage. He winked, but the guard didn't wink back until the scanner pinged all-clear. No extra identities, no secreted equipment of any kind. Then the guard grinned.

Dax raised his mask, but he held the smile with his eyes.

The guard thumbed Barringer's image on his data pad. "Already in the system. Password? For private messages, and the like?"

Dax pretended to think for a moment, his eyes following the curve of the cellar's stone archway, then back down to catch the guard's with a gleam. "Perrugia."

"Sounds like a wine," the guard replied. There was definitely more interest in his voice now. A small breathlessness. He waved Barringer inside.

"Easy to remember," Dax murmured as he stepped past the guard. The guard had already turned toward the next person in line.

Dax didn't bother to look back once he was inside. The guard had been cute, but Charlie Barringer's image in the database was at least a year old—it made him look like a kid. Roo's idea of a joke.

Do the job, Dax. He counted doors on the way to the kitchen. Two on the left, then one marked "staff quarters." Two on the right, both unmarked. Seven more down a hallway to the larder. He tried a handle. A room filled with cheeses. The pungent scent of real dairy overwhelmed him. He'd need to get used to the smell if he wanted to start a restaurant in the city, but he had to swallow hard.

Another room held serving trays, all aged silver and gleaming white porcelain. A third door didn't budge.

"Stay on your own route, mate," a woman in chef's whites called. She pointed a serving spoon at the floor's tiles. Thin lines glowed green for kitchen, deep merlot for cellars—matching the shade his workband had turned at the door. "Llyria doesn't like people out of place."

It was different than other estate parties he'd worked—Roo hadn't mentioned. Or she hadn't noticed.

The merlot line ran up a flight of three steps. "I thought the cellar would be in the basement? That's what they told us."

"Older wines, yes. But temp-control storage is through there," she replied brusquely. "Where's Vanier? I thought he was coming himself?"

"Later today," Dax said smoothly. "Sent me ahead to get things organized. Said to tell you he hopes you still think well of him." It was only a small fib. The sommelier had more of a reputation than Dax did. The payoff came in the form of the sous-chef's nearly merlot-colored blush.

"He did?"

King had taught Dax to build in small opportunities for chaos wherever he could on heists. *Everyone wants to be liked, Dax.*

Dax knew his smile, a replica of King's, was perfect for that. Even over his mask, he worked the distance between himself and the chef with a wide-eyed nod. The young woman was positively beaming in the kitchen's heat. She picked up an apple and a peeler, staring at both intently.

Vanier certainly wouldn't mind finding himself cornered by a very interested sous chef.

With a shrug, Dax followed the lit path to the staff bunk room and dropped his overnight kit in a secure locker—paying the fee for it, since Vanier hadn't. The fabbed mattresses were thin and hard, but he didn't plan to stay.

Roo had grown up entertaining fancy society folks under Nan's watchful eye, going to private tutors in the Skirts and the city to improve her diction. Dax had studied on the streets, showing off his skills by swiping as many trinkets from Roo as he could. "This is real thieving. Artists don't work this fast, this smooth," he'd said. Then he'd smile and she'd laugh and clap her hands.

"You're such a charmer."

Dax stuck his hands in his pockets and wished he had the family Timex. When Roo had swiped it back, he'd definitely let her. She'd needed the confidence. But should she be leading the job? They needed a real thief, with real dazzle.

When he was ready to get to work, Dax climbed the stairs and let himself in to the wine storage room. As the door closed in the dry, coolness, light came up from the floor panels. It haloed his feet and illuminated his reflection in bottle after bottle of the best pre-Mess vintages.

Dax whistled. "These are worth more than me."

And this wasn't even the cellar. This was the everyday stuff. Graves—or whoever he'd hired—had good taste. The feeds said Graves rarely drank, maintaining a pristine reputation. Dax made a note to check downstairs. Wine, like precious metal and data, was tough to trace when it fell into the right hands.

"Can't keep the best for yourself," he murmured. "When the Canarviers are here."

Private Feed for Approved Investor-Subscribers

Graves Biosecurity Forward-Looking Interactive Statement for Investors (Green Book or Enclave ID required)

Investor #[redacted] question:: What is the marketplace timing for your new research developments?

GB: As the go-to and most reliable source of bonded work-bands, GBS provides dozens of coastal markets, onshore and off, with ironclad security. From DNA to biomarker checks, we filter through Turbulence-related background confusion with ease. As the leader in safe technology-hardware, wetware AND loyalty add-ons (Safeware 1.0)—we support over a hundred families in the maintenance and curation of their valuable assets.

Opportunities abound: Offshore Enclaves' expansion of workband and slapcuff toolsets and Safeware applications. While we have yet to break into the citizen-band market, we see that as a natural outgrowth of our production endeavors. Our enhancements of Safeware into a more extensive and reliable product is ongoing.

Investor #45 question: Graves Biosecurity seems to be building alliances in high places. What risks and rewards do you expect?

GB: A data leak one year ago [experience PFAS #442] provided rich opportunities to clear degraded and outdated products from our line. We continue to upgrade security and note that all business relationships are subject to risk.

Investor #[redacted] question: I'd like more clarity on my question, above.

GB: Of course. New Developments are on the way. An exciting time for Graves Biosecurity is here! With enhanced data sets, extraordinary new developments in Safeware 2.0 (guaranteed to promote longer-lasting loyalty for your family), and additional research, your investment in us is secure.

For more information, or to expand your investment, click *here*.

Graves Biosecurity: Keeping What's Yours, Yours [Public Feed for New Washington Citizens of Specific income levels – twenty credits for interacting]

Graves Biosecurity - Keeping What's Yours, Yours – proudly announces:

- six new in-lab apprentices and promotion of four apprentices to research roles
- appointment of a new CFO following the departure of Rylan Stonecliff, who retains a seat on the board
- new offices in New Washington, at the Public Works laboratory

For our private clients we also announce: [feed-limited view]

- new pheromone adjusters for your personal safes
- new titanium storage implants
- new safe training seminars and coaches for kidnapping, pursuit, and evasion
- in development: smaller, more comfortable workbands for children

All That Glitters

At exactly seven o'clock that evening, Llyria's enormous carved oak doors opened. Guests flowed up the main drive, a river of silks sparkling with precious gems. Most wore masks that barely glittered around their eyes, setting off rather than hiding their features.

They passed beneath a delicate awning of flowers and cameras, chips and citizen bands glowing momentarily as Llyria confirmed their bio-signatures. The first perfect shoes touched the foyer tiles and waiters—fully masked in service livery, noses and mouths hidden—swept into the main hall with trays of wine and champagne, perfectly timed.

Roo stepped from the chrysanthemum garden into the reception line. She smoothed her black skirts with gloved fingers. Adjusted her mask. The first notes of a waltz drifted from an open window. She noted that she wasn't the only solo guest in the crowd. Still, those nearby focused on her mask, her profile, her gown. Was she being imaged? Would she appear on the feeds soaking up and selling what they could of the guest list? Was someone comparing her features with this year's debuts? Feeds were wonderful entertainment, but terrible for thieves. She approached the awning, saying a small blessing to the tech she'd woven into her stolen mask, and to her contacts—which she'd reprogrammed to match the identity of the guest she'd borrowed.

"Pucky, Beau! Good to see you again!" She waved shyly at an older couple in line. The nickname—a gift from Mason Graves's database—made the woman's face light up. She spoke more quietly. "I'm glad you're feeling better."

Beatrice "Pucky" Williams's brows wrinkled, trying to place her. Roo smiled brightly. "Elizabeth Greene. One of Naomi's daughters."

"Oh, Elizabeth! I hardly recognized you. Lovely." Pucky beamed. Roo curtsied. The line moved forward, with Roo as one of them. There were at least four other couples Roo could have greeted, but Pucky had been a coup. The guests around her relaxed, any determination to ferret out interlopers dampened.

Roo adjusted an earring while the couples in front of Pucky and Beau complimented each other's choice of designers, before falling into gossip that made the feeds pale in comparison.

"That's not her best evening set," a tall woman—Ann Raphaelle McClain, known to friends as Dodo—whispered to her wife—Deborah McClain-Daniels. She jutted her chin quickly at a woman ahead of her.

"That's not nice, Dodo!" Her partner replied with a laugh.

"Well, I'm not nice, am I? I don't have to be." The woman tugged a glove straight and frowned as their entrance stalled. "Oh, look. They've caught someone trying to sneak in, haven't they."

A woman wearing city fashions, with a very obvious camera-jewel, struggled in the grip of a guard. Three sky-colored drones dropped to the lawn at her feet and were crushed by the guards. The line moved forward once more.

"I suspect that won't be the last of them. Apparently, Evangeline encourages one of her fan feeds. Not that her father knows."

"You know, Dodo, they could throw you out too. Our hostess makes friends and fans without having to hire them. Perhaps you could take lessons?"

The dig was sharp, but McClain chuckled. "She is particularly strong at forging connections. I admire it. And how sad, since her mother went so young. She should be here to see how—"

"Oh, look who's come from offshore." Dodo's wife cut across the conversation, smiling as more couples joined the receiving line. Few but Roo were close enough to hear when she whispered, "Ann, Sam Benford has forbidden people to speak of it. We don't need to flout. Especially not with Judge Benford possibly attending. Ps and Qs, dear. This is not the feeds."

Ann grumbled. "But it's *interesting*." Roo hoped to hear more, but had to dip a quick curtsy as Dodo looked her up and down. Then the McClains embraced the Williamses and greeted the new arrivals. "How was the flight?"

"Bumpy!" groaned one member of a very blonde quartet. All four wore complimentary, jeweled masks. "I've never had a good hop from Atlantic, but this one has me vowing never again. At least Enclave weather is always good."

"At least we can come and go when we're in port." Their companion clapped a cold glove on Roo's bare shoulder and kept talking. "Those poor Ocean fools must get travel approved by their Enclave. Operate on a strict schedule. Imagine! You couldn't get me back on the hopter tonight for anything!" The crystal beads of the offshore guests' masks moved in complex patterns that dazzled like the sun itself had dropped them off. Roo stumbled. She didn't know these guests yet—not enough time delving into the database. *Improvise. What would Dax say?*

"You look smashing, and not at all rattled," she murmured as she passed beneath the awning. She turned her wrist to a concealed scanner, feeling the band beneath her glove warm as it registered.

"Elizabeth Greene," the house murmured. "Ann and Deborah McClain-Daniels." She'd passed the next test.

Dodo sniffed at the gleam of an eye scan as her palm glowed briefly, the color tuned to match her pink gown. "No one trusts neighbors any longer."

"Dari, Vaden, and Moré VanPerl," the house announced in quiet tones. "With cousin, Annelemma."

The guest list continued to unfurl behind her as Roo stepped into the main hall. She looked for Dax among the wine and champagne bearers. Didn't see him. Her tablet had notified her when he'd made it through security, so she knew he was here. But where? The plan required him to be in the hall.

All around her, guests greeted and gossiped. The main hall warmed until it was stifling. Finally, Roo spotted a young man, leaning on the second-floor balcony railing, taking in the grand hall's glitter. He caught Roo's eye and winked. Even with the biologic modifications, she knew that grin. Her brother had traded his sommelier's uniform for a stolen tuxedo. It fit perfectly. A purloined golden mask shimmered beneath the tumult of his dark curls. Her stomach churned. He'd only been here for five hours and he was already off-plan. Two young women hovered near his elbows.

Roo couldn't scold him in the grand hall, and he knew it. *Provocateur. If King were here—*

But King isn't here.

Roo barely dipped her head in reply. She had to trust that he'd read the situation well. That was part of the performance. The black and midnight feathers of her mask, gathered the evening before from bits and pieces around the house and grounds, trembled at the motion. They framed her eyes in a way that drew out the green in her contacts, but not too much, and matched the hand-sewn blue accents that crossed her bodice and moved down the cascade of her silk skirts and low-slung bustle.

Her fellow guests were similarly toying with the line of propriety. The bigger the gown, the more elaborate the hair, the better, as long as it was tastefully done. The effect was magical, but Roo knew, all magic was really money.

A guest in trim military blues lifted a glass in her direction. An invitation. *Not yet,* she smiled, then circled away from him, joining the crowd heading toward the ballroom. Beyond the threshold, music swelled. Her heart raced, anticipating the next beats of the Grand Heist.

Deep breath. This part she could do in the dark if she had to. Lift the light stuff, but only what would cause the most upset later. Roo's fingers twitched, recalling every practice session with King and Dax. The proper way to fold one's hand, curl a little finger, twist and lift. Over and over again, on dolls, on Nan's aprons while the bus rolled the Skirts, on moving targets in the streets around the city.

She'd felt so powerful, then. Like she knew secrets no citizens even suspected. *How long ago that had been.* Her heart sank. She knew now how small and vulnerable they were.

No. She was not going to let King's absence upset her. She heard Nan's admonishments in the music's weave and the hall clock's swing: *small things first, then big. No extra risks. No bravado. Keep it simple, and stick to the plan.*

This was the moment no one knew she was among them. Her favorite part of a heist. When she could be anything or anyone at all.

The real excitement—at least for the guests—would begin as soon as Dax triggered the calling card. She hoped he'd constructed it as close to King's usual calling cards as possible. It must seem as if the Canarviers performed with a full count. Once the card dropped, anything missing, from a spare tuxedo to earrings and credits, would be blamed on the thieves.

Thieves who themselves couldn't break the event contract, even as the guests inevitably joined in the game and made their own rules. It amused her that the rich enjoyed stealing from each other. That they were no different, no better, than anyone else. Long ago, Dax had been outraged when he'd first watched an elderly man pocketing six teaspoons during his first performance. "Why should they get to keep what we've worked and planned for?"

Nan had shushed him. "Don't they always?"

King had just laughed. A deep belly roll of appreciation for the game, and his family. The memory made her miss him even more. *Stop it. Focus.*

Roo found a good perch by an ornate champagne fountain. The tumble of bubbles ran over a replica of New Washington. The Belt Way, marking the divide between city and outskirts, held crystal coupes. The city wall and older buildings, upon which newer ones rose, the vertical farms and hopterpads, even a detailed museum with paintings and sculptures showing through the windows, all drowned in champagne. As the waterline of the surrounding basin rose, swallowing the first level of buildings, partygoers grabbed glasses and, laughing, came to the rescue.

Roo took a glass as well, then bent to fill it. As she did, she picked out several interesting targets around the room. She pulled her dance card from her sleeve and left the glass on the floor.

"Surely you are escorted tonight, madam?" A stern voice sounded close behind her. The man who'd raised his glass to her. His blue suit, which on closer inspection appeared closely styled but not actually military. His sienna-toned skin hinted at cocktails beneath an ocean Enclave's dome. *Maybe he came with the Atlantic guests.*

She studied the black cutwork of her sleeves. "My date fell ill, sir." Aimed her gaze up at him.

"That won't do. You are escorted now." He beamed from behind his green leather mask. The tooled leaves smelled strongly. *Was it actual leather? How much could I fence* that *for? Especially to one of the experimental lab-vans in the Skirts.*

"Rylan Stonecliff," he said and tapped her dance card. He offered his arm.

She wavered when his name came up as [/.] on her card. Was he who he said he was? Ironic, for her to worry about that, here, now, but her training at Miss Farmer's had kicked in. She hadn't seen a Stonecliff in the dataset either.

He watched her gaze indifferently. That was much more interesting—that he didn't mind her doubting him. Against her training, Roo took his arm.

Though Stonecliff smelled of whiskey, he swept Roo around the room energetically for several dances.

Dax had taken the floor as well, becoming the epicenter of a complex pavane. Three women followed him now, jewels glittering. *Careful, Dax.*

He said something that made them all laugh. He was definitely not keeping things simple.

When the music quieted, and the whirl of dancers slowed, Roo found herself conveniently near the doors. She watched over Stonecliff's shoulder as Mason Graves appeared on the wide staircase.

Applause bubbled up. The host eyed the cameras and his guests, straightened his jacket, and turned to the front doors. Evangeline Benford, her father, and five of her closest friends entered the main hall.

Evangeline wore a ruby-and-gold mask. The "feathers" in her headdress were hinged golden tendrils, wired to move with each breath. She lifted one feather from her crown as Mason descended to her. The crowd's attention focused entirely on the pair.

When they met on the first stair, a few risers above their guests, Evangeline slipped an arm around his waist, leaned up for a kiss, and playfully held the sharp quill against his neck, just above the collar.

The crowd gasped. Mason's jaw tightened. But then he chuckled, and said, with what all the feeds later acknowledged was a heart-bursting level of pride, "Happy birthday, my very own jeweled bird, with your precious feathers."

"Oh, Lord," Stonecliff whispered in Roo's ear. "They got a choreographer."

Roo stifled a giggle. Who was this man? A late invite? A competing thief? Her spine straightened and she pulled away. Security? *I should have been more careful.*

Stonecliff sensed the change. "A person of resources, in this Enclave, needs a firm resolve to remain independent. I see you have that." His tone was the formal playfulness Roo had heard among Enclave kids at Miss Farmer's. His gaze remained politely focused on their hosts. But he didn't let Roo go.

As the couple entered the ballroom, Mason raised a dark, glittering colombina mask to his face with one hand, and spun Evangeline with the other. Choreographed indeed.

Stonecliff turned Roo back toward the floor, following their hosts, and then lapping them. "Graves." Stonecliff inclined his head. Mason Graves missed a step. They spun past another couple. "Andrews," Stonecliff bowed to the woman on his left. As he did, Roo saw a pale scar running from Stonecliff's earlobe to his jaw.

He caught Roo staring and winked. Then bowed low to hand her off to Andrews, if she chose to go. Andrews was, according to the database, another offshore Enclaver. Roo did choose, determined to learn more about Rylan

Stonecliff later. Graves had startled at his greeting, which made her very curious.

As they parted, Roo's fingers lightly brushed his lapel as a goodbye. She curtseyed to Andrews, slipping Stonecliff's pocket watch into her bustle with a deft twist. Then Andrews sped her again across the dance floor.

They made it too easy.

Dax slipped from the ballroom soon after Mason and Evangeline made their entrance. He'd enjoyed the dance while he set the calling card. Roo's cautious next beat had him meeting her in the rose garden, or a backup location near the shared greenway and the first cherry trees.

He sniffled, sinuses already swelling from something that never bothered him in the city: pollen. His pilfered guest mask provided little protection. *Can't wait to retrieve my service mask.*

His stomach growled. He had a few moments before he needed to meet Roo. He blew his nose on the fine handkerchief in the borrowed jacket pocket—tiny stars and a knotted monogram embroidered on pale silk—and looked toward the kitchen. A server was headed for the back stairs, carrying a large prep tray that smelled delicious. Dax followed his nose.

At the bottom of the narrow staircase, the butler struggled to manage the next door and the tray together.

"Let me," Dax said.

"It's no bother," the server demurred. Dax helped anyway. "My thanks." The server tilted the tray for Dax to sample a few items. "Cured meats and eggs—all entirely legal in the enclaves of origin."

The eggs were mottled several shades of brown. Dax took one and bit down. A savory brine filled his mouth. He smiled and chewed, trapped. *Gah. Horrible.* He couldn't let on the egg was too rich for his tastes. "Delicious," he said, and kept chewing.

When the server disappeared down the hall, he spit the rest into the kerchief. In the kitchen, he tossed the kerchief in the roaring fire where the chef was preparing a vat-grown boar's head for the next evening's dinner. A chef's assistant began to shoo him away, but noted his tuxedo, and ducked her head instead.

Mustn't offend the guests. Dax turned back to the hall. *Now I'm thirsty and still hungry. Great.*

Dax loved food. He and Aanand had talked about opening a pop-up. Catering opportunities were great ways into parties. He needed a cover—even King had said so. *But maybe rich people food is not it.* He lifted a glass from a passing tray without asking its contents. The bubbles in his drink went straight to his nose. *Misery.*

"You can't drink it so fast," a soft voice murmured. Valencia, who he'd met in the ballroom. While dancing, she'd said she was a friend of the hostess. "You'll get used to this."

"Used to what?"

"The noise, the cameras," she laughed, pointing. Overhead, a small dragonfly hovered, recording. "You seemed uncomfortable."

Dax grinned. "These? Nah. They're everywhere."

"Not like these. Privacy filtered. Graves has some standards, or Evangeline does. My room was camera free when I scanned it last."

His flirtations were making him late to meet Roo. But he couldn't have a guest following him. "Care to dance?" He offered a hand to sweep Valencia back into the ballroom. Then he sneezed.

She wrinkled her nose. "Are you ill?"

Dislike of illness in the Enclaves was understandable, given the Mess, but Dax knew these same people wouldn't blink twice if Skirters got sick. "Cherry trees." He gestured outside.

She didn't look convinced. "I'm on my way to the powder room."

"Watch out for thieves," he said, laughing.

She grinned. "I heard they hired some! But where are they? Do you know?"

"I was just kidding." Dax sneezed again and Valencia lost interest. The beads of her dress and mask clattered quietly as she disappeared down the stairs and Dax turned for the rose garden, moving fast.

The antique hall clock chimed the hour. The musicians took a break, after playing a galliard. A DJ began to set up. King would have been horrified by the slapdash mingling of history and art, though it was in keeping with Llyria's ballroom pastiche. Roo was almost glad he couldn't see it.

She spent the pause by the champagne fountain, counting people in the ballroom. She'd danced with most, except Mason and Evangeline. That was fine. Let them keep their cufflinks and jewels.

It is past time for the calling card. I'm going to strangle Dax.

Stonecliff had disappeared too. Graves's mood had lightened the moment he'd gone, Roo noticed. *Very curious.*

Mason and Evangeline stood at the center of the ballroom when a tall, white-haired woman approached them, carrying a delicate box. She wore a simple wrap over an even simpler silk ball gown—all the highest quality. Her mask was elegant, but practical. "I cannot stay, but I wanted to wish you a happy birthday, darling. And a wonderful weekend."

"Aunt Minerva, we are honored." Evangeline sank to a full, kneeling curtsy with grace. Beside her, Mason Graves looked stunned and delighted. He bowed as well.

"Enough of that." The woman waved her fan in a small circle as guests murmured. *The judge. She came.* Minerva Benford looked embarrassed by the attention, but as Roo watched, she bent to adjust her shawl, smiling with pleasure. "You two look stunning. You'd best do well by her, sir."

The last words, aimed at Graves, made the entrepreneur blush. "I plan too," he stammered.

"You are the reason we are together, Aunt Minerva," Evangeline said. "I wouldn't have considered his suit if you hadn't pointed out his finer features." The crowd chuckled. "Although we have to work on tennis and hunting. Innovation, friends"—she turned to the assembled guests—"that's what makes the recovery work. My Mason is an innovator."

She opened the box lid and smiled. Lifted a Recovery Court deed for her majority to her chest.

Minerva gestured with her fan. "And you will be as well, with a forty-two percent share in this Enclave."

That's quite a gift, Roo thought. The crowd seemed to agree, cheering. Evangeline looked radiant. Graves, beside her, beamed. Judge Benford walked from the ballroom and out the main hall. A half-car sat on the drive. The guests parted before her and closed to talk excitedly in her wake. "She drove in her own half-car!" "Those shares of the Enclave were originally hers—didn't you know? Judges can't hold property, of course." "How generous and magnanimous." "What a sacrifice she's made."

The DJ began spinning a modified waltz by an ancient group called The Cure. Roo considered dancing again, but Dax finally appeared.

"Ready when you are." His eyes were puffy above his mask. He offered his arm. "That was some entrance."

"I've been ready." She moved with him into the waltz, turning the room's compass points until they found the patio above the gardens. The sprinklers had gone off as if someone had set them in jest, and not many guests were outside. The damp did terrible things to expensive fabric and hairpieces. "Which entrance do you mean? I'll bet you the judge bribed the DJ for that moment."

"I meant the hosts. The judge was good too." They reached the rose maze at the center of the garden. Roo disassembled her outfit quickly. She fed her mask and feathers to the bushes, then ate her contacts. "Goodbye, Elizabeth Greene."

"Gross," Dax whispered.

"I'm not leaving biodata for Graves's lab goons. Besides, the contacts are organic, Aanand promised. No worse than a fabbed protein bar."

"Hopefully." Dax grinned. *Not reassuringly.*

A sweep of her gloved hand and a murmured command made the decorative seams and cutwork disappear. She removed her bustle and rolled it into a ball. Then she whispered the resulting jumble of fabric table-linen white. "Conversion B-2." She reconfigured her skirts. Her transformation was complete before the waltz ended.

Under her arm, the bundle clinked as watches, jewelry, decorative data, and money clips settled.

Dax discarded his tux jacket and mask into the bushes. From inside a large marble planter, he retrieved his server's coat and an apron for Roo.

"Useful spot."

"I know what I'm doing," Roo bridled. "But we need to discuss the risks you're taking."

"Not risks. Embellishments. Guests want excitement—they want to feel alive. When they realize who they were dancing with?" He gave her his most winning gap-toothed grin and opened his vest to reveal two golden feathers—ones the hostess had recently been wearing. Roo saw subtle outlines of earrings and rings in his pockets. "They will never forget it."

"Dax. Nan made us promise to be careful." She tried to breathe calmly. *How will we make it two whole days if he is already this brazen?* "At least drop the feathers. They're too risky for the first night."

Dax laughed. "Maybe."

"And the card. We are late." *Canarviers are never late. King's first rule.*

"I set it on a pressure timer. Don't worry, Roo. Graves will hit it soon. We aren't late. We have the time."

Roo smacked her brother's shoulder lightly. "Why are you never worried?"

He sighed. "I am worried. About doing things the same way time after time. If we don't evolve, we're going to get caught. Again. We're out of backup funds. We can't bribe our way out of the next catch. This is our chance, Roo. Let's give it everything we've got." He squeezed her arm and sucked in his cheeks to look emaciated. "Which we can't do if we're starving like newbies in the Skirts. Let's see what's in the kitchen."

Her stomach growled. She hadn't had anything but fabbed nutrition bars for two days, and the kitchen did smell wonderful. "That card had better go off soon."

As the DJ's waltz ended, Mason cleared his throat. Evangeline, dancing with a new Graves Biosecurity client, looked over expectantly.

They'd planned their entrance, the first dances, Minerva's entrance, and Mason's response to the thieves' challenge to perfection.

Except the damned performers hadn't showed. That was even worse than Stonecliff appearing unexpectedly. *Outrageous.*

Mason could hear guests grumbling. He felt the same way. *Unbelievable, having to worry about your own robbery going right.* Had Holt spooked the thieves with his enthusiasm?

Worse, there was Stonecliff at the back of the room, laughing at a private joke with Sam Benford.

"Perhaps our next entertainers are afraid to face you," Evangeline, suddenly at his side, murmured so that only he could hear.

Good idea. I should say as much to the guests. He stepped forward onto the ballroom's new pastoral mosaic. The installation, a hillside scene with himself and Evangeline as shepherd and shepherdess, was a birthday gift he'd planned months in advance. It had been installed as the house was finished, then concealed under a false floor. Now revealed, their twined fingers lifted a rose skyward. Mason stepped on the rose and prepared to speak.

Copper-colored smoke streamed from the floor. Mason coughed as holographs appeared throughout the ballroom. He forced an amused smile, even as his chest convulsed from the smoke. A holographic orchestra played muffled notes. A shadow couple swept across the ballroom, masked.

Behind them, the room was filled with two types of guests. Those he and Evangeline had invited, and, interspersed among them, a gallery of historical rogues. A guest yelped as a gallows appeared in the smoke, readied for captured thieves. The sepia couple stopped their dance before it and turned masked faces to the audience.

Mason's guests applauded. Even several who clutched purses and wallets to their chests.

One dancer, wearing a feathered mask much like Mason's, addressed them in a clipped cadence:

"Like Charlie Peace and the five-fingered queen,
daring Vidoq, Cartouche, and Duval;
we slip among you, we test your gathering;
As Wordsworth wrote,
"Because the good old rule sufficeth them, the simple plan,
That they should take who have the power;
That they should keep who can."

The holographs faded and a gilt-edged calling card drifted to the floor. The voice rang out again across the ballroom:

"Time is a thief, sir, and the thieves have the time now!"

The card landed at Mason's feet, the troupe's name lit in holographic flames: *Canarvier*.

Multiple guests' excitement broke the silence.

"Oh, they're the best."

"Where will they strike first?"

"At billiards later tonight? By the pool tomorrow?"

Mason heard laughter and applause. Then someone cried, "My watch!"

In a rush of missing earrings, keys, clips, and bracelets, everyone felt the thieves' touch, too late.

Mason's heart lifted at the excitement. Evangeline had been exactly right.

Across the room, Sam Benford clapped approvingly, Stonecliff by his side. Sam's bald head gleamed in the light as if he'd had it polished.

"Our cameras better have captured everything, Holt," Mason subvocalized. With that footage, Graves's PR team could pair his ballroom entrance with shots of him capturing the performers.

"Yes, sir," Holt confirmed. His voice was gruff. *He's probably grinding his teeth to dust*, Mason thought.

Mason's fingers dipped to his left inside pocket, patting the case and the ring resting within. *Not time yet. Good to know it's still there.* Then he raised his eyebrows to the cameras, and then faced his guests. "The thieves have arrived then. I thought they'd lost their nerve."

Guests whooped and clapped. Some pulled out their dance cards, comparing names and faces. There hadn't been many strangers. Even the ocean-set were familiar from the feeds.

Mason straightened his tuxedo jacket and picked a bit of blue lint from a sleeve. His diamond cufflinks sparkled, each "G" perfect, and unthieved. "It is traditional, I am told," a fond nod at Evangeline, who curtsyed, "for hosts to buy back items that we don't recapture. The weekend's schedule will become all the more exciting now that thieves are about!" He paused, as they'd planned. "Please note your losses at the guestbook in the main hall. Meantime, for those who wish to play along, we offer a bounty of one million credits and a peacock feather for each thief caught. Happy birthday, Ev. Let the games begin."

Cheers filled the room. *What a host. What a party.* Waiters circulated more drinks. The traditional birthday songs began and increased in volume.

"We will make every effort to sort out and free anyone mistaken for a thief," the birthday girl added when the singing died down. Everyone laughed. Even Benford raised his glass.

Mason's toast was still raised when Rylan Stonecliff approached, hand extended. The man dared to wear a military consultant's uniform, here. And Mason couldn't say a thing about it with everyone watching. He came close to Mason and murmured conspiratorially, "I hope your safe is good. And fast."

Evangeline swooped in. "Rylan! I'm so glad you could come."

"A last-minute thing. Your father said it would make you happy." Stonecliff clinked his glass against Evangeline's before moving back into the crowd.

Mason deflated. *They'd added Stonecliff to the guest list? And hadn't told him?*

"He's a dear part of the family," Evangeline said, noting Mason's expression. "And it does make me happy. He said it's been ages since that little thing of yours."

It's called corporate espionage, Ev. Mason couldn't say it out loud. *And ages aren't long enough for me to get over my ideas walking out my door in that man's pocket. Allegedly.* But the Benfords didn't know—they were too close to the man. Mason summoned his best smile as Sam Benford joined them.

"Happy birthday, darling." He patted his daughter's shoulder as one might a rare and delicate sculpture. "Well done tonight. I never would have figured you'd risk thieves, Graves. Good work." At this, his neighbor's approval, Mason's smile broadened. Perhaps things were working out better than he thought.

New Washington Feeds: Meet Your Neighbors, *Enclave & Towne* (City Edition)

(Citizen-Band Subscription Required)

We are delighted to be reporting from inside Mason Graves's new mansion, Llyria, for the most dazzling event of the season so far: Evangeline Benford's twenty first-birthday weekend. While we can't provide a running score due to contract issues, we can tell you that the host has hired thieves, and they've definitely made a spectacular entrance!

Stick with this feed (micropayment engaged) to hear every bit of gossip and intrigue our reporters can discover!

Meantime, in a related, special report: Two members of the Lee family, Stephanie and Dallas Lee, were spotted at a popular bar a few nights ago. Now working several jobs in New Washington, the pair were open about their feelings for their former neighbors, and the fact that Grand Heists seem to once again be part of the social fabric.

User 3243523 captured the following:

Stephanie Lee: There's definitely pressure to throw parties. To have the best of everything. We were in over our heads even before the event.
Dallas Lee: Part of it is trying to keep up with everyone else, I expect. But after the Grand Heist, we saw our things in our friends' living rooms when we went to ask for help, for God's sake.

S. Lee: And Benford . . .
D. Lee: Let's not, dear. We're in public.
S. Lee: [undistinguishable] as if we'd shown weakness, and must be removed, before that spread. We could have found a way through, given enough time. But we weren't. Instead, we were ruined.
[someone asks about the troupe the Lees hired]
D. Lee: They played by the rules, observed each line of the contract. We can't say anything bad about them.
S. Lee: Not that we don't want to. [laughs]

[Feed removed]

The Baker's Dozen

From her nest deep in the laundry chute, Roo watched through the cameras as guests all over Llyria questioned the staff, and each other. *Everything's going well so far. No real slip-ups, even with Dax's enthusiasm. And people are having fun. Dax is wrong about that.*

The well-dressed, late-night crowd peered into every corner of the house—closets, cabinets, under furniture—delightedly seeking thieves.

The chute door squeaked open above her head and Roo doused her tablet. She'd made a hammock halfway down from the table linens. Her singlesuit matched the patterns and creases around her.

"I will not be going through the household's dirty laundry, Dodo!"

"Well maybe someone should—no one knows

much about Graves, I mean, who are his people?" The voices echoed down the chute.

"Dodo! Shhh."

"I can't imagine there is much laundry to speak of anyway. Come on, one peek." And the McClains peered into the space. "Nothing here." Dodo sneezed. "Let's go out by the pool. I heard they have merfolk and a casino."

Roo opened her eyes after the door slammed shut, and said a silent thank-you to Sasha for the fabric's camouflage.

She needed to get moving again, but she also needed to run some calculations.

Nan and King always said it was bad luck to count a haul before a job was done, but they needed at least ten million credits tonight. *That's not being unlucky. That's being cautious.*

Tomorrow's haul might cover half of the credits, if not more. It was going to be a spectacular performance. She tapped into the music gallery's cameras and scanned the room one last time. To her eye, the gallery's curtains hung a little heavier than they had before she'd prepared the room. But Graves's staff, who stared at monitors all day, focused on motion. They forgot how curtains should drape, especially if they'd looked that way since before the party began.

The tea services and silverware Dax was supposed to be taking care of tonight would likely bring a nice pile of credits in the sellback. But she didn't want to be caught short, and they had to expect some losses.

Holt's men would find at least one stash of belongings before Nan arrived to collect the next batch. That was part of the plan—give them a small triumph now and then. A way to feel like they were winning.

Given how frequently Holt had begun running searches in the past hour, they might find two caches. But they wouldn't find them all. The ball gown pickpocketing had been a nice take.

Should I tell Dax to flip the guest rooms earlier than tomorrow's dinner? She'd planned that beat as a finale, with the thieves appearing to escape from the upper windows after the meal, when they were really already gone, courtesy of more calling-card holograms. But they'd done something similar at the Johnsons' party last year, hadn't they? Maybe Dax was right. Maybe she was playing it too safe.

She was glad her brother was training to take over the troupe. She loved the work, but she wanted real, legitimate jobs: higher-level espionage, fixing services, background research, data diving. *Things Dax would probably call boring.*

Maybe, just maybe, if she ever got a chance to be boring, she'd find out what had happened to their mother. King and Nan had forbidden her to look, saying all they'd found was dead ends and the wrong side of MilPol's bad sense of humor. But if Roo set up her own investigation agency someday, on the other side of the wall, they couldn't stop her from trying.

Her tablet pinged softly. The last dragonfly that Roo had repaired in the shed had worked its way through the vents above the security room. She could hear them planning over the earpiece she'd added to its tiny body.

Holt was so technical—in tune with Graves's philosophy of superior technology—running sensor scans, metal and heat detectors, laser grids, camera sweeps. They'd forgotten it was easier to fool technology than a person. "Every generation forgets this," Nan had told her once. "And then they remember again."

Nan and King both agreed that the best Grand Heists had pacing, much like a waltz. Teams that grabbed everything they could the moment their calling cards dropped, and didn't stop or take time to breathe and reassess? They got caught. Roo was taking time. Reassessing the whole security grid again, taking it apart once more. Making her incursions look like data—before the latest round of passwords took hold.

She fed the system new scan algorithms that looked like they came from Holt's assistants. She adjusted the mirrors she'd hidden near cameras to create pure data garbage for security. Confusion built as the system itself seemed to throw errors. Roo watched carefully. She'd done a good job on the house, shutting down access before Holt detected her. But was she being overconfident?

She spun the charm on her wrist. *No, this is going well.*

She set new password-churners loose on the house's main systems. The maintenance request had gotten her fairly far before Holt had shut it down. By then, she'd acquired two staff keys, plus the main information on the guest and contractor databases. Even once she'd been shut out of that access point—Holt's team was good—she'd gained a better understanding of how Graves Biosecurity organized their data sets. Identification numbers, hash tables, the particular fractal pattern of their AI simulator, all of it. That could be valuable later.

But Holt's intrusion detection algorithms were getting smarter over time. With the dragonfly in the vents now, she could see much more.

They had to be careful. Even as much as Sasha's technical skill was helping—and not one sensor or guest spotted her hiding place when she set the smart fabric to conversion H—any mistake could be the end of things. But not yet. *Perhaps if they had enough credits left over after freeing King, I'll ask Sasha to make a suit for Dax. He would like that.*

Her tablet finished running the calculations. They were going to need to work faster in order to hit their goal. On the house map, sommelier staff were clustered by the hot tub, the fire pit, and the gaming tables. Charlie Barringer included. *Not a chance Dax would miss the mers. How to get to him, though.* She'd abandoned her socialite persona and was a member of the staff now. Tomorrow, she had to meet Nan, and return through the staff entrance as Ro Villon, aerialist. All without getting caught in the meantime. Her eyes narrowed at the map. There was a tunnel from the maintenance area to the pool shed. Right next to the laundry room. That would work.

She tapped the magnets holding her hammock up, dialing their attraction to one-third. The hammock slid silently, letting Roo sink a floor before she kicked out the back panel of the chute and slid through the access crawlspace to the maintenance tunnel.

It smelled like grease and chemicals, almost as bad as the Skirts.

"All in, all in!" A roulette wheel rattled. Dice tumbled across a felt-covered table.

Dax, masked now and bearing a tray of drinks, listened to the guests talk. Vacation homes—too big and distant to steal. Investments. Their favorite items from the Recovery.

"The Court declared these were my great-grandmother's." A tanned and toned young man in swim trunks flexed to show off several gold bracelets to a merman lounging on the pool stairs.

Two more merfolk—from an offshore water-ballet troupe—did flips nearby. Their green-and-blue hair sparked with tiny bee lights. Their tails were real, although temporary. Splicework was delicate, and the mers could only tolerate a few hours with their skin modified to gills and fins before they'd start to transform in unspeakable ways. Their sponsor and his physician hovered nearby, ready to pull them out and apply emergency cellular patching the moment they showed signs of sickening.

With mers in the pool performing, few were swimming. Most Enclave and city families had only heard of that kind of modification.

"They are beautiful." "Do you think it hurts?" "Shhh, Val, that's rude."

"Only when we stop swimming." The handsome one on the stairs flipped his tail. The guests laughed delightedly.

Dax knew that mer scales and Aanand's biologics—the contacts and face grafts that allowed the Canarviers to masquerade as Vanes in the city and disappear at parties—were related. *But some aspects of offshore life take modifications too far, even for me.*

"What if they got stuck that way? Out at sea?" Valencia didn't quit, despite her new escort's hushing her. "Or someone from Ocean decided to conscript them?" She shuddered, took a beverage from Dax without seeing him, to his relief, and kept walking the pool's circuit.

"Or what if something bigger and more evolved tried to eat them?" Roo appeared beside him, her service mask up, a plate of fruit in her hand.

"That's disgusting."

"You were thinking it too." His sister chuckled, turning to circuit the gaming tables. As she passed him, she blinked rapidly. *Change of plan. Meet in five, staff tent by pool house.*

Good, Dax thought. She was finally listening. She'd been in the house for two days, the Grand Heist had been on for hours, and their performance was adequate, but dull. Like scared shadows of the real Canarviers.

Where's the spine-tingling element that will show everyone, including the hosts, the time of their lives? We're on the hook for six spectacles, and we've only bagged one so far. Clock's ticking.

Nan and King had been worried about this job, and with good reason. *Security's everywhere. But we've run plenty of tough jobs.*

Dax made his way to the catering tent, and into the shadows behind it. Roo arrived a moment later, her tray piled even higher with cantaloupe wrapped in vat-grown prosciutto.

"Ohh. Real fruit." She lifted a piece to her mouth.

"You're going to drool on your magical outfit." He handed her a napkin. "Tell me you're shaking things up."

She dabbed at her chin. "I'm working on it. Thinking about moving the guest room heists up in the timing. We need more lifts."

"That's not—" Dax paused to keep his frustration in check. "Enough. By far. No one's going to book thieves if they get boring. Plus, we have contract obligations."

"Dax, we made a plan, we're adjusting it. Carefully. Tomorrow. I need you to listen, gather information. I have to work deeper into the house's security before we try it. They keep changing passcodes and patterns. The chief—Holt—has shut down a few access points already. I need time. *Then* we can wow them. But if I can't override the doors and threshold sensors before tomorrow, I need you to let Nan in. So please don't do anything to get caught tonight. Sleep in the staff quarters. I'll see you at dawn with the new plan."

"How will I know if you need me or not?"

"The kitchen window will be shut if you're needed."

I'm supposed to be up looking at windows before sunrise? Before he could protest, she'd slipped back out with her tray.

Why is everyone in this family suddenly so cautious? Starting with King, at the Dutton gig. Look where that had gotten him. Canarviers, never late, never caught, never boring. So much for that.

The roulette wheel rattled and guests shouted. A mer splashed their tail in the pool. Out on the lawn, someone began to sing. *Will anyone notice if I speed up the plan a little bit early? Roo's already considering the guest rooms. Why not be proactive?*

He patted the Timex he'd lifted from Roo's pocket and wrapped onto his wrist. It ticked as evenly as ever.

Late night was when every guest did what they wanted most, and no one said a word in the morning. Dax had joined them in the past. He always learned something interesting. And interesting was exactly what he was looking for now.

He hid his tray. Traded his jacket and mask for a gray tux slung over a pool lounger. Pulled out a jar of Aanand's secret hair grease and turned his dark curls blonde. A bit of putty in his teeth and his signature gap disappeared, at least temporarily.

He blended into the party's late-night dregs, complimenting just the right element in an outfit, flattering that person in just the right way. *Still got it.*

Laughter by the pool caught him up. Time slipped by. He listened as young heirs and soon-to-be heirs gossiped and laughed.

There was an enormous noise near the catering tent—pots and lids and serveware tumbling to the floor—and laughter. A young couple darted away from the tent, trying to sneak drunkenly back to their rooms. Dishwashers cursed. It was past time to find their staff cots and rest. Dax's crowd laughed and shook their heads. "Kids, man."

"Have we heard about that entire family who'd lost their business, and then their chips, and had to go live in the Skirts?" "That's a rumor. I heard they got whisked to an offshore Enclave." "These thieves? A bit duller this year, aren't they?" Dax soaked the conversation in, but the "dull" remark rankled him.

He waved for another round of bubbly, though he wasn't drinking any himself. These Enclavers were the dull ones. So predictable. Having the same conversations their grandparents probably had, before everything happened. And their grandparents' grandparents before that, all the way into historical times.

Dax didn't know much about history—recorded lessons came with a city apartment, but the family only had the apartment a week each month, tops. Still, he'd gotten enough to understand one thing: history was what the wealthy made happen to the poor.

How could Roo like being around these people at Miss Farmer's? Dull, boring, and bored. What these people needed was adventure. Dax chuckled. *Which they've conveniently, literally hired me to produce, haven't they?*

"If I was a thief, I'd get Graves's safe. Find his files—learn how the guy broke into Enclaves as fast as he did. My father says—"

"As if you know where Graves's safe is hiding. I bet he has it bio-locked, anyway."

"Maybe his office, but not the safe. Guy's got no family to do that for him—if he's got one, it's a rental."

"You're kidding." Dax leaned forward. This was exactly the kind of information Roo had wanted. A rental. And it was the opportunity Dax craved: a chance to dazzle.

"Rental or family, there's no way to avoid the safe kicking your ass if you try anything. No one's broken a safe in years. Not the new upgrades especially. And Graves is behind those. Stop dreaming, Sebastian."

Sebastian laughed, showing off his perfectly white teeth. He threw his companion into the pool. Dax decided to join them. Tomorrow, he'd dazzle them: steal the water right out of the pool, lift someone's inheritance. He permitted himself one drink. Swam the starlit pool. *I am definitely not boring.* But it was getting late and he needed to be up early for the next scheduled performance. And at least three spectacles, if they were lucky.

"Valencia! I'm tired," he called. She'd ditched her previous escort for the slightly familiar new guy at the pool.

She laughed and emerged. Then she turned her back to him so he could wrap a monogrammed Llyria towel around her shoulders. "Why so tired? Perhaps you are the thief, and not some cousin of—who did you say again?"

Dax had, very carefully, not said. "You know who. Stop playing."

She tipsily smiled at him, her strawberry-colored hair tousled and curling at her cheekbone. "I could turn you in, maybe. Go shopping with my reward." Her lilting voice stopped with a laugh. "Aw. Don't look so concerned.

I'm teasing. Besides, the search is more fun the longer it lasts."

It was all part of the game. If she risked turning in the cousin of the son of someone her parents knew, or had in mind for a business-enhancing marriage, she could be ruined. Valencia knew it too. Even looked a little angry about it. She handed him another drink.

Dax was taken aback by the thought that these rich kids were as constrained by the world as he felt. He didn't want to lose his family's support. But he had options—the street, for one. People like Valencia didn't sound like they had many options. At least not ones that they could think of on their own. They were trapped too.

Dax kissed her ear and laughed as she shivered in the cold night air. "You could turn me in." He turned her to face him. Looked deep into her eyes as he tapped a gentle finger on her lips. "But you would miss out on a great party."

The girl laughed again. Louder. "Serves them all right." She led him away from the pool and through the kitchen. They left wet footprints on the stairs going up to the guests' quarters in their wake.

Dax wasn't going to spend any night in the cramped basement with the snoring sommelier—who probably wasn't spending the night there either. Besides, Roo had told him to blend in and gather information. He'd definitely gotten some about the safe. He was doing what all the other Enclave kids were doing. He sipped the drink. Wasn't that blending in?

Yes, that's the plan. My plan. And I'm going to stick to it.

The antique clock struck a double note in the hall. Mason, jacket off, cue held just above the billiard table's slate surface, almost slipped. One ball wobbled, but no one said a word.

He waved off a glass of champagne. "Bring me a scotch."

"You're wound too tight," Evangeline whispered. "You can't let your stress show to Papa's friends."

He knew this. Mason disciplined himself. No stress about the three cameras in the ballroom and more on the stairs and in the hall picking up nothing. Absolute nonchalance about how the feed coverage he'd planned to use in his promotions was useless. He was just playing pool. Having a marvelous time.

His cue made a rough sound on the green felt.

"Scratch," called a woman watching from a barstool. Her curls mimicked the adornments on the walnut bar. She'd discarded her mask. Layne Andrews. A Graves investor. She reached out a delicate hand and Mason met it with a firm grip. "Wager the next one? We had thieves once. It was stressful."

The bartender prepared another scotch, in case.

Mason shook his head. Someone else could pick up Layne's bet. And Layne, probably.

He held the peat-tinged single malt on his tongue: casked offshore during the Mess, beautifully managed and preserved. He wanted that power someday, to make things he loved last. *To do it, you must smile and relax while someone robs you blind.*

Perhaps with a chase, or traps, he would enjoy it more. But this group was slipping things from pockets, then disappearing into the walls. That wasn't engaging at all. *I should have signed the other crew.* They hadn't even tried to chase the safe. Not yet, anyway.

Mason put his glass down with a walnut *thunk* and left the billiard room. He wove his way past chattering guests who all greeted him warmly. He finally found privacy in a back hallway used by the bar staff. "Holt, report."

His other hand went to his pocket, checking for the ring case. *Yes, still there.*

In his ear, Holt's voice sounded dry and controlled. "We've got a mask in the bushes, sir. And one small stash of guests' property."

Mason waited. Two billiard balls smacked together and rolled in the distance. *Was that it?* "You've had an entire evening and much of the early hours, and you've only got a stray mask and a bag of trinkets? What are our loss estimates?"

"The mask was reported missing by a guest soon after she unpacked. It's clean. Losses include a dozen serving trays from Versailles, several crates of wine, and the collection of antique fountain pens from your library."

It was too much. Time to accelerate the timetable. "This ends tomorrow, by cocktails." He enunciated each word. "I want the staff rechecked. All of them. And reach out to MilPol. Maybe we need experts to catch a thief."

"Has anyone seen Mason?" Evangeline's voice came muffled through the wall.

"He was just here," the bartender answered. Evangeline said something Mason couldn't hear, which made the group in the billiard room laugh.

It's past time to return to the guests. But Mason hesitated. To have Evangeline see him angry like this would be a defeat in itself. *Get it together.* "I'm coming down, Holt." Mason spun on one heel of his uncomfortable shoes and walked quickly toward the security bunker.

New Washington Educational Programming Feed

(proof of city residence required, watch time logged and compensated)

Headline: Atlantic Enclave arrives off New Washington's coastline

Atlantic Offshore Enclave partners with both protected cities and corporate locations for provisioning and deliveries. Their local feeds are abuzz with opportunities to visit New Washington's exciting pop-ups and local regions of interest.

Atlantic, one of three offshore Enclaves currently recognized as a partner by the protected cities, provides valuable supplies and recovery assistance.

Visits from Gaia2 and Korii Enclave are also anticipated. Citizens sighting Ocean Enclave are requested to contact local precincts. Information regarding whereabouts of other offshore Enclaves are always appreciated, even those suspected to be lost at sea.

*

This educational programming is sponsored by Miss Farmer's Academy—engaging with this feed nudge will gain your account three credits:

Miss Farmer's—An Enclave Apprenticeship Awaits

Where peers from across the Enclave community work toward full employment alongside future decision makers of influence.

Train for careers including: Architecture, Biological science, Catering & planning, Design, Data security, Medicine, Property management, Security, Science (general), Safe fitness and self-defense, Safe management, Teaching (youth, private), Teaching (advanced, private), Terraforming design and safely.

Limited scholarships available, wave for tour information. Have citizenship status available at time of inquiry.

The Falling Star

TWENTY MINUTES BEFORE the Enclave's predawn mist sequence began, Roo walked through the back pantries of the kitchen carrying a steaming tray of pastries. When she reached the large window that looked out over the drive, she set the pastries down. She slid a gloved hand carefully between hanging cookware and positioned a mirror in each lower corner of the sill.

Soft laughter came from the service stairs. Roo checked to make sure the window's security grid had been redirected, then crept through the pots, her wardrobe's hood covering all but her eyes. After applying a tiny silicone bead to the window, she opened it soundlessly. Then she climbed onto the sill and looped a length of silk through the handle. The black fabric of her skirts expanded to its full length in a long rope. As the cook's assistants entered the kitchen,

Roo rappelled down the outer wall to the driveway on her ball gown.

The misting began after she'd gathered up the fabric and tucked it away. She'd hoped to have time to recharge the wardrobe, but the newly chill air wasn't suitable. The wardrobe would have to use the kinetic heat of her next performance, which might suffice for a short time. Eventually, as Sasha had instructed, Roo would need to get the whole thing into the sun.

Not now, though. The shadow of an Enclave van passed by Llyria's gates. A line of performers—musicians and acrobats—began to straggle up the pathway toward the house. Roo smiled, relieved to see Nan among them. She slipped into the line, letting the wardrobe go gray, and prepared for the next phase of the Grand Heist.

"How's Dad?" Roo used King's signal, her eyebrows raised in question.

Nan shook her head and blinked. "He refused to see me. How are you? Your brother?" The line moved forward slowly. She murmured, "Impressive guest list," and touched Roo's sleeve, passing her the estimates for the day's haul.

Roo stretched her arms high, then touched her toes. She applied a new set of contacts and changed her hair color while she bent. Swapped out a new workband. But she didn't answer Nan's question about Dax.

"Hmph. Just like his father, that one," Nan whispered. "I should have come earlier."

"Shhh." Roo straightened. Now she was a red-headed performer standing with her chaperone, carrying ropes and gear.

"Badges!" The guard at the entrance stopped them all. "Eyescans and work contracts!"

"Villon Aerialists," Nan told the guard. She gestured to several young tumblers in the line, and Roo, then bent to the scanners. Roo followed. The guard waved them through.

The musicians behind them fussed. "Demanding last

minute that we report at the crack of dawn for security, while the sprinklers are on? You are lucky our instruments are protected." A viola player cradled her case.

"And insured," the performer Virolich grumbled, watching his cello move forward on its suspensors. "Then what do we do? Sit until guests are ready?"

"At least they're paying us by the hour," musician Anna Thoth replied. She began regaling the cellist with stories from her latest tour. "The ship I helped launch was so new they had to build a special dock for it on the Atlantic Enclave. I'm amazed it was accepted. It made the Enclaves look like the Skirts."

As Thoth chuckled and joined them on the other side, Nan murmured, "Someone's always richer than the rest. Keeps everyone striving."

Thoth peered over her glasses at the group of tumblers, then Roo and her companion. "We could rehearse a little. Make sure everyone knows the timing? Nice to see you again, Ro."

Roo smiled—Ro Villon had danced for Thoth concerts several times over the years. "Nice to see you too."

Nan led the aerialist troupe to a small side room in the conservatory to change. When Roo's turn for the washroom came, she began transforming her wardrobe once more, emptying her pockets first. Nan would watch her tablets and tools. She'd use the rest. Her fingers brushed a small object as she searched for the Timex. Roo startled when she pulled out a small earpiece. *Something I forgot to put in a stash?* She didn't forget. *A message from Nan? It must be.*

She put the tech in her ear.

"Ahhh, hello, Miss Greene. I had wondered if you would find my gift."

Roo struggled to recognize the voice, modified to sound like an insect's buzz. It took all the control she had to stay in the washroom, instead of running. Someone had tagged her. But they thought she was Elizabeth Greene.

She didn't respond. She lifted her tablet from the pack she'd planned to give to Nan and tried to trace the source of the earpiece's signal.

The speaker continued. "I believe your skills, on very subtle display yesterday evening, would be useful in the right company, young lady. Should you be interested in expanding your career beyond play thievery."

Discovered. But not caught.

"Let me in!" A tumbler banged on the lavatory door.

"Just a moment!" Roo said.

"Ah, you are there. I need you to do a small task for me. In return, I promise you a lucrative career, Miss Greene. Or should I say, Miss Canarvier?"

Roo couldn't reply over the awful realization that she was unmasked. *Was this how they—whoever they were—had trapped King?*

"I assure you, I had nothing to do with the interception of your father," the voice continued. "And I will help you free him, if you wish it. But in order to do so, you must go to Mason Graves's office and retrieve any items in his safe by—"

Her head jerked up. She stared at herself in the mirror, half made up for the next performance. "Absolutely not. We won't violate our contract." The words were out of her mouth before she could stop them. "This is a trap."

"Not everything is a trap, my dear. This is an opportunity. If you don't accept? Then it becomes a trap. I will let you get back to your performance."

Caught. Roo swallowed, or tried to. *By whom? Not Graves, nor his creepy security chief. By one of the guests? By another thief?* "You want me to break our performance contract *and* commit espionage?"

"You really have no choice. Bring what you find to this address by Sunday morning." The earpiece screeched out an address near the MilPol precinct and began to heat up. Roo pried it from her ear before it melted.

She stood in the washroom, shaking, as Nan tried the handle from outside.

"Miss Villon? Are you all right?"

"Fine," Roo managed. "I'll be fine." She had to be. Roo twisted her remaining bracelet charm, focusing on the cool metal, the smoke-brewing chemistry within. King wasn't here to help her decide what to do. *Everything's up to me.*

She unclasped the bracelet and tucked it away with her tools. Put King's workband in the bag as well. Glanced at her tablet. The earpiece's signal was coming from an upstairs guest room. She shivered.

"Miss Villon, it's time! The musicians are in place."

Chin up, costume on, and still shaking, Roo stepped out into the gallery's bright light.

Mason wore an ornately patchworked sweater that Evangeline had said would make him look casual. She'd paired it with striped pants and a white collared shirt.

He carried his still-uncomfortable shoes, padding down the back stairs to the kitchen in sock feet, hoping for coffee. He'd stayed in the security room with Holt until dawn and only managed a quick nap before getting up again. Today was going to be rough.

The party coordinator awaited Mason beside a steaming tray of bread.

"Can't serve the tea as planned this afternoon, sir. Two of our services are missing." She bowed her head slightly; her voice had a frustrated edge.

Mason stifled a curse. Evangeline and three friends had sequestered themselves with her stylist, getting hair and makeup done. She would be upset about the tea. And even more so if someone told her he'd been cursing. But he couldn't help it. The losses were becoming untenable.

Just beyond the kitchen, guests chatted, cups and

saucers clinked. *Coffee.* He leaned in the direction of the breakfast room, but the coordinator held his gaze. "Put it on my bill," he said, waving a hand.

She smiled tightly. "They are quite expensive sets."

Can I afford twenty-two more hours of this? Mason counted events in his head: the gallery concert—he'd looked forward to surprising Evangeline with the details of that; tennis and croquet on the grass courts—he played neither; cocktails, dinner, more music, the next morning's hunt. Then it would be done. Everyone would go home. He could return to business and Dr. Tsalta's research. He tried to picture himself in a moment where the thieves were already caught, everyone's belongings were returned, he and Evangeline were happily engaged, and he had Sam Benford's full approval.

There. That did the trick. Mason relaxed. "You aren't by any chance involved with this nonsense?"

"The thieves? That you hired when we had organized respectable performers like the Villons for you?" She flared. "I would never. How dare—"

"I apologize. It is early." He would make it up to her, after Holt cleared her again. "I will feel much better after a cup of coffee. Would you?" *If the cup hasn't also been stolen.*

She frowned, then gestured for one of chef's assistants to get the cup while she ticked off additional losses. Her tablet shook in her hand. Stress? Nerves? Mason knew Holt would sort it out.

He sipped noisily at the cup when it arrived.

The mid-morning sun cut through the music gallery windows, gilding the circular balcony. The railing where Roo perched glowed like a wrought-iron halo above the two-story room.

Overhead, crossbars wrapped in delicate bee lights led to the central beam that usually supported Llyria's large and historically accurate fabbed-crystal chandelier. The light had been carefully removed two days ago.

Dark-green velvet curtains covered the walls, lit at intervals by the glow of hidden gallery lamps. A marble floor that Mason had purchased after hearing it might have come from Venice rang with footsteps as guests entered through the main doors. Each footfall sang in Roo's ears: *caught caught caught*.

She shook her head to clear her thoughts. *Stay focused or fall.*

Roo swung out from the railing to the chandelier hook. Few noticed her yet; all eyes were on Mason's updated art collection, framed by the parted curtains. Roo knew from the subtle holographic commentary that one was a Hopper on loan from the Neo-Renwick Gallery. Another, a Ringgold quilt from the former National Gallery. An early Bosch, rescued from Philadelphia. A Calder sketch from the old library on the sunken mall.

Whispers carried to the ceiling thanks to the room's acoustics. *Oh, how lovely. She's been such a good influence on his taste.* Knowing chuckles followed.

Enclave & Towne—which was both a print magazine for the Enclaves and a highly expensive feed for the city—had run a feature on the couple's interest in pre-Turbulence art, Evangeline's charity work with several New Washington galleries, and her plan to bring long-sealed masterworks back to the walls of the city. Several of those expensive pieces were on display, static-mounted to float within the frames, at the request of Mason's insurer.

"Don't stand too close, Pucky," a gentleman called. "Anything more than a breeze and security will be breathing down our necks." More laughter.

Roo shivered at the thought.

A bright spot of conversation bloomed by the door.

Evangeline, wrapped in a cream silk shawl and matching tea gown, clasped hands as she entered. She remembered names and birthdays and kissed the air near cheeks. From what Roo could tell, Evangeline wasn't using the guest list data. She remembered everyone. And those she remembered were happy to see her. Mason entered in her wake, nodding tensely and repeating names and greetings in a gruff voice. He wore a patched sweater: modeled on a Skirts quilt, but new and clean.

To Roo, the platinum-haired birthday girl looked like a delicate shell amid a sea of brown, black, and white foreheads and noses, perfect hairstyles and bald spots.

Which one of them thinks they've got me? She wondered.

Evangeline turned to Mason. Her smile brought out his smile. The entire room relaxed.

Roo kicked her feet and the chandelier hook from which she hung swung gently. Far below, a cello struck a deep note. *Almost time.* For the first time in her life, Roo felt unprepared.

The heavy curtains shifted to block the light from the windows. Their motion revealed musicians and hid the art. In a large frame sat the cellist, backlit. His body curled like a shadow around the instrument, coaxing its notes louder and deeper. A gallery light at his feet began to glow, until his face was revealed.

"That's Virolich." The pleased whispers grew louder. "They're going all out."

"Oh, Mason," Evangeline's voice belled up to the ceiling. "I love it."

For a moment, Roo found herself rooting for the couple she was robbing.

Like Dax's apprenticeships at a coastal liquor distributor, which he'd used to charm his way into connections with sommeliers and bartenders, Roo's training had begun with dance, trapeze, and silks. The Villon acrobats—a group Nan assembled and trained—became well known, even if her face was not. She learned to love being part of a group in motion. Watching everything from on high.

But she'd never been this high up, with so much at stake. Not while someone below not only knew her real name, but was testing her. She searched the crowd again for a giveaway look. *Nothing.*

The violas appeared at the conservatory's far wall, accompanying the cellist. By the time they took over the melody, Nan had positioned the tumblers all around the room. Anna Thoth sent a cascade of flute notes over the violas. Guests applauded as they recognized her.

"I thought she was still on the *Marcelaine* yacht launch!" Evangeline squeaked. Her friends oohed and ahhed.

"Only the best for you." Mason put an arm around her shoulders. Then he turned and beamed at an older, balding man at the edge of the room.

That must be Evangeline Benford's father. Roo counted back through her dance partners from the ball. She hadn't met him. He couldn't have planted the earpiece.

The serenade swelled, calling Roo's attention to the immediate task. The musicians combined harmonies as waiters circled the gallery's outer perimeter with mimosas, subtly drawing guests away from the room's center.

Into this space, Roo dropped the end of a long stretch of flame-red fabric. As it puddled to the ground, a few eyes caught its glow. Faces turned upwards.

She hung upside down from the chandelier hook, as if held up by shadows. The rest of the room dimmed, and the musicians swept into a new piece.

Cello and flute laid highs and lows, the violins kept a steady staccato, and Roo, clothed head-to-toe in a skin-toned singlesuit, marked with softly glowing "jewels" at her toes, torso, fingertips, spine, and brows, let go and plunged.

Guests applauded her fall. She intersected with the silk and wrapped herself in it to stop her descent. Several twists later and her aerial ballet swept her around the room on the flame-colored swath. She felt the pull of the guests' curiosity—would she fall again, on purpose or not?

The new composition, which Thoth had written specifically for Mason and Evangeline, lasted four minutes. As Roo scissored her legs to lift herself back to the ceiling's shadows, her eyes searched the crowd. Not only for whoever had caught her, but also for Dax. He was supposed to be dressed as a waiter. *How could he be late?*

Her hand slipped but she caught herself in time. Then she let go on purpose, arched her back and dove groundward, before she stopped mid-plummet.

How could he not be here? Where was he? She caught Nan's eyes. The old woman rose and sent the younger tumblers on a circuit around the room. They danced, cartwheeled, and waved sparkling wands. Nan slipped behind the curtains.

We're in the backup plan. Not good.

Curling into a chrysalis as the crowd cooed and laughed at the smaller stars on the gallery floor, she began to lift herself again, pulling the remaining fabric around her. All eyes turned to her as the silk disappeared into the dark. Roo slowly lowered the palm of one hand into the light to signal goodbye.

The room fell silent, then dark, except for a circle of footlights. A guest chuckled nervously. Then the curtains rose to the ceiling. Light streamed in, glasses clinked, and guests softly patted their pockets.

Applause began in earnest once the guests realized they still had all their belongings.

Roo watched, heart in her mouth.

"Look!" A silver-haired matron with an empty glass was the first to shout. She pointed at an empty space. "The Hopper!"

"The Ringgold!"

Around the gallery, beside the musicians and the gallery doors already swung shut by security, hung fifteen heavy gilt frames, each emptied of their contents. One small Picasso dangled, stuck, from its frame.

The frames had been a lucky break—Mason's penchant for showy tech was known, but Roo had struggled to find the right ionization frequency.

She let out a breath.

Each wand—slim, ionizing pads tucked inside children's toys—had released the frames' static bindings. Dax had been meant to gather the artwork and stow it in the curtain pockets Roo had sewn two nights prior. But he'd missed the whole thing.

The art theft would make the feeds, fast. It would pay a large portion of King's bail as well. Even without Dax. Roo chewed her lip.

What had happened? I can't help King and Dax too. Not when we've already been found out.

What a horror, turning your spectacular gift into this, Evangeline murmured, squeezing his hand. *But we must smile. Laugh. We'll get them.* Mason heard the words, breathed in his ear, like the coolest of breezes. Then she stepped away.

"Oh, brilliant! Well done, thieves!" Evangeline clapped and the guests cheered loudly. "I didn't expect that!

Mason managed a brittle chuckle and matched her tone. "Nor I. This is going to cost a pretty credit." *More than I have. And these vultures are clapping.* Peering around the furnishings as if they could discern the trick to the disappearances.

"Luckily, they haven't yet stolen my birthday tea!" Evangeline added. "Please come out on the lawn and enjoy it with me! I am afraid we'll be using fabricated cups. as the service was nicked last night!"

Her delight alarmed Mason. *Is she trying to ruin me?*

The Lees had been pushed out in that manner. Was this easier than refusing an offer from me?

She caught his expression from the corner of her eye. As the last guests moved from the room, she squeezed his hand. "It will be all right. This is theater, darling. That's all."

Once again, he'd underestimated her. Mason was grateful she hadn't let him embarrass himself in front of everyone. "You are brilliant. Ev—" He was ready to get down on one knee right there.

"Sir?" Holt interrupted. Not in Mason's subdermals. Right behind him.

"Go ahead." He waved Evangeline toward the door where her friends waited. "I'll join you in a moment."

She leaned in to kiss his cheek in thanks and whispered, "The guests need this to be fun. I believe in you."

Fun. Mason smiled until she disappeared, then turned to Holt. "How did this happen? Weren't you watching?"

"Not a second away from the monitors. They didn't set the frames off until this last one." Holt gently lifted the dangling Picasso.

"I want the performers questioned. The musicians. Even the aerialist. And that old woman too."

"I have them waiting to go downstairs." Holt pointed at a puckered set of curtains. "Except the aerialist. She's still changing. He looked up toward the ceiling, just as the red-haired aerialist came downstairs wearing work clothes and a service mask. She headed for the doors.

"Not so fast," Holt stopped her. The young woman looked petrified. "You have some questions to answer, Miss Villon. You too, Madame Villon." Holt took Nan's elbow gently with the other hand, leading the aerialists and musicians down the hall to the basement. Mason followed.

Holt slowed his pace. "Sir, you should stay with the guests."

"I'm in no mood," Mason said. *Plus, I plan to turn on every last security setting you have downstairs. There will be no more losses.*

New Washington
Enclave & Towne Feed

(city residence or citizenship required)

We're thrilled to continue broadcasting from the birthday party of the century. Everyone looks magnificent. I must say this is the most exciting weekend I've attended in years, all very obviously Evangeline Benford's magic at work. Here are the photos and images so far.

Look at the scenes from the ball! The thieves' entrance, and the spectacular DJ.

The Canarviers are on the premises! Visit our archive to read about their previous exploits.

So far, the count of losses has included over two million in small objects, plus several service settings. We hear rumors of missing data keys, but no one has confirmed.

This morning's aerialist performance is accompanied by the famous Anna Thoth and Virolich! Click here to download their latest compositions.

We'll keep you posted—thank you for participating and supporting *Enclave & Towne*!

Select a room or holo for a list of lookalike clothing and furnishings, or place a friendly wager on where the thieves will strike next.

** Update**

Well, the thieves have stunned the house and its guests—and maybe taken things too far! Priceless works of art are missing. The host seems to be losing his temper. Meanwhile, the risks of a Grand Heist are being debated across the feeds, following the Lee tape. We are all wondering whether Judge Benford will make a statement or not.

Stay tuned to see what else *Enclave & Towne* can show you! Wave in the chat with your guess as to Mason Graves's current loss totals. Can he sustain this? We'll find out.

The Disappearing Banquet

Roo had only seen the basement rooms from dragonfly height. She wasn't prepared for the low ceilings and sharp lights.

With Nan left sitting outside, Holt pulled her into a narrow alcove and pointed at a bench. He raised a scanner to her mask. "Off. And the contacts. Out."

"Can't sir. They're medical–if I take them off, I can't see. And–" Roo began as meekly as possible.

"Check the performers' contract," Nan called out. "You lot can't remove medical accommodations. Imagine, leaving a young girl without her vision at an event like this."

Holt was good. Roo had watched him question staff for hours. He'd been respectful, but stern. The youngest he'd dismissed quickly, afraid of bad press for the house; he'd treated

Virolich and Thoth like the celebrities they were. *Thankfully,* Enclave & Towne *is upstairs.*

But he was getting no answers, and growing more frustrated with each interview. He had only two performers left to question. Roo let herself tremble. "Could you release my escort please?"

"When we're done with you," Holt said evenly. He began to pull the door closed.

"Can't, per the contract." Mason Graves stopped him. "I'll get the escort. Sit tight."

"Contracts. People think they're so smart. I've met smarter people cleaning bathrooms." Holt spat on the floor.

Roo smiled, memories of toilets she'd scrubbed while dressed as a housemaid a few floors above this room vividly clear. She bet Holt didn't mean her. "You mean—"

"Enclave brats, playing these games. Hiring criminals so they can look like heroes. My father fought during the Mess. This playing with vices is disgusting."

Mason returned with Nan, and Holt cleared his throat. He tapped a metal box clipped to his belt. "Just answer a few questions regarding your whereabouts and we'll have you on your way."

"I was in the basement, then the kitchen, then the conservatory for the aerials." Roo let confusion show on her face, though she was being truthful.

Holt tilted his head and smiled kindly. "I have to ask questions of everyone, don't worry. You only arrived a few hours ago. Things have been disappearing for days. You'll be fine." He unrolled a micro-expression reader and a pulse-band from the box, synced both to his tablet, then held them out to her. "Put these on."

"Artists aren't criminals," she protested. "I'm with the troupe." Musicians' contracts were quite specific about how they could be scanned. Anything that interfered with their art was specifically banned by the city. And the pulse-band Holt held didn't look standard at all.

"Not every artist is a good person. Even if they're a musician." Holt's voice turned brittle.

Nan already had a pulse-band on her wrist, put there by Graves himself. Roo's grandmother blinked, but didn't say anything. Holt wrapped the band on Roo's wrist, above her workband. "I hope that's not too uncomfortable."

In reality, it was very uncomfortable. Prickly.

Nan blinked faster. Canarvier code. *D-R-U-*

"It's my own special software. Picobot sensors and a bit of something to loosen tongues. Undetectable afterwards, not that you'll remember."

G, Nan finished. Each letter slower than the last, until her eyes closed and her lashes rested on her cheeks, twitching slightly.

"You can't—" Roo began, but her words sounded strange. She giggled.

"Are you certain, Holt? This didn't work on the gardener." Graves sounded doubtful.

"They're the last to question. We must try. And I dialed down the dosage. They won't remember, either way. Perhaps sir, for deniability?"

Mason Graves stepped out of the room, his face grim.

Now Roo shivered for real. She'd practiced resisting questions. She was skilled at fooling scans and detectors. But this? Was very new and extremely out of contract. "—should report you."

"You won't," Holt muttered. "Just tell me what I need to know, and you can go. Name."

Roo couldn't resist the question. "Roosala Vane." She swallowed. Not her aerialist name. She'd given him her Enclave name.

"Interesting. How long have you been with the troupe and where are you in school?"

"Eight years. Miss Farmer's on scholarship." *Stop talking! Why can't I stop talking?*

At that, Holt grunted. "Truth."

Roo leaned forward to tell him more about school, about her friends, but Holt moved on. "Where did you go in the house before the performance?"

"Basement, kitchen, washroom, conservatory." She told him about the music gallery's upper balcony, the guests below. Her words flowed with his questions. Whatever he'd given her removed her will to resist. She hated him for it.

But all the memory games King had made her play, the layers of identity she'd created for herself, with his coaching? Almost all of those held fast, despite everything. Because King had known she might need multiple identities to accomplish her dreams. *And more than that*, Roo admitted to herself, her mind wandering places she didn't normally let it go.

Because in her heart, she wasn't the girl from the Skirts anymore. Throughout Holt's questioning, she never once said Canarvier. She really was Roosala Vane.

Beside her, Nan replied to questions with grunts and nods.

"What time did you arrive at the house?" Holt's voice grew tighter.

Ahhhh. He does make mistakes. He hadn't asked what day. Lucky. Roo knew she could answer this truthfully, even in a drugged state, without giving anything away. "Early morning."

But just as Roo was feeling good about the way things were going, Holt leaned forward. His voice was gentle. "And where are the paintings?"

Roo blinked. Her mouth opened of its own accord.

She had to answer, though she tried not to. "They're in the conservatory."

"Truth," Holt grunted again after looking at his screen. "Pheromones don't lie." He removed the band from her wrist. He opened the door. "Kid knows nothing. Send her and her escort to the recovery rooms where we're keeping the gardener before you let them go upstairs. I'll talk to the caterers again. And to everyone who searched the room."

"And the guests, sir?" The assistant sounded nervous to Roo's ears.

Holt paused. Graves spoke from just beyond the door. "No. Everyone would think it rude."

As Roo helped Nan rise from her chair, she thought she heard Holt spit again. She felt badly for whoever had to clean the security bunker.

"Performers," Holt muttered as they left. "Not worth the credits."

In the recovery room, Roo blinked hazily and rubbed her wrists. She and Nan sat on a single cot. The other was occupied by a sleeping boy. "Valo?"

The gardener looks unhurt, but how can I know for sure?

"Nan. We have to get out—"

Nan stopped her with a gesture. The room was probably bugged. And Dax was missing. And King? It was just the two of them now. Them, and someone who knew who Roo was.

The windowless room felt too hot. It began to spin. Then Nan put her arm around Roo's shoulders. "Sit still. Let it work its way out."

Nan always knew. When King had pushed Roo and Dax too hard, it was Nan who'd bandaged their scrapes. Helped them try again. Roo leaned into the hug and put her head on her grandmother's shoulder. She couldn't risk speaking, or even hand signals. This had to be enough for now.

She had to decide what to do about the terrible voice. If she told Nan, her grandmother would stop the heist, and everything would end. If she didn't, could Roo risk confronting a safe? She didn't know. She had only a few minutes to decide. Nan needed to be seen leaving with her charge. When the guards let them upstairs, they gathered Nan's large bag, which had been searched and tossed back together, from outside the conservatory.

“Where are we supposed to serve cocktails?” the party planner was complaining to a guard who’d blocked the room. The guard gave no answer, but Mason Graves’s voice boomed from down the hall. “Just open it up. Everything in there of value is already gone. Or use the library. There are plenty of expensive books in there.”

Roo shivered as Llyria’s owner strode toward them, face mottled with frustration. A server stepped around a corner, then retreated in order to stay out of the way. Not Dax, though Roo had hoped. Graves opened the conservatory door himself. “Apologies, ladies. We had to be sure.”

Inside, empty frames encircled the room, curtains swung in the breeze. Graves winced. “The library is better.”

“I need to get my silks,” Roo said. Graves jerked his head and let her through.

She climbed to the balcony landing where she’d left the red fabric. It too had been inspected, requiring Roo to refold it carefully on the gallery floor. “A moment more, I can’t risk tangling it,” she called as Nan made impatient sounds.

What was she going to do, and how? Roo brushed her finger along the stitching at her wrist. “I’ve got to get this.”

Finally, Roo gathered the fabric and slipped it, and a number of fine canvases from the nearby curtains, into Nan’s bag. Then, she returned to her escort, a coat draped over her shoulders. Together with several tumblers, the Villons exited through the service doors and into a waiting work van.

“You forgot to change your slippers,” Nan said. It was the beat they’d agreed on. “Falling star,” she added.

The next beat was disappearing banquet, then—oh then. If Roo went back inside, she’d have to take up the challenge, or risk being revealed. They had enough—barely—for King’s bail. But not Dax’s, if he’d been captured. She had to go back.

Anna Thoth shook her head blearily. “I am reporting this entire escapade to my manager. I feel so strange.”

“I’ll get the slippers,” Roo agreed. “But we’ve made everyone late enough. I’ll catch the next van.” Nan smiled and Roo took in every angle of her face. She looked so tired. "Help King." She gestured. "Get him out."

She waited until the van had disappeared before slipping behind a hedge and shifting her outfit to catering whites. She used more of Aanand's cream, aware she was overexposed now. Her hair darkened again. Waited a moment more and then pulled up her mask.

By the time she'd helped clean up tea, she figured Nan had made it safely back to the city. Less than twelve hours remained in the heist. *And it is mine to lose.*

Dax's first mistake, he realized on waking, was obvious. *I definitely did not make it back to the staff room.*

The pillows and bedding were pink. Some kind of fruit pattern was stenciled on the walls. The room looked like a cyclone had hit it—clothes everywhere—and his head felt much the same. Had he had too much, or had someone altered his drink? His head was too muzzy to tell.

He lay there for a moment getting his bearings. Took note of a particular gown on the floor. *Valencia. This is Valencia's room.*

Worse, the sun was beating down on the tennis courts outside, and the glare hurt the inside of his eyelids. It was long after he was supposed to be at the next beat. Falling star.

His second mistake was trusting Valencia. He vaguely remembered showing Valencia a couple thief tricks and winced. Sometimes it worked to trade freedom for lessons. *Not this time.* His right arm ached. He realized it was attached at a painful angle, to the headboard, with Graves-logo slapcuffs. *Those need DNA from whoever put them on to open them. Or MilPol.*

Roo was going to murder him, and then drive him to the precinct herself, if Valencia didn't do it first. Dax squinted at the window, trying to make out the time. He was already late, he suspected.

"Hello?" he called. No answer.

Slapcuffs were difficult, but not impossible. They just took time to get out of. He twisted one way and then another, but the cuff only grew tighter. The motion dislodged a note, on Llyria stationery, with a lipstick kiss. The paper landed upright on the floor, just out of reach.

Hello, stranger, I've left you some water and a painkiller. Don't try to escape. I'm keeping you here until I'm ready to turn you in and collect my reward, or maybe give you as a present to my bestie. But I want to enjoy the party a bit more first. Sleep well. ~ V

Dax groaned. *A Canarvier, caught.* Then he laughed. He stretched and bent until he'd hooked the letter with his toes. Then he tucked his knees to his chest, snagged the letter, and pressed the kiss to the cuffs. They began to dissolve on contact.

Moments later, he was free, though he was still stuck upstairs.

If Valencia spotted him downstairs, she'd turn him in immediately. And then Roo would really murder him. Game over.

Dax gathered his clothes–the quills he'd stolen were missing, but Valencia had left the Timex. She'd hidden his shoes. That was a problem. How to get away, unseen, barefoot?

There were no good options. He sorted through the bad ones as he listened at the door for guests. *Prowl the nearby rooms to find shoes that fit, increase the take Roo was worried about.*

Now, I really need to do something spectacular, to get Roo, Nan, and King to forgive me.

Dax poked his head from Valencia's room. *At least I don't have to break into the upstairs.*

A long hall padded with white wallpaper and thick cream carpeting stretched the full length of the wing. Hallway doors looked nearly identical. Each bore a gold stamp at head-height above a scanner: an oval with a spiked crown—some old-time fruit. *Why use fruit as decor? Except the fabbed, cubed kind. That's delicious.*

Each fruit shape had inset letters: XI, XII, XIII. Then it got confusing with Vs. *Roo would know what that means.*

At the end of the hall was a guarded door. The owners' wing? Off-limits, according to the contract. But, making a place "off-limits" to thieves was intentionally tempting fate, wasn't it?

Graves's office would be back there. Along with any number of secrets. *That's tempting. Contracts are negotiable. If I find the right Graves Biosecurity secret, I can use it as retroactive leverage. Get something more for the troupe, and the family, long term. Make the Canarviers truly legendary. Besides, Graves demanded two dazzling events a day. We've only done two, if the aerial performance worked. We're not going to make six without a big spectacle.*

Those who tempted fate got what they deserved. Especially if the fate-tempting thing behind this door was Graves's safe. Dax shuddered in reluctant anticipation.

Nothing in the Skirts or the cities could compare with what Enclave folks thought was okay. Breeding or renting someone trained in self-defense, then surgically adding titanium mesh and blood-locked storage? That was messy work, even if the safes were coddled as valuable offspring, given anything they wanted: cars, wealth, companions.

When they'd been kids, Nan told stories about safes made of steel and iron that weighed thousands of pounds. Dax would have loved to see one of those. But they were hard to move fast, and when the Mess happened, most ended up under water or ash. The Reclamation and Recovery required safes that could run and think on their feet. That's probably what had spooked Nan about Graves, and this job.

If I'm going to lead the troupe, I need to get out of Mason Graves's guest wing with a haul big enough, and spectacular enough, to fix everything.

Footsteps came down the hallway. A rill of laughter and

talk of thieves. Dax ducked back inside Valencia's room, leaving the door cracked. Three pairs of shoes—heels containing moving butterflies, fabbed leather loafers, and a pair of sculpted gold feet over the wearer's own—passed the door without hesitation. They opened a room nearby and tumbled inside, laughing drunkenly.

Dax leaned against the door, relieved. Until Evangeline Benford pushed it open, and Dax toppled to the floor.

"Valencia said she'd left me a present. And here you are." The heiress clapped her hands together, delighted. Then she got serious. "I don't have much time, so you need to think fast. I am going to offer you a trade. You do me a favor, I'll give you a head start on escaping. Or I collect my prize now."

Dax didn't blink. *Improvise, damn you. Play the game.* He forced himself to shrug. "I like trades. What do you need."

Evangeline Benford blushed. "I would like to know the contents of the host's desk—his whole office, in fact. Now."

"Trying to get to know your boyfriend better?" Dax winked. It wasn't the first time a guest had asked a thief to retrieve valuables during a performance. King had done it himself on occasion.

"I would like you to take me along." She spoke quickly. "But I only have a few minutes before I must be back downstairs. Do this and I will not declare you caught."

Dax sighed. "Not a chance." Enclavers had no idea how many of them tried this kind of thing with thieves, at least once. That's how thieves got themselves caught. Most thieves. "Why not make your daddy's fixer find what you need?"

A family like the Benfords would definitely have a fixer on retainer.

Evangeline frowned. "Stonecliff? No. I want to do this myself. Papa's protective. A little paranoid. I don't want him to reject Mason. I just need to know he is who he says he is. Will you help?" Evangeline held out her hand, as if to shake on it. Woven between her fingers were the two quills Valencia had taken. "Do this for me? Without any more questions, and you can have your time, and both of these back."

She wasn't more than a couple years older than him, at twenty-one. But for a brief moment, she aged: her eyes had slight shadows beneath them that makeup and polish couldn't cover. Nan had been right that the Enclave was as hard on its residents as the Skirts were.

Roo would hate that he was wasting time even considering a favor for the hostess who'd caught him. But it could, possibly, get him into Graves's office, and maybe near the safe.

"These get us past the bio-lock." Evangeline pointed at the second jeweled quill. Barely rust-hued at the tip. *She'd dragged that feather along her boyfriend's collar, and I had the key in my pocket the whole time.* "So, thief. Will you help?" Evangeline's voice was bright, even hopeful. But her eyes were dead serious.

"It *is* your birthday." He cracked the door open as she laughed. The hall was empty, except for the guards at the end. "How do you plan to get around those two?"

Evangeline lifted the window shade. From the pool, Valencia screamed, "Thieves! I saw them! Heading for the green!"

The guards' earpieces crackled and one strode down the back stairs. The other stayed for a moment, then the earpiece garbled a word that sounded like "Stonecliff" and the second guard took off running. Evangeline pulled Dax down the hall and took his arm. "I have a privacy screen. No one will see us."

When they let themselves into the master suite, Dax gaped. The place was enormous. But Evangeline was already at the office doors. She pressed the quill against the lock pad. "Welcome, Mr. Graves," the house said. And they were in.

Evangeline went to the desk, Dax used the quill again, and she pulled a drawer open. "Empty." Another drawer. "Papers. Plans." She lifted the lid of the desk and squinted inside.

"That's a pretty piece of equipment." He stretched a hand to the mechanisms in motion.

The heiress's palm whispered, "Hurry, Ev. They're looking for you." Valencia's voice.

"Don't touch a running instrument! Mason's a scientific genius. I won't let you interfere with an experiment." She frowned, looking around. "It's not here, and I have to get downstairs."

"What's not here?" Dax was sizing up the paneling in the room.

"I was sure he had a ring. My aunt hinted a month ago that she'd recovered a sapphire-and-diamond set belonging to my mother's family that I've never seen, except in pictures. A piece of jewelry her people used to leverage support for themselves through the Mess—can you imagine? Of course it was lost long ago. But Mason rented a safe for the whole weekend—I bet it isn't just to protect a few feathers. If it's what I think, I want to hold that ring just once when it's only mine. Before it becomes his too—and represents something new." Her voice grew wistful. Then she paused. "Besides, if Mason is about to propose, I want to prepare myself so that my reaction is perfect, and Papa's also."

Ahhh. Dax understood now. He'd been around Enclave people long enough that he could read their problems like a wine menu. This one had nascent societal doubts, perhaps mixed with a misguided sense of adventure that might land her in trouble someday. But not today; not while Dax was on the job. "Best hustle. I'll clean up here. If I find anything, I'll get word to you."

Evangeline frowned. "If you take anything else from this room, I will have you locked up for good." She backed out of the room, shutting the doors behind her.

Dax knew he needed to get out of there too.

And I will, as soon as I do this one bit of dazzle.

As the afternoon drew to a close, tennis- and croquet-weary guests began to return to their rooms to change for cocktails. Mason and Evangeline waved to them from the ballroom patio.

She'd wrapped her left arm around his waist, and Mason was enjoying the closeness. Her untouched glass of iced wine sat on the balcony railing, capturing them in perfect reverse on its curved reflection. He looked good with her beside him. He rested his hand on her hip and pulled her closer. His lips began to form a question.

But Evangeline shifted, pulling away from him to tuck a loose tendril of hair back into her elaborate updo. She lifted her glass and gestured at the guests, smiling brightly. "They're all having a good time, I think?" The wine's surface rippled and swayed. "Are you? Having a good time?"

He smiled. "The chase for the thief this afternoon was quite exciting, wasn't it. Even if we only caught Stonecliff."

Why is she still worried about my mood? Mason hoped the party planner hadn't complained to her about his mood earlier. No, he'd made sure that was straightened out, the planner well compensated. *Or did she sense my nerves, just now? Did she guess what I was about to ask?*

The antique ring case nestled in his pocket. His heart beat faster. What heart wouldn't at a time like this? "How could they not be having a good time, Ev? We're employing half the city to entertain and feed them, not to mention rob them." Mason ran his free hand through his hair. He took her left hand and kissed it. "I admit I suspect they would have been as pleased with one evening of thieving. I know I would have."

What this was costing him. He couldn't even think of it. Once he and Benford merged forces, though, it wouldn't even matter.

"Your home, and you, deserve to be shown off for a full weekend, like a proper estate," she replied. She spotted Benford, dozing by the pool. Smiled fondly. "Papa is loving the event. I'm certain he'll offer you a partnership after this weekend. If"—her eyes lowered to the setting sun's reflection on the cut crystal of her glass—"if you still want that."

Mason had never seen Benford in anything but business attire. He was surprised at how scarred the man's torso and arms were. Then he remembered Benford's service during the Mess. MilPol. Of course.

He had to agree that he'd done right by Benford and Evangeline this weekend. And that she was pleased. Nervously so. Was this the right time to ask her? She'd just hinted it was, hadn't she?

Mason's fingers brushed the small box in his jacket pocket again.

To do it properly, he knew he should ask in front of everyone at dinner. But he'd been keeping an eye out for the right time all weekend, in case one presented itself. And right now was the perfect, quiet moment with Evangeline.

Slowly, he withdrew the box from his pocket. He turned toward her, noticing how the afternoon light framed her profile. How quiet she was.

"Evangeline," he began. He reached inside the box.

"He'll definitely offer it to you if we catch the thieves," she added.

His fingers touched the soft velvet, searched the lid, lifted the cushion. Scrambled at the space where the ring had been. And was not, any longer.

He tried hard to hide his sharp intake of breath. The box had never left his side. He'd considered returning it to the safe, but with him was even safer, wasn't it? How could a thief have found it?

His hand shook. That ring was worth far more than he was at the moment.

"Oh, silly! I was kidding, Mason! We will catch them." Evangeline still gazed at the pool, the grounds. She'd noticed his silence, but hadn't seen how pale he'd grown. "We'll catch them and announce it at the perfect time. Tomorrow morning and not before." She stepped back from the patio railing, kissing his cheek on the way. "I need to get changed. So do you."

The evening's colors, according to the party planner, were champagne and absinthe. A suit awaited him upstairs. A panicked laugh started to bubble up through his chest. It blossomed to a hiccup. The ring was gone.

"Mason?" Evangeline turned when he didn't move. He heard her voice as if he was underwater. The moment dissipated around him like vapor.

"By tomorrow morning, the thieves will have taken this house down to the wiring," he stuttered. He reached out and took her glass. Tipped his head back and drank the whole thing at one gulp. She stared at him. *Get yourself together, Mason. You can get another ring. What jeweler wouldn't love for Evangeline Benford to have their ring on her finger?* He cleared his throat. "We've found a few of their caches already. And we'll have the rest back, and more, but by this evening, and not tomorrow. And I'll never do another party like this again."

"You won't have to, darling." She kissed him again, her lips cool on his. He closed his eyes to slow his breathing. She must remain unaware of how much he'd just lost. When he opened them, she'd slipped away, heading back into the house to change.

Mason stared after her, into the darkness of Llyria. At the space where she'd been. His fingers searched the empty box once more and he shivered.

Roo, her service mask damp with sweat, pushed another pile of laundry into one of the machines in Llyria's basement. She lifted the empty basket to her hip. Dax's workband had gone dark hours ago. He'd missed the morning event and now cocktail service too.

Vanier was stomping through the staff quarters yelling about having the young man's head, workband, and city license.

"I'll kick that boy to the Skirts," he growled, passing through the laundry to hand Roo an apron stained red with wine. "He's got great hands, but terrible timing."

Roo winced in quiet agreement, but said nothing that might give the troupe away. *Where are you, Dax?* She'd heard the shouting, and watched the guards race to the green. But it hadn't been Dax. They'd caught a guest.

Overhead, the party rumbled like a distant storm: bursts of conversation and occasional footfalls, a reminder that the performance still had hours to go.

She risked a glance at recent security footage. Saw a guest room camera shimmer, as if a thief had rigged it, badly. Then a hall camera. Was Dax trapped upstairs? He was going to get caught. Roo shivered, remembering what Valo looked like in the recovery room. She had to get up to the guest wing to find him.

When Vanier climbed the service stairs, Roo picked up her basket and followed, past the first floor, then, before the guest wing door, she pressed a panel and let herself into the bridge to the owner's wing. If she made it back down before dinner, she'd have time to pull off the disappearing banquet. A job she'd run alone before, while Dax and King did the guest rooms.

There were six courses to the banquet; she could let the first two be swept in, and then steal the rest. Llyria was focused on everyone still lingering in the garden, and the hallways. She had a half hour to find Dax, and if she couldn't, she would be the only Canarvier left. She didn't have the closing card. She would have to declare defeat, with six hours on the contract. *Everything's forfeit if we go.*

Roo thought about the threatening voice. The "opportunity" she'd been offered. *If everything's forfeit, what do I have to lose?*

"Conversion C." She shifted her wardrobe once more, to the singlesuit that would block any heat-readings. The fabric transitioned more slowly this time. She knew she'd pushed Sasha's work beyond recommended limits without a recharge. There wasn't time to remedy it.

Dax needed help, even if he didn't know it.

The only layer of Llyria's security that Roo hadn't managed to work her way into was the master suite and office. She'd left it alone, per their contract with Graves. Now, she had no choice. She could satisfy her blackmailer and get Dax, all at once.

She ran the last of her code through the password tumbler. It failed. She had one last chance. She activated the dragonfly she'd dropped in the security suite just before the interrogation. Waited as it flew, then landed on the security deck.

"What's this? Indoors?" a guard said. "Kill it." Another ordered. She heard a smash and the bug went dead.

Hers was a choice of last resort; the tiny energy flare she'd set the bug up with as a worst-case self-defense only scrambled Graves's security data for a few seconds, but it was enough. She used the chaos to lift a housekeeper's identity and password through the system.

As she watched, the white Llyria crest on her guest band turned gold. Giving her access to Mason Graves's suite.

She moved quickly, but when she reached the office, she saw the door was already ajar. *Oh Dax. No.*

Inside, the desk and floor were strewn with papers. The thick curtains had been pulled askew, revealing a mullioned window that overlooked the service entrance. A valet's room through a side door, cracked open, showed more chaos. One of Evangeline's feathers stuck into the hardwood floor, badly bent. *Dax, you idiot.*

She peered inside the valet's room. It was a beautifully appointed suite, tricked out with entertainment modules and an upscale food printer. No windows though. And the lights were off. Roo could barely make out a man sprawled on the hardwood floor in the corner.

Dax? She rushed forward.

But it wasn't Dax. The stranger moaned and clutched at his side, where a titanium-lined wound gaped open. Someone else had gotten to him before she could even make up her mind whether to try.

Gotta get out of here. Out of Llyria. The Enclaves. Possibly New Washington. The Canarviers were in over their heads. *But where was Dax?* The safe was curled around the spilled contents of his cache, as if he'd tumbled from the bathroom, just beyond.

When she pushed open the door to the suite's dark bathroom, it stuck, blocked by another body. Dax. A sharp smell filled the bathroom. Chlorafoam. Illegal in the protected cities.

Choking, she pulled at Dax's arm. He didn't budge. She tried to shift the door. The gas spilled further into the room in thick waves. "Roo," Dax gagged. "Window."

"Safe panic button activated," Llyria's voice echoed through the room.

"I won't let them catch you." In the alcove of the valet's room, at the center of a house that broadcast alerts across all channels, Roo pushed on Dax's shoulder. "Get up!"

"Stick . . ." Dax muttered, "to the plan, Roo." His hand fell open, letting a broken Timex watch slide to the floor.

And then the lights went on.

"You'll all be relieved to know," Mason raised a glass of dessert wine to the dinner tables scattered around the large dining room and in the hallway, "that the Canarviers have been defeated." He paused dramatically. "With your help!"

A scattering of cheers and applause built, lifting the guests from their seats. Waiters entered the room and circled with trays of hastily poured champagne. Evangeline raised a sparkling glass to Mason as he tucked a winner's peacock feather into his own dinner jacket's breast pocket.

"Well done, darling!" Her smile lifted his heart.

She wanted that feather, Mason knew. It would do until he located the ring.

He was rattled, but he couldn't show it. *They were in my private quarters. They attacked my safe.* The safe had assured him everything remained secure, which was a relief. But Mason could not shake the feeling that his carefully built world was weakening. He could not let that happen.

When everyone held a glass, Holt entered the dining room, pushing a catering cart. On it, trussed, sat a young man. He wore a service mask, his clothing was torn by struggle, his cap removed, revealing tangled curls.

The crowd closed its well-coiffed ranks around the table, eager to see his face revealed.

The young man struggled groggily with the cords at his wrists.

"You think you're so smart," Mason whispered near the thief's ear. "Sneaking through the guest rooms, my private quarters. You have violated our contract. Once I'm done, this Grand Heist 'tradition' will be history."

The boy's cheek was flecked with his spit. Mason swallowed. "How many more of them are you? Where are they?"

The guests had stopped applauding.

The thief didn't move, or speak, even with two of Holt's interrogation patches slapped on his neck. Mason whispered again, "Where is my ring?" His mouth was close enough to the thief's ear that he could smell it. *Disgusting.*

A chair squeaked on the floor. Several brisk sets of heels left the room. "Mason." Evangeline touched his arm gently. "Our guests are uncomfortable."

She emphasized each word, trying to get his attention. Her nostrils flared, as if she was also uncomfortable.

The boy moaned. "Rrrr."

"What is he trying to say?" Mason pulled his arm away from Evangeline's gentle fingers.

"Roosala Vane," Holt murmured, making a note. "Aerialist alias. Left for the city earlier. We'll locate her."

The aerialist. The one everyone had loved. Rage pounded

Mason's ears. She'd been in his house, under false pretenses. Taken his art. The ring. Invaded his private quarters.

"The thieves will not get away with this." The guests that remained were watching intently. Most had never seen the power of Graves Biosecurity this close up. *Let them.*

The boy groaned again. "Where is Roo?"

Where was Roo indeed. "We'll catch her," he whispered. "What you're doing is illegal and immoral. Yet you sell it as entertainment. I will put all your kind out of business and ship the lot of you to the Kuiper Belt."

Mason stepped back into a silent, and much smaller, ring of guests. Many had put their glasses down. No one laughed. He didn't care anymore. "This was a game with a contract. The Canarviers broke that contract, and the reality is that this is no longer a game." *Especially not once we find the others.*

Evangeline ran from the room, her friends in a tight knot following.

Mason turned to go after her, his heart realizing before his brain did that he'd overstepped. He could fix this. But Benford stopped him. A strong, calloused hand splayed against Mason's chest.

The old man looked like he was ready to chew up Mason and spit him out. "You must make improvements, Graves. Immediately. Your temper. You will control it, before any business between us proceeds. Make it right."

Mason bowed his head slightly as Benford released him. What he'd heard was both a caution and a promise. They would have business together. Benford had acknowledged it. "I will. I promise I will."

Roo saw the safe rise from the floor and lean back against a wall as the lights came on, blindingly bright. His lip was swelling, but he brushed himself off, then picked up a glass ampoule from the floor and tucked it back inside his cache. Sealing it, he turned his head toward the thieves, chuckling. "There's no easier way to catch a thief than greed. Made a good go of it, though."

A trap. The safe had been a trap.

Far down the hall, she heard Holt, laughing. She searched for the window—any means of escape.

Earlier that day, she'd imagined herself back at the apartment after a completed heist, preparing to go back to school. Now? She braced her hands and feet against the floor and pushed herself up. The gas was making her woozy. It had the same effect on the safe. The man lurched for her, but missed.

She had one chance. The office window. It meant she had to leave Dax.

Leaving meant she could try to help Dax later, if Graves decided to prosecute for breach of contract. Leaving meant she could help King and Nan.

The safe lunged once more and she dodged him. His grasping hands tore at her uniform and then locked around her ankle. Roo reached the mullioned window and kicked him away, hard. Free of the safe, momentarily, she pushed the window open and pulled herself through the gap. On the other side, she held on by her fingertips, high over the driveway.

The security bolts whined. The office door opened quickly. Holt shouted, "Take the boy into custody."

Roo released the windowsill. She fell.

A moment later, the blacktop driveway rushed up to catch her. She landed painfully, then rolled out of sight into the bushes.

When she put pressure on her left leg, Roo bit down on her lip hard enough to draw blood. Blood was better than screaming, which was what she wanted to do. The splitting pain in her leg didn't let up. Roo almost vomited. She moved her arm, and there was more pain. The ground spun around her.

Roo pulled the last charm from her pocket. She would throw it and escape in the haze. Hide on another estate. Buy herself a few minutes at least.

Time blurred as she fought another wave of nausea from the motion. Below the office window, the garden lights looked like small stars; the dining room's glittering chandeliers too. Motion below the chandeliers demanded her attention. Holt's team brought her brother before the party's guests.

Mason Graves loomed over the captured Canarvier, interrogating Dax in his dining room. Evangeline Benford turned away, alarmed. She looked out the window. Her grey gown glowed with the last of the day's light.

The young heiress's eyes fixed on the sunset reflected in Roo's bauble. Her mouth formed an "O" as she gave a soundless cry. She locked her eyes on the bushes that hid Roo.

Oh no.

The hostess ran from the room. Roo needed to move.

She tried, but it was too painful. She couldn't make her body listen. Her family captured. King as good as gone. They'd lost. No. She, Roosa Canarvier, had lost. Not just the Grand Heist. Her future was gone. Holt knew about Roosala Vane. There would be no return to Miss Farmer's. No Sasha.

A hand grasped her ankle painfully and Roo twisted, trying to fight. To sink farther into the hedge.

Instead of Holt's thick fingers, this hand was manicured and glittered with rings. Evangeline's voice rose triumphantly. "The last catch of the party!"

Roo's vision darkened and narrowed to a tunnel. Her ears became a nest for bees. She heard Evangeline but couldn't see her.

"No one's ever caught the Canarviers before, until Mason and I! We will NOT have my thief dying of head trauma. Holt, carry her to a guest room. Summon a doctor, and your best guard."

Holt grunted a reply. Roo felt strong hands slip beneath her and gently lift her from the bushes. Then she passed out from the pain.

Enclave & Towne, New Washington

(Enclave subscription required)

We have a second night's official accounting—and it's enormous. The thieves certainly had the run of the house. There are even rumors that a thief broached off-limits areas.

But, nevertheless, Mason Graves and his security team won the day by thwarting the Canarviers before dinner on the second evening. While this may have disappointed some guests (visit our discussion area to learn more), most concede that Graves more than proved his skill with security. Several guests, however, seem to have departed the party early. We will endeavor to uncover the reasons why!

Meantime, our reporter was present at what seems to be the proposal of the year—perhaps even more dramatic because it seems to be a spur-of-the-moment profession of love, instead of the usual well-planned business merger we often see in the Enclaves. How exciting! Although a bit rushed and without a ring, Mason Graves continues to astound many in the community. Take a look:

[video of Llyria's dining room]:

> Mason Graves approaches Evangeline Benford, who is standing with her father at the far side of the table, talking quietly. Benford stiffens as Mason touches Evangeline gently on the shoulder. "Is all settled to your liking, Ev?"
>
> She turns, but does not step back from him. She beams, as if very pleased, and twirls a golden feather between her fingers. "I am content, yes."
>
> At that yes, Mason's smile returns, fleetingly. Then he

dips his head. He sinks to one trembling knee, his eyes on hers.

Evangeline's remaining friends cease talking, and stare. Evangeline puts three gloved fingers to her lips and blushes, confused. "Mason?"

With an awkwardness that could be interpreted as either unprepared or completely smitten, Graves stammers. "I am swept away, over and over again, Evangeline. By you. Would you—consider a life with me? Our two houses, merged?" He holds his empty hands out in supplication.

To the shock of all in the room, Evangeline Benford puts her hands in Graves's. "I would consider it, yes."

"She said *yes*!" a young friend (ID: Valencia Moreno) shouts. Evangeline hugs Mason quickly before she is borne away by a circle of her friends.

*

The *Enclave & Towne* cameras later caught Sam Benford pulling Mason Graves aside, but we have erased that portion of the video for privacy. We can only assume Benford gave Graves his blessing.

Registered User 4532: Perhaps the ring itself was stolen by the thieves. If so, it will be recovered in the accounting shortly.
Registered User 231: We will look forward to future reports about the state of Evangeline Benford's left hand in the near future!
Enclave & Towne: Wagers are being taken in the comments about how much the proposal was weighted by Graves's losses—surely the Benfords can absorb that too.
Registered User 7899: Evangeline Benford shone through the evening, triumphant. She practically glowed at the end of the second day, even though the Sunday's plans were cut short by the capture. I heard her father has promised to continue the party tomorrow, although the hunt will be a private affair.
Enclave & Towne: Perhaps we can convince one of the riders to take a camera along for us.

The Stolen Child

Roo dreamt in shards: Nan's bus rolling over the Skirts' rough road, her father's laugh, his stories. Thieves like Rocambole and Charmet escaped Miss Farmer's through a tunnel. Jack Murphy swung from the balcony at Llyria. The Comtesse de la Motte and Nezumi Kozō joined Dax in a dance as children from the Skirts turned sepia in the shadows, picking pockets. Roo drove the bus. She climbed a distant seawall. She tried to keep pace with the thieves as they ran each heist faster. Her dreams shifted. She was a guard at Toulon work prison. Victor Hugo and her father split rocks in the middle of an endless stone sea. As she watched, water flooded in, and King was pulled under. She screamed for him, but the walls of Toulon collapsed and crushed her leg, her arm. She tried to shout again, but her tongue was made of water.

When she finally surfaced from her dreams, Toulon's stones evaporated like mist on an Enclave lawn. She lay in a darkened room. The house, quiet. The party, over.

The remnants of Sasha's wardrobe slumped across the back of a chair. *Oh no.*

Maybe I can fix it. "Conversion–" Roo whispered. The outfit didn't respond. The chair's pattern–a pale fence, a unicorn, a dark background of flowers–showed through gaping tears in the dress. *Maybe it just needs to charge. If I can get it into the sun–*

There was a window, the shade pulled. She leaned for it, her side aching. She felt bruises in the same places the dress had holes. Llyria's hedge had made both.

Her mouth tasted like dust; the sharp edges of her dreams cluttered her mind. *Where am I?*

None of Llyria's rooms that she'd seen during the Grand Heist looked like this. Carved, high bed frame, ornate chair, the curtained window, a tree branch silhouetted on the shade.

"She's awake." She heard Evangeline's voice outside her door. Remembered her crowing in triumph. Mason Graves's outrage framed in Llyria's windows. And Dax? Where had she last seen Dax? The doorknob turned. Roo grunted and tried to rise.

Her leg and arm buzzed with numbing pressure. Compression braces. Expensive ones.

Pushing back a thick damask comforter, Roo stared at a brace's pulsing lights. The brace was still thick, its exolayers hard. Small timers counted down: ten hours and three minutes to go. Roo tapped the screen and saw they'd been healing her for nearly eighteen hours. Most of a day, gone. How much will this cost? The Canarviers would never be able to afford it.

Worse, it was Sunday. King would be sent to Alaska today, if he wasn't already gone.

"I've let my father know. Holt, please wait here."

Evangeline's voice was clearer now. The door cracked open.

Think, Roo. Escape routes: door–no. Window? Yes.

She dove for it, dragging medical gear and bedclothes over the end of the bed. Her fingers reached for the shade, tilting it as her feet tangled in the comforter and her oversized pajamas. She landed on thick carpet.

"Oh! Someone help!" Evangeline shouted, and footsteps sped toward them.

Roo's head spun. A wave of nausea overtook the pain in her leg and arm.

From her new position, she could see a wedge of sky beyond the skewed screen. A branch, festooned with thick, dark leaves. A giant blue flower turning gold at the edges. The tree grew close to the window. There were branches within arm's reach.

This wasn't Llyria. Mason hadn't planted trees near his home, or Roo would have used them in the heist. But Holt was here. And Evangeline. The latter was tucking the comforter around her. A thick floral pattern, dark against the muted creams and whites of the walls. There was a crest lightly outlined on the wallpaper in silver: a winged insect–maybe a bee?–and a boar. She searched the room for her tablet and tools. Only Sasha's dress was in view.

Several pairs of gentle hands lifted Roo back to the bed.

Evangeline scolded, "You must rest!"

Rest. How could she do that? *We lost. My family is in trouble, as am I. Even though we lost, we did grab several hauls, including some very important works of art.* She was obviously being held as leverage against getting the heist haul back.

Remember your rights as an artist. King had drilled that into her and Dax, along with what to say if she was captured during a performance. Roo spoke those words as loudly as she could manage. "My troupe's contract with our client mandates we cannot be held captive for longer than an hour. I demand release, or to be taken to the nearest precinct."

Evangeline's fingers paused just above the comforter. The rings on her fingers glittered. "You were gravely injured. We were all so afraid."

Afraid? Roo narrowed her eyes. "You won." Her voice creaked.

Evangeline, wearing a riding outfit quite different from the smoke-colored gown Roo had last seen her in, held out her hands as if to take Roo's. "Don't worry. That game is over." Her eyes filled with tears. "We were all very afraid for you for a moment there! And you are not a captive, any more than I am."

Roo didn't believe that for a minute. *How badly have we failed?* Her heart pounded, remembering Dax in Llyria's dining room, bound. *We broke the contract. No.* I *broke the contract.* "What does Graves want in recompense?"

Evangeline's fingers felt like a cage around Roo's hands. Roo struggled to sit up. She tugged her hand away. But Evangeline took hold again.

It wasn't Graves holding her captive, Roo realized. At least not directly. Why are they fixing me? She recalled the guests at the party, discussing Evangeline's philanthropy. *Am I someone's pet project?* She squirmed at the thought. That wasn't the kind of thing you could ever repay enough.

"I will find a way to pay for"—she examined the expensive exolayers—"all of this. I can work it off if I have to. I'm very good with—"

"Nothing like that is necessary, I assure you." The young woman let go of Roo's hand and tugged at the pillows so that they supported Roo's new position on the bed. A small laugh escaped her lips, more nerves than anything. "It's all okay now. You've been through so much. Papa will explain everything. I promise."

"Papa?" Evangeline was a Benford. Papa was Sam Benford. The man who built the Enclaves. Ex-MilPol, and someone who both Nan and King had done their utmost to avoid.

Roo sat bolt upright. *I need to get out, immediately.* "I demand release or to be taken to the nearest precinct." She whispered it this time.

Evangeline patted her hand again, though her fingers fluttered faster, unsettled. "Papa's waiting for us. And some lunch if you are hungry. But only if you are ready. You slept longer than our physician predicted."

Finally letting go of Roo's hand, Evangeline brushed a stray platinum curl behind her ear. Three gold bangles slid down her arm to her elbow. They got lost in the rolled sleeve of a silk jacket printed with peonies. "Nurse? Do you think our patient is ready for a small adventure?"

A privacy screen dropped from a monitor on Roo's bedside table. A real nurse replied over a speaker. "She is, if she doesn't exert herself. We had a chair fabricated."

A chair? How much would that cost? And a real nurse. *They're giving me the kind of attention Enclavers get without even thinking about it. Why? Probably because they hadn't considered any other way.*

"I'll be right back." Evangeline turned and strode from the room, the long jacket belling out behind her like a floral shadow. A hint of perfume lingered even after she was gone. Perfume! Roo hadn't the slightest idea how much that would get on the Skirts market.

Once alone, Roo struggled to rise. The medbrace wires and the memory of King's voice in the dream tangled around her. The thick pillows that Evangeline had fluffed beside and behind her felt intractable. *You are a master of your craft. Surely you can escape pillows.*

She sat a few inches higher. The nurse's privacy screen had dropped again. *So, even though they must know I'll be out that window the minute I get a chance, they're not watching me that closely.* Evangeline had called for Holt, though. He'd be stationed outside the door.

If Nan is negotiating the haul, and trying to get Dax and

me back, how can I help from this side of the wall? Roo tried to make a list of ways. First by not causing more problems. She would need to pay attention, escape if she could, without damaging anything else. Second, by waiting until the braces were off and her head had cleared. Her thoughts felt as round and soft as the pillows surrounding her. Uncomfortably so. They must have given her painkillers.

She would have to get in that chair, and go where Evangeline took her, at least. Then she would make a better plan. "Nurse? What time is it? And what day?" She had a guess from the braces, but needed to be sure.

"Today is Sunday, miss," the nurse answered. The face was young. The wallpaper behind her matched the silver bees in Roo's room. "You've been asleep for eighteen hours and twelve minutes. Your injuries have already healed substantially, but we are watching you for signs of concussion."

Sunday, noon. *I might still have time to help King, somehow.*

"Healed substantially, but not fully?" Evangeline had said a short adventure. Roo wondered how far they were from the Enclave gates.

The nurse paused, reading data. "Not yet. You need another forty-three hours off your feet, according to your statistics. You had a serious break, a dislocation, and there are old injuries we've seen fit to repair with the Benfords' medical bay here at Centenaire. As well, you are receiving vitamins based on the tests we ran, and an anesthetic. That will affect your balance. Exertion in the next few hours will risk further injury."

Roo blanched.

"Are you all right, miss?"

"Where I'm from, those kinds of injuries would take forever to fix. If they ever got fixed. And three million credits on top of it." Roo shook her head. "I forget my manners. Thank you for helping me."

"Of course, miss." The screen darkened .

I'm not healed yet. I can't run. It's Sunday. They're loading King on a transport this evening. Which is five hours from now. If I can get far enough from here to catch a work van, or contact Anna Thoth or Virolich, perhaps they can help. They have important friends. Roo shifted on the bed. *Until then, I have to play a new role here: captive.*

And if I fail at that? Who will help the Canarviers?

The most uncomfortable spot in the MilPol general holding pen where Dax spent all of Saturday night and Sunday morning wasn't the fabbed cot, nor the tile floor.

It was the focus of King's gaze, which tracked Dax wherever he paced, from the short-term holding pen a few feet from Dax, and across a static barrier. They'd already given him his cold-weather gear for Alaska. The others scheduled for shipping were unpacking their bags and crowing over the coats and equipment, spare as it was. King hadn't opened his.

"Dad, please listen," Dax tried for the fifth time. The number on his gray coverall read 55426. His stomach gurgled. MilPol had handed him the coverall, a protein bar, and the full list of charges Mason Graves had leveled against him when Holt had handed him off to the precinct.

Breach of contract, all ensuing and prior infractions of burglary and assault, false identities (four), impersonating a food service professional . . . the charges went on and on. None of it was sitting well in his stomach. Dax needed to get free of the hold, and soon.

"Stand back from the barrier." The wall of his cell shimmered. Dax stepped back. He didn't want to get zapped. "Prepare for cellmate."

The wall shimmered again. A shadow outside became a dust-grimed face and a gray coverall. No shoes. Protein bar in hand. The static barrier thinned as someone outside shoved and a smaller figure stumbled through, hissing at the current. The wall shimmered again as the tech logged Dax's new roommate. "Bard Lowenstein, citizen, New Washington. Accused of insolvency. Witness: Recovery Court."

When the witness against Dax had been announced to be Mason Graves, everyone in the precinct had perked up.

"You're one of the thieves then."

"Seen you all over the feeds."

"Didn't do so well this time?"

He'd ignored it. King's cellmates across the barrier–two insolvents, one vice violation, and an agitator–had chuckled at him until King stared them silent. Then he'd turned that gaze on Dax.

In the few days since Dax had seen him, King's beard had grown scruffier, the bags under his eyes, darker.

"Say something, Dad. Don't let them pack you off to Alaska without telling a good story at least. You always do." Storytelling was in King's blood. He'd been regaling Dax and Roo with the glories of the family business for as long as Dax could remember.

Now he was silent.

The thought of King going to that place in this state, knowing that Dax had ruined the family business, was too much to bear.

The charges–most of them–should go away once Nan returned the goods. Graves had sent him to the precinct as leverage. That was common practice. But the other charges? The feed video that Dax was sure had appeared after the guests went home? That would stick. There would be no more performing with his face that famous. No more working in the Enclaves.

Worse, though Nan was thankfully safe at home, she couldn't possibly take care of everything by herself. Would anyone–performers or vendors–take the risk of being associated with her now? Friends like Aanand and his family might. They'd been keeping the bus moving in the Skirts. But without the winning repayments on the heist, Nan wouldn't have enough credits to get back into the city before next month. Much less help Dax or King out. They would have to start all over again.

"Dad, we have to talk to Aanand." They had to find Roo, help Nan. Try to get King back from Alaska somehow, someday. Before Holt had handed him to the MilPol drone, Dax had seen his sister lifted on a stretcher. They'd had no further news in the precinct hold. Where was she now? Dax remembered shouting to her, groggily. Glass breaking. The sound of everyone running.

At least King didn't know how badly it had all gone. Dax frowned. "If you'd been with us–if you'd helped–you have some responsibility here too, Dad. At least talk to Nan."

Around King, inmates shifted on their waiting bench. Most were itching for some small drama to relieve the stress of waiting for transport to the water mines. But everyone knew that starting a fight in the hold was an expensive charge to a prisoner's hold fees. No one wanted to be accused of participating.

Dax didn't know how far he could push that boundary, yet. He just wanted King to give him some answers.

"Responsibility." King heaved a sigh. It wasn't much, but it was something. Maybe there was still time to talk. The transport didn't come for another hour. What Dax wouldn't give for more time. "Responsibility is the pleasure of kings. Not the domain of thieves."

"We're not real thieves, though, Dad. You said it yourself. We're performers. Magicians." Dax moved closer to the barrier. "Maybe we can find someone to speak for you. Help the city and MilPol understand. Aanand's parents know lots of people. We still have a little time. If we do it right, maybe they'll send you to another city, not to the mines."

Travel between cities was, for most people, rare and difficult. But the mines were impossible.

King set his jaw. His cellmates turned back to their

own business, checking through their packs. He looked at Dax, standing close enough that the hair on Dax's arms rose, then blinked and made four quick gestures, challenging Dax to keep up.

"*Were* performers. Real thieves now." King's eyes closed, relieving Dax from the stare, but closing off any possibility of argument.

And Dax was ready to argue. Aanand had told him for years that Dax could earn many more credits if he joined Aanand's gang. "'Performance thief' isn't real work," Aanand had said, repeatedly. "Come out for another delivery day at least. Grab some supplies." But Dax had sided with King and Nan: "Art is always real work."

He would use his one permitted message to call Aanand now and get help, but they needed to reach Nan too. King could do it with his unused message. If Dax could at least convince him to help, to stop freezing everyone out, which wasn't like him at all.

"Dad. Help me out," Dax whispered.

King didn't open his eyes. He bent forward and put his elbows on his knees. He held a hand out, almost touching the barrier between them.

Dax wanted to grasp that hand so badly. The barrier would zap them both, so he hesitated.

A good zap might let me feel something besides shame over the heist, and failing King. He leaned in, gritting his teeth as his skin went pins and needles, then grew searingly hot.

"Stop," King said. Dax's ears buzzed with static. He pulled his hand back. Heard ". . . the honor of thieves," and then buzzing. Then "protect Roosa"—which didn't make sense because King didn't know what had happened yet. But then he looked down. King was speaking and also using the family's signals. His big speech was to distract their cellmates, and probably MilPol surveillance too. So they might miss the gist of what else he was saying.

Three fast gestures and a fist. What King signed made Dax bite back a shout.

"I stole them, years ago. I thought I could fix it. Or keep you all safe. I failed."

"What did you steal?" Dax whispered. He couldn't help himself.

There were few gestures in the Canarviers' shorthand code for the next words. Letters, half hidden, mixed with coded signs as King began coughing. "Serena Benford. And her unborn child."

Dax stumbled back from the barrier. His ears buzzed so loud, he felt like he'd jumped into the barrier and it had zapped him senseless.

"I based the chair's design on a Renoir I curated for Papa's gallery," Evangeline said as she helped Roo settle into the fabbed, high-backed wicker seat floating beside the bed.

Evangeline had returned, hair styled, makeup done. She'd wrapped an expensively thick, cream shawl around Roo's shoulders to cover the medical wires, patches, and braces. Many of the weekend's bruises also.

She walked out of the room. The chair, and Roo, followed her down a wide, daylight-filled hallway to an elevator hidden behind wood paneling.

The elevator let them out into the bright light of a portico walkway. Roo gaped at how many peonies and irises grew along the border in a riot of colors. "Papa loves his gardens," Evangeline said, catching her looking. "Grandmother did too."

The blue veins at Evangeline's throat ran so close to the surface, Roo imagined she could hear them pulse. So delicate. She and Sam Benford both. She'd probably struggle to survive in the Skirts. Roo suspected Evangeline, like the peonies that lined the walkway, required careful tending.

She was treating Roo as if the same was true of her.

"We'll have my aesthetician come see to you. A proper polish will feel wonderful, all the grit gone."

Roo grimaced. A few days ago, that would have sounded nice. "Why bother? I'm just going back to the dust."

Evangeline slowed, her mouth a perfect "O." "I didn't mean offense. People will want to meet you soon. They should see you at your best. Especially my aunt Minerva. She's a judge and she's picky." Evangeline almost sang the words. "We'll make a day of it."

"I won't be here that long," Roo dared.

Evangeline didn't seem to hear. Her voice echoed down the portico, even the bit about the judge. No security followed them, at least not visibly. Roo peered around the wings of her chair, looking for cameras.

Was there no cost for joking about judges at Centenaire? Roo wondered as they passed stately white columns, each arch revealing the rolling hills and a view of the sea. *Maybe not for the Benfords.*

Even the seawall was transparent near Centenaire—though a thick wave-distortion caused the air to wobble there. The estate was all light, windows, flowers. Roo's soft shawl was embroidered with peonies. She let her fingers play across the fabric, tracing a floral tendril. No security. No cameras. It was confusing.

"Grandmother's favorites." Evangeline gestured at the irises and peonies, misunderstanding Roo's searching gaze. "She rescued several varieties before the land went near Charleston."

A perfectly manicured pink fingernail pointed out each shade—the blues especially. Some were nearly purple.

Roo's own fingernails were rough from work and the spill from the window. She hadn't seen flowers in such quantities beyond Miss Farmer's greenhouse. The cities were focused on food crops to support their populations, especially with the Enclaves buying up most of the fresh greens. Flowers could wait until the Restoration was complete. "Beautiful," she whispered. Her mind calculated how much the flowers would be worth. She couldn't help it.

The walkway ended at the other end of the mansion, at a broad glass door. Evangeline could have taken her through the inside hallways, but she'd chosen outdoors. A luxury, Roo realized. "Why show me all of this?"

Evangeline rested her arm on the back of Roo's chair and smiled down. The light made a halo of her hair. "I want you—and everyone—to love this as much as I do. This is the future. I've wanted for so long to have," she paused, "someone my own age here. And now I can. I am determined to make up to you every moment you suffered out there."

Roo had been right. Evangeline intended on making a project of her. She shivered. Looked up to see where Evangeline was pointing when she spoke of "out there," and "suffering." The heiress's hands tilted toward Roo.

Her first impulse was to make a break for the seawall. That wouldn't be safe, according to the nurse, for at least five hours.

If Evangeline was truly feeling sympathy for her—in a philosophical, philanthropic sense—perhaps Roo could ask for help. Freeing King. Maybe even Dax.

Roo pressed her lips together, struggling to control her expressions. "I don't know that *suffered* is the right word."

"Oh no, of course not," Evangeline replied quickly. "You have so much to teach me. We will start now, at lunch."

The clock in the bell tower—Roo stared at the actual belfry, a structure straight out of King's books—chimed noon in a gorgeous carillon. "The bells came from Westminster," Evangeline said. When Roo stayed quiet, she added, "That was in London."

The feeds provided simple post-Mess geography as well more detailed maps of the protected cities, but only within reasonable traveling distance of New Washington.

London was a name to charm with, filled with rogues and castles and intrigue. And long, long gone.

On the last chime, the giant glass doors swung inward as if set to reward punctuality.

With a wave, Evangeline started Roo's chair forward. Roo held up her hand as she'd seen Evangeline do. The chair didn't stop. Roo dropped the edge of her shawl over the wheel. The chair stopped.

"I'd like to drive," she said.

"It will listen to chips—when you have one." Evangeline walked forward a few steps, as if unaccustomed to anyone refusing to follow her. Her wide trousers swung just above her tapered heels; her blouse flowed with a similar watery grace. The top was loosely tied with a bow, and her bare shoulders were sleek with muscles that implied sports, without too much exertion.

After a moment, she turned. "Are you well?"

The word made Roo want to fight. But the Benfords had enough power to frighten even Nan, and King needed their help. She smiled, her face tilted up at her host. "I'm uncertain what's expected of me? An apology? A disavowal?"

No way will I disavow my family, but once I know, I can better negotiate terms. Roo was determined.

Evangeline frowned, her lips pursing just like they did on the few feed videos Benford occasionally allowed. "No disavowal. No apologies. You'll never need to apologize for who you are." She began to wave the chair forward but, to Roo's relief, stopped herself. "Would you like to continue? We will make him wait otherwise."

This time, Roo lifted the shawl. The wicker chair moved forward, and Evangeline followed behind.

They passed into a circular room with a view across the estate. Greenhouses dotted the edge of the bright-green lawn. A map of the Enclave graced the floor below them in different-colored woods. Above them, a cloud-and-cherub ceiling seemed to float. Roo stared at the mural, which was more skillfully reproduced than those at Llyria. No cameras here either. Just paint.

How did anyone function in a world without cameras? She knew how to pass through spaces where cameras thought they saw one thing, instead of another. But here? She couldn't use that tech to fool anyone. She wished she could wrap herself in the remains of Sasha's wardrobe and invoke a conversion to make herself disappear. *Sasha. I have to speak to Sasha. Tell her I will fix everything. And oh, I wish King were here to see what this is like.* Oh *King.* Evangeline had said she could ask for anything. Roo usually hated asking for favors, owing people. She preferred to take what she needed.

At the end of the round room, shadowed against the bright window behind them, two figures sat at a large table. "A model building," an old man's voice said. "Jefferson's design. Five hundred years old."

The table was set with four delicate pink-and-gold plates. Crystal glassware broke the light from outside into rainbows. A security guard stood at attention close by: Holt.

"Papa, history? Now?" Evangeline moved ahead and bent to kiss the old man's head.

"I thought Stonecliff would enjoy it," Sam Benford said.

Beside him, the other man rose, the light catching the scar on his cheek. Roo startled.

"Hello, miss. Greene, wasn't it, once?" Stonecliff's voice was soft. Not unfriendly.

"Rylan, let that be a bygone," Benford ordered. He stood as well, waiting.

"Sir," Roo said. "And sir." She stared at them.

"I can see this might be uncomfortably formal, miss." Benford said. "But we must talk of important things, before the weekend concludes, preferably before the hunt. Do you agree?" He stepped around the table, toward Roo.

Roo did a quick assessment of the table, her heart

thundering so loud she thought the chair might shake. Rylan Stonecliff was some sort of fixer, or advisor. And Holt was here to represent Graves. Of course.

Benford cleared his throat, waiting. He wore a dark blazer and pale-green shirt. Canvas pants with quilted padding at the sides. Hunting boots. "Please do not be afraid. I wouldn't have invited you here if I wasn't on your side." The old man's eyes searched her face for a reaction.

Roo had teachers at Miss Farmer's do the same. The room would go quiet. The pressure would build. King had taught her and Dax to wait; a void of silence would often get people to reveal more than they planned.

Evangeline stilled, uncomfortably.

But Benford knew how to manage silence. And he was winning at it. Roo was out of time to help King. She had to speak, but she wasn't about to ask the most important question right out. She refused to be controlled, especially by the richest man in the protected cities. And certainly not with Holt and Stonecliff standing by. "What do you ride for a hunt? There aren't horses here, are there?"

She was aware she sounded hopeful. King's books had illustrations of horses.

Stonecliff chuckled. "Wouldn't that be grand."

Benford laughed too. "Sadly, we can't reclaim horses yet. A few families are working on the various design problems in other Enclaves. We ride equadrones."

Roo must have looked confused. Evangeline came to her rescue. "Modified mechanicals with some horse-programming. Not too much."

"Yes," Stonecliff laughed, "there's something about horse-wit that doesn't work well with drones."

Only Roo and Holt were quiet now, as the three chuckled at Stonecliff's joke. It felt all too jovial. Holt smiled uncomfortably at her, but she looked away.

"Where is my family?" Roo asked. She would ask about King after she gauged Benford's reaction.

Benford flinched slightly. Was it her tone? "In time,

dear. I understand the urgency. Please. Stonecliff has some data that might be of use."

A fixer then. Benford's tone was not quite that of an invitation. But it wasn't an order either. Roo held her chair still. "Your daughter says you want to help me."

"Yes, certainly. We have made several provisions for–"

She cut him off, aware that Holt had risen to the balls of his feet, that Stonecliff was leaning forward, that Evangeline had placed a hand to her throat. "My family–Kenneth Vane is to be sent to the mines this evening." Roo thought fast. With Holt here, they knew she was Roosala Vane. "Urgency is an understatement. If you mean what you say, you must stop that from happening. And help set my brother free."

King had said that slow negotiation worked best with clients. Sometimes shock worked even better. Roo suspected that no one had spoken to Sam Benford like that in a long time.

He held himself rigid. Evangeline gasped.

And Stonecliff clapped. "She is dazzling. I told you."

After a long pause, Benford closed his eyes. "I cannot set that man free."

Roo tried to push back from the table. The chair did not move. "Then I would rather be at the precinct with my family." She watched the color drain from Sam's face.

Stonecliff rose, holding a data chip out to Roo. "If you would consent to stay and listen to what Mr. Benford has to say, you may feel differently."

Benford gestured that she should take the chip. Roo did not take it. "I will ask the precinct to delay Mr. Vane's departure. I cannot promise they will, but I can ask. And I will inquire after the others in your troupe as well. As a sign of good faith that I mean what I say. We want to support you."

Roo left the data chip on the table, but smiled at them. Even at Holt, standing behind Benford.

"That is very kind, Papa." Evangeline pressed a hand

to her collarbone. Her other hand squeezed Roo's shoulder, nudging her to respond.

Roo's heart lifted. "You can do that, just like that?"

"It's slightly more complicated, but we can do it." He gestured to Holt.

Roo stiffened. But before Holt came any closer, he knelt so that he was at her eye level. Then he bowed his head. "I am sorry, miss, for my part in how you were treated. I have transmitted our request to MilPol regarding their prisoners and will keep you apprised of their situation."

There was no anger in Holt's voice. None of the vitriol from the interrogation. He raised his head. His eyes held tears. "I'm loyal to the Benfords' service," he said. "I'll betray none of them. Anything you ask me to keep safe, I will do to the best of my ability."

It was said with the force of a loyalty oath. This felt like much more than an apology. Roo, with a shock, realized it was more like a promise. "What is Mason Graves's security staff doing saying this to a failed thief?"

"I was seconded to Graves on my patron's behalf. To keep an eye on him. As the merger moves forward, I may return to my true post with the Benford family."

Roo shifted in her chair as the guard rose and stepped away. Benford reached out his hand. It hovered above her shoulder. The air around Roo grew close and fragrant with cologne. "We didn't know." The old man's voice shook. "We thought all was lost."

Evangeline dabbed at her eyes. "What a birthday. Welcome home, Renata."

Roo shifted, searching the room for who else was joining the table. Renata? She saw no one.

Stonecliff smiled, taking in Roo's confusion. "I've been employed by the family for twenty years, trying to recover what was lost in a robbery. Many founders' families use my services. A job I was hoping to recruit you for, before I learned who you really were."

"Roosa Canarvier," she said weakly. *And you are the strange voice from the performance.*

"Renata Benford." Stonecliff tapped the data chip. "The bloodwork is undeniable, and Kenneth Vane's confession this morning only fills in the gaps."

Roo's skin crawled. The prisms of light from the rotunda's windows played across the table and her feet. She'd asked for a favor, and the Benfords had not yet said what they wanted in exchange.

She fought for control over her voice, desperate not to offend and ruin King's chances. "My name is Roosa Canarvier. I want to leave this place. My family's contract with Mason Graves did not include being transported or held captive. You cannot restrain me. I wish to leave or be transported to the nearest precinct."

Stonecliff's eyes sparkled. "Such spirit. But why choose prison over family?"

"Thank you, Rylan, that's all for now I think," Benford said.

The question stopped Roo cold. Did he mean Nan? Was she here? "What of my family?"

"You misunderstand," Evangeline said. She waved to doors that swung open around the rotunda. Three silver domed carts were escorted toward the table, as Rylan Stonecliff left them alone. The staff lifted the domes, showing an exquisite array of fruit, cheese, and pastries. All real. Roo's stomach turned to stone.

Evangeline spooned berries onto Roo's plate—strawberries, blueberries, something orange—then some on her own. She didn't ask what Roo wanted. "You are our family. We are yours. The medic confirmed your biodata. Mr. Stonecliff has verified the history."

Sam Benford once again extended his hand. He patted her chair and folded his napkin in his lap. "Those people? The Canarviers? They stole you and your mother. And now we have you back."

New Washington Found Footage Group #34

Subscriber 23422: Hey all, I think I found her again. This time it's a scrapped protest surveillance. I can't tell the date—when did the first water mines disaster happen?
Subscriber 3435: 2134. Or was that the second one?
Subscriber 23422: Here's what I found. It's maybe out of order. She's lost weight, but she is definitely the same woman. The file's completely bit-rotted.

A closeup shot of a woman. Her eyes, the color of the ocean, her hair, short and dark. She doesn't look directly at the camera, but it's obvious she's aware that it's there. She lifts a sign: "Don't steal from your future, build your future up." She shouts and yells, raises a fist. She throws something.

*

A group, marching on a downtown street, masked and wearing bicycle helmets, office trash cans, anything they could find. Garbage rained down on them from the buildings above. News drones followed the group—maybe thirty strong—as they converged on a municipal building. City Public Works.

*

A closeup of the same woman. She's bleeding from a cut above her eye, there's a bruise reddening on her lip. She's still carrying the sign. She's still yelling. A MilPol drone sideswipes her and takes her down. The MilPol guards descend. They slapcuff everyone they can find.

*

Subscriber 23422: My cousin's a Mudlarker, and he dug this out of a report that blipped on the municipal MilPol feed. It could be provenance:

New Washington South Wall Precinct Dispatch

Arraignment Report Dossier: Public dissent, disruption; incitement
Fourth arraignment notes for [redacted] aka Cere Vane, local activist.
Last seen lodging with one of the Vane families.
Last seen working a common kitchen in the Skirts.

Seen and captured at the Mine Disaster protest of [redacted], the feed privacy protests of [redacted] and [redacted], and the Equal Air for All Domed City protests of [redacted]

Suspect has refused family and legal support. Has suggested that mining is murder, reclamation is murder, and recovery is mono-economicism. [term added to feed watchlist]

Recidivist status: When asked how she wished to become useful to society, she inquired as to why she needed to be useful in order to be part of society.

Suspect remanded to Denali.
* addendum. Denali weather brutal, localized fires. Suspect record closed.

Subscriber 11238: Too bad about your cousin. And about this woman, who isn't the same person at all—look, this is a connected dossier. She's definitely a Vane, not some missing socialite:

New Washington Cohabitant License Termination Record

Re: Kenneth Vane and Cere Vane
Due to the transfer of one or more persons in this record

to the work-restitution program in Alaska on [date] following their involvement in unauthorized protests, this civil union contract and all shared assets are dispersed. Asset records are transferred to the nearest non-offender, in this case, the subject's mother Nancy Vane, bookkeeper and cleaning services.

By Reclamation Court order on behalf of the protected cities founders.

Subscriber 23422: I'll find the connection. I promise you.

Fooling the Bees

WHAT EVERYONE—ENCLAVE guests to local feed gossips—must believe as soon as possible, Mason knew, was that he barely noticed the weekend's losses.

His ambitions depended on the Grand Heist haul return going smoothly. Both in person and on the feeds.

As he dropped the fanciest fruits from the party into one of Llyria's high-powered kitchen blenders and hit purée, he contacted his creditors and planned his strategy. Seamless return of belongings. Payments when those belongings couldn't be found. Smiles all around.

Given his reactions at dinner the night before, that was going to be a job. The feeds were full of gossips this morning, buzzing like bees.

"I've seen that you took heavy losses last

night," one of his usual investors coughed. "How long would you need my credits?"

"Not long at all." The wedding could happen quickly, if Evangeline agreed. He turned so the creditor could see the documents on the table: an embossed folder featuring a silver bee and a boar.

"Oh in that case, by all means." The creditor sounded like they were smiling. "You will of course put your latest research down as guarantee."

Mason couldn't pause as he agreed to the terms. The transfer came quickly. *Seamless.*

Strawberries, apples, oranges. Even a pineapple. Into the blender. Each handful of fruit cost more than most city residents' annual guaranteed wages. Each had been carefully tended from blossom to fruit by at least three teams working in shifts at the vertical farms in New Washington. Except for the oranges and pineapple. Those came from the offshore greenhouses.

Evangeline had declined to use supplies from a private town the caterer recommended. "I've told Papa that, going forward, we must encourage better labor practices." The caterer had named an enormous sum, Evangeline had waved her hand. And that was that.

Now, alone in the kitchen, in all of Llyria since he'd sent the staff away, he practiced his best poker face in the reflection of pots and pans. "Of course, Mrs. Sweeten, your jewels are here." "Certainly Mr. Grouse, I understand you couldn't possibly have meant to pocket the fountain pens. Just a slip."

The shriek of the blender macerating the leftover fruit into another purple slurry made Mason smile.

He'd hire all new staff, once the dust cleared. The kind who wouldn't judge, or gossip. A full-time tailor, a personal physic. Properly observant chefs and body-men. The kind loyal to a family. The Benford kind. And he'd do it with Benford money.

At least Evangeline still believed in him. Her "yes"

after the thieves had been rounded up and taken away? That word still rang happily in his ears. He'd done it.

After the chaos of the dining room, Evangeline's delight at having captured the last thief came as a relief. The proposal—especially without a ring—had seemed spontaneous, and the guests that remained in the house had applauded.

Sam had taken some convincing. After Mason allowed the acrobat-thief to be taken for medical care instead of where she belonged at the precinct, he also let Stonecliff—who they'd caught with the belongings of a fellow guest—free. With that, Evangeline had lobbied on Mason's behalf.

"I know we can and will pull off the remainder of the weekend with grace," she told her father. Sam had acknowledged the plea with a stern nod.

The embossed invitation to the Reclamation Court for official document signing and green-book interview sat on the kitchen counter beside him. The bee, the silver filigree—within reach. If Mason could pull this off.

Benford had graciously offered to store his remaining valuables at Centenaire and to host the last birthday event—a hunt—himself, as a gesture of support.

Graves hadn't dressed for the hunt yet. This morning was a collared business shirt and casual slacks affair. He'd change after.

He'd cleaned his office enough to make sure his tests on the lab variant had been unharmed and were still running. The results would be finished after the hunt. He'd take the rest to Centenaire. When he did that, Benford promised to use his influence to have comments about Mason's temper at dinner removed from the feeds.

Benford's skill at smoothing things over was equaled only by his hatred for the non-service feeds. With an elegant hunt, the gossips would be distracted. The noise would die down and everyone would find another disaster to focus on.

"The party planner is here, along with Holt," Llyria announced.

Excellent. The planner had retrieved the items removed by the performers. On his tablet, she and Holt escorted two large hovercarts of objects up the main stairs.

In the carts, boxes of small items were already divided into categories: watches, credit clips, cufflinks, necklaces, one tiara, earrings, trays, service items. Wristbands, more than a few. A roofhopter fob, though the hopter itself was thankfully still on the grounds.

The larger cart held decor. Two tea services. Art, safe in preservation portfolios. Everything they'd been able to recover from the Canarviers' negotiator or find stashed around the house.

Mason left the kitchen and met Holt and the party planner in the main hall as they finished transforming the carts into tables.

The party planner smiled tightly at Mason. "Guests—or their representatives—will arrive here, then the items in their declaration-of-theft forms will be distributed by Major Holt, here. Any unfulfilled items will be credited by you, graciously, at the end of the line." She emphasized the word "graciously."

The antique clock ticked softly beside them, closing on noon. Two days ago, that clock had chimed the start of a ball. Two days ago, he'd had a ring in his pocket.

How things had changed. How Mason had changed. He felt alive now. Ready for what the future held. "Of course. I will be the model of propriety," Mason promised. The feeds would be watching—as he'd agreed with Evangeline.

The planner had also agreed to an "off the record" sidebar with *Enclave & Towne*, paid for by Graves, which would also help his image. *Enclave & Towne* offered a matching sum for in-house feeds from the party, once Graves and Holt had vetted them. Evangeline's idea.

He'd heard her fighting with Sam about that. She'd won.

At noon, the clock's chime coincided with the great doors opening once more. A few guests, their vehicles waiting outside, came to offer congratulations and collect their things, but most sent their staff. Several of the latter arrived with birthday cards for Evangeline, and one engagement card: mostly silly holograms with personal feed shots from the event.

Reconnecting guests with their pilfered items was relatively quick, although the Duttons proved a problem. It had been their first party. They had no idea how to behave. "Our form includes several damaged gowns, and an indemnity clause against further losses or implications in vice," a staff member intoned quietly, as if ashamed.

"Not to worry." Mason smiled. A model of propriety. Vice implications among Enclave families were highly rare. Dutton was too new to know that. "And I hope to see Jayson on the hunt later." Though he really didn't. The party planner smiled, pleased. All was going quite well.

When Stonecliff himself climbed the main stairs, however, Mason ground his teeth and Holt rose from his chair.

"Surely you didn't lose anything, Rylan, while you were looting the guests' pockets?" Mason reviewed Stonecliff's form. It was blank. Not one thing was due to the man. "Why have you returned?"

Stonecliff smiled brightly. "Let's not be petty. It's just a game, Graves. I was in the neighborhood, having lunch. I wanted to collect an apology from your staff for being so enthusiastic about your security." He pointed to a small bruise on his chin, near the scar.

Holt reddened. "I am most ashamed that your person was harmed, sir."

Mason regarded the cameras opposite the table. He smiled. If this was the only injury Mason had to deal with in the course of the weekend, well, he would make it look very good for the feeds. "We offer our apologies and regrets, sir." He bowed.

Stonecliff beamed. "Well done, Mason," he whispered.

"The feeds will eat that up." Then he extended a small, wrapped box. "I also came to offer congratulations to you and Evangeline, as I was unable to do so last night."

If Stonecliff was offering congratulations here, rather than at Centenaire, later, that meant he might be leaving town. Mason could only hope. "You're not riding out with us later?"

"I am in fact!" Stonecliff sounded delighted. "Sam offered me a decent position in the group as well. Just behind you. It should be a lovely afternoon. But I have several errands to run in the meantime. I'll see you at four."

When his former CFO disappeared back down the stairs and his motorcar—an old Bentley rebuilt with an electric engine and modern components—pulled away, Mason let out a breath.

"You are lucky he's not filing charges himself," the party planner muttered. "That was his message."

Mason grimaced. That had been recorded too. He'd need to filter it for the feeds. Rylan Stonecliff was only a pebble in his shoe now—something he might have to live with—but only that. He set the box aside and promptly forgot about it.

When his creditors had suggested Stonecliff and several others for the C-suite of Graves Biosecurity, the company had been on the verge of its pheromone breakthroughs. The safe equipment and biometric scanners he'd been selling widely in Denver and other protected cities were doing well, but Safeware? That changed everything.

He'd viewed the appointment as a vote of support as he expanded. That Stonecliff had left suddenly, at nearly the same time as a number of data files had been duplicated, had both infuriated Mason and secretly delighted him. He'd attracted Enclave espionage! He couldn't prove it, and Stonecliff's friendship with the Benfords kept him from publicly protesting, but Mason, and Holt, still held a grudge.

That Stonecliff had let it be known he was out of town, and then appeared at the party? The man delights in chaos. Now it's my turn to mess with him. The new Bio-Safeware formulas. The variants. Those were Mason's. And Mason's alone.

Besides, Stonecliff was a green-book. He'd refused a chip on the hopes that he'd be appointed a judge someday, but that hadn't worked out. The man jumped from company to board of directors to family trusts, fixing things for several different clients at a time. Everyone he'd touched was kept from publicly challenging him by his society status. If he spoke out against someone attempting to get into the social register—like Mason, for instance—it would take an immense show of power to fix that.

Soon, Mason would have that power.

Initially, Mason had attempted to get into the register the same way the Duttons had—by applying for a founders' award, using his safe research. When Stonecliff arrived, he'd assumed he was being vetted. But then the biennial candidates had been announced, and Mason wasn't on the list. He'd been crushed.

Then Judge Benford reached out, through one of his creditors. She wanted Mason to meet her niece. She'd promised nothing, and Mason had hoped for nothing. And now, here he was.

Mason would soon have the standing that people like Stonecliff and the Benfords enjoyed from birth. The lasting security. Especially if there were several little Graves-Benfords running around the green. An heir. And spares. Maybe even a safe.

When guests and staff slowed on the stairs, the party planner began disassembling the tables. The snick-clack sounds of empty boxes collapsing flat was a relief to Mason's ears. He was nearly done. Soon he'd be putting his valuables in Benford's safe, and then riding out on the hunt. Soon, Stonecliff couldn't throw him out of sorts any longer.

Mason finished distributing the last reclaimed spoils from the Grand Heist to a butler from the Atlantic Enclave. The man smelled of brine.

He turned to the preservation portfolio that had come in with the carts. One more thing to take care of: returning the art to Evangeline's favorite museum, and closing the insurance account.

He opened the portfolio and peered inside. Only six works stared back. A small quilt and five paintings.

"Where are the rest?" Mason's voice echoed in the hall. Losing priceless pre-Mess artwork, from one of Evangeline's charities? That was the kind of loss that even his creditors would flee from. Worse than insolvency; Evangeline's belief in him might be shattered.

"The Canarviers' representative says they are still in the house," the party planner said. *Is she chuckling? Are her eyes dancing with amusement?* "They said to check the curtains in the music room."

"Holt!" Mason hissed. His voice echoed from the speaker in his security chief's implants.

Holt reddened and subvocaled, "We are rechecking now, sir."

Mason's belly soured on a repeat of Saturday's outrage. The thieves were still making him look bad.

Then he remembered the cameras: *Enclave & Towne*. "How brilliant of the Canarviers! They were excellent craftsmen. It's too bad this was their last performance. Historic, really."

He gestured at Holt to turn the camera feed off. He ignored the party planner's murmur of dissent. When Holt acknowledged it was done, Mason turned to the planner once more.

"I need to dress for the hunt. Where is the rest?" He said it so mildly, she almost missed his question.

"Of course, sir. Is there anything else missing?" the planner murmured. "Perhaps another guest has—borrowed something? Surely not though." Was she wearing a mic? A camera? Probably.

He'd presented Evangeline with the winner's feather and a promise. *Her ring isn't here.* Minerva Benford had said the ring had been traced to Evangeline's fourth-great maternal grandmother, from before the Mess. There were few like it left—a precision-cut midnight sapphire surrounded by diamonds and platinum—and no fabricating the provenance that came with a Reclamation Judge's guarantee. Nor the way it caught the light in its facets. Judge Benford had made him guarantee it to her with Llyria's deed. Which he'd backed with the Safeware research. Which was now backing his creditors. "Surely not," Mason assured her. His voice sounded hollow.

Holt bent to disassemble the last table, and subvocaled, "The Canarviers say they didn't take the ring. My interrogation confirmed it. They have filed a hardship against repayment, as multiple members of their troupe—including both apprentices—are being held against contract."

Holt waited until after the heist distribution was complete to tell me this. Smart. Couldn't have me flying into a rage on a feed.

The clock sounded three fifteen. Mason was exhausted from the distribution process, late, and still needed to change for the hunt. *I will deal with the matter of the ring later.*

He smiled for anyone who might be watching. Kept smiling as he turned to inspect the clock. The planner took the last table and departed the hall.

"We will find it, sir," Holt subvocaled.

"Thank you." Mason bit every word, still smiling. "Search again and then study the surveillance before the feeds see any bit of it. Anyone who came near me, I want tracked. If they try to sell a ring—any jewel—I want to hear first. Let the pawnbrokers know. And call the safe. I'm late and he's not released until we transfer the remaining valuables."

Whoever had it would try to sell it. The gem had been visible in a salvaged Cartier catalog from hundreds of years before the Mess, and on a portrait of Serena from before her marriage to Sam—the provenance was undeniable. Judge Benford had said the ring was lost in a robbery, and although the judge had recently discovered the ring's location, she'd waited to share that information with her brother. "It will be the surprise and joy of Evangeline's life," she'd said. "My brother can't keep this kind of thing a secret." She hadn't explained further.

Had Benford's physic found it on the thief recuperating at Centenaire? If so, could he somehow play that as a very special way to propose? He would think on it. But if Evangeline or Benford didn't say they had it, he couldn't show his hand.

Which was, admittedly, empty.

"Sir." Gabriel, summoned by Holt, appeared at the top of the stairs, his own bruises from the struggle with the thieves mending well. He descended much as Mason himself had done a few days prior.

"The ampoules please, and the documents. I'll bring them to Benford's myself." Mason held out a hand.

The ampoules were locked to his personal biokey, but he'd still feel better once they were at Benford's. *Especially when my own chief of security can't find a simple ring.*

"Thank you, sir, I am doing much better," Gabriel replied to the question Mason hadn't asked. Then he hesitated. "I counted them after the fight with the thief. But it seems I counted wrong—"

"What does that mean, exactly," Graves said quietly. He stared at the intricate marble pattern on the floor of his home.

"I mistook one ampoule for a shard of tempered glass in the confusion, sir. I assure you that my insurance will cover any loss."

Mason felt the air around him compress as he

whispered so low that the departing party planner couldn't hear it, nor could the cameras. "Which ampoule?"

Roo waited impatiently by the rotunda window as the hunt assembled on the Benfords' lawn.

She was expected to give the Benfords an answer when they returned from the hunt. Their offer: apply for acceptance into the family, agree to a family chip, and they would try to help King and Dax.

She would make them wait as long as possible. Her braces were growing thinner, ticking down. Soon they would vanish. And Roo would as well.

She watched the group don goggles and masks, then carefully adjust static veils—protection for venturing into the unrecovered areas.

There were Evangeline's friends, all in a knot of tan jodhpurs and impossibly white blouses. And the Duttons' new gear with bright monograms. Rylan Stonecliff sported a bright-orange jacket and a hat to match. Evangeline had a tiny hat that tilted her veil over her goggles. And Mason Graves, when he finally arrived, wore padded green pants and a coat that belted twice at the shoulder.

None of the group seemed to have a job to get to, even though the city worked round the clock to reclaim itself from the Mess and expand.

Roo didn't have any more time to play. She had to get word to Nan, she needed to talk to Sasha, though she didn't want to, and she had to find a way to free King, without giving up her freedom.

Benford—she wasn't yet comfortable calling him Sam—had paused King's transfer to Alaska, but not canceled it. *For how long? As long as I behave?* Roo bristled. They said she was not being held hostage, but they were lying.

"I admit I've been extremely protective," Benford

had said, after spearing another piece of pineapple. "But someone disappearing, and no sign, no matter where we looked, no matter how much we paid—it was very upsetting. I couldn't lose you too."

"What was she like?" Roo asked. *What happened?* She didn't ask. This stranger couldn't be the mother that King told her and Dax about, with her eyes like the sea and her voice that sounded like a bell.

"I remember her singing," Evangeline said. "And she loved to dance with me. And she loved the gardens."

"Yes," Benford whispered. He fussed at the pale-blue chip in his palm, lost in the memory. "And old books. I'd just bought her a volume of something—Dickens, maybe. Or Carroll." He paled, as if he was remembering. Then he reached inside his sport coat to a pocket above his heart. Lifted out a small, oval frame. Not a hologram or a feed grab. A tiny painting of a young woman in a pale dress. Blue eyes. Dark skin. Long fingers clasped in her lap accentuated by a large, blue gemstone ring the color of midnight. The young woman in the frame looked very much like Evangeline, but with dark hair. Also, if Roo squinted, a little like herself. "She was my world."

Roo blinked hard, her eyes itched. King had filled her life with stories of Cere but no pictures. She was a mother who feared nothing and no one. Who planned impeccable heists, who fought for the rights of those in the Skirts, who was among the first jailed for agitation, and sent away. She'd disappeared in Alaska. King hadn't stopped looking for her, but he'd also made sure the space where Cere should have been in Roo and Dax's lives was filled to overflowing.

Yes, Roo had wanted to find out what had happened to her mother. She had many questions to ask. *But I don't carry around a locket that seems to weigh much heavier than it should.*

Evangeline wore a similar locket. A missing mother, a lost wife. *A tragedy,* the guests at Mason Graves's party had said.

Roo's few memories of Cere were so different from that still portrait. So present. A brilliant smile. A deck of cards that appeared and disappeared. She'd disappeared too, before Roo turned three.

She'd never wanted to marry. King had said their promise to each other had been worth more than a document and a city sanction. She'd been a parent, an artist, and a protester. "How did she come to be taken from here—from the Enclaves?"

"What we know," Evangeline said, "is what Stonecliff has found for us. There are so few records, but there is footage from that night. She was caught unaware and kidnapped. No ransom. Papa kept that quiet. He only recently told me she hadn't died the way everyone thought, from a sudden illness. He'd said that to keep the family name unsullied."

"Unsullied?" Roo stared at Evangeline, then Sam. *I want to leave now.*

Sam Benford tapped Evangeline's side of the table for emphasis. "There was so much chaos then. We were focused on emerging into a better world. We still are. When I learned she'd been arrested at a riot, we tried to help. She must have been brainwashed. She didn't want any of it. And then she was gone."

"But you're Benfords. You could have interfered—" Roo burst out, a hand raised over her plate. "Not just for her, for everyone sent away. You could have the world better with them, instead of on top of them—"

Clink. A server dropped a spoon. Evangeline startled. "We focus on that work now in Mama's memory. Once you're recovered, I'll show you. You might want to help us become even better at it, when you are ready."

Benford tried to pat her hand, but Roo slid it to her lap. He gestured to her face instead. "I can see her spirit and mine in you. You are absolutely a Benford. When you've been added to the family ledger—the green book—we'll be much better able to answer your questions. You will continue your education, receive an allowance. Anything you wish. Even if you decide not to stay here. As long as you accept the family."

She could return to Miss Farmer's. Finish her project. That at least was a relief. An allowance—like some of her classmates had? A dream. Perhaps travel to another Enclave—not the distant ones, which were still a risky endeavor even for those as rich as the Benfords, but somewhere like Raleigh or Pittsburgh. Or an Enclave that came near the coastline. She could keep going from there. After she told Sasha about her wardrobe. *Or what's left of it.* Roo toyed with a piece of pineapple. It was very juicy. This was a tempting trap. What would Dax do? He'd say: *Play along, Roo, until you know we are safe.*

She risked it. "I want to hear this story from King himself."

"We could go first thing tomorrow. It will require us changing some plans with the Recovery Court. Would you, in exchange for this, give us a few days to know you better? And you, us?" Sam's voice wove equal parts sorrow and hope.

Play along, Roo, but do not answer. "I would like to learn more about Serena also." The words felt sticky, like the fruit. Too much so. She pressed her mouth closed, afraid she would be sick at the table.

But maybe there are clues here, to the mystery of Cere. To the mother I've only known through King's memories. How had she vanished? How was she lost?

Sam smiled at her question. He held out the locket. "Would you wear this while you're with us? As a sign of our favors for one another?"

Roo knew when she was being tested. *If I say no, I may anger my hosts.* She held a hand out.

Instead of passing it to her, Benford stood up and settled the pendant around her throat. She tried to hide her shiver as the cold metal touched her skin.

He secured the clasp. "Thank you, Renata. You have made us very happy." He squeezed her hand.

I have not accepted anything. She tried to believe that.

"We must prepare for the hunt. I do not think you are in any shape to ride. And perhaps you would like some time to yourself to decide?" He stood, then pulled Evangeline's chair back.

"Thank you, that is very kind," she said. He hadn't noticed her sharp breath at the name. *So far, Sam sees what he wants to see in me. That could be dangerous, if I fail him.*

"I could stay?" Evangeline said. "Papa and Mason may have more to do with this event than–"

Benford shook his head. "I need you with me, to keep me from throttling your fiancé, if nothing else. Are you certain he is what you want?"

"More than any other suitor," Evangeline said, although she sounded worried. "If I must marry to satisfy the inheritance contracts, then yes, I am certain. I can stay in New Washington. I can continue my work. Besides, Aunt Min likes him. You are always too worried." She kissed his cheek.

"At least I'd hoped he could protect you," Sam said. "That's all I want. Now that you have a seat on the Enclave Family Trust, it is even more important."

Sam Benford wasn't so different from King, Roo thought. Once he'd settled on Dax to inherit the family business, he'd decided Roo must hack society, by working on the Enclave side of the wall. He'd hoped the next generation of Canarviers would have access to better. He'd charged Roo with making that happen. She'd tried to do that with her project. But instead, she seemed to be reaching more of his goals with the failed heist. Roo shivered.

Although, now that I'm here, with the Benfords offering everything on a silver plate, all I want is to run home. Or at least back to Miss Farmer's.

She heard Evangeline murmur a few steps from the

table, "Maybe I can also protect myself, Papa." *How interesting.*

The servants cleared the table when the Benfords left. Outside, preparations began for the hunt. The drones were pulled from one of the greenhouses and arrayed on the lawn. Riding gear set beside each shiny carapace. The rotunda echoed with silence.

A Benford. Me. Impossible.

For a single moment, she allowed herself to dream. She could make the world better than they had, if she had their resources. *Books and food for the Skirts. More opportunities. I could clear Dax's record, bring him here. Help ease Nan's days.*

Roo knotted the fringe on the shawl and shook her head to clear it. Nan would tell her if there was any truth to this. She had to get a message to her now, before she dreamed more possibilities. Tomorrow was too far away.

Finally, the gathered guests mounted the drones that floated on the lawn like large, dark beans, and disappeared.

When they were gone, Roo looked to the servants for familiar faces or a nod of recognition. She saw no one she knew. The masks and uniforms made them a unified, supportive, distant whole. The way the Enclaves liked it. They did notice her staring, though.

A woman with hazel eyes and a long braid mostly tucked beneath her cap came to kneel beside her. "You sure you wouldn't like something more, miss?"

I want a kitchen hob, and the means to make myself something that will crackle when I bite into it. I want Dax to point out how ridiculous this shawl is. I want a roofhopter or a motorcar that will carry me away from here, or at least a way to move faster on my own. This chair only has one gear: graceful. I need a wristband, so I can get out of here.

"Do you have a fabricator?" It was worth a shot. The Benfords seemed to have everything else, and Evangeline had produced the chair somehow.

Roo's braces were thinning. Almost time to run.

From his cold seat in the precinct hold, Dax's only source of distraction from Sunday night's imminent transport collection was watching his fees piling up.

His cellmates' charges were rising too, but that was small comfort. Dax couldn't convince King to contact Nan, and he needed to reach out to Aanand. Desperately.

But when the transport detail came, they emptied the room of everyone but King.

"Who's looking out for you, buddy?" One of King's holdmates muttered on the way out. King looked as confused as anyone.

Was someone looking out for him, or using him? Leaving King to rack up hold debts was benefitting someone. A guard finally tapped on the wall. "Benfords requested you cool your heels here instead of Sitka for now. Friends in high places, eh?"

Dax's hold mates regarded him with suspicion now, and King too. Dax felt much the same: was King telling the truth? Not one of his stories? Was Roo a Benford? Was Cere really one of them? *I don't remember her at all, but from the stories, she would have hated that.*

"Dad, call Nan. Now." Using his one call, he could straighten everything out.

King sat silent. As he pondered his new situation, their debts continued to soar. The city charged precinct room and board, such as it was. And cleaning fees, even though bots did that. Then there were the hourly supervision charges, recording fees, and fees to log the fees. Each was carefully broken out on prisoners' sleeves so everyone in the hold could see the impact of their infractions. *Better than some protected cities,* Dax had heard. *Aanand says Denver prints them on the forehead. Albuquerque, around the neck.*

Finally, King signaled the guard to make his one connection. It had been nearly a week.

The minute he did, Dax asked to contact Aanand, via one of Aanand's aliases. Everyone in the Skirts had aliases. Few had as many as Aanand. It would be a race to see who arrived first. And who could risk leaving work first.

Nan beat Aanand by three minutes, according to the fee-counter on Dax's sleeve.

Dax tried to listen to her conversation with King, tried to catch her eye, but the privacy static made it difficult. He heard her coughing—she'd had that as long as he could remember. From the Mess, she'd said, and a fire. She usually kept it down with homemade lozenges and breathing exercises. Sometimes medicine that Aanand's father got her from his connections. It sounded worse today: aggravated and deep.

Even though he couldn't make the words out, he could see her hands moving. Updating King. *The goods were returned. We're out of credits. No word about Roosa. She's not here?*

King didn't know. The guards didn't say, but everyone could see that she wasn't. *Did that mean she was a Benford?*

Nan frowned at King, "Did you do what they're saying? Attack a Judge?"

Judge attacked me, King signed, as he said "No."

"Why? What were you doing?"

King folded his hands. Nan sighed loudly. She signaled to Dax. "Your arm okay?"

The safe had roughed Dax up pretty thoroughly. Dax rotated his arm to show her. He'd fixed it himself to avoid hold medical fees.

Nan frowned. Signed, "We'll find a doctor. And get you both house arrest. We'll keep the apartment after the take is declared returned. Graves would consider your release, but claims there are still items missing."

There were always going to be items missing. That's not how this worked. They couldn't afford any more delays. They were down to the bus and its contents for trading, before the Grand Heist. They couldn't lose the bus, but everything inside was fair game. Including King's library. *It isn't like I read much of that except to make calling cards. Good riddance.*

Dax needed to get out. Even though he was being careful about what he ate and drank in the hold, not only to avoid the fees, his stomach was curdling. The hold facilities were uncomfortably public.

Before Dax could ask Nan about his mother, or anything else, Aanand arrived. Pulled up in front of Dax's hold. "Hi Nan. Saw you on the feeds, Dax. Bad luck."

"You're lying," Dax said loud enough to rouse his cellmates.

"Truth. Could make a pretty pile of credits to sell my stories about you to some gossip rag right now, not that I'm thinking about it." Aanand laughed.

"You wouldn't." Dax had been neighbors and friends with Aanand—finding the same sorts of trouble, getting pinched for shooting down delivery drones, teasing Roo for studying so hard, all of it—his entire life. Aanand's parents were helping Nan as much as they could, letting her keep the apartment over their week, moving the van.

Aanand looked like he was thinking about taking the payday. "Lots of credits going to Benford- and Graves-related feeds this morning, after your . . ." he paused dramatically, "performance. Loved your last act, by the way. Graves had it broadcast everywhere."

Dax groaned. So, the Canarviers' faces—at least Dax's—were public. His last name was common as sand, but the connections to Roo, Nan, and King were available for anyone who dug deep enough. "The troupe is ruined." And his future.

His stomach churned.

"Maybe," his friend said. "I've got some ideas." His hands folded and unfolded. *Llyria Guest List?* His fingers spelled out in Skirts signs.

Nan got up from her meeting with King and patted Aanand's shoulder before she left.

Dax watched her go, then said, "Nan could use more help, if you're feeling like checking in on people." He kept the under-conversation going while he spoke: *I don't have the list. Roo shared it with Nan. She didn't want us to resell the data when she grabbed it, ever. I bet it's worth something.*

Aanand winked agreement. "I'll make sure she's all right. You need anything?"

Dax needed to tell Aanand just how badly he had to get out of the hold, but Aanand hadn't sprung for privacy. And Dax couldn't afford it.

"Just news—anything about recent employers?" He meant Graves. It was a delicate thing to say he had something on the guy, right here in the precinct hold. Then it clicked. Aanand was asking him similar questions, without using signals. He was being careful too. Dax shifted uncomfortably on the cheap fabricated bench. Aanand had to see there was something more. He had to cough up the funds. Finally, Dax gave in and signed, *Private conversation?*

It was shocking how quickly Aanand slapped his work band on the wall. The privacy screens dropped around them. There was still city surveillance, but no one else in the visitor's area could hear.

Aanand tried talking trash about party guests. "Evangeline's friends are fine, yeah?" Dax winced. "But the Duttons seem stiff. And that guy, what's his name, Stonecliff?"

He steepled his fingers, then shook his wrists, as if nervous. Folded his hands in a particular manner: *Don't you watch the feeds? There were founders at the party, folks from Atlantic Enclave, maybe even Ocean.* Aanand shuddered, muttered. *One of the new social registers too. And one of the founders' fixers. I have investors who want to know what they were up to.*

To anyone listening, their conversation was a combination of banter and negotiation. Two friends trying to do business.

"Find Roo, maybe she can help."

"That's another thing." Aanand looked angry as he spoke. "Saw a clip of her being wheeled about Centenaire like some prize. Evangeline's next charity project, maybe. Most clips get doused by Benford's security as soon as they pop up, and they're blurry, but it's her. Living the sweet Enclave life, while you're stuck here."

Aanand held up at tablet. A still of an estate property. Roo in some medical contraptions and a ridiculous shawl being floated across a lawn. "Your sister's not locked up. She's folded on you, I'd say."

Dax watched his sister's blurry image on the feed, relief and confusion wrestling in his gut. She'd seen her jump the window. Had heard the shouts. And watched the stretcher evacuation from his MilPol bindings. She was all right. But maybe she was more than that—was she already settling in with a new family? "She's playing them. Roo wouldn't fold."

A folder, in the Skirts, was someone who might ask you out for a drink at the end of a workday, and sell one of your kidneys on the black market before you woke up, hungover at the start of the next. *Roo was not anything close to a folder. How dare Aanand call her that? No way can I tell him what King said now. Aanand might doubt all of us if I do.* "Roo's not the kind to betray anyone she loves."

"Wouldn't she? With that fancy scholarship and fancy friends?" Aanand's hands worked double time. *Nan said Graves was waiting on more missing goods. You think Roo's hiding them?*

Dax thought back to the apartment, and Sasha Limére's cut when he'd been trying to be friendly. He felt smaller just thinking about that moment. "I remember. But that was to benefit all of us."

Aanand sniffed. "Is it doing that? Look at yourself. I can smell that hold stench through the barrier."

Even when they were kids, Aanand would tease Roo, trying to make her cry. He'd tear pages from King's books, saying they were too moldy. He'd tell her she was one step away from being put out on the salt flats to desiccate.

Roo would always stand her ground, face turned from Aanand's latest fault-finding. And Dax would step in, often fist-first, until Aanand laughed it off as a joke. Then they'd all go play. It was never really meant to be mean. Just Aanand's way.

Part of why they were friends was that Dax understood this. When they weren't getting in trouble, sometimes Dax would share information from their heists, and Aanand would show him what his family's van-lab was developing–biological stuff, ways to heal cuts, and disguises. Plus Aanand's own inventions. Drone-augments, mostly.

Roo understood this. She was the one who kept Aanand's data clear of all his small crimes, and helped him make new aliases, wasn't she? At least she had.

It was a good partnership between families. *If the Canarviers are really done, maybe I can have a future with Aanand's teams.* Dax hoped the information he had now could smooth that path. "Maybe there's more to the story."

Now, though, Aanand wasn't joking. "Your fault if you don't believe me. I'll try to help your Nan, but I can't promise for how long. Come up with something useful and we'll see."

He began to stand, and the wall started to go opaque.

"Wait." Dax tapped on the wall. The fee hit his sleeve like a shock. "There is one thing." He signed quickly. *Graves had these ampoules of liquid in his rental safe. I might have swallowed one.*

Aanand listened intently to the rest of what Dax had to say.

Enclave & Towne Feed

Enclave & Towne secured an exclusive interview with Judge Minerva Benford at the Graves masque. Viewers should note the timestamp—this conversation took place prior to the proposal. We hope to update the files with a word from the judge on the outcome, and have submitted further questions to her office. In the meantime, the feed below is available free after interacting with the following informational programming feeds.

New Washington Educational Programming Feed

(city residence required)

Remember: You benefit as a citizen of a protected city!

Working to help the Reclamation, renting, or owning property in a protected city, brings you:

- Lifelong educational feeds
- Basic feed access beyond education: safety and health updates, changes in leadership news
- Basic annual income with accounting required
- Basic fabricators in all city-run bodegas
- Basic bodega coupons for essentials as defined by city regulations
- Basic medical support to maintain public health
- Free messaging to city regulators and Recovery Court judges (three per month per household)

Help those who need it access city services by offering reclamation work, providing jobs, and spreading the word. The protected cities benefit you!

*

E&T: Our viewers want to know whether you approved the entertainment for the ball this evening?

Judge Benford: My niece approved everything, and her judgment is sound.

E&T: And yet you have spoken out in previous interviews about vice in New Washington, specifically entertainers like the Canarviers.

Judge Benford: As I said, I trust my niece's judgment. The city is safe, and these entertainments are unnecessary, but I appreciate how they're showcasing Graves Biosecurity innovations.

Update: To our questions regarding the proposal, a potential Benford family merger, and Mason Graves's rumored losses from the party, Judge Benford's office has replied, "We have verified that Graves remains in good financial standing with the Enclave, and we have no further comment at this time."

The Hunt

MASON'S EQUADRONE FOR Sunday's hunt was a loaner, and, as such, hadn't been customized. The midnight-blue chassis curved a touch too wide. Already, the seat was starting to rub against his tailbone.

When the party hit rough terrain and couldn't hover, the equa extruded eight legs and compensated, but it had a cadence Mason couldn't master. His entire skull ached, and his subdermal comm channel kept turning on accidentally.

He was careful to conceal his discomfort as he rode the wetlands shoreline beside Sam. Luckily the whole party was wearing protection, complete with gloves and static-veiled hats. That worked on the mosquitoes swarming in thick clouds above sunken buildings in the Georgetown archipelago just as well as it dissuaded the feed drones attempting to follow the riders. *Bloodsuckers, both,* Mason thought. It kept his companions from seeing his grimaces and glares. It also helped with any other risks—*though snipers and kidnappers are more of a Skirts problem, really.* Luckily, they weren't going near the Skirts.

How can they find this thrilling?

Beside him, Sam Benford's classic black equa—which he'd named Apotheosis—was well matched to its rider. The older man seemed to glide along the waterways of Georgetown and around the deep basin of Foggy Bottom as if he was born to it.

He'd replied to Mason's overture about running more footage from the party, carefully edited to Mason's benefit, with a firm "no."

Behind them, in a tight knot of her friends, Evangeline rode her own equa sidesaddle. The pale-cream drone had extruded a settee-seat and a grip for the purpose, mimicking a unicorn's horn atop the chassis. Her friends had copied the style to varying degrees and the entire group talked their way through much of former Alexandria as if they were at tea. *They're definitely preparing some feed fodder. It's unfair.*

Mason had no need to be part of that conversation—he didn't want to explain not having the ring with him—but he did wish for a softer seat. He had no interest in trying to spot a rare pigeon, or to scan the horizon for an undiscovered wreck as the tides receded. Several more adventurous members of the hunt, seated as high on their equas as they could get, carried high-powered binoculars, nets, grabbers, and metal detectors for that purpose.

Still, Sam expected him to ride in gentlemanly fashion. Which meant that he was jostling above the remains of the Emstreet Bridge when Dr. Tsalta called.

"I have some results."

Mason quickly reined back the drone to a slow hover. He gestured the others to ride on ahead.

"Go on." *And let this be good news.*

His own equipment, which had cost him trillions of credits, had only produced a confirmation of Tsalta's original assessment: that there had been a change in the sugars on the antibody mechanism. He needed more data in order to reach out to his investors.

"Do you know how many different things had to go wrong in the lab for a control transfer to completely reverse?" Tsalta sounded genuinely excited.

"I need to keep this short. I'm not currently at my desk," Mason reminded her. "Just the results."

"Yes. Of course. I've reproduced the errors and recreated the formula," she said quickly.

Was it possible that some hunt riders heard Mason shout "Hallelujah"? It was. But they didn't turn to see who was cheering.

"That is to say, I've recreated it in the lab. I don't know if it will generate results in vivo—with the control weakening while the controller grows stronger. That could have been a fluke. We need more sibling/relative sets to test it, and we need an antidote as well."

"At this point, you have my full support to do anything you need to do." Make mythical creatures that fly, he was about to say, but Sam was looking back for him. Time to get back to the day's business. "Go ahead, Tsalta. Make the formula your priority. Success will make this lab legendary." *It will at least make me a legend.*

When Mason began to rejoin the party, the equa's footfalls felt almost jaunty.

He was almost to the rest of the group when a mer rose from the waters and, with an actual net, tried to scoop him and his drone under. He screamed and the riders ahead turned back to watch.

Was this a part of the hunt? Was he being made entertaining? No. Evangeline's shouting. She's got her hand up, so does Sam, they're calling for—

The net was made of strong fab. The mer was close enough for Mason to see he was bio-masked, not altered.

He whispered, “Your creditors want a word.” Everything smelled of sewer and sea. This was not entertainment.

—they're calling for help but it's too late.

His equa sparked as the salt water got in the seams. The attacker grappled Mason's veil and that sparked too. *I am going to be cooked.* Mason struggled, trying to yell for Holt, but the jolting had shut his coms off again. Mason prepared to defend himself the way he'd done back in Denver. He reached for the knife he always hid in his sleeve. The hunt would be appalled, but Mason wouldn't die.

With a blinding flash of light, Stonecliff knocked the attacker into the water. He held an electrified baton—military grade. The mer's tail floated up and his head stayed down. The attacker turned gray as they watched, and sank, tangled in his own net. “Well.” Stonecliff brushed himself off, then righted Mason's equa. “That was exciting. Stay with the group, would you?”

Mason, breathless, agreed. “Absolutely.”

Evangeline, who had left her own mount and was trying to run toward him, was being restrained by her friends. The rest of the hunt was filming. Then Holt and the Benford guards encircled them. Safe.

He wanted to collapse, but too many were watching.

Mason looked to Sam, then Stonecliff for support, and winked. “Just a small entertainment at my own expense, to make things exciting!”

He struggled to control his breathing. To tuck the knife back where it belonged. To calm Evangeline with a smile.

“Oh!” “How brilliant!” The riders clapped and helped themselves to refreshments from beneath the equas' saddles. Evangeline stared at Mason, not falling for it.

“Shall we turn back, then?” she asked. Her voice wobbled.

She is definitely upset. But still cares about me. Mason didn't hate that result, even as he was holding himself as rigidly as possible. In fact, with Stonecliff giving a resounding answer to the creditors, he felt pretty good.

He'd survived an attack—possibly by his own creditors—thanks to the Benfords' power. He took in the crisp, dense air through his mask. The whole world felt charged with possibility. And he had the formula! One that might—possibly—provide longevity, even lifespan security! *At least it will secure my entire future.* He didn't feel scared. He felt more alive than he'd ever been—he could ride through the wastelands forever. He hadn't lost his temper. No one had seen him panic. And he hadn't died. "Let's go a bit longer. Your father said you wanted to see the salt flats. Perhaps we'll spot some *more* wildlife."

This drew a laugh from the riders. Evangeline, even. She spoke to Holt and her own guards, making sure they'd follow more closely.

But Stonecliff shook his head. "We'll only spot more dust and the usual noise from the Skirts. They've scared off the wildlife with their constant circles. We should head back."

Just like Stonecliff, not wanting to let anyone forget that he'd played the hero. Mason wondered—had the man known what was about to happen?

Then Jayson Dutton, on his own loaned equa, called out to Stonecliff, "Know a founder or a judge willing to change the contracts then? My cousin says we can't touch them if they're moving."

The entire group grew quiet. "Surely you're not proposing attacking the Skirts?" Evangeline asked. She stared at her former suitor, alarmed.

"More like a hunt, to make them pay commuter tithes at least."

The group grew even more silent. Dutton had made a grave error. "There's nothing Enclavers like more than someone who makes social errors. At least temporarily," Stonecliff whispered to Mason. "You're getting a lucky break."

"Another old commuter law, yes," Benford said, smoothing feathers. "One with value for the protected cities. We get a boundary between us and"—he gestured toward distant, unprotected areas beyond the flats—"and a consequence for anyone who falls beneath New Washington's standards. Doesn't that seem worthwhile?"

Dutton bowed, allowing the point. Mason noticed he seemed a bit pale under his veil. Perhaps he'd realized he sounded too violent for a day's ride. Mason came to the new Enclaver's aid. The feeds might even say he was magnanimous about it, especially after the adventure he'd created. "Let's continue then. To the flats!"

The hunt turned, each gleaming equa chassis reflecting the dust-shadowed sun like a dozen tiny stars. Evangeline settled herself on her mount again, having shifted it from sidesaddle to standard western seating. "Hiyah!"

Mason did the same, feeling much more comfortable now.

The party headed away from the water, a thin row of brightly clad riders taking in the ruins of the Mess.

"We mostly use this for staff needs and repairs." The maid hesitated between Roo and the estate's main fabrication room, near Benford's security offices. They'd taken the elevator down two floors below the main house. "You don't need to—"

"I like doing work," Roo said. Once she had access to the fabricators, maybe she could find a way to re-fab Sasha's dress. Or make the disaster up to her, somehow, before she turned in her final. Sasha would be waiting to hear from her by now. And King. And Nan. She had to try.

Four fabricators took up one wall of the room. Each was large enough to print a free city fabricator, supplies and all, Roo realized with a shock.

She drew a walking stick on the fabricator's screen, with arm cuffs and a firm hand grip. After some thought and a quick check of her leg's strength—better, but tired easily—she commanded the fabricator to print two of them.

The fabricator didn't respond. A light blinked.

"What kind of material, miss?" the maid interceded. Her fingers waved options into view on the screen: metal, bamboo, even a rosewood composite. Roo had worked with basic, free fabs—soy constructs for food, with flavors if you were lucky, and carbon fibers and fullerenes for everything else. Both options were grayish in color. The Benford fabs had every shade imaginable. The maid pointed at a peach-tone. "This is the color of the year according to *Enclave & Towne*."

As the machines silently extruded peacock-blue carbon-fiber canes exactly as she'd drawn them minutes later, Roo watched in shock. Even the nicer fabs at Miss Farmer's made noises like large blenders.

When she had what she needed, Roo lifted herself from the chair and tried the walking canes. They were light, comfortable, and still warm to the touch.

She pulled the peony shawl closer, knotting it at her waist. Pulled the braces' dregs from her leg and arm. "Thank you," she said to the maid. "These are exactly what I needed."

The maid blushed. "No need to thank me. And if you don't mind, please don't think twice about sending me to do this. I've been trained on fabs. Besides, most things on the property are handcrafted, and Mr. Benford would be upset to learn that you even knew where the fab room was. You or Miss Evangeline."

She sounded worried.

I've crossed a line of propriety. Everything about the Enclaves had an order, Roo knew this from the jobs she'd worked. But she knew it from the opposite side. *And I still messed it up. Did my mother have the same experience? Does this mean Evangeline and I are sisters? No. Med data can be wrong. The truth about my identity will be cleared up soon. Or maybe my history is too much to let me stay in society. Blood isn't always enough, and I certainly don't have the credits to match it. Or the upbringing. So, what will happen to me then?*

She paused. *If I'm not a thief, I am a pawn. I will not let that happen to me. I am an artist. I can improvise.*

She demurred the maid's help and found her own way to the elevator and back upstairs. She returned to the walkway, and the flowers. Something buzzed over a peony. A moth? A dragonfly? It didn't look like either. She heard the telltale drone clicks and watched it fly to a greenhouse close to the seawall, far down the property's lawn.

Halfway between her and the greenhouse, Roo's eye caught a metallic gleam beneath one of Benford's trees. An antique half-car. Was it the one Rylan Stonecliff had arrived in for the hunt? Maybe.

She wobbled a little on her sticks and cursed the feeling. *I did fall from a window yesterday. This isn't bad recovery time. A car could be useful; I could get to Miss Farmer's, and maybe then back to the city, before tomorrow morning. The perfect opportunity was waiting with its convertible top down.*

No one seemed to be watching as Roo walked to the vehicle. She slipped into the passenger side. Ducking down, she thought about the vans she'd traveled in, and the lessons Nan had taught both her and Dax about keeping the Canarviers' bus moving.

First, find the ignition—what kind it was, what fuel switches it uses. But, despite the antique look of Stonecliff's car, the internals were all sleek padding and upholstery. There were no visible controls. Only a chip reader.

Everything in the car was keyed to Stonecliff's identity.

If I had my tools back, I might be able to hack something. But I'd still need a chip to drive away—my own or someone else's. Roo frowned. She flexed her hands. She wouldn't want a chip for anything in the world.

"Miss?" A familiar voice interrupted her thoughts. "Did you fall? Do you need assistance?"

"No." Roo cringed. She quit studying the controls and looked up through the windshield. The maid from the main house, the one who'd helped her with the fabricators, peered into the car. "I needed to rest a moment. A lot less recovered than I thought."

The maid smiled. "I understand. And with you being so kind before, let me help you back home now? I won't say anything to anyone about this."

Home, Roo thought as she let the maid help her out of Stonecliff's car. *Where is home now?*

The hunt returned to Centenaire three hours after it departed, muddy and gleeful.

Roo paced the walkway of the Benford's estate as the party landed on the lawn, hoping to catch Sam and ask another favor. The hunt dismounted. Riders exclaimed. "We saw a live deer!" "What a grand surprise!" and "Well done, Graves!" They discarded protective outer layers beside the drones for staff to clear away. The party began to disperse with a few last calls of "congratulations!"

Mason waved triumphantly as Evangeline pulled him past Roo, and indoors. "You could have been killed! What—"

"Shhh. That was all part of a bit, you heard Dutton notice it was the same mer as at the party. Nothing to worry about." Graves smiled at her, before catching sight of Roo. "Oh, you're still here. And walking about." His glee seemed to fade dramatically.

Roo glared. But Evangeline reached her right hand, still warm from the ride, to clasp Rooa's elbow. She held Graves's hand with her left already, so now Roo felt connected to him through her. "We should all talk, sooner rather than later." She smiled, the ruddy, dust-lined goggle marks still bright on her cheeks.

Roo thought carefully what she would say to him. Not nice thoughts.

"Unfortunately," Graves said, "I need to address a business call I received during the ride."

He wormed his way out of the confrontation, and Roo tried to get her disappointment in check. "I thought you'd be riding in the Enclaves?" she said. That was the only thing that made sense. Going out of doors anywhere else was more than uncomfortable.

"Oh no." Evangeline pointed at the veils on the lawn. "We had protection! We rode Alexandria and Georgetown and thought about turning toward Annapolis, but no one felt like diving. And–there was a bit of excitement that it seems Mason arranged." Her voice drained away. "But then we looped around near the Skirts and finally to the dustpan!"

The dustpan. The salt flats. A shiver ran down Roo's spine. The dustpan was deadly and completely misnamed. It was an expanse of salt ridges and eroded earth–and here and there, the front windshield or headlight of an old car peeking through. The salt hadn't yet taken everything down to chalk and rime, but it was trying. The winds were doing a fair job, too.

"That's a no-man's land. What if someone saw you?" Getting caught in the dustpan by MilPol was grounds for being shipped away. Immediately.

"We paid our fees to the Recovery Court." Evangeline waved her hand with no concern. She saw Roo's expression and her brow wrinkled. She rushed to explain. "They don't *really* mind as long as we don't leave any trace beyond drone tracks."

The glass of water the maid had given her when they returned from the driveway was still cool. It was gently lit by the setting sun that filtered through the Enclave's drone-dome.

They don't *really mind.* Roo sipped at the water and permitted herself a small frown. "They always minded us."

Evangeline, misinterpreting Roo's expression, patted her shoulder. "You'll get to go with us next time, now that you're properly healed. I am so glad you are feeling better! And that you had the staff make you those smart walking canes!"

Only another day more, Roo promised herself. So that King has a chance. "What fees? Next time?"

"Well, the fees support the city, of course. You'll love it. It's always an archaeological adventure! We find new things every time. Papa has a whole room of artifacts. Would you like to see?"

Roo balked. "I was hoping to talk to Mr. Benford now."

Evangeline smiled. "He *would* love it if you'd call him Sam. I think he was going upstairs, to tuck away his latest find. Come see, then we'll get dressed for dinner."

A glimmer of hope. "Dinner in the city?"

Evangeline brightened. "If you'd like—I can ask the staff to make arrangements? There are several good restaurants. What do you like?"

This was one step closer to King. "I couldn't say." Roo had worked in a pop-up near the apartment in New Washington. She'd helped Nan clean restaurants, sometimes. But eating at one was new.

"Papa will have an idea. Come." Evangeline led her down the main hall, into a library twice the size of Nan's bus. Though Roo wanted to linger, a hidden door opened when Evangeline waved her hand, and they stepped into a smaller elevator and rose into another wing of Centenaire. "Did you not like the chair? I thought it was pretty," Evangeline asked as they rose.

"I wanted to be able to get around faster. I'll need to when I return to Miss Farmer's." Sam Benford had said she'd be allowed to continue her education. That meant Sasha. Making sure she got credit for her wardrobe. Telling her everything that had happened. Sasha would know how to help.

The elevator stopped and the door slid open. Evangeline paused on the threshold, with Roo trapped behind her, still in the elevator. "To Miss Farmer's? Why? Papa's got three tutors coming to interview with you after we return from court tomorrow. Each teaches a different field—data science, obviously a love of yours, astronomy, environmental arts, art history and botany, like me–I chose the list, but we can connect you with more researchers in any field. Why continue–" Her voice dropped as if the walls could hear her, "with something as limited as Miss Farmer's?"

The words felt like a slap. Miss Farmer's had been the best step up from apprenticeships available in the city. It was how she would find employment. She had left her work there. It was where Sasha was. And in Evangeline's world, it was severely lacking.

Outrage tangled with curiosity. "What do you consider limitless?"

Roo couldn't help but think she wasn't the only person who might want to know. Dax might be curious as well. Maybe–though she hated the thought–the feeds would also, if Roo found she needed the credits.

Evangeline thought for a moment, her eyes sparkling. "Science. Philosophy. Botany. Art. All limitless. Even design is limitless–wearables, terraforming, everything."

"That's not what I meant–" Roo had wanted a practical answer. But Evangeline was throwing wide the doors to a dark room where even the shadows seemed to sparkle.

"This is what I mean: Papa's cabinet of wonders," Evangeline said. Her voice had turned tentative. She watched Roo's face, gauging her expression. The lights came on. Beyond the doors, more than a dozen cabinets rose to the ceiling, made of what looked like mahogany and glass.

The wonders–in terms of the room–were unsettling. Skulls. Fragments of magazines, preserved in liquid to keep them from disintegrating further. The open air would have turned them to black mold in an instant. A handbag's vivid red–a color the reclaimed world hadn't managed yet, Roo knew from Sasha, because scientists couldn't reproduce the spider eggs to make the dye. A real airplane engine.

Everything in the room felt heavy and dead.

"Things from the Mess. With no provenance." Roo kept her voice calm.

"The Turbulence, yes, and from before that too. Look—" Evangeline pulled open drawers below the cabinets. "Papa rescued these from Philadelphia, and these from Baltimore—there were museums full of medical curios, maps, animals—this is supposed to be a dodo's egg. Can you believe it?"

Evangeline's delight was as obvious as the horror Roo felt. But something more too: she was knowledgeable about these things. She was a collector—a scientist? "This is definitely not something your feeds know about you."

"Oh." Evangeline quieted. "Please don't tell them. Papa would be furious if they found out. He's so protective. He sends his people in to redact almost everything when they can."

Roo nodded, understanding Sam's reticence even as the thief half of her tabulated the haul from a room like this. She had to stop once she was in the quintillions of credits. *No one had that much money. Did they?*

Then another thought crossed her mind. *Has Evangeline collected a Roosa for herself? Who will she be showing me off to?*

"What's wrong?" Evangeline paused before pulling out another drawer.

Roo felt the rush of falling out of the window again. "Dustpan, drowned, burnt, and salt things. To someone who grew up like I did." She paused, trying not to slip. "In the city. Some would say these are haunted objects." *Nan would say this.*

"I know. We've had scholars and scientists here to do research—it's important to share the discoveries. Like universities used to do. Maybe one day—will do again." Evangeline beamed, misunderstanding Roo. "And that's not all. Sometimes he trades for things from very far away. Imagine."

"Indeed," Roo echoed, softly. Sometimes the past was

worth leaving. Still, she couldn't help wondering "What is it like to grow up in a place where so many lost things mean nothing but curiosity? When we found things"—*when King did, really*—"my Nan would light a candle for whomever had loved it last."

Roo imagined reaching through the glass to hold an object that had touched that part of time, when the world was different.

Evangeline stared at the cases. "I'd never really thought about who—" She grew quiet.

"We keep these items in trust for the future, Renata. So that we can always think about those who came before us." Sam stepped into the room from a large office just beyond the last case. "That's our charge. Our purpose. That's why we are working here, experimenting and testing, to build a better world. Come up one more floor, to the gardens—it was Serena's favorite place." Sam led her to the elevator.

"Shouldn't we be getting ready to go? Isn't your fiancé waiting downstairs?" Though her feet ached from walking, Roo was itching to go to New Washington. A real, living city, with her family in it.

Sam folded his hands. "Ah. Mason was in such a mood. Don't let it trouble you. He's in the garden now, waiting for us."

"We must get past it," Evangeline said. Her face had darkened for a moment, but then she brightened. "We will."

Roo had seen the flicker of doubt. *The "everything" Mason Graves very likely needed to get past is me.* "Upstairs? What about the city?"

"I'm sorry, dear. We need to dine here after all. There is no way I could have security ready, or get the feed-mavens blocked before tomorrow. And there was a legal issue I needed to address. I won't risk you or your sister out there without protections in place." Sam looked sincere in his regret.

Roo knew her disappointment was visible. “I am not hungry.” Her stomach growled, betraying her. Centenaire felt a lot like the precinct. “I need to speak to my friends and family.”

“Papa,” Evangeline said. “We aren’t children. I am not, at least.”

“As of yesterday! Give me a little time to get used to it.” Sam clutched his chest. Then he turned to Roo. “Please have dinner with us. I’ve made tomorrow’s arrangements. You will be added to the green book at lunch, and then we will go see the Canarviers. If you would like to speak to anyone in the meantime, we can get you a tablet.”

A tablet. “Yes, please. Now? I’m afraid I’m too tired for dinner.”

“We’ll have one sent to your room,” Sam said. His disappointment was clear.

Roo didn’t wait. She headed for the elevator and her room. The longer she could put off giving them her answer, the better.

New Washington City Feed

Canarvier Fan Group #3

[Log] Rumored associations and sightings for various Canarviers—[UPDATE: Images redacted. Account deleted.]

[Log] Arrest count from the Graves Grand Heist, includes video and photos.

User 121: Did you zoom in on that shot of the house? Looks like someone crashed through a window until they re-fabbed it.

User 133: But they carried the thief out from inside – so someone else escaped?

User 6: How many Canarviers are there?

User 21: At least four, sometimes more. But everyone brings in specialists and apprentices these days. It's hard to get an exact count.

User 34: There's one MilPol arrest for burglary on the date of the Grand Heist—possibly more? Here's the booking document for the right date and time. Daxian Vane has got to be a Canarvier, folks. That's thief one IDed . . .

[Booking document removed from discussion by moderator.]

User 12: Is Graves really holding one performer against return of goods? I heard that he also caught an Enclaver by mistake? What an enormous error for him, if true.

User 34: I've heard the same about the Enclaver—AND that it was his former business partner. Lot of water over that bridge, I suspect.

User 21: How embarrassing. But is Graves actually holding a performer? Or does someone else have them?

User 12: why do you ask?

[reply removed by feed monitor]

User 6: Who's taking bets as to what their haul was?

User 12: Can't collect on a haul if you lose a heist. Their take is zero.

User 133: *Less* than zero if you count booking fees and supplies. They must be scraping.

[Log] Spotted: vendors using similar products to Canarvier holographic calling card.

[Log] Working group: a room to discuss Canarvier strategies (see also Rockville troupe, Delavay troupe, Potomac troupe) and successful heists. [Deleted, please proceed to other troupe feeds.]

[Log] Known Canarvier heists over the years [incomplete].

The Horse-Trading Gambit

THE STATE-OF-THE-ART TABLET was made of a sleek fabric that could wrap around Roo's wrist or stretch out like a book. When she connected to the city's network, there was no lag. Roo tried contacting Nan first.

But Nancy Vane didn't answer. Roo tried again.

On her third try, the tablet said: "This citizen exceeded their account for the week."

At least the city still considers Nan a citizen, Roo thought. *But exceeding accounts isn't like Nan at all.* She worried as she readied herself for the second call.

When it connected, Sasha narrowed her eyes and whispered, "It's after lights-out! How is your father? Where are you calling from that gets around a non-disturb? Did you get good photos?"

Roo scrunched her nose. "No good photos."

She looked around her room, trying to find a way to describe the situation to Sasha. She couldn't find the words.

Sasha filled in the silence. "Bad luck. Are you finishing your finals at home? Can I come to get the wardrobe?"

The school was only a short drive away, but to Roo, Sasha and Miss Farmer's felt unreachable.

"I can bring it to you. Hopefully tomorrow." Roo steadied her voice so she sounded more certain. She assumed Centenaire security was listening. *Good. Let them.*

Sasha sat up straighter. "Roo, they've packed up your things like you're not coming back. We thought your father died."

Not yet. Not if I can help it. She'd been in tighter spots. Quite recently in fact. "Sasha, I'm coming back, I promise. Can you wait one more day?"

Her friend looked concerned. "I can try. I'll have little time to alter anything, but I must make some changes. The Graves party is infamous now–and everyone's talking about the person who tried to impersonate Elizabeth Greene. A child of the Benfords' former inner circle, Roo! If my dress is connected, that will cause an enormous stir here."

"I am so sorry." Early on, Roo had suspected her truths–being from the Skirts, the tales of her mother–would drive Sasha and everyone else at Miss Farmer's far away. But this was much worse. "I assume you'll disavow me once it's known I took liberties with someone else's name."

"Assume differently," Sasha chuckled. "It's fascinating."

Fascinating. Roo felt, for a moment, like her old self again. She met Sasha's gaze and held it. "I promise I'll come tomorrow, as soon as I can."

Sasha smiled, her face fading into darkness. "I can't wait to see you."

When she closed the call, the screen went blank. Roo

had no one else to speak with, and no interest in seeing what the feeds were saying.

The remains of Sasha's dress hung like an accusation on the chair.

Roo lifted the wardrobe in her arms. *If I can use the fabricators to mimic the cloth, maybe I can mend the stitching and programming. At least enough to be useful.*

The dress was heavy. There was still a lot of cloth left. But it didn't reconfigure when she asked it to.

Sasha had said it needed to charge. That must be part of the problem. She would mend it tonight and find somewhere sunny to charge it in the morning, while they were in the city. Then she'd bring it back to Sasha.

It felt good to have a plan. Roo opened her bedroom door.

Outside, a maid napped on a chair. She startled awake when Roo came out.

"Miss, may I get you dinner? Mr. Benford said you felt tired."

"I'd like to use the fabricators," Roo began, then paused. Her knowledge of the fab room would get another maid in trouble. "If there are any available?"

The woman held out her hands. "Give that here. I can have it mended. Or we can have more designed in a day, as Miss Evangeline does."

Roo clutched the wardrobe close. She imagined Sasha's expression at seeing a botched repair on the cloth. That she was even considering amending Sasha's design to fix it was bad enough. To let someone else try would be worse. "Thank you. I'm so used to doing things myself. If you would just point the way?"

"I'm afraid I cannot." The maid's voice shifted from friendly to firm. "Mr. Benford suggested you rest until we leave tomorrow. Would you like something to help? A sleeper?"

"Just some tea, please." Roo needed a minute alone.

If she sent the maid on an errand, she could get to the fabricator.

The maid smiled and subvocaled the house, the same way Holt had done at Llyria. "It will be right down. Kitchen's been alerted."

When the tea arrived, a steaming porcelain cup on a tasteful tray, the maid waited until Roo had finished it. After she removed the service, Roo realized she was exhausted.

The dress would need to wait until morning.

When Roo woke, the tree outside her window cast a shadow across the floor. It was well past ten.

She startled upright, angry that she'd overslept. *There'd been something in the tea. Or the maid misunderstood me when I'd asked for that instead of a sleeping patch. I will need to be more specific.*

The medic's privacy screen closed as soon as she sat up, and the maid knocked at her door.

Or, she reconsidered, *this maid is a guard, and I might as well be at the precinct.*

Her bargain with Sam hinged on this afternoon. Her arm and leg felt much better. Her head as well. She would need to give the Benfords an answer about spending more time with them, and the current situation made *No* nearly definite. But that could wait until after she'd made sure Dax was safe and she'd seen King.

Roo slid from the bed. A pair of blue slacks and a teal blouse lay across the chair. Similar colors to Evangeline's Grand Heist gown, in bamboo silk. Not anything close to Sasha's smart fabric.

She looked under the slacks, and in the closet behind the chair. Then under the bed. *Where was Sasha's wardrobe?* There was nothing. Just the blue silk.

She had to get the dress back and take it to Miss Farmer's. This afternoon. She'd promised.

Roo was still holding the clothes aloft when Evangeline bustled in, the medic behind her.

"You're not changed. We can't be late. Court building airspace will take some time to navigate. Papa's personal physic will make sure you're safe to fly." Evangeline's face glowed with a light sparkle of powder and a soft lavender lip cream. A gold bead sat at the corner of each eyelid.

The medic looked over Roo's injuries and checked her eyes. "She's stable. No concussion. Just the ankle needs to be braced for a few days longer." She held out a revitalization patch. Roo shook her head. "No more of whatever that is."

"It's ginger and nutrients." The medic was patient. "Some caffeine. So you can be at your best."

Roo refused. Her grip on the fabric grew tighter. "You ran tests on me. Took my blood. Gave me a sleeping tea last night."

"You indicated you wanted a tea, not a patch." The medic switched off the light she'd shone in Roo's eyes. "And we wouldn't take blood without your consent. But you left enough strewn around when we stitched you up after your incident with Llyria's window. I sent that to our labs. It's not an official match, that's for the Recovery Court to report. But I'm glad Benford's finally got his spare. That will make everyone happier."

"Everyone?" Roo said, not following.

The medic cleared her throat and left.

"Don't let her worry you!" Evangeline lifted the outfit from Roo's hands and smoothed out the creases. "We'll get going, take care of a small legal matter, and then enter you in the green book." She was practically singing.

"What small legal matter?" Roo accepted the top back. Then the pants. "Graves filed charges?"

"Oh, no. It's only the Greenes. They're furious you

stole their daughter's identity. Impinged her reputation. Nothing to worry about. They're always mad. We've got it all in hand." Evangeline picked nonexistent lint off the silk.

Roo reddened. She'd been performing, but libel? She doubted it was in the Grand Heist's contract protections. "What happened?"

"A guest expressed surprise to them that Elizabeth Greene had attended our party—I'm guessing Dodo or Pucky—because Papa and the Greenes haven't spoken officially in years. We invite them, and they do not attend. It's a bit of a game." Evangeline shrugged. "Then, when they heard Graves was holding a female thief against return of goods, they did more digging, filed charges with MilPol, and demanded you be turned over. We're negotiating reparations, which is why we moved up the court visit. If you were to go out in the world unescorted, before they accepted? Zoom, off to Alaska with you." She chuckled. "I'm kidding. They probably would just sue you some more and send you home. But don't worry, Papa's taking care of them and the rumors. It will be fixed soon."

Doubtful. "Do you know anyone who has ever just been sent home?" Roo certainly didn't.

"Lots. Kids get into trouble in the city often. Not me, Papa wouldn't have it. But my friend Valencia got a slap on the wrist for a stupid escapade last month and they let her off after her father took away her roofhopter. What a mess."

Hardly a mess. Roo folded her temper into a small, neat square in her mind. "What's it like, to be able to get out of trouble as easy as that?"

"Well, it's expensive! That's not all that nice," Evangeline winked.

Roo chose her next words carefully. "Where is the outfit I was wearing when you . . . found me?"

"We put it in the garbage. The fabric was interesting. But very dirty and torn. We'll get you something new."

That was too much. "I want it back. It was borrowed."

She couldn't lose her temper if she wanted to see King. And she desperately wanted to see him. He would make everything make sense. And then she'd see Sasha. *With* the wardrobe in hand.

Evangeline nodded. "I'll see what I can do. Come on, we must hustle. Papa's waiting. And Aunt Min. I guessed your sizes with this outfit; we'll get you everything you need in the city after today."

Aunt Min. Minerva Benford. The white-haired judge from the party. "Why is she waiting?"

"She'll verify you on the courthouse's secure connection to the green book, after the other judges give you their official stamp. All must be carefully done and documented, since ours is the only wide-network connection between protected cities and particular offshore Enclaves. After that, she'll approve Mason's offer, once she and Papa agree." A knock at the door distracted Evangeline.

"Aesthetics." She waved a young man in, as if this was her room, not Roo's.

The aesthetician frowned at Roo. "Fast or subtle?"

"Fast," Roo said, pulling on the pants. She was going to get through this day, then get what she needed from the Benfords. Whatever it took. She set the information about the green book and a broader connection than a city feed aside to think about later. Even at Miss Farmer's she'd never heard of such a thing.

"Something classic," Evangeline agreed.

Ten minutes later, Roo's brown curls were pulled into a chignon. Her eyes and lips were lightly detailed with what Evangeline called "city chic:" a gold waterline, gold dust across her cheekbone and collarbones. Her brows ached from a fast shaping. She barely recognized herself.

They finished and Evangeline rushed her through the halls and into the elevator, which lifted silently. The gilded doors opened onto a Victorian garden, filled with scent: lavender and roses. Roo was so startled she had to pause to catch her breath.

"Our mother's favorite place. I like to care for it myself, when I have time." Evangeline beamed. "You can come here whenever you like."

The garden spanned much of Centenaire. A low hedge maze filled the center, and benches and pots of well-tended plants lined the high stone walls.

In one direction lay the wetlands and the ocean sparkling beyond the seawall. Overhead, the sky looked blue, the clouds white, but that was partly the Enclave dome's effect—a series of ever-shifting micro-drones and static barriers that not only kept the dust out and managed the weather, but filtered the light too. The sky in the city still had a yellow tint. If Roo stared close enough from this height, she could see the shimmer of the dome as the Enclave's drones shifted to accommodate and filter the wind.

In the other direction from the ocean were more Enclave estates. Broad green stretches of lawn, trees, rooflines, and wide windows. *How many houses? Thirty? Each safe beneath the dome, everyone who wanted to be outside, breathing clean, filtered air.* The dome's shimmer caught the sun and Roo could see where the green ended and the bumpy road began.

"I miss her, very much," Evangeline said. "Though I barely remember her."

"Me too," Roo agreed. She stared at the horizon, blinking. She was used to controlling and concealing her emotions for an audience, but Evangeline's honesty threw her off. Sadness made the skyline wobble as if she were back in the city. But this time, it wasn't the heat; the dome gentled the sun's glare.

Evangeline took her elbow. "You all right?"

Roo nodded, but then she spotted the roofhopter, parked a few meters away on the roof, and felt her knees buckle. Dax had long wanted to ride in one, just once.

As they approached it, she slowed and looked back at the maze. Her mother had walked here. She tried to remember each detail, as she didn't want to see it again, after today. Her family was more important.

Evangeline climbed into the sleek black vehicle, behind the pilot. "We're going to be late!" When Roo boarded, Evangeline secured their seats by pulling a bar down from the roof.

Then the roofhopter rose and turned faster and more gracefully than Roo had ever managed on the silks. She screeched and clung to her seat. Evangeline, beside her, seemed unaffected. She pointed out the window. "Look, the city—and the sea!"

The pilot replied, reciting:

There is a pleasure in the pathless woods,
There is a rapture on the lonely shore,
There is society where none intrudes
By the deep sea, and music in its roar:

When Roo turned from the scene out the window toward the front seats, blinking in confusion, Evangeline chuckled. "Papa loves poetry."

King does too. Roo's heart clenched at the thought of him reading poetry while the sunset cooled the Skirts.

A broad blue cataract opened beyond the seawall. On the horizon, another dome glittered—a distant, floating estate.

Evangeline finished the pilot's verse:

I love not man the less, but nature more,
From these our interviews, in which I steal
From all I may be, or have been before
To mingle with the universe, and feel
What I can ne'er express, yet cannot all conceal.

The pilot joined in the next line, so the two said in tandem, "Roll on, thou deep and dark blue Ocean—roll!" And Evangeline beamed.

Roo smiled awkwardly. Even with all the verses King had recited to them, she didn't know this one. She made a guess. "Was that Byron?"

King had hated the man and every word he'd written, and didn't shy from letting people know it.

"Yes–Lord Byron is a favorite." The pilot turned and smiled. Sam Benford was flying his own plane. "It's something, isn't it," he said, without specifying whether he meant the poem or the ocean. He shook his hands as if to relieve tension.

"You fly your own roofhopter?" Roo had assumed there would be more staff. But Sam did this–*if I stayed, might he teach me?* She dismissed the thought as soon as it tempted her.

"Have since I was your age." Sam began pointing out city landmarks, as if she was visiting from another city. "Having a chip makes it simple. Though this one's giving me a bit of trouble lately. Look–there's the seawall. And Public Works. We've made so much progress."

"Trouble?" Evangeline looked at her own hand. "The chips are supposed to be more reliable than most protected cities' networks."

At the same time, Roo rebelled against Sam saying 'progress.' "The city still doesn't have clean air. Just the Enclaves." She couldn't help it. Evangeline seemed too worried about the chips to pay her notice.

Roo had tried to research the chips and local networks at Miss Farmer's. It hadn't been easy. The latter were easier to secure, and harder to take down than the old, interconnected world-grid. The former kept green-booked families and founders connected wherever they were–to their accounts, their equipment, and, with the right protocols at locations like the courthouse, Roo was beginning to understand, to a much larger community. Too much thinking about the chips had earned her teacher's censure, but that connection was tempting–Sasha certainly thought so.

"It's nothing to fret about. Holt's looking into it," Sam

said, guiding the hopter into the landing pattern for the courthouse.

Roo wondered at what a malfunctioning chip might mean. *Could they be tampered with? Another reason to avoid getting chipped.*

She let her eyes drift the skyline until she found what looked like the Vanes' shared apartment. Where Nan was. It was too far to be sure. *Just get through this day. Talk to King. Find the dress. Go home.*

By the time they landed atop the courthouse, it was noon.

Mason waited uncomfortably with Minerva in the courthouse atrium as the Benford's roofhopter reversed its small thrust array and began to land. The courthouse's old stone walls muffled landing noise, but the wave of dust across the fabbed-glass dome signaled an imminent arrival.

Evangeline had broken the wonderful news at dinner that the first green-book induction meeting had been moved up. "So soon!" Mason said, trying to mediate his excitement.

"The process takes time. Best get things moving." Sam had said, distractedly. He held a grievance that had arrived by courier after the hunt. A courier—with a printed document, no less—meant an entity outside of New Washington.

After a long pause, Sam folded the paper, then folded it again, drawing his fingers against the edge to create a sharp crease. "This should be quickly cleared up. We'll address it at court tomorrow."

Mason was happy it was Sam's concern, not his. He had his hands full reassuring Evangeline about the attack.

She glanced at him over their meal, and worried at the scrape on his cheek. "We will double security from now on."

"It wasn't anything, Ev. Even Stonecliff agreed, and we don't agree on much."

Her concern woke his memory of the mer rising from the water. *The creditors—could they know I've lost the ring? The ampoules?* The credit issue wouldn't be a problem, very soon, unless the creditors got there first. He waved it off. *Soon,* he knew, *I'll be able to wave for anything I want.* "It was a lark. A joke. Perhaps, after court, you'll join me at the lab? I would like to show you something much more exciting."

His offer was to both Benfords, but Sam demurred. "I have another meeting in town."

Evangeline flipped through her salad with a delicate fork. "I missed the last visit. I'd love to see what you're working on."

He beamed. "Science. The world-changing kind."

"Perhaps science made of carbon, compressed by centuries," Sam joked dryly.

Mason coughed, inhaling his drink, but he recovered. He would find the ring soon.

"Papa!" Evangeline's blush had been so pretty, with the sun shading the dome oranges and pinks.

And now the hopter was landing, the blades scattering bits of paper across the roof and the atrium's own domed gallery. The hall where he waited was lined with paintings from the previous Recovery Court, hundreds of years prior. Those judges had brought London through its first terrible fire.

The new judges were doing the same, both in New Washington and in other protected cities around the reclaimed world.

The Fire Judges' clothing and appearances were so different from modern judges. One nearby portrait showed a man draped in furs and pearls. *Someone had obviously enriched himself while righting the community. Luckily that didn't happen here.*

Judge Benford, and others like her, Mason knew, were inviolate. They even avoided having children to maintain their status. It was an honor to stand beside her, even when she was in a mood.

Minerva's mouth pursed like a teapot spout. She'd greeted him with a raised eyebrow. He'd shaken his head. No, he hadn't found the ring. She had not said a word to him since. Mason focused on the paintings to distract himself.

Then the Benfords were in the hall, with a flurry of civil servants all around them. Sam signed several documents and bowed to his sister, while Evangeline came to greet Mason.

He reached out to take her hand. It felt like a feather in his palm. He rubbed her fingers with his thumb. She seemed nervous. Why?

The answer became apparent when the thief emerged out of the flurry. Mason gaped, then tried to compose himself. It had been charitable to heal the thief. Reflecting well on the family. To bring her everywhere like a pet was something else entirely.

"Shouldn't she be in a precinct hold?" he asked Evangeline quietly. *Or on the moon?*

"We need her to be here. Please follow my lead," she cautioned.

Judge Benford cleared her throat, waved all of them through to her office, and sat behind a large desk. "The process of adding members to the family rolls is often a glorious occasion."

She didn't sound like she thought it was glorious today. She sounded like she had indigestion.

Mason spared another look at the thief. At her posh hairstyle and sleek outfit. "I don't understand why she's here," he finally said. Evangeline bit her lip.

With more gusto than was considered polite, Sam said, "My daughter has every right to be present." He stared at his sister, pointedly.

Mason swallowed. Time, scientifically, couldn't speed up or down based on heartbeats. A single beat crossed the same arc of time in seventeenth-century London, or twenty-second century New Washington. Even stopped hearts, like Mason's own, at that moment in the center of the courthouse, eventually started again.

Daughter. "I didn't mean Evangeline, of course—" Mason fought to right things with his future father-in-law. Evangeline patted his hand, but she looked so tense. *What was happening?*

A stenographer entered the office and closed the door. They began taking notes when Minerva spoke.

"Although happy, this is rather unusual," Minerva said. "I have been made aware of"—she gestured at the thief—"new developments in the family history, irregularities in identity, and a charge of libel. Identities, not to put too fine a point on it."

Mason stared at the desk, rather than risking a glance at Evangeline. *What does this have to do with the green-book induction? Or me?*

"My brother has also become more wary of the irregularities in your history, Mr. Graves," Minerva added. Mason felt as if the floor was breaking beneath him. "And now we are all here."

"Horse-trading," Sam said. He clapped his hands together, rubbing them with gusto. "Let's get to it."

Horse-trading? Mason tried to think of why anyone would want to trade a horse.

The thief protested, "I am not a horse." She looked as shocked as Mason felt.

Nor am I, Mason agreed. But he didn't say as much. He'd promised to compose himself. This must be about the ring. He could explain.

One cold look from Minerva froze the words in his mouth. "Nevertheless. Before I can begin your interviews, the family must agree that both of you deserve to be here. Mason Graves, do tell us who you really are."

Mason nearly stopped breathing, until Evangeline squeezed his fingers. "Go on."

Did she know the truth? "I am Mason Graves," he began. "Of Denver."

"And were you educated in the way that you told your investors, your fiancée, and before that, myself, apprenticing at both the Bohr Clinic and the Bergen Institute?"

Mason paled. Minerva knew this. She'd suggested he get those bona fides. *Why is she doing this, here, in front of Sam and Evangeline? She knows I can't lie in court, in front of her.* "I did not. I paid those scientists for their support." He closed his eyes. "I am self-taught, in most everything."

Everything he'd dreamed, derailed, because of a tug-of-war happening between Minerva and Sam that he didn't understand. All being recorded. *I will only tell them as much as I am forced to. I hope Evangeline will let the engagement stand. I hope Sam will as well.*

But instead of leaving, Evangeline beamed. "You are brilliant, to have done all of this on your own."

He held her gaze, as it was easier than looking at Minerva. "No one in the Enclaves would accept me without those bona fides." Nor would his creditors. "By the time I'd made my first fortune, I didn't think it mattered anymore."

All his cards were on the table now. Mostly. Mason's temples throbbed.

Minerva folded her hands on the desk. "There, brother. Your turn."

Sam smiled at the thief, who stared straight ahead, frozen in her chair. "This is Renata Benford, my daughter. Also known as Roosala Vane, Roosa Canarvier, and Ro Villon. She has been raised in the Skirts, unbeknownst to the family, by a man named Kenneth Vane, aka King Canarvier, who listed her as an apprentice."

Mason couldn't believe what he was hearing. Evangeline squeezed his hand tighter.

"And her profession?" Minerva's brows couldn't become any more pinched.

Sam chuckled. "She is a thief. And an acrobat. And a fine hacker."

The judge's frown deepened. "Those are a great many

vices. They bring chaos, not order. Society needs order. And there is one more alias, is there not?" Minerva steepled her fingers. "Which is why we are here. There has been a libel grievance filed."

Sam held out both hands as if this happened every day. "She stole the identity of a member of society. Elizabeth Greene, of Atlantic Enclave."

"Which is a high crime. Do you understand that, Renata?" Minerva's tone was far different than Sam's had been about that issue.

The thief blanched. "I understand that crimes rank higher or lower, depending on who you are. And please call me Roo."

Mason couldn't believe the cheek.

Minerva didn't seem swayed either. Under her breath, she muttered, "If you are not Serena's daughter, you are doing an excellent impression."

The stenographer didn't record that.

The judge raised her voice again. "These admissions have been entered with your names into the family's private records, provisionally," Minerva said. "Upon verifying that you are who you say you are, Miss Vane, and upon producing the mysterious ring you claim to have procured for my niece, Mr. Graves, we will clear each of your files and your applications will proceed to full family membership in society. Until then." Minerva swept her hands out as if she was weighing two very heavy objects. "Do you understand?"

Despite his confusion about Minerva's denial of the ring's provenance, Mason's heart felt incredibly full. He still had a chance. "I do."

The air smelled of flowers as Evangeline released his hand. "You did well."

His fingers tingled.

Minerva inclined her chin to say that she agreed. *I passed a test, I think.* Mason wondered how many more tests there would be among the Benfords.

The judge turned to the stenographer. "Please tell the Greenes that the court has approved restitution for their injury. Sam Benford will provide it. Do you understand the implications, Miss Vane?"

The thief doesn't look like she understands. The Benfords are taking full, legal responsibility for her. How unfairly lucky she is.

Mason still couldn't fully believe that Evangeline might have a sister. That everyone else in the room seemed ready to do so shocked him. *I know how much Evangeline mourns her mother. That she might have a sister must be so tempting. Even if it is someone who, until two days ago, was robbing my house. But she'd fought for me too.*

He stared at his fiancé. "Did you just bargain for me?"

Evangeline tilted her head. Her eyes danced, as her father winced. "Maybe a little."

He owed her everything. He caught himself wondering if that was something she'd considered. "You could have told me. Do the feeds know already? What will we tell them?"

"I hinted at it, last night. As best I could." She gestured to him to calm down. "Papa is taking care of the feeds for now."

The thief was arguing with Sam, apparently more unhappy than Sam. She wore a necklace identical to Evangeline's. *She looks nothing like my fiancée. Maybe a bit around the eyes, but is that worth a whole inheritance? She's shorter and her manners are terrible and did she just curse? Here? I have to keep my composure. I must stay polite.*

He failed. "Did you consider that she might be lying?"

Evangeline frowned at him. "Mason. No." She turned toward the thief, following as the stenographer and Minerva shepherded her into a corner of the office.

Mason was having a hard time keeping his temper. Until Sam returned with a contract rolled out on a tablet. "While Renata's being certified, we can begin to sort this other business, if you like. Benford Holdings and Graves Biosecurity. Take a look at these. I'll return shortly."

The acquisitions documents. Sam was accepting him. That smoothed the way, a little.

"A libel accusation? That was the legal matter?" Roo turned on Evangeline the moment she and the stenographer left their chairs. Minerva opened the office doors for a medic.

"We didn't want you to worry," Evangeline said. "You were gravely injured. And the Greenes are furious. You verified her name at the masque. They made a big fuss because they're always looking for ways to better Papa. But soon it will be sorted." She gestured Roo toward the medic. He held out his hand for Roo's arm.

Roo didn't move. "What if I refuse?"

Evangeline quieted. "We will lose standing and money. The charges will convert to crimes. You, your brother, and Mr. Vane will all go away for a very long time, on an array of vices."

That's no way to treat family, Roo thought. She held out her arm. "And what if your medic was wrong?"

Evangeline didn't reply. Sam joined them as the medic pushed microneedles deep into the inside of Roo's arm. *Ow.*

"The green book requires more thorough sampling than accidental spillage," the medic said. "Especially in unusual circumstances. Bone marrow." A light went on in the sampler. "Now you both."

Evangeline and Sam proffered their arms, sleeves already rolled up. "I don't understand what you see in Graves, when there are other suitable matches," Sam said.

"Independence." Evangeline smiled. "And creativity. Aunt Minerva thought I would work well with someone who was brilliant, but didn't have the same experience in society." She winced as the needles struck.

Sam coughed. "She has always looked out for you, and

the family, in her own particular way." He didn't blink when the sample was taken. "Soon we'll know for sure."

Despite her intentions to leave immediately after this, Roo heard the hope and desperation in Sam's voice. *If I lost a child, then thought I found her, I'd feel the same.*

"I regret," she told him, "all this trouble." There was so much about Sam that reminded her of King.

"Verified," said the medic.

"Not trouble, not at all." Sam embraced her. "Renata. I knew it in my bones."

The chair Roo sat seemed to tremble. *No. It's me, shaking. This is real.* "What did King do?"

"A word, Sam?" The judge frowned. She attempted to pull Sam into the hall, but her brother balked. He took a slim box from his jacket pocket and stared at it, brow wrinkled.

"Stonecliff asked me to return your citizen band from the robbery to you. I expect you wiped its data remotely after the attack, but you should have let someone here run a check. We had to recalibrate security at the house. Some tech still isn't working right." Sam lifted his gaze to the judge. "So, Minerva, if there's anything else you'd like to tell me, you can say it in front of my daughters. Your nieces. It's safer when the whole family is informed, wouldn't you say?"

"Ah. I'd been hoping to get that back. Sentimental–my first band after the Judgeship took my chip. Thank you." The judge sucked her teeth. She seemed shaken by the reminder of the attack. "And I am happy for you."

"For us all," Sam reminded her. He reached and arm toward each daughter.

"It's only–" Minerva took in Roo's appearance from head to toe for the first time. Roo shifted uncomfortably. "She's been in the wild, as it were, for her entire life, Sam."

The judge blinked when her brother flushed with anger. But she pressed on, this time speaking directly to Roo. "We don't know what you've been taught or who by.

Serena had her own beliefs, ones that got her killed. And your half-brother is pure chaos. This family lost much in the Turbulence. We are building it back. We cannot be associated with chaos."

"And your interests? You still believe that you can control Graves's? Really, Minerva, that's enough," Sam growled. "I will deal with the founders. They will see reason. You handle Graves. We have made a deal. This is family."

"What are you proposing, Aunt Min?" Evangeline asked. She gestured for Mason to join them.

"A series of thresholds. A public presentation, quickly, before the feeds can make a stir." As Minerva spoke, Roo felt a cage closing around her.

"At the next Trust meeting," Evangeline agreed. "A coming-out. We can send word today."

"I would prefer not to," Roo said. No one listened.

"I can manage the feeds," Sam said confidently. "We've been doing it for years."

Minerva shook her head. "Sam, I keep telling you. The feeds are becoming like water. They'll find a way around any blockade, eventually. This sort of thing is what they thrive on. We will announce an early Enclave family Trust meeting for Wednesday. And she will need a chip. Immediately."

"No." Roo spoke fast. Her clothing felt too tight. The room, too hot.

Minerva drew herself up straight. "No?"

Evangeline tried to intervene, but Minerva, incensed, spoke even louder. "This family's work is too important, young lady. How else will we know we can trust you to act in our best interests? Serena was an agitator long before she was removed from the Enclaves by those—people."

Roo ground her teeth. "You seem to have decided already. So have I. No chip."

The older woman stared at Roo, willing her to back down. Roo stared back.

All was silent as the medic cleaned up his gear, and office staff bustled outside. A second judge entered with the official documents and the dedicated green book network.

Mason Graves interrupted. "If I may? Roosa is an adult. A–citizen–and capable of making her own decisions. If she won't consent to a chip, what if she agrees to remain under your supervision until such time as we know more about who she really is?"

Roo was stunned. *Mason Graves coming to my assistance?* Evangeline looked surprised as well.

Minerva loomed over the three of them, her jaw moving soundlessly. She composed herself and lifted her chin towards Mason. "That is a good idea. Do you agree Miss–Benford?"

Roo pressed her lips together. She'd delayed their demands for a chip. That was something. And King was still safe. She wanted to speak to him more than ever. But she did not trust Graves for a moment.

Hopefully Sasha could wait until tomorrow. Her friend's face, fallen in disappointment, failing her finals, flashed through her mind. Then King's and Dax's figures–turning away from her–toward a terrible and far away future.

I have to make a choice. This is the only way forward, for now.

New Washington City Feed

Found Footage Group
(Citizen Verified Subscription Required)

Subscriber 77897: I found more video from the same location—old Enclave security tapes—about thirty minutes after the previous footage:

House Feed Video Surveillance, Samuel and Serena Benford Residence, New Washington Enclaves pre-market [date redacted]

Redacted from public records, per Chipped Citizen Request.
Camera #45 shows Benford's vehicle landing on the lawn. Someone his size/description runs to the house. He speaks briefly with someone off camera: "No, leave MilPol out of this. We can't have this kind of thing happen here. We'll take care of it ourselves."

Subscriber 77897: This is proof they covered it up! Serena Benford was kidnapped and they covered it up lu sell Enclave shares
Subscriber 8765: or to try and protect her. MilPol wasn't exactly kinder and gentler twenty years ago. Did you see that they took several people with them to the court building today? They're discussing it on a Benford Fan Feed—someone I know follows it—Graves and someone else, who'd been at the weekend party where Graves proposed.
Subscriber 9982: do you think there's more fo—

[group closed and deleted. Participants cautioned they have invaded private property]

The Investor Attack

THE COURTHOUSE ROOF deck held one MilPol transport and several private vehicles. A visibly new hopter's platinum-tinted frame reflected Mason's still-shocked expression. With his status in question until he could produce the ring, he was out an unspeakable sum for the transport. Which he did not have.

That, plus the possibility of a new Benford heir, had Mason in a tailspin. *At least I stalled the thief's chipping, even if I can't keep her out of the green book.*

The only thing he had going for him now was the variant formula. He focused on that, to keep Evangeline from seeing how worried he was. He'd promised Sam he'd mind his temper. He handed Evangeline into the aircraft, looking forward to spending some time alone with her. "Ready?"

"I hope you won't mind if I join you?" Minerva's voice behind him made Mason jump.

"Of course not!" Evangeline reached out to her aunt, as the roofhopter extruded another seat. Holt, piloting, hadn't asked Mason. Not that it mattered.

"Of course," he echoed, taking his seat. "Shall we drop you at your townhouse?"

"I thought I'd swing by the labs with you," the judge said. She arched an eyebrow. "See how your research is going. My associates said you were testing new Safeware formulas."

Mason's headache from the meeting increased. "I'd be delighted to show you." He was not delighted. *We have a missing formula. Unexpected results. And Dr. Tsalta is running secret experiments for me. Taking a Recovery Court judge to the lab is the worst idea.* "Holt, let the lab know Judge Benford is accompanying us." That would give Dr. Tsalta some warning.

The hopter lifted into the air. Mason watched the city drop away. They turned from the water, toward the vertical farms and, beyond them, Public Works. New Washington wasn't enormous, even by post-Turbulence standards. A few minutes flight and they neared the lab.

"Perhaps we should have *E&T* do a feed on your new hopter," Evangeline said. She looked lovely in the custom-fabbed seat, printed with extinct bird feathers in blues and blacks. "I do hope we are able to recover more birds soon."

"If you think a feed post would help my status?" Should he have gone with flowers instead? Evangeline's botanical hobby was extensive. The greenhouses at Centenaire—he hadn't thought about it enough. He would change the design.

"I don't think it could hurt. They are curious about you. Silencing curiosity only makes it worse." She smiled at her aunt. "Despite what Papa thinks. What if we give the feed what it wants?"

"You'll have to argue that with your father, but do be careful," Minerva said. The roofhopter cabin rattled as the pilot dodged some weather. "The feeds will always want more. They crave a show; a disturbance is even better. That's a trap."

Speaking of traps. Mason had to ask, "Will there be adjustments to your inheritance with a new sibling? Will she get a stake in the business?"

Minerva's face clouded. Mason regretted his words. Of course, when Sam came into his majority, Minerva had stepped back from family business, and away from society. That had to sting a little, even now. Even when she wielded significant power, it wasn't the same as Sam's.

Evangeline put a hand on his arm, coming to his rescue. "Don't be crude. I expect everything will become much smoother now." Her smile had an edge to it. He'd seen her deploy that smile when she was negotiating with designers. "Especially with your technology to help."

Minerva watched the lab roof grow larger. "It *is* convenient that Sam has fought so hard for her. You'll have more security. More options."

It all dropped into place. Evangeline may have found her lost sister, but Mason hadn't given much thought to why she'd want a sister. Until now.

Mason's headache evaporated. His smile grew to match his fiancée's. "What a gem you are." They wouldn't need to make a safe unless they wanted to. Evangeline would be bringing one to the marriage with her, whether the thief liked it or not.

"I'm hoping we can avoid the Safeware. It's an honor to be a Benford. She will come around." Evangeline squeezed his arm.

"She's a thief, Evangeline. She may not agree to this. We'll start the dosing. Then you'll have one less thing to worry about." He hesitated, eyeing Minerva. Had he gone too far?

But his mentor smiled approvingly. "It's all right,

Mason. I saw the promise in your work when you applied for the founders' award. Even when few others did. I trust your approach. An excellent way to limit the girl's chaos, even if Sam is being way too soft with her. He's still not gotten over Serena."

Evangeline looked hard out the window. They were nearing the roof, which shimmered strangely. "What is that?"

Mason stared, not believing his eyes. Someone had put a filter dome over his lab. "Holt. Report."

"I see it. The city channel is signaling." He broadcast the channel to the hopter's cabin.

A cheerful voice filled the space. "Graves Biosecurity, its lab, contents, and employees have been repossessed. You are not to approach, except with a bonded creditor, until the Graves accounts are settled."

Evangeline looked appalled. "Mason, what accounts? What creditor?"

Minerva's expression was harder to read.

Damn. Should he have signed Benford's acquisition offer immediately, instead of asking for time to review? He thought he'd have more leeway. "Holt, ask the city on whose orders they're operating." He'd get to the bottom of this.

But Holt never had the chance to ask. Because Minerva's eyes sparkled as she said, "Mine."

The courthouse extended a fabricated walkway toward the precinct so that Sam Benford wouldn't need to risk the street. While the material hardened, Roo waited nervously next to one of the ancient portraits. She'd learned all about the Fire Judges on the feeds—they were a model for the protected cities. But she hadn't noticed before how self-satisfied each of them looked.

"They did what was best for the world," Sam murmured.

The familiar feed motto. "And so will we." Masked office staff jostled past them as he stepped onto the walkway.

The smell was strong: carbon fab, the basic building block of the Recovery. She looked down through the thin separation between her feet and the air. New Washington's streets and canals were busy with traffic: basic fab supplies arriving, pedestrians in outdoor masks and goggles returning to work through building airlocks. Lunch pop-ups clustered near the new Dutton air-filters.

In the distance, the entertainment district pulsed with music, raising dust in waves over the area. A small flock of roofhopters circled overhead, waiting to land.

How many times have I walked below, feeling invisible in my mask, in this city. Never thinking someone might be walking overhead.

The precinct's sounds and smells soon overwhelmed Roo's senses. There were few places in the city like it. Too many people clustered together. MilPol drones coming and going. Sam tensed.

"You don't come here much." Roo wasn't asking.

"Hardly ever." Sam held a silk handkerchief to his nose.

"Perhaps you should." Roo walked faster, though her ankle throbbed.

When they reached the far end, a desk glowed before a low wall. Roo had never seen anything in the precinct glow before. Sam tapped his fingers against the top, letting his palm graze the surface. With a sweeping noise, the barricades withdrew. A human officer rushed into the hallway. "We were expecting you, Mr. Benford."

How pleasant everything is, Roo mused. *With enough money and influence.*

Sam barely nodded at the officer. "The Vanes, please."

"Which Vanes? There are several here." The guard paged through a list on his palm.

"Daxian and Kenneth Vane," Roo said. Were they both still here?

The guard tapped two names aglow. "One contract hold for burglary, one for transport."

Roo's head bowed in relief. *Not in Alaska. Sam had kept that promise.*

Sam looked concerned. "You've barely recovered, and it has been a long day already. Perhaps we should do this another time." He reached for her elbow, as if to guide her away.

Roo pulled her arms close. "They're having a much longer day in the hold. And this situation's left my Nan in dire straits. Dax could help her if he was free."

"Your Nan was helpful in returning items, and has been working for the city for a long time. I will see what I can do," Sam said. "However, you should know that she was aware of your past circumstances. Stonecliff's investigations show she knew the truth all along."

Roo swallowed. *Nan too?* All the times she'd cried on her grandmother's shoulder. Her bus where she'd learned to read, surrounded by books and family. *I need to know why they did this. There must be a reason.* "Can we see them now?"

Sam hesitated before waving his palm over the desk again. Roo realized substantial credits were being transferred when the desk glowed green.

The guard waved them forward, into an elevator that descended into the city's depths. They reached a holding floor, much finer than any Roo had seen on her visits to the precinct. An upholstered bench with a small table anchored the room, a foot from the door. The table held a cold glass of real water. Roo's mouth had never felt so dry.

Sam stopped outside the door. "I do not wish to interrupt. I will wait here."

As she sipped the water, a wall changed opacity, revealing Dax and King.

"You're all right." King took a step forward. He touched the barrier and snapped his hand back as if it hurt.

She stared at him. *Am I all right?* Years of treasured

memories had gained newly sharp edges. *All those stories you told, the history you made us learn. But you kept my past from me the whole time.* And yet, she still cared about him. How could both be true? Anger and confusion roiled her stomach. *What do I say to you? What will you say back?*

She stalled her reply to him by turning to her brother. "Are you all right, Dax?"

Dax didn't meet her gaze. He stared at her new clothes, at the shadow of Sam Benford just outside. "If you're really here to help, clear my fees—all of them: visitor, housing, and recording." He displayed the arm of his shirt. It was covered with charges.

"I *am* trying to help." *He's furious. Why?*

She watched his hands as he rolled his wrist, then steepled his fingers. Asking, *Are you running a con?*

Am I? The small bargains she'd made with the Benfords added up, but only until she could go home. She *was* negotiating. *Which, the more I know about Sam, was beginning to feel like terrible work.* But if this was a con, it wasn't one she wanted Dax mixed up with. He'd get in even more trouble.

No, she signed. A quick left-to-right motion with her fist.

Dax's face changed. "The next convoy comes tomorrow. We have no credits; our debts are compounding. Indigents fare worse than criminals, Roo. How will you help? Toss a few baubles over the wall?" He gestured at Roo's pendant.

She put her fingers to her throat. "I'll help any way that I can." The promise she'd just made to Judge Benford and Sam complicated everything. But she still had some negotiating power. "I will always try to help you, Dax."

Dax turned his face from the barrier. He muttered something to King. King bowed his head. He looked terrible. Dax's hands moved. *You sure seem comfortable where you are, big sis.*

Please believe me, I'm not, she replied. Had he seen what she said? How could she get him to understand?

Roo turned to the door, and Sam Benford behind it, in desperation. "I don't want to be any more indebted to you than I already am. But my brother needs help. Clear their fines. Free them. Please. I will remain at Centenaire for a few more days. I will attend the meeting."

King and Dax couldn't hear beyond the barrier unless Roo faced him directly. But King could read lips. "What are you doing, Roo?"

She turned back around, preparing to face the man she'd believed was her father. He used Skirts signals to speak before she could say anything. *Do not make bargains with these people! They won't be fair ones.*

Her heart broke. "What bargains have you made, King?" Roo said, loud enough for Sam to hear. "You taught me to do the right thing, or the next best thing if right wasn't possible. What did *you* do? What happened to my mother?"

As Roo spoke, Dax's precinct gear turned blue gray. The red charges disappeared. King's faded as well, but not completely.

A door buzzed. "Daxian Vane, report to house arrest." Relief washed over her brother's face.

She'd used her small amount of leverage, and it had changed everything. It felt so easy. But she knew she'd traded their prison for hers.

King pounded at the static, shocking himself again. "Have you asked what they expect of you?"

Roo stepped back from the barrier, shaken. A wave of feeling swept over her: anger. King was a hypocrite. *Is everything I thought I knew, wrong?* She closed her eyes, trying to calm herself. "Did you ever ask me what I wanted?"

King blinked and sat back down on the bench. He didn't try to defend himself. Roo realized that she'd wanted him to fight—for her, maybe. For the family he'd stolen. Instead, he stared at his hands, curling and uncurling them in his lap.

She sped out the door, past Sam, through the visitor's

hallways, and out, until she stood on the precinct stairs, gasping in the unfiltered air. Her walking canes were all that kept her standing.

A MilPol drone arrived moments later. "Do you need assistance, Miss Benford?" It projected a small filter. She could breathe.

Miss Benford. That's me. Roo blinked. She couldn't answer either way.

Sam caught up with her. "All is well. Your brother will be released with food chits and supplies." He patted her shoulder, comfortingly. He didn't say what would happen to King.

Roo didn't ask. *King would be fine. He'd always been fine. "Don't make deals with these people," he'd said. Still trying to control me. That is over.*

"Now I want to go to Miss Farmer's," she said. *At least I can tell Sasha what's happened. The day can't possibly get worse.*

Sam shook his head sadly. "I'm sorry, but you cannot. They suspended you this morning, based on the Greenes' complaint. You should rest at home." A car pulled up to the curb and Sam climbed in. "We'll meet the hopter on the road."

Home. Centenaire. "Can you help fix Miss Farmer's?" She was pushing her luck, she knew. She held the car door open, but didn't get in. "It is important to me. It was first place where I did anything beyond King's influence."

This wasn't a con, she realized. She truly wanted to be Roosala Vane, student.

"I will do my best, although Miss Farmer was quite concerned." Sam reached out a hand. It hovered over her arm. "I also would like a moment to get used to you being safe and alive. This has all been very sudden. Can you give me more time?"

Do not make bargains, King's words worked their way into her head. His hands twisting together and clenching. *But who else can I trust?* Sam's answer wasn't a no, but it wasn't a yes either. Roo slipped into the car. Watched the city recede.

As she rode away, she felt a tiny edge in her pocket. *A tracer? No. A microbead.* In the precinct, or in the office jostle, someone had passed her a message. Someone who still wanted to speak with her. She shivered.

What have I agreed to? And what have I already lost?

By his second hour of freedom, Dax relaxed on a hammock secured between two vehicles in the Skirts' slow caravan. He breathed the familiar smells his mask couldn't filter. The rebreather made everything taste vague, and distant, but at the moment, that was exactly what he wanted.

The small relaxipatch he'd added to the filter didn't hurt either.

"Thanks, man." He patted Aanand's head.

Aanand pushed a foot against the rear view of his family's oldest car, head in Dax's lap. "Glad to." The hammock swung.

Dax's back rubbed against the hinged double door of Nan's bus. He felt much better.

The sprint home through the tunnels beneath the city had been painful. But his insides were finally unknotting. Somewhere a few cars ahead, two kids were playing what sounded like tubas.

Another Skirter dropped in a horn, high and metallic. And then James, owner of the oldest van on the road, started to belt one out. "You never had it so good," he sang.

Dax sang along. "We're gonna have it all—"

"What will you do when we get paid? Find another city?" Aanand sounded troubled. "My dad's fleet could use a hand in Corporate-Raleigh. I know a guy in Knoxville too."

"Takes too long to get there unless the drones take you. And if they do, you're going where they want, not where you want." Dax didn't want to admit it, but he wanted to stay. King had remained in New Washington, and Nan with him, in case Cere returned. If King got hauled off, Dax would do the same. "Besides, would you want to go to an unprotected city? Knoxville, man."

"Company cities have qualities to recommend them. Square meals. Decent fabs. If you like to work." Aanand laughed. "Sorry your dad's still in pocket, but you need to make plans."

Dax didn't want to think about it. Or traveling between those cities and the Skirts—the dustpan, the wetlands. Anything could happen there, and no one was the wiser.

Same as the precinct. After Roo and her rich benefactor left, while Dax waited to be released, he heard a struggle in the next hold. Two MilPol had King by the elbows. They were taking him away.

"Stop it! He did what you asked."

No one listened to him. When guards came for him, Dax struggled too, but not as much. He figured he'd get to keep King company, watch out for his dad, wherever they were going.

The drone deposited him alone at the apartment complex, a precinct bag by his feet. The bag contained torn clothing from the Grand Heist, his paid receipt for accumulated charges, several protein bars, and meal credits. He'd been let go, but King hadn't.

He didn't stop to change out of his hold clothes or go upstairs. It wasn't their turn on the apartment, and wouldn't be for a long time. Finding out what happened to King had to wait. He had to get back to the Skirts. And fast. His stomach churned.

Stepping into the apartment's entry, Dax opened the door to an old basement. He pushed several boards aside and climbed down into the building's dank underbelly. Everything looked like it had when he'd been there a few weeks before, coming the other direction. It smelled like spoiled milk. Rats scuttled in the shadows. At the bottom of the stairs, deep in the dark, a sommelier's fabricant crate sat above a pile of old boxes. Dax pushed these aside and lifted the hatch below.

Soon, he was in the tunnels that worked their way beneath the city walls, then on his way out of New Washington, heading for the Skirts. And then he was home, and King wasn't.

"I want to be findable. Maybe I'll open a pop-up club until Dad gets back." Dax inhaled hard and his filter popped. He fixed it fast, then spent a minute coughing dust while Aanand pounded his chest.

"You've got no chops to run a business." Aanand laughed. "Management? Not your style. Come work for me." He'd been trying to get Dax to partner forever. "We'll split the credits from your latest intel. You'll see I'm fair."

Dax considered it. "Who's going to hire someone with a face that will put a security system on full alert purely by walking past?"

"You know we can fix that." Aanand said. "Free of charge. Plus, people forget. Give it time."

They watched the Skirts spin. Thanks to the filter patches, they spun with it. Then Aanand's tablet lit up. "Finally. Buyer's in. If you can verify your haul is from Graves's lab."

Dax nodded. "Definitely. But your buyer needs to wait a few."

"Tell me you're not still waiting." Aanand sat up, his face grim.

Dax grinned. "The hold's food turns your gut to stone, man. This filter's got medicinal purposes." His guts gave another twist.

Aanand groaned. "You're lucky you don't end up an organ donor. You should be more careful."

"Not today. I have plans for those credits." Dax rolled off the hammock and began to jog beside the slow caravan, his heart lifting with the Skirts' music. The buyer's bid was enormous. "Going to get my own place! With a bathtub! And a good fab. Anything I want, anytime. And start that club."

"Are you now?" Nan's voice drifted out the bus window. "Just how will you do that?" Her voice rasped. Her coughing had worsened.

Maybe now that I'm home to help, she'll do better. Dax shrugged. "You should be sleeping, Nan. You need rest."

The outraged shriek from the bus coalesced into words and laughter. "I will decide that, Daxian Canarvier, thank you very much." Then another coughing fit.

Of everyone in Dax's life, Nan was all he had left. She'd always been there, ready to call him on his wild ideas before he really got into trouble. He couldn't think about a time when she might not be there. A band of guilt and worry squeezed his chest. *If I hadn't screwed up, she'd be at work. I wouldn't be on house arrest, basically banned from the city. If Roo and I hadn't screwed up.*

"I'll print you some lozenges, Nan, give me a minute." Dax picked up his pace. He'd do that after he found one of the caravan's chempots. *Finally*. Relief mixed with worry. This had to be the payoff the Canarviers needed.

As Dax wove his way through the slowly circling vehicles, toward an outhouse, Aanand unhooked the hammock and headed the other way. He air-chatted Dax on the Skirts earpiece he'd given his friend. It only worked in range of his dad's bus, or Aanand's drones, but it was enough. "I'll be in touch soon. Let me know when you have proof. Promise me something?"

Dax chuckled. "What now?"

"Clean up before you call. You stink. The buyer's Enclave. You need to look professional. I got you a sand scrub at Rooster's."

"Will do." Rooster's flatbed held a heaping of clean sand. It did the trick in a pinch. Then Dax would trade for clean clothes. He'd look *professional.*

The outhouse came into view: an old electric car attached to a bigger camper by its charging cables. Pre-Mess hybrids still worked, no one knew how, and diesels had been converted to salt water, or hydrogen. But the sedans with the transparent roofs? Dax's neighborhood had mostly converted those to garbage haulers and chempots.

Dax handed the outhouse driver a fistful of city meal chits and tucked himself into the back of the car. The scratched moonroof showed him a clear yellow sky. A couple of delivery drones passed over, heading toward the city. Dax sat and thought hard about what a sky filled with birds would look like. He'd only seen birds on the feed. All beautiful and free, right up until they did a mess on your head, like Nan used to tell for bedtime stories.

After far longer than he'd paid for, and with the owner pounding on the outhouse's side, Dax was ready. He'd wrapped his hand in the precinct's carry bag and plucked the ampoule from the rest of his leavings in the fabbed chemdust. He closed the pot, processed the rest into pellets, and wiped everything down as best he could before exiting.

Two Skirters waited outside, walking right next to the car.

"I'll pay you what I owe, I promise," he told the red-faced owner. He tucked the ampoule in his pocket and ran for the nearest stolen fabricator. Then back to the safety of Nan's bus.

When he got there, Nan stifled a cough. "Hungry?"

"Not quite yet." Dax didn't want to think about food for a while. He pocketed the vial and gave her two lozenges. "All I could get with the precinct chits. Fab thinks it's running out of Southend, so it's charging double."

Nan shook her head. "We'll need to hack it back to a cheap location or people are going to starve. Roo would know how."

Roo doesn't care about the Skirts anymore, Dax thought. "She's busy."

"She's in danger," Nan said.

"From what? Too many bracelets? I don't think so." Dax bit his tongue before he said more. Nan thought Graves had let him go, not Benford. He stepped deeper into the bus, toward his corner. Nan had turned the front of the vehicle into a library–shelves everywhere. They were mostly empty now, the books buying extra days in the apartment. "We'll get the library back, Nan, I promise."

"The books have good homes, doing what they're meant to do." Nan handed Dax a half-bar of pressed protein. "Eat."

This was Nan's way of saying she'd missed him. He wasn't hungry, but he bit into the dry bar and tried not to think about how the color and texture resembled chempot pellets. "Thanks."

She worked her way past him, to her corner. Settled painfully on the cushions there, but left her privacy curtain half open. Dax and King had shared the other side of the bus. Now Dax had it all to himself. It felt too big. He went back to her side. She sat with cushions piled all around, working on a tablet.

Without looking up, she said, "A gardener who used to work at Llyria's seeking a gig. His mother too. Does Aanand's dad have anything? His mom?" She paused and looked at Dax, worried. "Aanand better not be telling the feeds that you're home."

"His dad's looking for help with his rental fleet. The biopharm's staffed." Dax paused. "But I might have work soon. A club, maybe."

Nan peered at him over her glasses. "I'll ask once more. Where would you two get money for a club? Does Aanand have another scheme to steal patrol drones and turn them into cleaning bots?"

That had been Dax's idea, but he wasn't going to argue. Nan had given Aanand, Dax, and Roo small, broken bots from jobs over the years. Roo had been the best at hacking them, but Aanand could turn them into magic: flying birds, stalking mice, even a few useful haulers to move disabled vehicles so that MilPol wouldn't relocate them. But they only worked for little while, even the cleaning bots. Aanand had no patience with power sources.

He stayed silent. Her fingers curled around his wrist. "Dax. What are you boys up to?" Her fingers were sharp, and surprisingly strong.

Just like she'd always known where street marks kept their wallets, she'd always known how to get his secrets. He shook his head, but his hand had drifted to his pocket. It was empty.

Damn, she still had fast hands.

Gripping his wrist, Nan's eyes bore into his. Her other hand flipped palm up, revealing the bag containing the ampoule. "Tell me what this is. Now."

"I found it in the Enclave." He hoped that would be enough, but one look at her face and he knew he had to keep talking. "Something from the heist."

Nan's tablet clattered to the floor. "You held something back from the client? What are you thinking. They will sell us for parts." She narrowed her eyes. "Is there more? A ring?"

Dax shook his head. *No ring.* "It was a brilliant lift, Nan. Excellent improvisation." Now he wanted to tell her everything. "Graves was keeping it in his safe. I swallowed it."

When Nan paled, Dax tried to reassure her. "Don't worry! It's sealed. Impermeable."

"How can you swallow something when you don't know what it is." If her hands hadn't been full, she would have swatted him. "Never mind. I know the answer already."

"What do we have to lose?" Dax laughed.

"You have a lot to lose! Still! We all do!" The bus rattled

slowly over a pothole. Nan's words turned to coughs and she let him go. She handed the bag back too.

Dax picked up her tablet and gave it to her, silently apologizing.

"Let me run a search." Nan already had the feeds open, tracking apprentices for Public Works. She was fast. "This one. Junior apprentice to Graves. Not dumb enough to record anything in a lab, but maybe . . ." She froze a reflection on a pair of glasses. Enlarged it. "Is that them?" A grainy image of a sleek ampoule, the size of a lozenge. Titanium bio-locked lid.

"Could be." Dax held the bag up to the light. The glass sparkled inside.

Nan went quiet, testing different paths through public data. She pretended to be an investor. "Graves is working on DNA and pheromone mood controllers. But they have way too many scientists assigned. Beyond what's in their books on city records. Let me see that vial?"

"Give me a minute." Retreating to his corner, he opened the bag. The stench was overwhelming. As he cleaned it with his shirt, he felt a tiny crack. Almost invisible. "Cheapass Graves, using cheap containers," he muttered, shaking the ampoule.

Half empty. Whatever had been inside, is in me, instead.

"Nan, what were they working on, exactly?" He kept his voice even, to avoid upsetting her.

Nan was quiet. "They don't seem to want anyone to know. They've got their data black-boxed. Why?"

Dax stepped around the curtain, trying to hide his shame and worry. One look and Nan knew. "Oh, Dax."

"Seventy-two hours–I knew I could swing that. I tried to get out of the hold faster, but–"

"It's broken, isn't it." She searched faster, with no new results.

"Don't worry, Nan." He tried his best grin on her. Even as Graves's safe had beaten him to a pulp, he'd been focused on lifting something big enough to matter. He'd felt the ampoules in the safe's half-opened pouch and palmed one in the struggle. Then he'd swallowed it. If the chlorafoam hadn't gotten him, he would have made it. The greatest heist ever. It was still going to be.

Even if, somewhere between there and here, the ampoule had broken. "I can still fix it. Aanand's buyer won't have to know."

He was digging through Roo's belongings for sealant to hide the crack when a fist pounded on the bus door. From the window, Dax could see Aanand's profile, next to a taller figure in a heavy outdoor mask. He checked his earpiece. Five messages.

The buyer's here.

New Washington Found Footage Group #34

Subscriber 23422: Look! More documents that may connect our missing lady after all:

New Washington Precinct Dispatch

Attention: Kenneth Vane
Regarding: Employment termination with the City of New Washington
Date: June 1 __ [year]

Mr. Vane, given your recent attendance at a protest, verified by New Washington MilPol, your access to Reclamation and Recovery Public Works facilities, tools, resources, and housing has been terminated immediately. Your status as a citizen will continue for six months beyond the date of this letter, barring any further misdeeds on your part. Turing this time, you should find other employment and accommodation.

*

New Washington Precinct Dispatch

Attention: Kenneth Vane
Regarding: residence termination with the City of New Washington
Date: August 1 __ [year]

Mr. Vane, your continued inquiries and research into the status of one Cere Vane has been flagged as an aggressive act. As you were instructed during your prior warning: there is no such person. Your actions have taken up valuable MilPol time and do not represent employment. Your residency in the protected cities is hereby terminated.

Subscriber 23422: No such person? Aggressive act? Who has that kind of power and interest in a case like this?

Subscriber 23422: Anyone out there?

[group feed terminated]

The Escape

"YOU WILL SHOW me everything," Minerva said. "A highly placed person at Public Works heard rumors that you've double- and triple-dipped credit from multiple investors to secure identical risks. I can't have one of your other creditors taking over your company before my brother does. And I won't approve the rest of your merger arrangements with things in this state. My associates have repossessed your lab until such time as you can clarify everything."

"I'm being framed," Mason protested.

Evangeline stared straight ahead, as if her eyes could bore a hole in the roofhopter's shell. "Is that true?"

If she'd ordered Mason to shrink to the size of a molecule, he would have done so. "I may be slightly over-leveraged at this moment, but that's how the game is played, Ev. Science needs capital to do great things. And we are doing great things!"

"Prove it," she said to him. Then Evangeline turned to her aunt. "Prove he's doing this."

Minerva unclipped her coat and pulled out a tablet. She showed Mason's books—the public ones, in the green, and then waved her hand so that an overlay of interwoven debts, bargains, and promissory voice recordings wiped everything out, and then some.

"There are creditors from different cities, offshore Enclaves, insurers, and other companies on here. Plus," she pulled up the liens on Llyria, "think how a fraud charge would impact you, if my brother was nearly undone by a libel accusation. Your green-book aspirations would evaporate."

Evangeline blinked. "I must reject the proposal. You didn't tell Papa or me the truth."

Mason's heart turned to glass and began to crack, until Minerva held up a hand. "My dear, was the money what you appreciated most about this man?"

Evangeline blinked faster. "No. I liked how he innovated—and the adventure of it. His big dreams."

She'd said *liked*. Not loved. Mason prepared to disappear back to Denver, or further if he could.

But Minerva shocked him. "Don't let go of that. Your mother forgot her dreams. Did you know that? She was my best friend, once, and I've dedicated myself to keeping what happened to her from happening to you. Our duties, our purpose—renewing this world—need both order and dreamers. You, together, are those things. And with my guidance, I can help you become the next step forward."

Evangeline wouldn't look at Mason. "Aunt Min, you are saying he's a *fraud*—you *hate* criminals."

Minerva smiled tightly. "You've been far too sheltered by your father, Evangeline. The crime isn't fraud. The crime is getting caught." She took Evangeline's elbow. "You say you want to help this world grow. To do that, you need to have a thicker skin, and a stronger sense of purpose. We will fix this. You will find strength in a partnership where, with my help, you hold the reins. The next generation will be better for it."

Evangeline did not look convinced, but she was listening.

"Please, Ev. Give me a chance." Mason surprised himself. It would be easier to let her go, to start again. But he didn't want to. He turned to Minerva. "What do I need to do? I must get my lab back. We're doing important work down there."

Evangeline said two words to him, finally: "Show us."

He agreed, and Minerva signaled the city to allow them entry.

On the way from the landing pad to the lab—Mason could hear via his subdermal comm the sounds of staff scrambling to greet them properly—he made a gut decision. He would show them the new formula. But not the variant. He needed negotiation room.

He opened the door to the upper laboratory, where two senior engineers, four scientists, and their apprentices assembled by the wide windows. The staff in the lower lab had been told to keep working, so Minerva could watch. "The larger mass spectrometers, the modified resonance machines you see down there, are generating the new Safeware 2.0 formula. It is stronger and longer lasting than the one currently on the market."

Mason pointed out trays of ampoules moving through the production ramps.

"What's on the bench in the corner, near the hood?" Evangeline asked.

So observant. He had to keep her by his side. "That's Dr. Tsalta's group. Research for new products."

Minerva looped her arm through her niece's. "Remember, niece. The desperate often embody innovation. Continue."

Mason lifted a small ampoule from the lab tray held by

a waiting scientist. Clear at the base, with a blue titanium bead-cap that turned green at his touch. "This is the original bio-serum."

He lifted another ampoule from the tray, this one with a red cap. "The new formulation uses a DNA bond to strengthen the pheromone bond. A blood transfusion between relatives, with this formula, removes any thoughts of disloyalty. We have also been working toward removing the relationship requirement."

"If not a relative, how could you guarantee loyalty?" Minerva asked, frowning. "That would be quite an advancement, given some of the early betrayals. I want to see it work."

Mason waved a waiting lab apprentice over. "The serum is the guarantee. We're not quite there, but Tobias has been taking the new serum for a week. No ill effects."

Evangeline stayed quiet as the young man came willingly.

"You test on your own employees?" Minerva didn't look concerned, only curious.

"They volunteer," Mason assured her. Another apprentice stepped forward. "Megan is Tobias's sister. Megan, tell Tobias to slice his hand."

Megan uttered the order reluctantly. Tobias lifted a scalpel from a nearby tray and drew it along his palm. His blood welled, but he didn't attend to it until his sister told him to do so.

Evangeline drew in a shocked breath. Mason hurried to reassure her. "It's quite all right. When Tobias's service is finished, he won't remember. And they'll be well compensated. Their family will receive enough credits to move up in society."

But Evangeline turned away, arms crossed, her hands cupping her elbows tightly.

Mason fretted. *I should have asked Tobias to do something simpler. How to distract her?*

Minerva, on the other hand, inspected Tobias closely.

"You've told MilPol about this, surely? The removal of a relationship requirement could interest them."

She knew he'd told them. He'd informed backers when he shared quarterly results last month. *She's fishing for something.*

Evangeline looked toward the lab doors. "I hadn't realized," she murmured.

"How did you think it worked, dear?" Minerva waved off her concern, and waited on his answer. "Go on, Mason."

He spoke with a confidence he didn't feel. "MilPol groups in several protected cities are also interested in a variant Safeware patch that eases interrogations. We were able to test that during the Grand Heist. It does need some refining."

"So full profits are still on the horizon. That is disappointing. Is there anything else that might make you more appealing in acquisitions, or distract your creditors?" Minerva looked around the lab. "I am trying to help you."

Mason hesitated. But Evangeline put a hand on his arm. "Don't keep any more secrets."

Her touch was electric, even here. Maybe she wouldn't leave him. He would do anything. Tell her everything. "Let's go down to the lab."

Dr. Tsalta's head and shoulders were sunk deep in the lab hood. She jumped when Mason entered, slowly withdrawing from the static ventilation barrier. "Ah, Mr. Graves. I was just running the variant through—"

She stopped when she saw the Benfords.

"It's all right. We have new partners," Mason reassured her. *A repossession is somewhat like a partnership. But if he managed this right, it might soon become more of a merger.* "You can speak freely."

Dr. Tsalta's voice shook. The repossession had upset the scientists, as he'd feared. "My results are confirmed. As long as we can keep it stable, Variant B is not an aberration. We can consider ramping up production, if we can reproduce it."

Mason beamed, deciding to think about the reproduction problem later. “This is very timely news.”

Will Minerva let the matter of a few credit overlaps go? With her protection, the others certainly wouldn’t attack him again, and he’d have time to certify the offer. *Will Evangeline stay?* He had to try. He’d been working on his pitch for customers already. He tried a few lines out on his most important audience: “Eons ago, Emperors drank mercury in pursuit of eternal life. That was misguided.”

Minerva snorted. “Very.”

“But in the course of developing Safeware 2.0, we discovered a different option for those lucky enough to have access. Something every founder and those able to afford it will clamor for. A way to extend life, perhaps indefinitely.” Now he had Minerva’s attention. And Evangeline didn’t look quite so upset. He resolved to keep going.

“Longevity?” Minerva said. “It’s a myth. A way to sell health shakes on the cheap feeds.”

Mason, who loved those very health shakes, disagreed. “I assure you, it’s quite real.”

“Let’s see it then.” Minerva held out a gloved hand, as if Mason could place immortality there.

Evangeline lifted her hand from his arm, chewing her lip. “Dr. Tsalta said ‘if we can reproduce it.’ Correct?”

She was so very observant. “Correct. So far, we’ve only been able to generate a few micro-ounces of the variant. But the subjects testing it are thriving. Overnight, they gained the physiques of twenty-year-olds.” *And their relatives fared the opposite.* Mason didn’t mention that, and hoped Evangeline wouldn’t ask. She didn’t.

Minerva looked at the balance sheets and narrowed her eyes at Dr. Tsalta. “That does seem research worth continuing. I will have a word with the city. And your creditors. I believe I can buy you five days. If you solve this problem, I’ll let the merger continue.”

Less than a week? Mason took a step back. “Science doesn’t work on that kind of deadline.”

Minerva leaned closer. "Yes, but creditors do. And your competition might. Who else knows about this?"

Mason thought hard. "No one."

"Keep it that way. I hope the formula is secure," Minerva said.

Tell them as much truth as possible. It's the only way. Mason led the pair out of the lower lab. "It is. I gave the ampoules to Sam yesterday. They're in his safe. He believes they're all the new Safeware formula. Not the variant."

Which, for the moment, they are. But that will change.

Minerva clapped her hands together. "Splendid."

Back at Centenaire, Roo crossed the rooftop garden with Sam. She hadn't spoken since the precinct, and he hadn't pushed.

She felt empty. Dax hated her. King had shouted at her. She understood even less than before. The family that had raised her had destroyed her real family.

They reached the walkway. The peonies had closed their petals for the night.

"Thank you," she said. "For keeping your word."

Sam bowed his head. "I am sorry it was not easier for you. I was only nine years older than you are now when I lost Serena. And you. But now everything is changed."

Hope lifted his voice, though he'd said the word "lost" like a businessman, still angry.

Sam sat on a garden bench, gesturing for Roo to join him. "Do you really want to leave? To be on your own again?"

Yes. Roo didn't sit. She knew her answer was projected on her face. "I want to go back to school. Finish my work. Follow dreams of my own. Just as Evangeline can."

She could see him thinking about that. Weighing his options. "I can see how the role of Evangeline's supportive younger sister might not appeal. Tell me your dreams."

Roo touched the microbead from court that she'd hidden on her cane handle. "I had hoped to find employment in the Enclaves, or offshore. I am good with data."

"As we've seen. You can do that work for the Benford family."

That's not a career. Roo stayed silent.

"I can see how you might feel, coming from a community based around monetary exchanges. But what if your skills had repercussions across generations? What if you could make a difference for the world?" Sam pulled a petal from a rosebush. "It may look like the Estates are frivolous exercises in wealth."

She couldn't hold her tongue. "It does."

"But they're more than that. They're a way to salvage what we value most—culture, art, knowledge, science—and reclaim it for the future. The terraforming. The gardens. My collections. Much the same as vehicle racing—boats and cars—in the twentieth century did for engineering and science, and rocket challenges began to do before everything got turbulent. Competition pushes creativity. Look at the Enlightenment. The Hagia Sofia, the Imperial Palace. The race to the moon. Many great ventures were called frivolous once. There are a lot fewer people on the planet now, but we can still make progress. We must."

"But those aren't merely triumphs of money. And many of those advances were turned into weapons, as you said you feared." Was she risking everything being this bold? She didn't know. Worse, Roo realized, she sounded like King. *Idealistic. Iconoclast. Kidnapper.* She stopped talking.

Sam laughed, from deep in his belly. "I wish I'd had the chance to know you when you were a child. You are fierce in every cell, just like Serena."

"I suspect growing up hungry has something to do with it." Roosa thought of the meals at Centenaire. Of the banquet tables at Llyria. "I'm not fierce. I am angry. The entire Skirts population is—"

"The Skirts has created its own problems. They exist at the law's edge, grinding our largesse in the dust. We give them the basics and still they break the machines, hijack deliveries. If they were willing to come inside the city walls, to work and contribute? Can you imagine what all that creativity might do? Don't you think they'd be taken care of too?"

Roo stared. "You can't write people off because they don't think like you do. I'm a thief from the Skirts, too, Sam. I don't break things. I move them around." Roo had no interest in discussing economics with someone who had never been hungry. "I would let people breathe. Experiment. Even those outside the community. I'd make sure they got what they needed."

Sam's expression grew stony. "Who do you think makes sure the basics are covered even out in the Skirts? We do." Sam got angry for the first time. His chest puffed and he stepped back. "Don't think that we don't, Roo. It's never enough."

Sam strode away, shaking his head.

Roo hurried in the other direction. *None of my families want me. And I don't want any of them.*

She felt for the microbead on her cane again. Someone had put in great effort to pass her a message. She needed a tablet. And time.

She called the elevator to the roof, hit the buttons for the basement fabrication room, let it close without getting in, and then pried the door open when the carriage began to sink.

Using one cane as leverage to hold the door open, she stepped atop the elevator and knelt. The cane cracked and she tossed it down the shaft.

She wobbled, but didn't fall over. As she rode down, she got a good look at Centenaire's inner skeleton. Especially the vents and the spaces between floors. When the elevator stopped on the main floor, Roo crawled into the space between the ceiling and the floor above, taking the other cane with her. Then she kept crawling.

Her silk pants and blouse were soon covered in grime, but she didn't care. This felt good. For the first time in days, Roo felt like herself.

As she crawled, she passed vents that looked up into dark rooms. An office. A library. She took in the shelves filled with books. When she came to a vent screen that spilled light into the crawlspace, Roo peered out, her eye at floor level.

The outfit Evangeline had worn the day before was piled on the floor. An unattended tablet lay beside it. Evangeline's belongings were strewn across the room.

Feet moved past the vent, and Roo held her breath. A maid was picking up and folding clothes, smoothing away Evangeline's life before her mistress returned. She lifted the tablet from the floor and put it on a footstool.

Roo watched until a bell chimed, and the maid left the suite in a hurry. *Where was Evangeline? Probably at dinner, or out with her terrible fiancée.*

She pushed on the vent screen. Stretched her fingers toward the stool on which the maid had laid the tablet. Something crunched beneath her arm, and she nabbed an earring that had rolled into the vent in all the chaos. Tucked it into her pocket. A fountain pen and a credit key on the rug came too. The last one could be easy to sell in the Skirts. *Or I can try to load it with the allowance Sam has bestowed on me. Maybe give that to Nan, for Dax.* That was a good way to help them.

A few gems glittered and caught her eye on a far table. A ring like the one in her mother's portrait? Sam probably had matching ones made–a fab was likely printing one for Roo now.

She was calculating whether she could risk going deeper into the room when she saw her gown–Sasha's wardrobe–crumpled beneath another pile of clothes the maid hadn't gotten to yet.

Evangeline hadn't thrown the wardrobe away. She'd stolen it.

Roo wriggled forward, hissing when she scraped her knee on the edge of the vent. Then she stretched her cane forward and hooked the fabric. Triumphantly, Roo pulled the fabric toward her and replaced the screen. Then she crawled on.

Soon, she was in her own room. She ached all over, but her heart beat fast and happy.

Still in her grimy clothes, Roo reworked the tablet, using Evangeline's access code. Only then did she put the microbead on the tablet's surface. Had Stonecliff reached out to her again? *What will he ask of me this time? How will I answer?*

She'd meant it when she told Sam she had dreams of her own.

But when the message loaded, it was not blackmail. "If you are able to, meet at the apartment after midnight." No signature. *The apartment. Nan!*

The masked office staff–Nan must have been among them! Roo couldn't believe she'd have missed it, even with a disguise. It didn't matter. Nan wanted to see her.

I am not alone.

Roo sat for a moment, her fingers on the tablet. She wiped the screen's memory, erasing everything she'd done.

How do I get from here to there?

Outside her window, beyond the tree branches, Roo heard the soft grind of many tires on the road. A large service vehicle passing by. A garbage hauler by the sound.

"Someone always has to take out the trash." Nan always said so. That was the answer.

Roo would take herself out, thank you very much.

When Nan opened the bus door, the buyer pushed in with a sniff. "Haven't been Skirts-side in a long time."

The man was tall, and when he removed his thick outdoor mask, a scar twitched across his cheek.

Dax palmed the ampoule. Aanand, on the bus steps, hadn't mentioned this man had been at the Grand Heist. When his friend's dark hair came into view, Dax waved a greeting, with two fingers down. The Skirts sign for caution.

"Tried to call," Aanand said. "You weren't picking up."

"Couldn't wait to see what Aanand told me you had." The buyer reached his hand out. The hand was scarred too. It had seen a lot of rough jobs.

Dax's eyes narrowed, searching the man's face. "You were at the masque."

"I was. You have a good memory. The ampoule, please." The buyer gestured for Dax to hurry up. He smelled of soap.

Nan rose from where she'd been researching Graves's company. "You can't just burst in here, Aanand, it's not polite." Her attempt to help Dax stall was cut short by another coughing fit. She covered her face.

The buyer proffered a linen handkerchief, which Nan waved away. "I'm afraid I am pressed for speed. I have clients who don't wait on ceremony."

Dax had gathered his senses enough to lie. "You should have waited. The ampoule isn't here. I hid it out on the salt flats."

Aanand signaled for him to cut it out. *Guy's dangerous.* But Dax kept up his act. "Go ahead, toss the bus. You won't find it."

The buyer smiled. "I think you are a better thief than that. Aanand tells me you swallowed it the first time. Did you do that again?" He stepped closer to Dax.

Aanand. You talked too much.

"Don't make me call for help," Nan said. "Our neighbors don't like strangers any more than we do."

Aanand looked afraid. "You said you had it, Dax."

"And you took my money, Aanand," the buyer growled. "Very well. It's too bad things have come to a head like this." He slapped a patch on Dax's neck. Another on

Aanand's. Nan tried to leap at him, but he pushed her back onto her cushions, and she stayed down.

Dax felt himself growing extremely willing to talk. He pressed his lips together.

"Where," the buyer asked, "is the ampoule?"

"Here." Dax fought the word, but it won. He felt his arm extending. He couldn't stop it.

He watched Aanand sink to the bus floor, beside Nan. "What keeps you from sending us to the moon, even if we do what you want?" Aanand mumbled.

The man plucked the ampoule from his fingers, opened a padded case, and dropped the container inside. "The moon is expensive."

He lifted a gloved hand, peeling it back just enough that Dax could see a military coms band. "Never mind the pickup," the man said. "Just take the entire bus. Drop it in the flats."

A MilPol unit already hovered above the Skirts, Dax could hear it churning the air. The bus began to rattle, then shook hard as clamps broke through the windows. The buyer stepped down the stairs and jumped lightly to the ground as the drone scooped the old vehicle, Aanand, Nan, and Dax, away from the Skirts.

Pieces of glass and the back bumper fell to the ground. Dax ripped the patch from his neck and cradled Nan, protecting her, as the bus swayed in the air, then flew over the Skirts and out to the sparkling white expanse that stretched as far as the eye could see. Dax spotted the drone and bus's reflection in shallow lakes. An irrigation ditch had cracked into a deep gully, covered in rime. The drone set down nearby, unhooked the clamps, and flew away.

Dax shook off the last of the drug from his head as best he could. "Everyone okay?"

Nan winced, then slowly tried to sit up. "Yeah. Dizzy." She closed her eyes again. Aanand, wedged into another corner, groaned. He'd landed on top of Nan's tablet, breaking it in two.

Dax tapped his earpiece. Got only buzzing. They were too far out to pick up any municipal signal from New Washington, and nothing from the Skirts. The only people who knew where they were, besides the buyer, were on Nan's bus.

That night, with Evangeline snoring softly in her room, the house silent, and the remnants of Sasha's wardrobe stretched to its limits, Roo climbed out of her window and down the walls of Centenaire.

She'd left her wristband on her bedside table and her remaining cane leaning beside. She was much steadier now, and the house could think she was asleep until they discovered she was gone. She had no intention of returning.

A half mile away, an Enclave truck's brakes squealed. Picking up the last of the late shift—dishwashers and cooks who didn't live at the houses they served. A garbage hauler followed close behind. She waited until the van was rolling forward, and then tucked herself in the garbage hauler's bottom rack. The truck was difficult to see, as it used reflective paint. No one in the Enclaves wanted to see a garbage truck on the main roads. Now Roo was hard to see also.

Huddled next to the garbage being removed from the Enclaves, Roo felt giddy. She was tucked next to a bag of diapers and it smelled terrible, but it didn't matter. She was going home.

As the van trundled toward the airlock, Roo held her breath. Would they scan the garbage and find her? The airlock beeped and the van rolled out onto the rougher roads. A rat squeaked and worked its way through the pile, and Roo tried not to move as it climbed through her hair.

At the garbage depot, she emerged from the pile—she'd

been at the bottom of the tip, so she was dumped at the top—and brushed herself off as best she could. Rich people's garbage was no better than that in the Skirts. Worse, even.

She left Evangeline's tablet, regretfully, behind. It had cracked in the jump to the street. The dump/recycling area existed on the city's edge, with an area Skirts residents could pay to access, and that was where Roo headed. Toward the city wall, and the access tunnel to the apartment.

She climbed a hill of garbage sorted from the recycling, feeling the heat of it though her feet. "A shining city on a hill," she thought. One of King's favorite poems.

Just beyond, the Skirts' lights moved slowly past the city. Purple bio glows and algae lamps lit up the dust. Roo made herself a makeshift mask and ducked under the wall.

It was nearly midnight when she arrived in the apartment's basement, clutching the small sack carrying her take from Evangeline's room. *It will help. It has to help.*

She climbed the stairs to the third floor. A figure waited in the dark hall. Not Nan. Taller. Whispering quickly, "Don't say anything. Give me my dress."

Roo smelled seamstress's tape. Miss Farmer's laundry soap. "Sasha!"

"Quiet. You don't even live here, do you." Sasha's voice was filled with doubt. "I didn't recognize anyone who came here."

As an answer, Roo pulled the sodden, torn wardrobe from the sack. "I am so sorry." Sasha would never understand just how sorry.

Sasha reached for the gown.

The smell of garbage overwhelmed the hallway. "You've ruined it. And me." She let her hands fall to her sides.

"I can fix it. There are fabricators—" Roo said. "I will find a way."

"You can't fix it. I have to turn in my final tomorrow. Worse, have you seen the feeds? Evangeline Benford's fans posted photos of the gowns. They've cleaned the images now, but there was one of my dress. Miss Farmer's seen my sketches. She'll know I conspired in that disaster. I'll be lucky to be expelled."

Roo bit back a sob. "Take this. There's more than enough to buy more fabric." Roo held out the credit chip.

"No thank you. You didn't think to tell me that you would be ROBBING the party? You let me think–Roo, this was my work. You can't buy your way out of destroying it." Sasha pushed past her, snatching the cloth from Roo's fingertips as she went. Roo followed down the stairs, but the door slammed shut. *Gone.*

Roo had nothing left.

She crouched in the hallway's shadows. Outside, the city pulsed with revelers and music. It felt like repeated punches to her chest.

When lights came on in the third-floor apartment well before dawn, she knocked, her heart in her mouth. Would those staying there let her back in?

The Vane who opened the door wasn't Nan. The apartment share had turned over to the next family; Aanand's father, Amos Vane, grimaced when he saw her. "You reek. Your brother was all over the feeds, and then he got my son involved. You lot are trouble. Get out."

"Wait–Dax is on house arrest–tell me where? Are he and Nan still in the city?"

Amos shook his head and spoke through clenched teeth. "Hacked his way back yesterday. MilPol came and took your Nan's bus last night. Aanand was inside with them both. I'm working to find out where. Which I can't do with a folder nearby."

"I'm no folder!" Roo was shocked at the accusation.

Amos shook his head from side to side. "Seems you're worse. Canarviers are bad luck. King especially. His transport crashed, just a few hours ago. Now, get out, before you ruin me further."

She ran down the stairs. She couldn't go back to the Skirts without the bus's shelter. She couldn't stay on the city streets. King was gone. And Nan and Dax needed her help.

When a predawn garbage truck passed by the wall, Roo waved the driver down with Evangeline's credit chip. They let her hitch all the way back to the Enclaves.

I'll help my family. Even if they don't want me to. Even if they never know it's me. I'll find a way.

City dust mixed with her tears to form an itchy rime on Roo's cheeks.

New Washington
Precinct Dispatch

Arraignment Report Dossier: assault, burglary
Subject 1 remanded to house arrest, Vane apartment #314
Subject 2 remanded to Sitka. Flight turbulence reported.
Record closed.

The Rescue

Roo ducked into the Benford greenhouse near the seawall and pulled a black coverall off a hook. She stuffed the clothes Evangeline had selected for her into the incinerator. Then she settled on the floor below a row of citrus seedlings to wait. She'd returned to Centenaire because she had nowhere else to go. But she wouldn't stay in long. *They don't even need to know I am here. I only need a few things. Then I'm gone.* When the Benfords were distracted, she'd slip in, gather things from the house—a tablet, a motorcar, anything that might help her find Nan and Dax. Then she'd get them to safety.

The pungent smell of warm garbage disappeared, but her conversations with Sasha and Aanand's father haunted her. *Bad luck. Destroyed me.* She'd wanted to help her family, and she'd lost them. She'd ruined her friends.

The outer door to the greenhouse opened and shut. Roo crouched lower, hiding from the gardeners. But the footsteps moving through the greenhouse were slow. The shoes, expensive.

Sam Benford's scalp reflected the greenhouse's lights as the older man peered at his outdoor drones, dormant in their charging hive. He inspected a blueberry plant.

He looked like he'd been awake for some time.

"I would be happy to lend you a driver, Renata. If it keeps you from climbing into the garbage."

He's guessing. Maybe. Roo held her breath and waited, hoping Sam would leave.

He stayed. "I understand, you know. What you said yesterday made sense, even if it was uncomfortable to hear. I'm ready to listen."

Roo stared at Sam's shoulders through serrated leaves. "How did you know?"

He tapped the place on his chest where the locket rested against her collarbone. "You didn't leave that in your room. I assumed you wanted me to know you were going. And that you'd be back."

Did she? Had she? "I hoped to find Nan. She never lied to me." *Not to my face, anyway. Now, you, on the other hand. Shipping King away. Everything else.* "But she wasn't there."

"She may not have lied, but she omitted enough of the truth. When Stonecliff told me at the ball that King had attacked Minerva, it was the first time we'd had a lead in decades—"

"Stonecliff said King attacked the judge?" He had to be lying.

"Stonecliff is an investigator. And an old friend who takes on all kinds of clients. After Serena was arrested and disappeared, everything went cold—we never knew who took her. Your Canarviers had changed names, appearances, keeping everything—including you and Dax—hidden in plain sight. It was Stonecliff's idea to put out word in the Skirts some time ago that we had new information about Serena. And when King finally took the bait, Stonecliff contacted me. That's why I was angry at King. He attacked all of us." Sam bent his head. Covered his eyes with his hands. "I am sorry that you felt the need to leave."

Roo stepped into the light. "MilPol took Nan and Dax away from the Skirts. Tonight. Their bus is gone." She spoke fast, before she lost her nerve. She couldn't say King's name, or what had happened to him. "Did you do that?"

Sam stared at the seedlings behind her. He shook his head. "I did not. How can I help?"

"I need open access to the city feeds. A way to search for them. I need a vehicle." It was a big ask. She didn't care.

"Holt will have a fit." Sam said this so dryly that Roo laughed.

"I figured you would too, which is why I was just going to take everything." She looked him in the eyes. Hazel, with crows feet. The smile lines deepened as the silence gathered.

"Roo, you don't need to steal what's already yours. I didn't listen to Serena's concerns before she disappeared. I couldn't understand her choices after. I'm going to honor her memory by helping you." Sam's eyebrows furrowed as he struggled to get his emotions under control. "Family matters to me. I want to make up for the past."

Family. Roo turned the word over in her mind. *I have nowhere else.* "Prove it. Call MilPol and tell them to drop Nan's bus on the lawn."

Sam looked out on the lawn as if he was considering it. "We can search for it ourselves. A roofhopter will make short work of it."

"That will wake the whole house. Your security will chase me down. Make me drink tea again." She shook her head. But then Roo spotted a dark shell in the back of the shed, covered with old sheets. The equas from the hunt. "I'm taking one of these. Now. Before the sun comes up on the salt flats."

"I am sorry about the tea." Sam sounded truly regretful. "Do you know how to ride?"

Roo shook her head.

Sam's eyes crinkled further, his expression shifting from surprise to what, if Roo knew him better, might be excitement. "I haven't done anything like this since your mother was alive."

He opened the shed and pulled one of the equas out. Handed her a veil and a helmet from the hunt: Evangeline's own. Got on and held out a hand. "I'll try to help. I must be back to prepare for the Trust meeting by ten, but hopefully, I'll earn your trust in the meantime. Let's go, quickly."

Stranded on the salt flats, Nan's bus heated up fast. The drone had dumped them near a ditch. In it, a car, buried in shale and salt slurry, was slowly being etched down to its whitened frame. Right now, the sun was baking them all, but the bus would sink and start to look like that the minute a weather front hit. Clouds were gathering on the horizon. They had to try to move, even on flattened tires.

Nan rewired the ignition in an attempt to start the engine. Aanand looked out over the flats, then sipped one of the last protein drinks from the bus. He passed it to Dax. "It's delivery day. Drones will cross the flats soon. We can get more."

One by one, Aanand pulled ten pieced-together, large-winged drones he'd modified from the Enclaves' discards. "You'd better be charged."

The bugs were, for once, charged. They flew into the sky, sharing enough signal that Aanand could track it on his own tablet.

As they disappeared in the distance, the engine, which Nan had cobbled together from spare parts for so long, ground tighter and finally sheared. At the earsplitting sound of gears breaking, Dax rushed to the front of the bus. "Nan!" The raised hood blocked his view. Dax could hear each wheezing breath, out of time with the engine's protests. "Nan?"

Nan pounded the front bumper, but there was nothing she could do. Dax stepped outside, next to the popped hood. "Come on," he finally said, trying to lead her to where Aanand sat on a salt hill. "Let's get you something to drink."

"We're low on supplies already," she waved him off. "You drink. I can wait."

"Luckily," Aanand called, "we had a pickup planned. I'm just going to get it a little earlier." He showed them the flock's-eye view of the flats. A fleet of offshore drones laden with cargo cast a tiny cloud-shadow on the white surface. "We're only going to hit the shipments that we need. Let everything else go to the city."

Aanand's flock swarmed six drones in quiet succession. The delivery drones grew confused about their path and stalled in the air. Aanand circled three more drones from a second shipment. The bugs swarmed and the drones fell to earth.

The boys, masks secured over their faces, took off running, their feet kicking up silt.

Out in the drifts, the cargo crashed into salt hoodoos and crumbled crevasse edges. Cartons tumbled from the boxes.

"You're much better at delivery day than when we were little!" Dax's shout was muffled by his mask.

Aanand laughed. "That's the job! Too bad you're not any better at it."

Dax helped Aanand disassemble the cargo, the shipping net that carried it, and the crashed drones. A good haul. Food fabs in sealed containers: a soy-and-seaweed alginate. "Flavor packets! And real water!"

"Remember our first lift?" Aanand hooted. "What a rush."

Dax didn't answer. King had been so angry when he'd come home with a roll of base fab from that delivery. *"Your mother and I wanted more for you."*

He winced at the memory. He remembered saying, "Then we shouldn't live in the Skirts." How rude he'd been. King had used the fab, though. Made a whole new set of untraceable equipment with it.

They unwrapped the water. And a package of base fab, except it seemed much lighter. Aanand cut the wrapper extra carefully.

In the distance, Nan had given up trying to fix the bus. She sat in its shade. He waved her over to get water as Aanand unrolled the wrapping. Nan waved back, but didn't move.

Aanand pulled out a large, silver blanket. "Was going to get this anyway today. Might as well have it here."

Dax recognized the fabric. "Saw a dress made of similar stuff once. It's from offshore?"

"It's growing very popular," Aanand said. "Someone's using a bit for a finishing school project, but I bet they don't know half of what it can do." He whispered a command and pulled the blanket over himself.

And was suddenly gone.

Dax kicked a foot in the direction Aanand had been, and the toe of his work boot connected with something thick that went "oof," just like Aanand would. All he could see was the salt and sky all around them.

"Fancy," Dax murmured. If Roo had gotten some of this for him and not just for herself, they could have had themselves a fine heist indeed.

"Expensive. I caught wind of it heading to New Washington yesterday. Was going to do the buyer deal, then get it." Aanand half-emerged from the blanket and grinned. The silver lining made it look like Aanand was in a safe pocket inside the world. "Got it anyway. Want to show Nan?"

Dax shook his head, a little unnerved. "Nah, Nan's feeling terrible. I'd like to get some help for her." *Soon*, he thought. "Can you boost a feed signal on your flock? Connect with your dad? If you fly them back toward the Skirts?"

"I can try, once it charges again." Aanand pushed at the depleted drone with his foot. "Don't worry. My dad is probably already looking for us. He saw the bus go."

They stopped talking as footsteps crunched the surface of the flats. Two figures approached, pale shadows on the pale ground.

Aanand ducked low, trying to pull Dax down with him. "That's too early for Dad, though. Raiders, maybe. Who saw the delivery fall. Hold on to your kidneys."

Nan. Dax pushed Aanand's hand off and started running. No one was going to hurt her on his watch. But when he reached the door, the figures had already boarded.

He heard a shout. Climbed the bus's steps. Saw Nan with her arms wrapped around both people, covered in flats dust. "I hoped you'd find us," she said, to the taller figure.

The pair wore thin veil-cloaks and heavy Skirts masks.

"You sold my books?" the tall one said, pushing down his mask to look around the empty bus shelves. Not raiders. *King.*

Dax shouted with relief. If anyone knew how to get out of an impossible spot, it was his dad.

"I did. Didn't think you'd be back," Nan said. She clasped the second figure's hand.

"Dad." Before he got the word out, Dax was wrapped in his father's broad embrace. "You got out of the transport?"

"It is a bit more complicated—a daring prison break, a valiant rescue—" King began, his hands up, ready to tell the story.

"A brilliant rescue," the other figure laughed, cutting King off. A woman's voice. "A few friends who helped me in Alaska did me a favor and shot down the transport after I heard he was being sent up." Her voice sounded like she'd been chewing stone. Or living deep in the salt flats for years.

King looked crestfallen he couldn't tell the story, but still couldn't take his eyes off the woman beside him. "You haven't changed a bit."

"Not one bit," Nan agreed. Her eyes were rheumy with tears. She shared her drink with the newcomer, then gestured her grandson forward. "Dax has, though."

Dax hadn't felt shy about anything or anyone for years. Now, though, caution kicked in. He hesitated at Nan's side.

Over the edge of the water jar, the woman studied Dax with clear blue eyes. *Same color as mine.* The deep weather lines in her face, pale against her dark skin, made her look older than Nan, but the eyes were younger. *This voice, and this face I've never known. Except that it is Roo's face too.* He searched her eyes.

Ma.

"She found me, Nan," King said. "Hacked the transport, had it drop me in the ocean. Had no idea what was happening, then found myself stolen right and proper."

"I knew, I always knew you were alive." Nan kept a hand on the woman.

Cere Canarvier–Serena Benford–turned to her son. "I owe you an explanation."

"When we get out of here," Nan interrupted. She coughed into a handkerchief and spat black. "We need to get to safety, and I need medicine. I don't want to get anyone else sick."

A clatter, and then one of Aanand's bug drones shot in the window. It buzzed Serena's short hair, then shot past King and stopped. Reversed. Turned its camera on Dax. Then dropped to the ground.

"I thought you were raiders! Not my dad's! The bad

ones!" Aanand climbed into the bus and stopped at the sight of Serena. "You look like Roo."

Serena laughed. "And you look like one of Amos's kids."

Aanand grinned and bowed. "I'm his business partner, now."

Dax felt as if he was talking to one of Nan's ghosts from the pre-Mess. "How did you find us?"

"We *weren't* looking for you. The drone drop got our attention. King jumped from the transport with nothing. We needed supplies. Lucky break we were heading out, I guess." Serena grinned. "Come with us–we're stowing away on the nearest ocean Enclave; getting off wherever they end up next, for a fresh start. Time's now. We've got transport rigged, just over the hill. Get your sister."

Dax stopped shoving supplies in his backpack. "She's not with us." He stared at King. "You didn't tell her?"

"I was waiting for the right time," King sighed. The bus, which had been noisy a moment before, became as silent as the flats.

Nan muttered, "King. Tell her."

Serena turned from the son she barely knew to face King, sighting him in her glare like a sharpshooter. "We said we weren't going to keep secrets anymore."

King sputtered, searching for words. Dax clenched and unclenched his hands. Was he going to be the one to say it? He didn't know her well enough to do it right.

"Roo's ensconced in a posh suite at the Enclaves," Aanand announced into the quiet. "She's a total folder, I reckon. Graves and the Benford clan got her. Feeds keep gossiping, posting sightings, getting banned."

"She's not a folder!" Dax shouted at his friend. "She's playing them. It's a long con."

Serena stared at Aanand. "Benfords? She's–no. That's not–" She rounded on King, and Nan. "You promised me. The one thing I made you promise me was that Roo would stay away from the Benfords."

"We tried. Then I heard you might be alive, and that

the judge had evidence—which was correct, in a way, here you are. But I got nabbed, and then the kids tried to save me and—" King swept his arms out, expansively, then left them out, as if hoping to bring everyone in for a hug.

No one moved.

Serena spoke in grim tones. "Everything I went through. And you let her go—just like that. We have to get her out of there."

"Why?" Dax asked. "Usually, Roo can get out on her own."

"Yeah, what's the hurry?" Aanand said. "She's probably shopping." Dax smacked his arm.

"Or," Serena drew a tight, panicked breath, "she's being lured in by Enclavers' kindnesses. She's making small concessions, and they're lulling her into a sense of security, maybe even duty. Eventually they'll take more than they give. Some of her organs, for instance. When they turn her into one of the family safes. I fought with Sam and Minerva about that over and over. It's wrong. They never listened. When I found out I was pregnant again, I grew afraid. And I ran—with King's help. Roo was protected. And then I fell for your dad, and had you." She gazed at Dax for a long moment. Then her expression shifted to anger. She spun to stare at King and Nan. "Except now she's back in that house, with those people."

Serena slammed out of the bus and stood in the flats, staring at the horizon. Nan stared out the window, coughing, then looked back at King. "You have to make this right. We need to go get Roo. Now."

Nan tried to speak again, but bent in half with coughing. When she finished, she lifted her head. "I'll only slow you down. I have enough supplies to be all right until Amos arrives. I'll let him know you're safe, Aanand. You all get Roo."

When Nan's bus appeared on the shining white horizon of the salt flats, it was a dark shadow listing to one side. It looked like it had been dropped from a great height. Torn shipping wrappers and broken drones lay nearby, but no one was inside.

"Dax! Nan?" Roo dismounted first, and walked around the wrecked vehicle, shouting names. "Aanand!" No one answered. Her legs wobbled from the ride.

She panicked until she saw the scrap of code, scrawled on the door. *Safe, with friends.*

Amos had said he was looking for them. It seemed he'd found them. But not knowing for sure where they'd gone, or how to reach them made Roo feel exactly like the bus looked.

She sat down hard on the sand, her mask working overtime to compensate for the speed of her breathing.

"There are many places for people to disappear in this world, if they want to," Sam said. Still on the equadrone, he startled at the slither of the glass and salt against wind. He tapped at his palm, nervously. "We should go back."

"I need to know they're all right," Roo protested. The flats stretched in every direction. "If we keep looking, we might catch up with them."

Sam's hand trembled. "I'm afraid we are running out of time." He looked like he was in pain.

"Are you all right?" Roo stood and stepped away from the bus.

"When my chip becomes disconnected, it causes great discomfort. But it should not be disconnecting. Even on the hunt, in places where the Enclave's signal is weakest, I didn't have this problem. Something's wrong." Sam sounded different out on the flats. Afraid.

She tried to reassure him. "There's no signal out here, that's normal. It's called the flats for a reason." It was one of many reasons the place frightened Skirts kids, who weren't afraid of much else. This was a very disconnected place.

"I am worried," Sam said, embarrassed. "These are

designed to be impervious to such things. But here I am." He stared at his palm, where the chip was dark. Then it glowed back to life. "I may need a favor."

The old man, her real father, looked small beside the bus, and smaller still in the expanse of salt devastation. "I said I would stay. And that I would come to the meeting of your Trust. I will keep my word, Sam." *What more might he ask of me?*

"You said you are good with data. Show me how good. I believe I'm being hacked."

He'd been worried on the flight to court, but Evangeline had said Sam was suspicious of everything. "You're so careful. How could you get hacked?"

Sam kicked at the ground, then turned toward the equas in the shade of the bus. "At first, this week, when it was a few small things, I figured it was a glitch. But Holt and I discovered a competitor had too much information about my plans for the acquisition with Graves. They claimed they were a creditor. And the Greenes knew you were with us, not Graves. There's a leak somewhere."

"But who would get close enough to do that?" Roo knew she had to be cautious about who she suggested. "Stonecliff? Your staff?"

"This all began after the Grand Heist, so Holt and Sergeant Theridge, my security chief, suspected your family at first. Minerva did as well," Sam said. He narrowed his eyes at her. Then chuckled. "But I don't think that's the case. You're the only one with that skill set among them, and you were too busy trying to get away, not break in. Stonecliff is both a longtime friend—he recommended Theridge to me, years ago—and a distant cousin, but I do worry he enjoys espionage too much."

Roo thought back over the past few days. "Might your sister be involved?" Minerva was pushing Mason's proposal, and the acquisition.

"If Minerva is involved, I bet she thinks it's for the good of the family." Sam frowned. "She's got influence with

Evangeline. Possibly because I was so protective. But she wouldn't risk—" He stopped and smacked his head. "Her wristband. She told Theridge she'd wiped it remotely, but it's possible someone could have tampered with it."

Stonecliff had given Sam the band to return to the judge, Roo remembered. But it was Minerva's band. "And when you touched it, it accessed Centenaire. Didn't your security chief run diagnostics?"

"She did. We found nothing. But now that Evangeline has a majority in the business, and is engaged, if someone is jockeying for power before the next generation takes over, she is in danger." Sam grew quiet. "Minerva's never been interested in power. Only in family and order. I worry that it's a much bigger problem. There are groups who would take the Enclaves' innovations and turn them into weapons. If they've hacked my chip, they could try for more."

"Weapons? You make flowers and trees," Roo wondered. "They might do better attacking Graves."

Sam nodded, but it was a bare thing. "They might do both. It has happened in one other Enclave, where research like ours on terraforming and plant repopulation, and even the equas, was copied and repurposed. Turned against them by their own guards. The people who had sworn to keep the families who saved them safe. That Enclave—well, I don't want that to happen here."

"Not Atlantic—" Roo began, staring at the dry salt flat. She was thinking of the guests from the heist.

"No. Graves's technologies, and similar products, are very popular out there. Ocean is the concern. They're talking to us less and less. But they lack the contacts on land to do any real damage so far. And they've been frozen out of the green book. That doesn't mean they—and others like them in some of the company towns—aren't trying to breach the successes we've fought so hard for here."

Roo shivered in the heat. But a memory tugged at her, from the courthouse. "Why isn't this on the feeds?"

"What would that do, besides get people upset?" Sam

asked. He paused. "Perhaps it *should* get them upset. I did Evangeline a disservice by allowing her to be chipped so young. I wanted to always be able to find her. But if she's been compromised as well, with all that's about to happen with the Trust . . ."

The equa hovered above the salt, its shell turned cooling white. The veils kept them invisible. But Sam's words made Roo feel exposed, and shook loose a memory: King's hands, the way they'd moved, folding one over the other. The way he'd blinked. He'd been using the family code. Saying *trap*. Over and over. She'd been so upset, she'd missed it.

What did he think the trap was? He'd taken Minerva's wristband. Had he set a trap for Sam? She would find out. "The chips—one of which you want me to have—come from offshore, made by your family there?"

"Yes, from Atlantic. Very trustworthy." He hesitated. He wasn't sure. "But everything is much more fragile than people think."

In the middle of the salt flats, next to the ruins of her grandmother's bus, Roo struggled to trust Sam. Sasha had always said not to show how much she was capable of. This could be another test, another trap. *But what if he was telling the truth?*

She made her choice. "I think the chips *are* hackable. At least in concept. We were forbidden from researching them at Miss Farmer's. If you let me access yours, I might be able to find out what's happening. I will need a few things—my work from school, for one. And I need to know who has access to your data." *Who knows where you are and when? Like now? Who saw us disappear this morning?*

"I control my data. As an adult citizen of the Enclave, it's mine, no one else's." Sam's words sounded reassuring, but Roo squinted until he admitted, "I installed an encryption tumbler in my office a few days ago. Even the family doesn't know."

"If the data exists, it can be managed, shifted, and hidden." Roo, like most, had never traveled beyond her own city. She'd grown up with New Washington feeds, and only occasional news from the broader world. But she'd often wondered what was changing in places beyond the city feed. Now that she'd seen the green book, she wondered even more. "My final project was about tracing lost objects back to their owners, but if I reversed it, I might be able to trace the hack."

One look at the bus and her eyes welled. "No one wants to lose what they have," she said.

"No one," Sam agreed. His tone was regretful. "I need a thief to help me stop a thief. But if I take you to Miss Farmer's to get what you need, I'll be breaking our terms with the Greenes. They could charge you again."

Roo grinned. She scrambled onto the equadrone. "Then we'll have to sneak in. Before anyone is awake. Now."

Sam hesitated. "You want me to rob Miss Farmer's with you?"

Roo pointed the equa for the Enclaves, and he climbed on. "You can be the distraction."

The feeds had much more to say about Mason, now that he was about to be a Benford. Not all of it nice.

I am much better than Jayson Dutton. The man is a simpleton, not a scientist. Mason grumbled. Once he was a Benford, Mason would follow Sam's example: erasing threads, deleting accounts. He would enjoy doing that. *But before I have those tools, I can use the thief as a distraction.*

Evangeline and Minerva might love the feeds. He, like Sam, no longer wanted to be part of the public entertainment. But sometimes needs outweighed wants.

His creditors circled—two had called that morning—and the lab was no closer to producing more of the variant formula. It was Wednesday. Three days to Minerva's deadline.

I have to take back control—both of my reputation and my company.

He reviewed the tapes from Saturday one more time, editing here, shifting timelines there.

He was going to make the Canarviers pay. All of them, starting with the closest thief.

While waiting for Evangeline on the rooftop garden, he made himself two new accounts on the feeds. Paid the exorbitant fees.

A cook set a coffee service and pastries down on a table nearby. It smelled wonderful.

He uploaded a snippet of video. Offered a few details to a reporter. He waited for New Washington to swarm.

"You are here so early," Evangeline said. She greeted him with a kiss on the cheek: a somewhat chilly one. Pulled her sweater closer around her shoulders.

"You said you wanted to have brunch, before the meeting. I need to visit the lab today as well, so early is better. The staff said Sam is already out somewhere." He'd brought over several suits hoping Evangeline would help him choose. Which one would impress the various cousins and members of the Enclave Family Trust? *I'd love to have Sam's opinion too.*

"Always working," she said. "Both of you. Mason. I have concerns."

His heart fell again. After yesterday's shock, Minerva had taken Evangeline in hand, and it seemed all would be right again. "I will make things better, I promise. No more lies."

"It's not that. The formula—both formulas—they're abhorrent. People should be allowed to decide for themselves what they are willing to do. I never realized safes work that way."

Ahhh. Sometimes clients occasionally voiced concerns like this. *I know what to do.* Mason reached out and held her hands in his. "Darling, they do decide. They agree to let the compound make them faster, and better, without hesitation. And when their service is over, they are better for it. It wasn't always this way, but it needed to be. I am helping them be better."

She smiled faintly. She would understand. It was business. He could even demonstrate. *What Safeware dose would be appropriate for the younger Benford sister? I can have it made at the lab today and get Holt to pick it up.*

Deciding that made Mason feel happier than he had for some time. "Now that you feel better, what does the meeting schedule look like? You must be nervous."

She smoothed her skirt. "I am, a little. I want everything to go right. We will announce Renata and celebrate the Graves-Benford partnership. Papa will speak. I have a report to present on the greenhouses. We'll have a tea—with some of those wonderful ices from the city. I've contacted *Enclave & Towne*, and a fan group. It's time we have a better presence there. Papa is too paranoid about them."

Mason chuckled, and showed her his tablet. "I was just looking to see how the heist piece in *E&T* came off. Well, I think!" He'd paid them quite a nice sum to ensure it would.

She lifted his tablet from his hands. Sat next to him and settled her back against his shoulder. "This is a good image of us. Who took it?"

"It's off the ballroom security camera. I haven't worn those blasted shoes since, Ev."

"Look at that, Stonecliff is standing with Renata. I hadn't seen them together." Her brow knit. "Do you think he took my ring? As a joke?"

Mason had considered it, although not as a joke. "We searched him thoroughly, when we caught him on the green. He had a few baubles in his pockets, and a few documents. We tidied him up and sent him on his way. No ring."

She turned and looked into his eyes. "Tell me truthfully. Are you happy it was stolen? Do you want the partnership with Papa but not with me?"

He heard the worry in her voice. Squeezed her hands tightly. "I would happily marry you tomorrow if I could. If you recall, I would rather not have had thieves at all." His tone was a bit sharper than he intended.

"I wanted to set you on good footing. Now—look at us."

She held her head in her hands. Then she pulled herself up and handed the tablet back. "Right. This is nerves. You are correct. The meeting is in five hours. I've already gotten a small gift for Renata and ordered her a selection of suits by a designer she likes. What can I get for you?"

He pulled her closer. "All I want is you."

The garden smelled of roses. Evangeline did as well.

Now that they were heading in the direction of Miss Farmer's, and Sasha Limére, it was the last place Roo wanted to go. But she needed her research, which was locked in Kerr-Moulthrop's classroom. She left the equa before the carefully tended gravel drive began. Sam rode ahead, stopping the drone in front of the Georgian facade. Inside, everything was still dark. Sam knocked on the door. Roo crouched in the shadows by the side of the school.

The matron who opened the door seemed both sleepy and startled.

"I'm here to see Miss Farmer, and to retrieve Miss Vane's things. I believe they've been packed up," Sam said.

Roo watched the dormitory window for any movement—there was none.

In a matter of moments, Miss Farmer appeared at the door, black hair in an elaborate bun. The style exposed the curve of her russet neck above a sharply collared blue suit. "Please do come in, Sam. It is good to see you again, if unexpected."

"Thank you, Sarah. I have a favor to ask." Sam stepped inside. Roo startled at hearing the headmistress's first name, even though she knew Miss Farmer was a title.

This Miss Farmer had been educated offshore, in all the niceties required by society, but she'd also apprenticed in environmental engineering in New Washington and the Enclave. She had several patents to her real name. A large citation from the Recovery Court hung on the wall of her office for all the students to see. But she'd stepped back from those interests to govern the school. To help shape the next generation.

Roo had never enquired why, although Sasha had once hinted that it was out of a sense of duty, and a friendship with the Benfords.

Roo slipped around behind the building, cloaked by her riding gear. She opened the basement access—a trap door in the ground—and climbed in. The sensors didn't detect her. The veil confused them.

Inside, she ditched her outerwear and goggles and crept upstairs, pushing the basement door open. A small drone, like a hummingbird, activated at the other end of the hallway. At the noise, Roo hissed in frustration. Miss Farmer's security was good, although limited by the privacy requirements of some of the families she served.

Kerr-Moulthrop's office was just across the hall. The door to the room cracked open. If she could get by the hummingbird, she could get in there. The hummingbird edged closer. It peered right at her, ticking.

She had no wristband. No way of proving that she was supposed to be there. Roo froze.

The bird hovered, then flew away. *The maintenance coverall from the Enclaves. Coming from the basement. A familiar face profile. Maybe the drone decided I belonged here.* Roo crossed the hallway into the classroom. *I used to belong here.*

The cabinet holding student tablets was locked with a motion code, but Roo had watched Kerr-Moulthrop unlock it daily for six months. She pressed her fingers against the pad, mimicking the pattern he'd used. The door opened, and her tablet rested in a stack on the rack inside. They hadn't erased it yet.

Roo's fingers twitched. She lifted the tablet, passing her hand across its smooth surface. A soft cough behind her made her freeze again. When she turned, Miss Farmer stood in the doorway.

"Miss Vane. Our agreement is that you are not to be here."

Roo nodded, gripping the tablet tightly.

"And so, you are not here. You may not return. You will leave school property here." Miss Farmer waited for Roo to acknowledge this.

"Yes ma'am."

"Your work has always exceeded school standards," she said over her shoulder. "A teacher is a particularly sheltered role for those who might need it. One's identity could be subsumed. One might find a safe place in a finishing school far from New Washington, if one needed to."

Roo stared, her hands cradling the tablet, at Miss Farmer's shoes. They had small straps that wrapped each slim ankle. "I appreciate that."

She could not leave the city, not without knowing what had happened to Dax and Nan. Not without trying to help Sam, so her conscience was clear. She couldn't accept Miss Farmer's offer of help, yet.

The shoes receded. Roo set her resolve. She had loved this place. Now it, too, was gone. She put the tablet back on the rack and slipped into the basement.

A rumble from the kitchen above told her students were gathering for breakfast. Sasha, included. Roo donned the veil and returned the way she came, gathering the shielded equa and meeting Sam on the drive.

She had what she needed. The microbead she'd rested on the unlocked tablet had lifted her work perfectly. *But,* she realized, *I can't test the code on Sam. If I am wrong, the hacker will know. I need a chip of my own.*

"You would do that, for the family?" Sam said, when she said as much on the ride back to Centenaire.

"It's the only way. Tell Minerva." She had to trust someone, at least temporarily, and today it was Sam. But she could also bargain more. "Tell her I want to horse trade. The chip, to find Dax and Nan."

New Washington City Feed

Benford Fan Group, Evangeline Subgroup

[Fee for anonymity]

What a week in New Washington—not only has Evangeline Benford been all but offline since her surprise engagement (still waiting on the ring), we haven't seen much out of Mason Graves either.

—I do not like him.
—you don't like anyone EB dates.
—that's not true, I liked Dutton. And now he's got a founders' award. He'd be a great match for her.
—or Stonecliff.
—Isn't he a cousin?
—distant cousin. Honestly, there aren't that many of them to go around. Can't afford to be too picky.
—sure seem like a lot of them to me.

Breaking news! we've been contacted by someone who says they're PR for the Benfords announcing a public feed broadcast and reception—after the Benford's Enclave Family Trust meeting—what could it be?

—Benford's backers must be curious as we are seeing a lot of traffic in and out
—Meantime, EB's been seen minding a chaotic charge, the mysterious Roosala Vane—who is she . . .

The Family Trust

Roo had barely slipped back into her room when Evangeline knocked. She cracked the door open, trying to hide her salt-stung, windswept appearance.

Evangeline was visibly preoccupied with preparations for her first Trust event. She put a hand against the door frame. "I've commissioned clothes. The designer you favored from the masque said she was busy, but her school indicated she needed graduation project. So here we are. Perfect, yes?"

Perfect, no. Roo, exhausted from the ride, was speechless. She didn't want to see Sasha ever again. "I don't favor any designer—" she began.

"There's no time to argue—I traced the source of your gown to Miss Limére. We *will* look like a unified family this afternoon. It's important," Evangeline countered. Her hand chimed with messages from the caterer, security. "So many details."

Roo eyed the chip, wondering if it had been tampered with too. She would find out soon, for Sam. "All right."

The outfits Sasha brought to Centenaire an hour later took Roo's breath away. One suit in particular had a goldfish that swam laps up and down the collar. Roo touched it, astounded, and the goldfish disappeared into the fabric's blue depths, only to emerge on a hem and swim its way back up. "Amazing."

"You like it!" Evangeline sounded delighted. "That's the one I chose for you."

Sasha stood quietly by the rack of suits. She tabulated the bill on her reticule. She did not look up.

Roo reached for the fabric again. *Sasha made this.* "I couldn't. I don't want–"

"Dearest, when you are coming out publicly as a Benford, you must BE a Benford. It's overwhelming at first, but you'll get used to it. Everyone will see how wonderful you are this afternoon–even Mason seems to be coming around," Evangeline added quickly, with her back turned as Roo stepped into an ocean-blue combo. "He's tough to crack, but he'll understand. He was like you once."

Roo cringed. *Mason Graves is not like me.*

"Once I–we–run the Benford companies, you'll need more polish. It only takes a little effort to smooth the way. Let's start with these–I'll let Miss Farmer's know they're satisfactory, Miss Limére, and that we'll be taking you on as Renata's personal seamstress."

The room had been the perfect temperature, but Roo shivered in the silence that fell. Finally, Sasha dipped a small curtsy to Evangeline. "Thank you, ma'am. I have plenty of work already."

Evangeline looked confused. *No one says no to her,* Roo realized. She tried to keep a straight face, but her mouth quirked. Sasha caught the look and glared.

"I have no need of a private seamstress," Roo said.

Evangeline caught the exchange and blinked. She pointed at the suit. "I'll just step out of the room while you alter that."

"You can stay," both Roo and Sasha said. But Evangeline was already over the threshold, leaving the door slightly ajar in her wake.

Roo glanced at her former friend. Sasha busied herself with a box of pins. "Go ahead, try it on." She held out the goldfish suit and averted her eyes.

The fish splashed and leapt as Roo pulled the outfit on. Sasha knelt and began to adjust the pant hem.

"I am so sorry," Roo said. "I've been awful in every way. I couldn't find a way to make things right."

"I am too." Sasha's fingers brushed the cloth near Roo's ankle. "I was hasty yesterday. Very upset."

"With every right to be." Roo touched Sasha's shoulder. Sasha took her hand. Pressed her cheek against Roo's fingers. *Her skin is so warm.*

Roo knelt too. Pins scattered on the floor. And Sasha, close, caught her breath, leaned closer.

A noise in the hall, Minerva's voice, and Evangeline's. Both upset, gave them only a second's warning. The door opened wide just as Roo straightened.

Sasha adjusted the hem of Roo's pants, again.

"Who authorized this?" Minerva, looking stern in a dark suit, held her finger on a feed about Roo. "Someone's uploaded a whole batch of images and stories about you to a fan page. Look at this discussion." She held up the tablet, pushing a holo into the room.

"Well, I think it's lovely, if quaint," a young Enclaver was saying on the feed while walking the green with an escort and an *Enclave & Towne* reporter. "Benford extending his charity to someone like her."

"I didn't authorize anything," Roo protested. Evangeline shook her head, denying it too.

"We will quiet the feeds down. I'll ask Holt or Theridge."

Evangeline said. Her own pantsuit had a broad, blue sash. She wore a matching set of gems in her hair, setting off her eyes: Sasha's design as well, Roo guessed.

"Holt is busy this morning with an errand Mason asked him to do." Minerva gestured at the holo. "And now this."

An older woman beside the first speaker said, "Water, food, housing—print all you need, at any kiosk! But this girl—a Skirter!—getting a chip, and an inheritance! The Enclaves didn't used to be a place where anyone could just sneak in."

A young man interrupted them, "Perhaps she could be useful, like a—"

Evangeline waved a hand to cut the feed. Lucky, since Roo felt she might burst into flames from embarrassment. People were talking that way, about her. Sasha had seen that.

Sasha's hands were on the suit's sleeves. The blue cuff brushed Roo's wrist.

Minerva looked furious. "They're making a mockery of the family. We can't have our purpose eclipsed by speculation. Important people will be here today, and listening in. You may not realize it, Renata, but the work of this Enclave, and others in the portfolio, support entire towns' restorations. The production of airlocks and drones, the reclaiming of homes from the Mess. There are outside forces that could send everything back to ruin. We work for order."

"I am beginning to understand," Roo protested.

Minerva stared at the suit Roo wore, then studied her face. "We must prove them wrong. Everything must go perfectly."

Sasha stepped away, clearing her throat. "I am finished here."

There was a knock at the door, and the family physic entered, carrying a small box.

"I am glad you finally decided to see reason," Minerva

said. Roo swallowed. The box was black, the size of an Enclave chip.

Sasha's eyes caught the box as she walked past it. She stared at Roo.

"Thank you," Evangeline dismissed her, as Minerva opened the case.

The chip glittered on a dark cushion. It seemed like a tiny, clear gemstone. *How does it store data?* Roo wondered. As the physic washed her palm with antiseptic, she felt faint. *How can I break it?*

Minerva caught her staring. "Second thoughts? With a flip of your wrist, you can have almost anything you want. You could even help those friends of yours in the Skirts." Her words were dry, but there was a glitter in her expression that made Roo squirm.

Roo held out her hand. The physician held her wrist gently, but it still felt like she was being twisted in two different directions. The chip would take her farther from her life with the only family she'd known. But it would let her help them, too. Even if they never knew of it.

"You could use it to start a small traveling book-thing, as a charity. Like your Nan–" Evangeline said, just as the physician pressed a sharp needle into the heart of Roo's upturned left palm.

Evangeline had been paying attention when Roo talked about Nan. *I will never be invisible again.*

The physician held a scanner over Roo's aching palm and read the results. "Successful connection. Welcome to the family, Miss Benford. Should we schedule the rest–"

"Not yet." Minerva waved him off, then smiled. "Welcome, Renata." Her words were terse.

Roosa. My name is Roo. Roosala. Anything but Renata. She felt woozy. Her palm throbbed and her fingers seemed made of metal. She shook her hand and the feeling dissipated. But the room still felt too close, and almost tilted.

Evangeline hugged her. "Sister! Papa will be delighted."

She noted Roo's pallor and gestured to the physician. "Give her something soothing."

Roo didn't want to be soothed. She waved off the physic. *I want to feel the full impact of what I've done. What I've accepted.* It hurt, immensely.

When the clock tower chimed two, they took the elevator to the rooftop garden. The broad lawn below filled with roofhopters.

"Far fewer than I expected." Minerva frowned at Roo.

"Shhh, Aunt Min, it's not her fault." Evangeline squeezed Roo's fingers in support. Roo winced.

Staff raced back and forth, putting the last details of the meeting into place. Roo watched the silver services come out, the glassware pile in pyramids. The faces of the staff, covered in service masks. *So many details that had once been my job. And Dax's.*

Her new sister smiled and greeted a couple by name. She asked after their children. Roo tried to keep track, out of habit.

When the guests moved toward the center of the garden, Evangeline touched her elbow. "I hope you are happy that you've decided to join the family, no matter Aunt Minerva's mood."

It hadn't felt like a decision. "Did I have any other choice?"

"For you, from me and Papa." Evangeline put a small round box in Roo's hands. When she opened the box, she found King's Timex. "They discovered it after the heist. We thought you'd like to have it."

Roo touched the watch. Thought of all that it represented. "Thank you."

"I paid for the repair myself." Evangeline sounded proud.

For a moment, Roo was lost in the dream of a family. On the Enclave side of the wall. She wished that Dax could be there. Then her hand throbbed, reminding her of what she'd just done. *At what cost?*

She'd lost Sasha. She couldn't afford to lose anyone else.

"Come, let's mingle." Evangeline led her through the garden. The sun was high in the sky, turning the blue roses purple and throwing short shadows along the walk.

After slipping the watch in her pocket, Roo rubbed the sleeve of her jacket, absently, between two fingers. There was a roughness to the cuff. Small, French knots. Sasha's stitching. *I believe in you. The real you.*

Roo's heart skipped a beat. Maybe she hadn't lost Sasha after all. As she walked the garden path through chairs and tables, the number of people attending the meeting grew. "So many people." The back of Roo's neck prickled, as it did when she felt someone staring at her. Roo spun quickly on her heel. Her suit jacket flared out and the goldfish swam in circles.

"What is it?" Evangeline asked.

"Nothing," Roo said. Overhead, security and PR drones hovered, the latter permitted inside the Benford estate on this one special occasion. *It's just the drones. It's all right.*

She held herself still as, in the corner of her eye, near the rooftop hedge, a shadow moved. A familiar shape, a particular set to the shoulders. King.

Then the shadow was gone. A ghost. Roo shook her head to clear the memories out, careful to not dislodge the chignon Evangeline's stylist had given her again. She was seeing things. King had been on a transport to Alaska. It had crashed in the wetlands. Amos had said so. There was no King.

The chip implant is making me imagine things. Worse, now they could trace her everywhere, unless she successfully hacked it. Or removed it with something sharp. *Reprogramming it is better.* Roo would find out soon if she could do that. She'd set her program running before Sasha arrived. If it worked, she'd be connected to Sam's chip as well, as he'd requested. *I'll look when I have a moment to myself after the meeting.*

Evangeline pulled Roo near the low stage at the front

of the chairs. Guests approached, congratulating them. Greeting her by name. *Renata. Renata. Renata.* How much she resembled Evangeline. How happy she must be to finally be home.

Even Stonecliff came to shake her hand, though Evangeline had stepped away. She offered him her unchipped hand, and he bowed to kiss it. "Pity. You made a lovely thief, and would have made a great spy, Miss Benford."

"Thank you, sir." She wanted to ask him about King, but he slipped into the crowd before Evangeline returned with Minerva.

Evangeline searched the crowd for her cohort, some of whom were among those out of town. "Valencia isn't here," she whispered. "I guess that saves me the trouble of seating order at the wedding."

Roo winced. "You didn't need to stand with me; it's ruining your friendships."

Evangeline squeezed her unchipped hand, "This is building my family, and my future. My strength. You are part of that."

Roo flexed her hand. She could feel every handshake as a stab in her wounded palm. She was glad this part of the event was nearly over.

Roo looked out across the lawn as a last roofhopter landed. The Duttons emerged, with Jayson in the lead, bearing flowers.

Minerva cursed quietly. "Look at Jayson Dutton. Newest Enclave shareholder, eager to meet the newest Benford."

Roo's eyes widened, alarmed, even as Evangeline reassured her, "It's not like Papa will marry you off to them. Besides, I won't let it happen," Evangeline said. She put her arm around Roo's shoulders. "One merger is enough. Let's see how your chip is healing?"

Roo lifted her palm and turned her hand toward the sky. The heart of her palm pulsed, but didn't hurt. A small chip gleamed white, just under the skin.

"Opal. It suits us." Evangeline held out hers. They matched. "We're almost ready to start."

Roo pressed her aching hand against the goldfish on her suit as Mason approached.

"Hello Miss Benford." Mason bowed deeply before the thief and spoke her name through clenched teeth. "May I present you with a small token of my regard?"

He handed her a sleek envelope. Inside was one of the thieves' feathers. "Your brother dropped this in my house, only a few days ago."

The thief took the feather, even though it didn't match her suit. She tucked it in her jacket pocket, nonetheless. "Thank you."

No, that won't be close enough. Mason had only had time for a small dose on the feather. *Just enough to let Evangeline see it in action.*

"It will look better in your hair." He lifted it, and went to tuck the feather into the young woman's chignon. Touched her ear with it.

Her fingers reached for her hair. But he'd been careful. Evangeline hadn't noticed.

"Thank you for the lovely gesture," she said. Her smile was genuine.

Good, it was already working.

Evangeline tugged at his arm. "Come see the Yangs, they want to hear all about your research."

"Let's take Miss Benford with us; this will be educational," Mason said. "Just for a moment before Sam starts talking."

"Come on, Renata," Evangeline obliged. The thief stepped forward without a second thought.

They tucked her between them. Renata, grateful to be finished with greetings, let them pull her away from the dais. At the other side of the stage, Minerva stood with the couple Evangeline pointed out. They'd been cool when they'd greeted Mason before, and now they nodded and stepped away.

The idea of this thief becoming part of society on the same day he was joining the family? Nearly impossible to accept. He'd put in so much work—what had Roosa Canarvier done that was anywhere close to his dedication? Even Evangeline had to see it. A more tractable thief would model the partnerships' products. Rather than make Sam look weak. They would all see it soon.

"How goes the project, Mason?" Minerva asked. Mason thought her tone sounded over-confident. As if she had information others didn't.

"Very well. We're ready to go into small-batch production of the new Safeware in two days or less. So far, in tests, it's proved very strong." He smiled broadly, emphasizing the *or less.*

The newly minted Miss Benford smiled, listening, but not interrupting. Good.

"And is there a way to make it permanent?" Minerva was wondering.

"No, eventually it will wear off, though it takes a while. A reliable safe can be dosed in their food regularly. Or in a wearable. Evangeline, ask Renata if she's finding everything to her liking?"

"Mason, you didn't." Evangeline sounded alarmed. Her cheeks flushed.

Oh no.

She sneezed and the glass of water she held splattered the thief's suit. Then she pulled the girl aside, glaring at Mason, and grabbed a napkin. "Let's get rid of THAT," she muttered. She swiped at the place where Mason had scratched Renata. Then dropped then napkin into her glass.

The thief's eyes began to clear. "What just happened?"

"Mason was testing something he thought would please me. But it does not." She glared at him.

"Evangeline, if you'll listen a moment," Mason said. She ignored him.

Renata tried to shake her head clear.

Evangeline's cheeks turned red. She took both of her sister's hands. "I am so sorry. He and I had discussed Safeware once, and then he didn't listen," she turned and spoke the words to him, pointedly, "when I told him I no longer wanted to put you through anything like that."

Had she meant it? He'd thought she understood. He'd been trying to impress her. And Minerva. He'd grown so practiced at anticipating what she wanted, especially when it aligned with what he wanted. But he'd been dead wrong.

Renata stared at her sister. "But you did, at one point, want to do that?"

Evangeline closed her eyes, ashamed. "Growing up, so many other families had too many children. Some were eager to be trained as safes." She opened her eyes and contemplated the sky above the rooftop. "It's very exciting. You get to be an assassin! A master of weapons! At one point *I* wanted to be a safe. It all sounded so impressive."

Mason thought of the rental safe, how quickly he'd moved. How well trained. This thief could never be as good. Perhaps renting was preferable.

"Mason, as I got to know Renata over the past few days, I realized how selfish that initial wish was. I failed to make that clear to you. We'll find another way to guard our family's most important things, as Papa has." She turned back to the thief. "I promise you will be protected, no matter what, Roo. And whether I marry Mason or not, he will apologize to you. He will make reparations."

"I will, immediately," Mason began. "I am so very sorry—"

"Welcome, families!" Sam announced from the dais. "We have exciting news to present to the trust today. A few voting items, and several people you must meet if you haven't already."

Mason would have to apologize profusely later. He took Evangeline's hand. She pulled it away.

"We have drafted merger documents between two established families. That alone is grounds for celebration. Before I say more about that, I have an announcement about this Enclave and the future." Sam paused until everyone in the garden grew quiet. "For too long, we have stood apart from the city we aimed to benefit. Our original intent was to rebuild and recover. We've lost our way, as several people have pointed out to me recently. Beginning tomorrow, I will direct our engineers to start the process of expanding the Enclave's bio-dome, so that it will eventually encompass all of New Washington." He paused, as the Duttons murmured. "Jayson, do not fear. Your work will play a large role. Even as others are looking toward tools of security and defense, we will use our resources to support clean air and beautiful skies for *everyone*, here."

The crowd gasped. Some applauded.

Minerva shook her head. "No, no. No." She headed for the dais as a puff of smoke rose from the stage.

Dragonflies lifted and circled around Sam Benford's head. They spread their wings. "The thieves have the time," was spelled out in letters on the drones' bodies. The crowd murmured in confusion.

"Someone is playing a ghastly joke," Evangeline whispered. She looked to her father for answers. Then she glared at Mason. "You didn't."

"I didn't!" Mason said. He tried to subvocal Holt, but got no response.

"Stay together," Sam said, so that only his family could hear. "Evangeline, stay with your sister." Then he stepped away from the crowd.

Beside Evangeline, Renata Benford had seemed cheered by Sam's surprise speech. A pleasant relief after the recent upset. But now her face fell again. Mason stared at her, baffled, as she stuffed her hand into a jacket pocket so quickly, the suit's goldfish jumped to her sleeve.

Her fingers emerged empty. "The watch. Oh no."

Live from the Benford's Enclave Family Trust Meeting

Enclave & Towne feed + educational feed, the latter funded by Sam Benford (all residents and citizens welcome)

The families of the New Washington Enclave Family Trust have gathered, and it is a slightly smaller crowd than expected in the rooftop rose garden. I can see Judge Benford mingling, and Evangeline Benford accompanied by Mason Graves, along with—it looks like the mysterious Roosala Vane. Apparently, an announcement is forthcoming among the families today regarding both her and Mason Graves.

Meantime, the Duttons have arrived in force, as have the Lius. A representative from offshore is here as well—all very interesting!

[E&T Update]
It seems . . . someone has invited thieves. Is this a prank?

*

[EB Fan club]
I can't wait to hear her speak today—it's time for Evangeline to come into her own! Her vision for the Enclaves must include more greenhouses: she's a skilled botanist, her designs for evening wear are meticulous and—

I heard she used a new designer—Sasha Limére—anyone heard of her?

Oh! Yes—she's a student at Miss Farmer's. SIGH likely will be whisked away offshore before we can hope for any knockoffs or thrifts.

.Look at THAT. Would you look at Jayson Dutton sucking up to Roosala Vane? What's that about.

Oh lord, the Greenes are not coming, that's bad. The Roosala Vane incident—did you hear? There was some sort of impersonation and—

Wait. When?

At the birthday—oh do you think . . . hang on, my cousin subscribes to the Canarviers feed. Let me ask.

[feed paused due to outage]

[Benford fan club]
DID YOU SEE?? They're proposing a dome over the whole city—a real dome! I wonder how long that will take!

Over the Skirts too?

Well, that's what he said—

[Found footage fan club]
I know this is just for footage, but look at this live reel of the Enclave Family Trust meeting—do these two look familiar? They look just like Her—the woman from the video. Do you think?

Nah that's—not everyone is related you know.

But what if—they're sisters?? That's . . . hang on, Benford just announced that they're doming the whole city, or going to try to . . . amazing . . . remember that footage from the protest? The Equal Air For Everyone riot? YEAH. That one. Where is it?

The Ghost Job

DRAGONFLIES WHIRLED AS Dax watched the crowd. He'd dropped the card a few minutes early—after all the roofhopters had landed, but before Sam Benford had finished speaking.

His parents had left him in charge of distractions. The timing was his decision.

And the time had been perfect, with Roo nearby, and Graves talking at her.

"We're ready to go into small-batch production of the new Safeware . . ." the man had been saying. *Interesting.* Dax drew closer.

Aanand circled the crowd, wrapped in his quarter of the silver fabric. Dax assumed he was lifting a few items from the guests, although he only saw a shimmer when the light was right.

Knowing he had the same invisibility, as long as no one bumped into him, Dax slipped into a space in the crowd near his sister. He risked stretching his hand into her pocket, intending to leave her a dragonfly. So she'd know he was close.

Close enough to steal her myself—but no. That's King's job. I will stick to this plan.

His fingers touched the metal and glass of King's watch in Roo's pocket.

Well, maybe one small change of plan.

He heard the rest of Graves's conversation. His fury grew. *How dare they drug my sister.*

After that, triggering the card was as simple as a finger snap, thanks to Aanand's modifications. The dragonflies swarmed in the cool air, kicking up the scent of roses and lavender.

But that was just for show. The Canarviers were here to steal only one item: Roo.

Much earlier that morning, Amos Vane's party-supply mover had circled the Enclaves. Dax, King, and Serena crouched in the back, hidden by the fabric, and uncomfortably close.

"Why didn't you tell me." Serena frowned at King. Her voice was quiet, sad.

She'd attempted a conversation with Dax, which was uncomfortable and looked like it gave her a headache.

Trying to get to know me in the back of a van while we rescue my half-sister? That's a lot to ask. Dax was sure they'd work it out, eventually.

Serena had pulled a decent fistful of fruit cubes from her pack and shared them around. Anyone who liked those couldn't be all bad.

"I was waiting for the right time," King said.

Serena's soft sigh of frustration told Dax all he needed to know about how long King had been the way he'd been. "Dad, what's the plan?"

"You start," King said. He put his hand on Dax's shoulder. "There's no better time for you to take over for real."

Dax thought for a moment and then snapped his fingers.

"The Canarviers are going to do one more performance. It's going to get everyone's attention."

Smiling softly, his mother nodded. "And while you're doing that, we'll find Roosa. And—"

"No ands," King said. "Keep the plan simple. The last time I tried to do too much, I wound up in the clink." He chuckled, though. "There's nothing you need from that house."

It wasn't quite the family reunion Dax had envisioned, but it was better than nothing. "No beats today. Only distraction."

"There will be roofhopters on the lawn. Meet us at the closest one to the house," Serena said. "Once you drop the card, Sam will try to get the girls inside, likely to his office. That's the most secure place in the house, or it was. We'll find them. Then I can fly us out."

"Them?" Dax squinted.

"Just Roosa," King said. "Kidnapping Evangeline Benford is not on my dance card today."

Serena grimaced, but didn't disagree.

The van stopped. They'd arrived. *I will have to trust that Serena knows what she's doing.*

Amos opened the hatch. "We're right by the green; the trees should hide you."

It was midday, the guests hadn't yet begun arriving. Aanand and Dax headed for the service entrance with the chairs, while King and Serena disappeared into the trees.

Now, Dax hoped they'd had enough time to get into place.

His breath caught as Sam Benford stepped back from the dragonflies, alarmed. The old man rushed toward the elevator, without Roo or Evangeline. *That is not the plan.*

No matter what Sam said, Roo couldn't remain with Evangeline and Mason another moment. As the crowd shifted around them, confusion building, she pulled her arm from Evangeline's grip and headed for the corner of the garden where she'd seen staff emerging. Her skin crawled, especially near her ear, from Mason's trick with the feather. *How dare he. How dare Evangeline consider turning me into a safe. The only reason I'm not leaving Centenaire right now is Sam.*

Behind her, Evangeline took control of the meeting, steering the trust through elements of the Benford-Graves merger. "The Enclave Family Trust will be the acquiring company, with shares of Graves Biosecurity subsumed into the broader array of Benford holdings as Graves-Benford Security."

As her sister spoke, Roo disappeared down the service stairwell, in search of the thieves. She was relieved to know Dax was safe. *But what is he playing at now? And who for?*

Roo was going to find out.

The service stairs were plain, unlike the Benfords' elevator, and slow to navigate. She skipped as many steps as she could, her ankle aching on impact, but holding. The goldfish on her collar mimicked the motion, leaping into a suit pocket.

As she reached the lower floor, she heard glass shatter—real glass—just beyond the stairwell. Roo pushed hard, but the access door barely budged. She eased it open just enough to slip through and emerged from a concealed entrance in a bookcase, just outside Sam's room of wonders.

Holt lay stunned and slapcuffed in front of the door, out cold. He looked like he'd put up a fight. Roo nudged him with her foot. The man groaned, but didn't rouse.

Feet crunched on the glass, fast. Running. *The thieves. It must be.* Whatever Dax was up to, she had to find them and stop them.

It didn't take long to see that she'd arrived too late. Displays had been smashed. A dodo egg lay on the floor, cracked. A brace of twenty-first century weapons was missing from its case. *Where had Dax gone, hauling so much loot? He must be hiding nearby.*

"Daxian Canarvier!" she whispered. There was no answer.

She searched the whole room. Finally, a shadow moved by the doors just beyond the display.

"Stop!" Roo repeated. She cornered the thief outside Sam's office. A mask revealed ocean-blue eyes above the dark fabric. But the singlesuited figure was too slight to be Dax.

This was no one she knew, nor anyone from the usual gangs. Still, Roo felt a shiver of familiarity. "I'm certain this area is out of contract, whoever retained you. But you are caught, nonetheless."

Whose side am I on now? Roo wondered as the thief flattened themselves against a cabinet. Their outfit took on the color of the wood.

Roo grabbed their wrist before they faded into the decor. "I said, I declare you caught."

The words felt so bitter in her mouth. She didn't want to catch anyone, especially a clumsy thief. But she could end this prank, find Dax, and learn who had brought them to Centenaire.

The thief struggled. "Roosa," they whispered. "Let me go."

Roo froze. That voice. So familiar, like a voice from her dreams.

The thief pulled down her mask. She looked like Evangeline. And like Roo. Her lips moved. She was speaking, but an ocean roared in Roo's ears, blocking the words. *Cere. Serena. Ma.*

"Run. Both of you. Now!" King's voice, behind her, punctuated by a dry cough. Roo couldn't let go of Serena—but she twisted to try and see King. *They are here. They are both alive.*

As she turned, Serena pulled herself from Roo's grasp, then pushed her toward the service stairs. "You must come with us."

But Roo tripped. She stumbled against Sam's office door, swinging it open.

"No, this way, Roo. Hurry—you are in danger," King whispered, even as footsteps pounded the hallway.

But the unlocked door had opened on tumult and ruin. Roo couldn't look away from the storm-tossed room. Weapons from the display case, documents, tablets, and blood.

She heard running behind her. King, fleeing. Dragging a protesting Serena with him.

Roo, stunned, stepped deeper into the room. *What have they done?*

Against one foot of his large desk, blue suit torn open, Sam sat, eyes shut. His white shirt was stained red, and gaped wide enough for Roo to see that his side had been ripped apart, a titanium pouch near his waist, emptied. More holes had been carved in his chest, by someone who hadn't found what they wanted. "Sam?" She touched him, gently. He was gone.

There was a clatter behind her, and shouts, as others followed Roo's path.

"Thief! Murderer!" Mason shouted from the doorway.

"Papa!" Evangeline, close behind, activated Centenaire's alarms.

From where he sat in the Benford security bunker, on a bench between a large stranger and the thief, Mason couldn't see the MilPol hopter circling, but the earth shook as it came and went. He lifted his slapcuffed wrists and tried to push a lock of hair out of his eyes. The room was filled with guards. Holt's boss, Theridge, ordered her staff to keep MilPol out of Centenaire. "They don't need to be here yet. Mr. Benford is injured, but recovering."

The lie was necessary, at least for the moment. Founders were conferring about Evangeline Benford's succession status, and the fate of the Enclave. Anything that leaked to the feeds would throw the city into chaos.

Minerva had been clear on that point, and Evangeline had agreed. *But holding me here? Surely there was a better way.*

"Holt, this isn't necessary." Mason's security chief had accepted medical assistance, after detaining him, as well as nearly everyone else. On Minerva Benford's orders.

"MilPol is eager to question guests, Graves. Would you rather be with them or with my team?" Holt said *Graves* like it was an insult.

"You have to believe I had nothing to do with this," Mason said for the twentieth time. No one believed him. At least Roosa was in similar straits. The thief stared at the stranger, and Holt, and struggled against her slap-cuffs, but hadn't yet said a word.

"Let me speak to Evangeline." Once they realized the thief they'd allowed in their midst had betrayed them, Mason would be freed. "Don't keep me here with these—" He gestured at Roosa and the stranger, who'd been stunned and patched into silence. The man looked as if he'd been dragged through the rose bushes on the roof and smelled like the Skirts. Another of the thieves.

Holt looked toward the ceiling, deploying white noise to subvocal. Mason tapped his jaw. "I'm not getting a signal."

But Holt turned away from him. *He's not speaking to me,* Mason realized with a shrinking feeling. *Surely, they don't believe I had anything to do with Sam's murder?*

When Holt finished, he doused the white noise and addressed the man beside Mason. "Your bio-signature matches a MilPol record, Vane. And Centenaire recognizes you—that's the only reason we're not turning you over right away. You've been here before, and Evangeline has a lot of questions for you to answer."

Vane. Like Roosala. There's evidence of collusion, Mason thought. But he remained bound. *Why hold me?*

"What about the others on your team? Who let you in? This one?" Holt demanded, gesturing at Mason. The bruises on his face were shifting from red to an angry purple. "When did you two begin conspiring?"

The man remained stubbornly silent, struggling against the interrogation patch on his neck.

"I didn't conspire with him!" Mason struggled against the slapcuffs. "Let me talk to Evangeline, or Minerva." They would see he was right.

Holt gestured at a security screen. "They're busy right now. Getting a grip on the estate. Securing the Enclaves."

The screen showed Minerva at the courthouse, transformed by grief. Her jaw was set in a way Mason had never seen before. She'd changed her suit, but her hair was uncharacteristically tangled.

"Canarviers won't ever contract with Graves again," the man replied when questioned a second time. His dark singlesuit had torn in places, revealing bruises on his arms and torso. "Right, Roosa?"

Roosa turned away from the man, and he seemed to shrink. A guard pushed him. "No questions from you. Where's the Duttons' roofhopter?"

The big thief didn't answer. Roosa didn't either. Mason shook his head. "I've been with the family the whole time."

"I need the truth, or I'm going to be on that bench with you," Holt growled. "You will talk."

At a knock, the security bunker door swung open. Evangeline entered. Her face ashen, with dark circles beneath her eyes, she took in the bench's occupants, one by one. Her gaze settled on Mason. "Papa worried you might one day stab him in the back," she said. "Did you? The thieves knew just how to attack Centenaire–a terrible betrayal." Evangeline chewed her lip.

"Just like you spiked that feather," Roosa said.

Mason started, and he replied to Evangeline, ignoring the thief. "I did not betray you, Ev. I would never. You must believe me. I was mistaken with the feather. I thought it was what you wanted. I am sorry." The feather had been a terrible idea, but he would never attack the Benfords. He had to convince Evangeline, before she left them with Holt again. "I was with you, Ev. I admired him. Roosa was the one who ran off."

As he spoke, his thoughts spun wildly. *She'd said yes to marrying me even though her father didn't trust me. What happens now?*

"Why kill my father?" Evangeline asked the thieves.

"I found Benford as you saw him." The man shook, his face haggard. "Roosa found us after. She had nothing to do with this. We were only looking for her. Cere–Serena–"

"My mother?" Roosa said, then corrected herself, to Mason's surprise. "Our mother? I thought I saw her, for a moment. But it was another of your holograms, wasn't it?"

"No," Evangeline said. "I saw her too. She tried to speak to me as she ran from the collection room." She twisted her hands together, wrestling with the memory. "Then she headed for the green."

"We will find her." Holt's boss glared. She signaled two guards to follow him and left Holt in charge of the bunker.

Holt returned to questioning the occupants of the bench. "How did you fool the house? There are gaps in Centenaire's records."

"Minerva believes Renata hacked the house," Evangeline realized. "And that she's the reason Serena fled in the first place. Is that true?"

King Canarvier shook his head. "She was trying to keep Roosa safe."

Roosa blinked. Her eyelids were swollen, her cheeks chapped. She met Evangeline's gaze with her own. "I didn't interfere with the house. But I have been tracing a hack that Sam was worried about. He asked me to do it. If you want, I can show you."

Evangeline straightened. "My father trusted you. Possibly more than he trusted me. We don't even know what the murderer was looking for." The pain in her voice silenced the room.

Mason stifled a groan. Sam Benford hadn't merely kept

his business dealings secret—even from his family—he'd made himself into his own safe. Trusting no one but this thief had gotten him killed. And now, here they were.

"We *do* know," Holt said after a pause. Mason shook his head, *no*. But Holt wasn't his security chief, in truth. He was Evangeline's. "They wanted Mason's ampoules. The ones he'd entrusted to Sam's safe the night of the masque."

Evangeline's eyes widened. "Mason's?"

"Sam demanded I keep them at Centenaire," Mason said. He stared up at Holt. "Did you find them?"

Holt shook his head. "We didn't find any ampoules on King Canarvier. Nor on Renata. Nor anywhere in the house."

Evangeline's brows pinched together. "But—" she whispered. "You saw how horribly they searched. Whatever they were looking for—whoever they are—they were willing to kill for it." She paled and sat on the bench to steady herself.

Mason encouraged her to lean against him. To his surprise, she accepted. It was a relief to be able to offer her comfort. "Whoever took the ampoules is the killer and the thief. If it's not Roosa, or these two, we will find out who it is."

"We've examined Centenaire's access records. None of them entered the private quarters. Everyone kept to the garden, except Roosa, yourself, Sam, and a few staff." Evangeline looked to Holt for confirmation. The security chief nodded.

Mason tried to contain a growl, unsuccessfully. "But what about your family friend? Where was Stonecliff? I saw him on the roof."

"Rylan?" Evangeline said, sitting upright. "He wasn't invited. He's not a shareholder and wouldn't have been in attendance. Are you sure?"

"He shook my hand," Roosa said, remembering. She flexed her unchipped hand.

"If Stonecliff was here, it wasn't on your father's behalf," Holt said. "And Graves is right, he wasn't on the guest list." Holt frowned, listening to his comm. "Ma'am, the house says that Stonecliff was *not* in attendance."

"But both Roosa and Mason say he was. And they don't agree on anything." Evangeline extended the tablet to Roosa. "I want whatever data Papa had you tracing. Now."

"Sam did trust you, Evangeline." Roosa took the tablet over Mason's protests. "Just not anyone else around you." She laid her palm on the tablet, regarded King for a long moment. "Tell me how you got into the house."

King shrugged. "We had Serena's chip, from when she lived here. She'd removed and hidden it when she left. I'd heard a rumor that Judge Benford found it. She was going to tell Sam. I tried to stop her, at the Duttons'."

"When Aunt Minerva's band was stolen." Evangeline stood up. "That was you."

King nodded. "Guilty. I didn't hurt her, though. The witness made that up."

"I'll hazard a guess at the witness's name. Stonecliff?" Mason looked to Holt for answers. "Did you know?"

Holt shook his head. "If I had, I would have locked the whole place down. I'll try to find that witness data."

"Why didn't you tell us?" Roosa asked King. "Why didn't you talk to Nan at least?"

King sighed. "Nan loved Serena as much as I did. I didn't want to get her hopes up. It would break her heart twice over. Like mine."

The thief turned back to the tablet, working on the code there. A tear dropped onto its surface, reflecting lines of data. "Sam's chip recorded everything until his death. It says the last person to enter his office was . . . Minerva."

Mason groaned. "Can't anyone see what's going on? This is a con. Minerva would never kill her brother. Stonecliff is setting everyone up. Holt? Are you involved? Your boss is one of Stonecliff's recommendations. Where is your loyalty?" Mason didn't care about alienating the man any longer. Holt had been incapacitated; his employer murdered.

"My loyalty is to the Benford family. I was chasing the thieves," Holt said. "One overpowered me in the display room. Watch." He displayed the scene. The very walls seemed to attack Holt, and then stun him with his own baton.

Mason deflated slightly. "I still think I'm right about Stonecliff."

Minerva's voice interrupted them, startling the room. "Holt, I've received a message that Evangeline must hear. I'm returning to Centenaire immediately. Tell her to meet me in Sam's office."

Evangeline stared at Holt's screen, then at Roosa, and finally at Mason. "If Minerva is involved, none of us are safe." She stood, upset but determined, "We will get to the bottom of this, before she gets here. Come with me."

When Holt pulled him upright, King groaned. Roosa tucked Evangeline's tablet in the pocket of her suit and looped her arm under the bigger thief's shoulders. "I've got you," she whispered.

Mason swallowed. He felt a twinge of jealousy. Even thieves had family and support.

Mason had long done without family. Even when Minerva took him under her wing, he knew it was for her own reasons. Then Evangeline had accepted him. And Sam, grudgingly. He'd started to want more. But if Minerva was involved in Sam's murder, Evangeline would have nothing to do with Mason ever again, he was certain of it. There would be no more chances.

As the roofhopter charged through the air, it rattled and jerked its occupants from one side of the cabin to the other.

Aanand cackled in the pilot seat, enjoying the turbulence, as Dax sat quietly behind him. "Dazzled the heck out of that gig, at least! Not quite perfectly."

Dax grimaced. *No. Not a perfect job. We bagged a roofhopter. But no Roo. And a few extra passengers.*

"We're heading that way." Serena pointed to the horizon. "A tower at the edge of Public Works." Her hand shook. "I'm so sorry, Dax."

"It's not your fault, Ma," Dax said gently. He looked at the shock baton poking her ribs.

After the card had dropped, Dax and Aanand had found the Duttons' roofhopter, as planned. They'd begun to prepare it for the family's escape. "How does this turn on?" Dax growled as Aanand tried to hack the roofhopter's controls. "Your parents better know."

But when Serena came running, they weren't ready for what came with her.

Shadows had moved quickly across the lawn, two figures backlit by the sunset. The hopter's door opened.

Instead of Roo, the buyer had climbed in, close on Serena's heels. "Hello everyone, nice to see you again. Take off immediately."

Dax bolted from the copilot's seat, dropping one shoulder in order to ram the man off the hopter's boarding rail. Aanand was right behind him. "Joke's on you, we can't."

"I wouldn't be so speedy, son," the buyer murmured, hitting him with a jolt from the baton. Dax fell to the floor of the hopter. "You gave me a broken vial. Which means you have something of mine, still. And I have several items of yours."

Then he pressed the baton into Serena's kidney and activated it. Serena cried out, "Stonecliff means what he says. He claims an associate of his has Nan. They're meeting us at Graves's lab."

Serena took the pilot's seat, groaning. She closed the hopter's doors and pulled a small metal chip from her pocket. She pressed it against the hopter's controls. "I never wanted to see this thing again," she said.

The machine whirred to life and lifted into the air.

"Where's Roo? And King?" Dax asked her as they flew. He could see she was in pain. He'd been hit with the same shock, and wondered why he wasn't.

"I assume trying to get out of a murder charge. Which wouldn't have been necessary if your sister had done as I asked at the party." The buyer, the man his mother called Stonecliff, took the seat behind Serena and Dax. He removed his glasses and cleaned them with a white handkerchief. "Amateur thieves, it is time to make your escape."

The kerchief turned red as he worked.

"What did you do?" Serena shouted over the roar of the hopter's thrusters.

"This is not her blood." Stonecliff looked straight ahead. "Do not worry. Now sit tight. You're all going to be extremely useful in the next few hours."

The vehicle dropped suddenly, as Serena began coughing, then regained altitude. Stonecliff pushed Serena aside, into a seat beside Dax, then took over the controls and righted the vehicle. They flew faster, until the roofhopter came to a screeching hover over the Public Works tower. Below, a repo lock shimmered.

Stonecliff turned to Dax. "Crack that for me."

"That's Roo's area of expertise," Dax replied. "You grabbed the wrong Canarvier." He kept an eye on Serena, who grew weaker as the minutes passed.

Stonecliff set his jaw and forced the vehicle into a dive. The hopter's shell shrieked as they passed through the repo drones' barrier. "We're landing anyway. Buckle in and hold tight."

A small EMP lit up the instruments. Then the hopter stopped working. They spun sickeningly in the air and crashed on the rooftop.

“I’m down,” Stonecliff subvocaled. “I’ll let you know when you can get in.”

Then he gestured to Dax and Aanand. “Get up, and bring her.” He stepped out of the vehicle. Repo drones clung to the sides of the hopter, trying to link together. Stonecliff raised the baton toward them and it sparked. “Or I’ll fry you all.”

Dax and Aanand scrambled to lift Serena in their arms, then followed Stonecliff into Graves Biosecurity.

New Washington
Enclave & Towne Feed

(subscribers only, premium fee)

[E&T Update] It's chaos at the Benford residence but we're hearing no one was harmed. We're also hearing everyone was NDA-ed before they were cleared and allowed to leave.

Apparently, several thieves were captured and are being held at Centenaire. MilPol has been advised it was a prank, but the Duttons have announced that their roofhopter is still missing.

The Benfords promise to send an update as soon as they have assessed the damage and discovered who sent thieves to their meeting.

*

New Washington City Feed,
Found Footage Group #67

(citizen's band required, subscription only)

[Subscriber 77897] I wonder if it was an attack. A real attack. By someone who had data on Benford himself? He had a lot of enemies.

[Subscriber 7786] Look at what I got off the Enclave & Towne feed—I used this image to do a facial comp and those two are definitely related.

[Subscriber 5341] Here's footage of Kenneth Vane attacking Judge Benford from only a week ago. Look at how he rips the

band from her wrist. What a monster! Is Vane involved? He employed Daxian Vane, who's been flagged as a Canarvier . . . Wait, what if you—have you compared that footage to the kidnapping? Have the Canarviers had it in for the Benfords all along?
[file removed]
[channel closed by order of MilPol]

[Mudlarkers group - subscription only]

—MilPol has released a dossier on Kenneth Vane; apparently, he was at the center of the ruckus tonight. The Benfords must be allowing it.
—Kenneth Vane is King Canarvier—I'd heard rumors. Now we know!

The Hostile Takeover

FROM WHERE DAX and Aanand sat, bound, on the upper floor of the lab, they could see a small corner of research tables below. Below them, a woman and three men helped Stonecliff round up the scientists. They wore uniforms similar to what Stonecliff had sported at the Grand Heist. All had fabbed tasers, unlike anything Dax had seen before.

Worse still, the woman had arrived carrying Nan. "Tell your dad, thanks." She'd winked at Aanand. She deposited Nan beside them.

Beside Dax, Serena murmured groggily, "Amos, you idiot." Aanand groaned.

"I'm so sorry, Ma," Dax said quietly. His voice sounded small in the large lab. "This is my fault."

"Shhh, Dax." Serena cradled Nan in her lap as she spoke. The older woman breathed shallowly. "I've gotten out of worse."

Dax smiled grimly. "But we haven't. Roosa, King, Nan, and me." He looked at Aanand, wondering how far he could trust his best friend now. "We couldn't do the job."

"You pulled the most amazing heist. And Dad's wrong," Aanand said. "He'll cut a deal with almost anyone these days. But I won't betray you, Dax. I'll make sure you get out of here, if we're not heading to the Kuiper Belt."

"I will not send you to space." Stonecliff looked up at them from below. "At least, not Dax or Serena. Nan's too weak to test the variant on. You might be useful offshore, however." He returned to the group of scientists. "Get back to work."

One scientist shook her head, refusing until the uniformed woman forced her back to her lab hood.

Stonecliff continued to speak. "If you all do what I ask, Dax, I will task Dr. Tsalta with making an antidote for Graves's formula. Otherwise, young man, you will live your life without your family, as your presence will kill them." He gestured at Nan's huddled form. "Surely you've noticed how well you're feeling?"

Dax had noticed. Even as the roofhopter had spun wildly in the sky, he hadn't felt sick. When it crashed, he'd barely felt the drop, while the others were bruised and battered. The shock from Stonecliff's baton hadn't bothered him. In fact, he felt healthier than he ever had.

But even as he realized this, Nan's cough sounded weaker. Serena's dizziness looked worse. Stonecliff wasn't lying.

He inched as far as he could get away from his family. "What does the variant do?"

"If Graves is right, it takes advantage of relational resilience. You—or whoever gets the control side of the drug—can live far longer than normal, and in much better ways. Longevity, friend. Fountain of youth. My clients were very excited by the possibilities."

"And Nan?" Aanand said. "What happens to her?"

Stonecliff smiled. "Very smart, young man. Eventually,

we'll need to replace her. That's why we've brought a spare. But if you cooperate, we'll try to keep everyone alive."

"My mother isn't a spare." But Dax could see it: the woman he hardly knew, who shared his genes, was weakening too. He looked back and forth between Stonecliff and Aanand.

"Going to be the end of me, aren't you," Serena groaned. Her eyes looked sunken, but she smiled at her son. "You and your sister both."

"He won't just yet," Stonecliff said. "And he'll be the source of a new kind of life for my clients. Who are interested living as long as possible. What Graves stumbled into—and what Dax swallowed—delighted the leadership of the Ocean Enclave. Their safes and other spares might be shorter lived, but the community will be stronger for it. Am I correct, Layne?"

"As always," the woman who'd brought Nan replied. Dax knew he'd recognized her from the ball. The curly-haired woman who had danced with Roo.

Aanand glared at Stonecliff. "My father thinks offshore folks are so much more enlightened. You're all just folders."

Aanand had known his dad was in contact with the offshore Enclaves. Dax signed as best he could, from the slapcuffs. *Are you a folder too?*

Aanand replied with a firm *no*. His eyes were wide, as if imploring Dax to trust him.

But Stonecliff chuckled. "Ocean *is* enlightened, young friend. While everyone else has been rebuilding, and celebrating, Ocean's been growing stronger, picking up what others don't yet value." Stonecliff unfolded a tablet. "I'll need a green-book connection to start the bidding offshore. And provenance. Graves's investors are going to call this an open attack on their interests. We need to get the rest of his shares to make this work. Then we'll auction at a trillion a dose. Time to play our last cards."

The group below turned back to the lab, and Dax pressed his fists to his forehead.

"They're going to use one of us to send a message," Aanand said softly beside him.

Dax realized his friend was right. "Maybe we can send a message of our own when they do." He gestured to get Serena's attention. "I don't know how much Canarvier code you know, Ma?"

"Some. Older signs, mostly. And Morse. I taught that to your dad." She grimaced. "While we were in hiding after the robbery. Before we fell in love."

There was so much Dax didn't know about his parents; so much he wasn't sure he wanted to know. Dax fought off a wave of regret. He hid it by teaching Serena and Aanand the new hand signs and codes he and King had developed recently.

Before he'd finished, the elevator doors opened. Layne emerged and approached Serena. "You'll be needed now, dear." She pulled at Dax's mother's sleeve and Serena rose.

Once Layne had her positioned against a nearby wall, she raised a sound shield. A low buzz filled the lab. Dax could see Layne holding a camera and instructing Serena in what to say, but he couldn't hear anything. When they finished, Layne doused the shield and stepped into the elevator. She rejoined Stonecliff in the lab.

Serena slumped to the carpet, exhausted.

Aanand elbowed Dax once the sound shield had faded. "We've got stop Stonecliff before he sells everything off or you'll never get a cure."

"I'm thinking," Dax muttered. His brain whirled. What would King do now? An idea began to form. *King would put on a show. And I,* Dax realized, *might be able to do it even better*.

Dax struggled until his bindings loosed enough that he could reach into his pocket. He held up two half-active repo drones he'd pulled from the roofhopter so that

Serena could see. "Give me and Aanand a few minutes to recalibrate these. We still have a chance."

Reentering Sam's office was harder than Roo thought it would be.

Sam's body had been moved by the family physician. She knew he was lying in his own bed. His chip had been retrieved, and she set it on Evangeline's tablet. Any data she'd missed earlier would be here.

Except for the state of the carpet, and the darkened chip, it felt like he'd walk back into the room at any moment.

And yet, Roo knew, *he won't. How can I miss someone I barely knew?*

Inside Centenaire, the clocks had been stilled. It felt as if time itself had stopped.

She'd thought nothing could shock her any longer. She'd felt numb after the chip had been pressed into her palm. Number still when she couldn't wake Sam. But now, with everything she'd learned from King about Serena, shock was all she had left.

"How do you do it?" she asked Evangeline. "How do you keep going?" She was struggling to understand this woman, who had seemed so simple on the feeds, and so infuriating in person, but who had returned the watch, and was trying so hard now to do what was best.

Evangeline drew herself up straight. "We just do. We always have. Minerva says the only way out is through—through the Turbulence, through everything. I expect it's a bit like a performance. You set your feelings aside, to deal with later." Her lip trembled.

Performance. That made sense. Roo wished she could comfort her sister, but Evangeline had already steadied herself to get through everything.

As they gathered in the office, Evangeline worked

with the reporter from *Enclave & Towne* to share news that Sam had taken ill, but that was all. It felt shockingly cold. But, Roo realized, she was buying the family time to find out what really happened, and who they could and couldn't trust.

Sam is dead. Discovering who'd killed him is what we must do first.

Before Minerva arrived back at Centenaire, Roo used her chip to project the family feeds, the chip data, blended with Centenaire's recordings, under Holt's watchful eye.

A hologram of Sam appeared. They heard him trying to reach Holt and get him to stop the thieves interrupting the Trust meeting.

In the room outside the office, cases crashed to the floor once more.

"For the love of all, what are you doing?" Sam yelled, before a shadow pushed him back toward the desk.

"Who is that?" Evangeline interrupted the hologram.

"They're cloaked, somehow. I can't see any data, nothing," Roo said. She shivered. The material seemed similar to her wardrobe from the heist. Someone had seen what the fabric could do, that weekend, and had procured more. Sam wouldn't have been able to see who was attacking him.

At a nod from Evangeline, she activated the data again.

Sam struggled with the figure. Outside the office, two thieves entered the collection room, with Roo in pursuit.

Roo closed her eyes. *We were just outside. We might have helped him.*

But they didn't enter the office, yet. Their voices echoed as Roo yelled stop, and warned that they were in the wrong wing, against contract. Meantime, inside the office, Sam fell. Roo struggled with the thieves outside. A blurred figure slid out the window. Then Roo toppled into the office. And Mason arrived, shouting "Murderer!"

The broadcast ended. Tears streamed from

Evangeline's eyes. Roo put her head in her hands, trying to feel something other than shock. "You didn't kill him," Mason said, reluctantly. The data looped back around. Roo let it replay, silently. The data was clear. Someone had been in Sam's office before Roo and Mason.

"No matter what this shows, I don't believe King Canarvier is innocent," Holt began. "He's a skilled hologram producer. He brainwashed Serena. He stole her away from you, Evangeline. That man—"

Evangeline stared at the image of Sam falling, again. At the murderer escaping. "No. The thieves aren't violent. They're performers. This is someone else."

"He attacked your aunt, a week ago!" Holt folded his arms. "Stole her Enclave band."

Roo stared at him. "Sam said the same thing. But Nan never told us she'd found an Enclave band in the Dutton haul." She turned to King. "What happened to it?"

King shook his head, trying to clear it. "I put it in the garbage. Before they arrested me."

"Someone else found it." Someone temporarily had control of Minerva's access to Centenaire. And Stonecliff had found and returned the band to Sam just before the chip irregularities began. Pieces of the puzzle began to fall together in Roo's mind.

"Whoever did this is still out there. It could be Minerva. Or Stonecliff. Or an associate. They wore material that cloaked them from the house—even their ID is unmarked. But I've found an irregularity. There's a record of Minerva in the garden."

"That's not irregular. That's where she was," Evangeline said. She peered at the tablet.

"But the chip says she was also in the office with Sam. At the same time." Roo pointed at the house data. "She didn't show up on the house map because Sam cloaked his office after his chip started behaving oddly. King doesn't know how to duplicate citizen bands. And I didn't do it."

"Minerva was upset about Sam's announcement, but she wouldn't do this," Mason protested. "She's no murderer."

For a moment, Evangeline didn't look so certain. She startled when Minerva entered the office.

"Of course I'm not a murderer. Thank you, Mason," Minerva said. "The murderer is Serena Benford. She killed her husband. My brother."

Now both Evangeline and Roo protested. "There's no proof of that."

King growled. "She would never."

"Silence! Or I will deliver you to MilPol myself," Minerva said.

King quieted, and Minerva continued. "On the contrary. Serena Benford is now holding the employees of Graves Biosecurity hostage. I suspect her of allying with an off-shore entity. She is not who any of us thought she was."

Evangeline and Roo stared at the judge. Evangeline shook her head slowly, "No. That's not possible."

Minerva handed Evangeline a glass of water. "You've been through a terrible shock. And you never really knew her. I did. I can see betrayal in her eyes. I will show you, once we get these people out of our–Sam's office."

Evangeline put the water down without drinking it. "They will stay. Roo is finishing a project that Sam assigned her. And she wouldn't come without the others."

"Very well." Minerva broadcast the call to the room. "Perhaps it will help all of you to see this for yourselves." She broadcast the call to the room.

Serena appeared, where Sam had just been, surrounded by Graves's lab equipment. Some of it broken. A woman stood beside her in a military-style uniform.

"Layne Andrews," Mason groaned. "In my lab."

Serena spoke slowly, "A group of your investors has requested evidence that this laboratory is still functioning. You will release all passcodes and order your staff to work with us. You will turn over your data. This is a hostile takeover."

Evangeline stared at Serena's face. King looked hard at the projection. "No. She wouldn't do this." He quieted, staring at Serena.

"I have to agree. Look behind her," Holt added.

Almost offscreen were several pairs of feet, bound. "Dax," Roo groaned, recognizing the shoes. "And Nan. And Aanand."

"It's very poor timing, with the merger hanging in the balance." Minerva looked at the carpet and put her hand on her chest. "Mason, did you have creditors from Ocean Enclave, or Atlantic?"

Mason sighed. "I thought Atlantic. But Layne—now I cannot be sure."

"Mason, Evangeline, they are demanding we go to the lab, to sort this out, within the next hour. I have a possible solution, but I will need the two of you to help. Otherwise, Graves, you've put our family's future in jeopardy."

Mason hesitated.

Roo stiffened too. Evangeline didn't look as if she wanted to leave the office. She wasn't going to let Minerva put anyone else in danger. "In jeopardy? Both of our families are already well beyond that point. Evangeline, are you feeling well enough to travel?"

"I am not," Evangeline said, with a look of gratitude. "Mason, you go with Aunt Minerva. I will remain here and try to calm the feeds. I can join you both later, if you need me to."

Minerva and Mason protested, but when Evangeline lifted the glass to her lips, Minerva agreed to depart.

Evangeline put the glass down without swallowing, and gestured to Roo, her voice breaking. "I knew you didn't do it."

"And I don't think Serena did either." During the video, Serena had gestured and blinked in a pattern Roo almost didn't recognize, although some of the signals resembled Canarvier codes.

King made a muffled noise. She turned to him, and, against Holt's protests, took off his gag. "What was she saying?"

King sighed. "She's asking for help. Dax must have taught her the newer signals. She's saying Ocean is involved. That Stonecliff is going to marry Evangeline."

"That could be a trap," Holt said.

"I don't think so," Evangeline said, shaking her head at the thought of marrying Stonecliff. "Tell me what's in that water, please. It smells terrible."

Holt sniffed the water. His eyes narrowed. "Safeware. Did Minerva give that to you? Just now?"

Evangeline stared at the glass. "She has no right to try to make me compliant. Roo. Tell me what else you saw on Papa's chip? And in the house data."

"Only one strange thing," Roo recalled an image. "An hour before Sam comes to the office. Before the party. Someone is there." She pointed. A blip on the recording. A camera being adjusted.

"Whoever did that, knows who killed Sam." Whether it was Minerva or someone else was impossible to tell.

Holt thought hard for a moment. "At the ball, you projected a hologram that felt very real. Could you do one of Sam?"

Roo squinted. "That would take time. But with King's help, yes."

King raised his eyebrows. "But do you want us to bring Sam Benford—with the utmost respect—back to life? Temporarily?"

"Yes." Evangeline bowed her head, took a slow breath. When she looked up, her voice was steadier. "Holt, you are brilliant. Do you still have the hologram projector from the ballroom? If we keep people—the Trust especially—from learning Papa is gone, perhaps we can trick the real murderer into revealing themselves. We can find who hacked Papa as well."

With a slow nod, Holt grinned. "It's in the security office."

Roo thought carefully. "I'll need feed images of Sam. And some chaos. You don't by any chance have a map of Mason's lab at the Public Works?" When Holt nodded, Roo took a deep breath. "King, will you help us?"

King Canarvier grinned. "It would be an honor."

An hour later, the floor of Sam's office contained a projected outline of Graves Biosecurity. And Minerva had messaged to say that Evangeline needed to prepare for a public merger in order to calm investors.

"Walk me through this again," Evangeline said. Roo thought she sounded less nervous than she should, and said so. "I need to do a kind of performance. For my family," the heiress replied. "You of all people should understand."

Roo did understand. "People see what they want to see—what they want most, what they're most afraid of. They help make the illusion real," she said. She stood in the center of the holographic lab, then stepped forward to an X on the floor.

"Are you talking about Papa, or Mason?" Evangeline kept pace beside her, counting the steps.

Roo smiled grimly, but held her tongue. The office floor glowed from the projected lab's big windows and outer desks. "When you reach this point, no matter what else happens, signal me. We'll activate the projection."

"You're not going to be there?" Evangeline sounded panicked. "I don't want to do this alone."

"You won't be alone. Mason will be there. Holt doesn't think he's involved in this, any more than I am. But security will never allow me in the lab, and he's already on his way there. I'll be nearby." Roo handed her Mason's shoes and a crystal hair pin.

"I've modified it to carry my signal. We will be in close contact the whole time."

"We are going to need a miracle." Evangeline suddenly sounded nervous.

"No. We just need a good ghost."

Once they left Sam's office, Mason balked. "Evangeline shouldn't be alone."

But Minerva turned on him. "Stop being a coward. Serena Benford's betrayals have weakened this family from the start. Sam was much too lenient with her, and lenient with Renata these past few days as well. We will make order of this chaos. And we will catch whoever is doing this. The family will be safe because your company, your discoveries, have value, and Evangeline too. I will not let them be stolen by a ghost from the past."

As Minerva gazed at Centenaire's wrecked collections room, Mason recalled the destruction in his lab from Serena's broadcast. "Everything is in ruins." All that he'd worked for. Even the people who had trusted him. Evangeline. His staff. "I will help you," he capitulated and prepared to go with Minerva.

"Ruins can only be rebuilt from positions of safety, Mason." The judge studied him. "You are a survivor. You will help me make this happen. We will determine an arrangement with your creditors that will maintain the trust. Even if it means postponing Sam's fanciful wishes for the city."

"Evangeline and Roosa will never agree to that," Mason said.

"Evangeline will see reason," Minerva countered. "I do not care what Renata wants." She took him to the roof, and they boarded the roofhopter. "Now call your lab, tell them we're coming."

Mason ordered a direct line to the lab. “Dr. Tsalta, please.”

“Sir.” Dr. Tsalta’s voice came through the roofhopter’s comms. She sounded shaken.

“Are you all right?” he asked, surprising himself.

She paused. Mason realized he’d never asked her how she was, before this. “I am, sir. But they are forcing us to proceed with our work. They are trying to copy our data.”

Minerva spoke. “Tell Layne Andrews that I will negotiate directly for the Enclave Family Trust with the creditor. I have a possible solution that will benefit us all.” She closed the connection before anyone at the lab could object.

As the roofhopter lifted from Centenaire’s garden, Mason subvocaled Holt a short message. He hoped the security chief would get it.

New Washington

Enclave & Towne Feed

Joint Graves Biosecurity Press Release

On live feed and *Enclave & Towne* in two hours, a spectacular event: the merger of two proud families, and strong New Washington businesses.

The Enclave Family Trust has signaled a longstanding agreement among the renowned Enclave families, as well as ongoing partnerships with numerous organizations beyond New Washington.

Graves Biosecurity provides biodata, safe supplies and training, and workband validation for protected cities throughout the world, as well as several offshore clients. Enclave Family Trust and Benford Holdings is the developer behind the New Washington Enclave, as well as the restorer of several museums.

Evangeline Benford and Mason Graves announced their engagement recently.

"I'd always hoped for a resource-considerate wedding," Benford said.

It turns out there will be a wedding, although details aren't forthcoming yet. Stay tuned!

*

[E&T Update] This is an unusual setting for a merger ceremony, in the depths of a research laboratory. However, given the week we are having, I can't say it isn't entertaining!

[E&T Update] Rumors of more happy news are circulating, and the presence of several Recovery Court figures and founders' families is even more exciting.

[user 12786432] cannot believe she's getting married in a lab

[user s78912163] do we think they're pregnant??

[user 21385r9] don't be crass.

The Merger

As Aanand adjusted the drones, Dax spoke quietly with Serena. "Are you sure Stonecliff is serious?"

"From what I know, he's very serious. There have long been rumors around Denali of a group taking in escapees. I avoided that, camping in the wastes, making friends with various groups offshore and on. I'm trying to help, Dax."

"But," Aanand said, "Dad said those people are pirates. More dangerous than anyone he knows." He had nearly finished with the drones. If they were going to get everyone free, it would need to be soon.

Serena shook her head. "There are pirates offshore. My friends and I? We're just troublemakers. If you'd like to join us, I'm sure you'd be welcome."

"The folks on Ocean sure sound like they're

trying to be pirates," Dax whispered. He scooched across the floor and set the drones carefully by the doors.

"We've heard some rumors to that effect. If Stonecliff is working with them, then they've just upped their game from corporate espionage to attacking a protected city business. That's an escalation no one needs at this point. It could swing us right back into the Mess."

Dax shivered. He'd heard enough of Nan's stories to know he didn't want that.

Aanand grinned. "We can stop them."

Serena shook her head slowly. Her short curls fell into her face. "You can't stop an entire Enclave, Aanand. You can shift things . . . sometimes it takes decades. Look at what you said Sam wanted to do, sharing the dome across the whole city. I'd asked him to consider that since before—" She paused. "Before Roo, even before Evangeline." She stared at Nan, sleeping in her lap.

For the first time in his life, Dax wished he could comfort her. "We'll get them back." The drones were ready.

A clatter above and a thud. Another roofhopter landing. Layne Andrews exited the elevator to greet them. She kicked the rebuilt drones aside. "We'll discuss your little toys later," she said. Then she snapped her fingers and Aanand's slapcuff shocked him into silence.

When the lab doors opened, Minerva Benford entered, followed by a very cowed Mason Graves. The woman King had attacked glared at the captives on the ground. Dax had only seen her fleetingly at the Grand Heist, but he recognized that ramrod posture. She wore a business suit now.

Beside Dax, Serena narrowed her eyes. "Minerva. Don't."

"Oh, Serena. The trouble you have caused our family." Minerva Benford bent over her sister-in-law and tucked a stray hair behind Serena's ear. "Now I have to clean up the mess, just like before."

"I don't need you to clean anything up." Serena struggled to stand. She glared at her sister-in-law. "You can't—"

"That's enough," Andrews snapped again, and the

slapcuff buzzed. Serena dropped like a stone, stunned. "Ocean has made many improvements on your technology, Graves. She'll be out for a few minutes. Anyone else want to have a go?" She glared at Dax.

He shook his head.

Mason Graves, for the first time since Dax had met him at Llyria, looked visibly shocked. Then Stonecliff appeared. The man paled. "I knew it."

"Welcome, Mason, Judge Benford." Stonecliff smiled and held out his hands as if Graves's lab was his to give.

"Let's get on with this," Judge Benford said, less shocked. "You and Serena were obviously working together. She murdered my brother. You commandeered the lab, based on investment claims. Now you want to test the variant and sell it to your clients. Do I understand correctly?"

Dax shivered at the coldness of her voice.

"Ah, you understand very little," Stonecliff said. "Where is Evangeline?"

"She is not here. We decided you could negotiate with the two of us. And we will decide how much profit you gain from your auction." The judge sounded as if she was passing down a declaration of fact, but Dax saw Mason's face behind her. It flickered with confusion.

"Dear, you are hardly in any place to bargain," Stonecliff said. "That band on your wrist? I've been tracking you for an entire week. Listening to your conversations, the agreements you've made to verify reclaimed objects, the bribes you took? Worse, I heard all your boring little petty spats. Recorded every one."

The judge paled. "That isn't as important as the family. Your little takeover ends here. Until the Recovery Court confirms succession, I will represent the expected primary shareholders—my niece—and those within the Enclave Family Trust, Graves here, and several creditors."

"Ah yes, but you see, dear, I have powerful contacts in MilPol and clients on Ocean Enclave. MilPol will be most interested to hear of your activities. And Ocean has been looking for ways to extend their territory. How would more turmoil benefit your family? Or your ability to control it to your liking?" Stonecliff smiled, showing his teeth. His scar rippled, pale against his cheek.

Dax shifted uncomfortably as Mason stared at his former business partner, and then at Judge Benford, his jaw growing slack with understanding.

Beside Dax, Serena had passed out on the floor.

Dax weighed the last of the small drones in his hand. How much disruption would it cause if he tossed it into the lab below? He hesitated. He didn't want to hurt the scientists. He activated the drone's recorder instead. He felt for the controls and pressed several buttons, hoping to connect to the lab's PR feed.

"What do you propose?" Judge Benford punctuated each word.

"A different kind of merger. Stonecliffs and Benfords, united. All the profits from the new variant, split among us. I marry Evangeline. Say it's what Sam would have wanted. And Ocean stays offshore, happily."

"I will never agree to this," Mason said. "Evangeline can't marry this murderer. And I will never allow my company to fall into this man's hands." He pushed forward, but one of Andrews's guards threatened him.

"You have no choice," Judge Benford realized. "With the merger announced, we have controlling shares."

"Then it's simple." Stonecliff smiled. "Who knows, after all you've been up to, it might well have been you who killed Sam. So, really, this is in your family's best interests too."

The judge frowned, thinking. Serena roused beside Dax. "You can't do this," she said, weakly.

But Judge Benford frowned. "Call Evangeline. Tell her to come here. She will listen, I am certain."

Stonecliff began to issue orders to prepare for the merger, calling in favors and demanding two Recovery Judges come to the lab to act as witnesses. "We'll need some sort of celebratory décor, I suppose. Food and flowers. Make them tasteful. And fast."

In the upper lab, Mason closed his eyes. He felt nauseous. "I don't think I can do this, Minerva."

"You will do this. The negotiations were quite clear. You will represent Sam's wishes, Mason. By giving Evangeline away, to Stonecliff. The merger will protect the family's interests, and then the Enclave Family Trust and Ocean's investors will share the company. You will be allowed to stay on, in some capacity."

Evangeline had arrived by roofhopter soon after Minerva explained everything. She looked angry, but she obeyed all of Minerva's orders. She wore a pearl-colored suit and a large, jeweled pin. She looked calm. Too calm.

Mason stared at the woman he loved. She wasn't just obeying her aunt. Her eyes. She looked like she'd been given Safeware. Based on how Minerva was instructing her, that's exactly what had happened. He had to undo it. "Ev, no. This isn't what you want. Wake up."

"It is all for the best," Minerva said. "Stonecliff has been quite clear."

Mason squinted into the lab, where the guards held the scientists and four thieves captive.

Evangeline came to his side. "I brought your shoes, for the ceremony."

I hate these shoes. She knows this. He stared at her.

"You can do this." She squeezed his hand. When Minerva wasn't looking, she winked. It looked like the motion took effort. But she was in there.

Mason felt something he hadn't experienced since Denver. Fear. Minerva had threatened his future, and it hadn't mattered. But she threatened Ev now. The thought of losing her was unbearable.

Long ago, Mason hadn't cared who he lost. He'd figured any sacrifice was worth it to have the kind of life he deserved. But now? The thought of Evangeline and Stonecliff. The thought of all she'd been through. He had to try to shock her out of the Safeware. He had to tell her the truth, all of it.

He couldn't believe all his hard work had come to this. "Ev, I have not been honest. I bribed your aunt to introduce me to your family. I raided the ruins of cities to get where I am. I'm not worthy of the society you are part of. That your father built. I had nothing in Denver. No family, no support. I found a way through, and I aspired to having everything someday, but I didn't truly know what that meant. I just wanted to win. Meeting you? Changed me. It changed everything. I understand how important family is, above all else. And now I've ruined it all. I am so sorry."

Evangeline listened, her expression never shifting. "You've ruined much, but not everything. You are just starting to fix things," she whispered. "I once had some doubts about your intentions, your honesty. But now? I can hear your sincerity."

Mason studied her closely. Her face looked placid, but her words. She *was* in there. He squeezed her hand. "Tell me what to do. Tell me how to help stop this."

She risked a small smile. "Aunt Min was right about one thing: You are creative. That still intrigues me. I should tell you–"

Below, Minerva knocked her knuckles against the glass. A judge had arrived from the recovery court. Stonecliff stood beside them. And Layne Andrews, of Ocean Enclave. The woman had been a guest in his home, all the while working with Stonecliff.

Of course. Stonecliff had truly betrayed everyone. Me. Evangeline. He even had a live feed running. He was going to take everything.

To his surprise, Mason didn't feel angry. He felt cold

and methodical. He would end Stonecliff once and for all, to keep Evangeline safe. As Sam had wanted. The room felt like it was running out of oxygen.

Evangeline took both his hands in hers. "I am not about to give up on you. You have work to do, rebuilding my trust, but I believe in you. If you could do all that you just told me, you can help fix this world. Now trust me. Put your shoes on. And hold this for me." She pressed a sharp, cold object into his hand.

He stared at the sparkling midnight sapphire in his palm. The ring. His ring. He raised his eyes to meet hers. "You had it this the whole time." The betrayal overwhelmed him. She'd let him sweat through Minerva's interrogations—she'd ruined her own engagement. Why? "The whole time?" was all he managed to repeat.

"We all have secrets. Now you know one of mine." She winked.

Instead of enraging him, the wink dissolved his anger. Replaced it with what felt strangely like respect. In her place, he might have done the same.

"Evangeline, we will begin." Minerva spoke sternly. Mason understood that Ev couldn't make her aunt wait. That she must have some plan. He changed his shoes, then followed Evangeline into the elevator.

Minerva waited below, smiling grimly for the feed cameras. The Recovery Court official waited with her. Dr. Tsalta, standing with the rest of the scientists, looked stunned as the outer lab filled.

"Nothing better for Graves Biosecurity and the Enclave's survival than a family merger," Minerva said when she welcomed them. She looked furious, but behind her, Stonecliff looked elated.

Mason smiled uncomfortably. His shoes—the ones he'd worn a week ago to dance with Evangeline—had a new tightness to the toes.

At exactly seven in the evening, Mason and Evangeline stood in the Graves laboratory—lit in soft ambers for a ceremony where he would give the woman he loved to the man he hated.

Minerva lifted a finger, signaling the judge. The man began to speak. "The city of New Washington, the protected cities, and the offshore Enclaves and founders welcome you, Rylan Stonecliff, and you, Evangeline Benford, to your merger."

Mason shivered. He'd never felt angrier. He caught Evangeline's gaze and held it. He would make this up to her.

"Please say a few words, Mason. In Sam Benford's honor," Rylan Stonecliff said.

Layne Andrews moved back, recording, and Mason stepped forward. "I will not–" He felt his shoe click slightly.

And that's when Sam Benford stepped out from behind the assembled scientists. Mason jumped backward, startled. But Evangeline steadied him.

"Congratulations, Evangeline," Sam said. He leaned heavily on a cane. His eyes drooped and his skin looked gray. The guests stepped back to let him speak.

"Sam!" Stonecliff said, looking at the cameras, then Minerva, uncomfortably. "What a relief to see you well. We had wondered, given the rumors on the feeds."

"I am among you, so I must be alive," Sam wisecracked.

The scientists murmured, concerned. Minerva stared. She mouthed her brother's name.

"I am among you because of the latest advancement from Graves Biosecurity," Sam said. "The researchers here saved my life."

"We did?" Mason whispered.

But Evangeline squeezed his hand hard. "Yes, darling. We did."

"This is brilliant!" Layne Andrews cheered.

"More brilliant than you can imagine," Evangeline said. She didn't let go of Mason's hand, but she rubbed her eyes with her other hand. Contacts glittered in her palm.

She turned to the feeds, clear-eyed. "My partner's team"—she gestured to Dr. Tsalta and her white-coated colleagues—"has discovered that a specific adjustment to the Safeware pairing can provide unusual and unexpected results. They are results that one Enclave wishes to steal. Prior to this ceremony, and under my own auspices as an Enclave Family Trust majority shareholder, I placed an IPO on the feeds for the Graves-Benford Security Public Trust. The entire city of New Washington and the Skirts are invited to visit the new, free Trust facts feed, and bid on shares in this entity now. The company will immediately cease production of Safeware products, but will continue to study longevity, without familial consequences. Moreover, we will continue my father's wish: to expand the dome across the city and the Skirts."

Layne Andrews had stopped recording and started shouting, trying to interrupt the broadcast. But Dax, in the lab above, kept filming. And Mason realized Evangeline's pin was also a camera. The one Holt had taken away from the party crasher at Llyria.

Mason turned to her. "What are you saying? You meant every word up there?"

Evangeline smiled at Mason in that way that melted his heart. Then she held out her hand. Mason put his ring in it. She turned to her great aunt and smiled even more brightly as she placed it on her right ring finger. Her fourth great-grandmother's ring, on her independent hand. Minerva Benford gasped.

Rylan Stonecliff made a choked sound. "You cannot do this, Evangeline. We've already made a deal." His hands shook.

"I'd like to think of it as more of a friendly takeover. Papa! Come up here. And Mama, hello." She beamed at her father. Then at Serena, above.

Sam smiled back at Evangeline. All around him, scientists held up recorders, sending live videos to the feeds. Tablets beeped as regular citizens and Skirters donated funds and became part owners of the new firm.

But as Sam walked toward them, Stonecliff caught

Evangeline's hand. He pulled her close and whispered sharply, so that only she and Mason could hear, "What are you playing at? Who is impersonating your father? He's dead. Sam is dead. I know he is."

Evangeline patted Stonecliff's shoulder and whispered, "How do you know that, Rylan?" She gripped his shoulder tightly, so he couldn't get away. Then she spoke louder. "We know it all seemed very dire—especially recently. And Mason's not been entirely truthful. He kept back some of the new formula. But Roosa—Renata Benford, my sister—was kind enough to help us save Sam. She wanted only the best for our father."

Minerva's shock showed on her face. She was the color of old wax. "Your . . . sister. Healed my brother?"

Evangeline smiled. "With Mason's formula. Perfected in this very lab." She looked at her fiancé proudly, her other hand on his arm.

Mason, for his part, didn't move. Evangeline was brilliant. He found himself frantically trying to keep up. Sam, alive. And Evangeline taking over.

"I must talk to my brother," Minerva said. She stepped toward Sam.

Then Mason heard the thief's voice whispering, very close. Evangeline wore a tiny, fabbed earpiece.

When Evangeline replied, "Finale," Minerva, in her confusion, didn't notice. Nor did Stonecliff.

Then Sam Benford said, very clearly, "Stay where you are, Minerva. I'll see you later." He began to walk away, disappearing in the crowd.

Minerva shrieked and tried to follow. "You will speak to me, Sam Benford. You cannot make any more decisions for the family without me."

"That's enough," Evangeline said. She gestured to the security team. Holt opened the doors, gently moving the scientists in the lab out of his way. He helped Serena to her feet. Gently lifted Nan in his arms. "We've all heard you, Rylan. You killed Sam Benford. You set up King Canarvier."

Guards came down the elevator. Two took Stonecliff and Andrews by the elbows.

Another guard stood close by Serena, while a fourth collected Minerva.

Evangeline faced her aunt. "And you wanted the ability to control the family's fortunes so badly—which Sam was starting to suspect—that you risked bargaining with Stonecliff to do it. Stonecliff found out that you've been falsifying provenance for valuables from those who put their trust in you as a Judge. I saw the recordings. Dax has it all. This judge isn't here to witness the merger. They are here to take you into custody."

She looked into the feed cameras. "And to certify the public ownership of Graves Biosecurity."

"You can't do that! I'm a Benford too," Minerva shouted.

"Not anymore," Evangeline said. "I am proposing, as the head of the Trust, that you and Stonecliff both be struck from the green book. We will no longer recognize you. No one will speak for you."

Mason's heart felt full—this time with awe. He'd worked so hard to gain control, to make sure he had the best of everything. Just like the Benfords. But only Evangeline had been willing to risk it all. Now one Benford was being led away in custody. Along with Stonecliff. While the thief and his fiancée had rescued him.

No, Roosa's not a thief. She's a damn fine hacker. Sam had been right. And the Canarviers? They were highly competent in their own fashion. It just hadn't looked like what he'd considered talent. He was learning otherwise. *Given the chance, maybe I can put that knowledge to good use.*

Evangeline put a hand on his arm, calming him. "Don't worry. I'll make sure you have a good position in all of this. So you can help undo the harm you've created and build something better here in New Washington."

"Is that a job offer?" Mason stared at her with astonishment.

"Let's call it an extended date." Evangeline smiled.

Outside the laboratory, Roo sat behind a dumpster with King, running the hologram. They'd modified their masks to allow them to control Sam's voice and reactions in the lab, while Mason's shoe projected his image inside.

Everything was going according to plan, until a MilPol transport circled low.

Then guards escorted Minerva Benford in slapcuffs toward the hopter, with Stonecliff and Layne Andrews right behind, similarly cuffed. Serena Benford was the last to emerge from the building. Guards secured each of them on the transport.

"Ma." Roo couldn't stop herself. As one MilPol guard looked down, Roo backed further into the shadows. King nearly leapt over her. "I will end them," he whispered. "I will get her back."

Roo caught him by the coat and held on. "Holt said we can't. Not yet. You're a fugitive too. We will figure out how to help her. I promise. We'll clear both of your names. Somehow." The building's rough brick dug into her shoulder, tearing her jacket. She didn't loosen her grip until the security detail climbed into the roofhopter and departed. *I will find them, and free Serena, no matter what it takes.*

When the transport departed, Aanand helped Dr. Tsalta carry Nan out. Roo could see that Nan she was smiling, weakly. Dax waved from behind the door. *They are safe.*

When Roo let go of King, he rushed to his mother's side. She shouted to her brother, still in the building. "You're alive." She wanted to hug him. And smack him. What was he waiting for? "You took too many risks. But you stole Stonecliff's heist right out from under him. Not bad."

"And you engineered a superb spectacle," Dax shouted

back. He held up a hand to stop Roo from coming inside. His grin had a guilty slant. "Alive is one thing I can't seem to escape. I really did swallow some of that formula."

Evangeline and Mason emerged from the lab and into a circle of feed cameras, Evangeline's arm tucked firmly in Mason's. "We'll find the antidote for the formula, Dax, Roosa. We promise."

Then she dipped her head to King and Nan. "I understand you can tell me much about my mother. I am looking forward to hearing everything."

King chuckled, grimly. "Perhaps, with your connections, she can tell her yourself one day."

Dax gestured to get Aanand's attention, then pulled a bright object from his pocket and tossed it. Aanand caught it and approached Evangeline, holding out the Timex.

"Whoever runs the job, gets the watch," Dax shouted. He grinned. "Welcome to the team."

King's deep laughter broke the quiet. He clapped happily. "Well done, Daxian."

Roo looked at what was left of her family, gathered for the first time in the glare and dust of New Washington. Her sister. King, Dax, and Nan. Even Aanand. There were a few missing parts, but they'd find Serena again. And, perhaps, there might be a few new additions to the troupe.

She winked at Dax. "We are a team, no matter what."

"Canarviers," Dax chuckled.

King looked at them both, and then shouted loud enough for the guards on the roof to hear, "Canarviers!"

"You survived! You are stubborn and so difficult, and you must tell me everything," Sasha said as she ran to the car. "Did you really bring Sam Benford back to life?"

Roo took Sasha's hands in her own. The chip in her palm felt less uncomfortable now, though she was thinking about having it removed. She squeezed Sasha's sewing-scarred fingers gently. "So many questions. It's best you know everything. Come for a drive?"

As the car pulled away from Miss Farmer's Georgian building, Sasha blushed, her freckles darkening on the bridge of her nose. "You know you could have asked me for help."

"I could have. I wanted to." Roo's heart felt light. Sasha, looking over her glasses, actually seemed as if she might be crying. "I wasn't sure if you wanted me to."

"I do want you to. Ask me," Sasha breathed, and then kissed her fingers and her cheek.

Roo laughed, delighting in the idea of asking Sasha to help with many things. She had an excellent idea for a new family business.

Acknowledgments

A Philosophy of Thieves is one of those books—authors know the ones—that I kept writing even when it felt like the world kept telling me to stop. The first threads of this story began weaving themselves together in my mind before I'd published any novels. I put it down because I needed to work on another project, or because I got discouraged. Then I'd pick it up again. And every time I did, there were people who encouraged me, reminded me that this was a story worth telling, and didn't let me give up on it.

The story didn't let me give up either. The Canarviers broke into my dreams, their manuscript appeared at the top of a pile when I reorganized my office, and, as time went on, their shenanigans and their world became the place in which I most wanted to work.

Writers, don't ever let the world tell you that your story isn't worth writing. Write your story.

I am forever grateful to my agent, Andrea Somberg, for being among those who refused to let me give up. She's a fierce advocate, and wonderful at seeing all the possibilities of a project.

To A.C. Wise, Bernie Mojzes, A.T. Greenblatt, Siobhan Carroll, Sarah Pinsker, Stephanie Feldman, Rachel

Hartman, Kelly Lagor, Lauren Teffeau, Sarah Mueller, Chris East, Chris Gerwel, Curtis Chen, E. Catherine Tobler, Kat Howard, Raq Winchester, and Nikki Braziel, thank you for your brilliant insights and sharp eyes on what feels like millions of variations of this story that crossed your desks. To Sarah Guan, who saw especially what this story could be, and asked so many great questions key to making it so. To Jennifer Etheridge and Jeff Hugel for security and logistics consulting. To the usual suspects, my pen & ink friends, and my family, especially Tom, Iris, Sue, Chris, Geoff, and Denise, I'm very grateful and not the least sorry for trying to pickpocket a few of you. I'll get those treasures back to you shortly. To my students who teach me as much as I teach them, every day. And to my teachers (some of whom found their way into the book), thank you for everything.

To everyone at Erewhon and Kensington Books for believing in the Canarviers as much as I do—Diana Pho, Editorial Director and heist fanatic; Viengsamai Fetters, Associate Editor; Cassandra Farrin, Publishing Director; Kelsy Thompson, Production Editor; Erin Roll, Copyeditor; Mickey George, Proofreader; Steve Thomas, Cover Artist; Seth Lerner, Art Director; Shannon Gray-Winter, Senior Marketing Copy/ARC Manager; Martin Cahill, Campaign Manager; Kasie Griffitts, Sales Associate; the extended Kensington management and production team, and the sales team at Penguin Random House—thank you so very much for all your hard work and dedication.

Discussion Questions

These suggested questions are to spark conversation and enhance your reading of *A Philosophy of Thieves*.

1. When we first meet Daxian and King Canarvier in *A Philosophy of Thieves*, they are entertaining a party of successful entrepreneurs. How might you evade capture in similar circumstances? How might you outwit one of the thieves?
2. King Canarvier values the history of his craft. He teaches others by resourcing artifacts and books for use in his performances. How could such elaborate preparations make the Canarviers better than others at their chosen form of theater?
3. The effects of the Mess (aka, the Turbulence, if you're wealthy) are etched into the surfaces of New Washington, with familiar places transformed, but still visible, and some even usable. If you were a time traveler, how might you be able to find your way around the area?
4. Roosala Vane can shift between city culture, Skirts culture, and Enclave culture smoothly, and yet, in order to stay in any one of these places for good, she

may have to give up people she dearly loves. What kind of choice might you make in her situation?

5. What would you do with a wardrobe like the one Sasha Limére designs for Roosa?
6. If you attended the Graves' party, would you be on the lookout for thieves, enjoying the food and other entertainments, or trying to acquire a valuable or two of your own? How might you go about doing so?
7. While Mason Graves is ambitious and accomplished, the risks he's taken to get where he is are something he desperately wants to hide. How far would you go to belong? To gain wealth? To be successful?
8. Evangeline Benford's upbringing has been as overprotective as it's been luxurious. How might someone in her position develop different coping mechanisms as they grew up? What might her family (multiple people, as well as the family trust) be worried about on her behalf?
9. The New Washington city feed conveys news in the form of education, information, and gossip to a curious audience in *A Philosophy of Thieves*. In a space where these are intricately intertwined, who gets to say what is truth and what is fiction?
10. Why would an analog watch like King Canarvier's Timex be important to him, and his family, in a place like New Washington?
11. The book is set in a post-event(s) world, where many things have gone wrong, and society is only now righting itself, in various ways depending on location and wealth. There is a sense of loss and grief buried beneath the surface—how does the way different groups treat artifacts and valuables reveal their experiences?
12. Would you rather live in the Enclaves, the New Washington, or the Skirts? Why or why not?